Sprinkles on Top

ALSO BY KIM LAW

Sprinkles on Top

A Sugar Springs Novel

KIM LAW

Published by Montlake Romance, Seattle

www.apub.com

Amazon, the Amazon logo, and Montlake are trademarks of Amazon.com, Inc., or its affiliates.

ISBN-13: 9781477824672
ISBN-10: 1477824677

Cover design by Georgia Morrissey

Library of Congress Control Number: 2014904439

Printed in the United States of America

To Kristin Anders, for your awesome idea for the mirrors . . . and not for the crappy idea concerning legal matters (which my editor, thankfully, made me remove).

Prologue

N ot interested." Zack Winston snapped his mouth shut and focused on the two men staring back at him from the other side of the linen-draped table.

Low lighting and the slight clink of utensils on fine china surrounded them as he waited.

What he waited for, he wasn't sure. What could they say? He'd made his stance clear. He wasn't interested in getting to know them. That train had passed years ago.

And he most certainly wouldn't be heading north to visit their "quaint little town."

"I hope you'll reconsider," Cody said. Though the men were identical, it was clear he was the angrier of the two. He'd shown up with a chip on his shoulder the size of Zack's bank account. "We're not talking about moving there." Cody was working to remain polite, but Zack could see that he wanted to tell him to go to hell. Good for him. The feeling was mutual. "Just visiting," Cody continued. "Sugar Springs is small, but it's a good town."

"Cody spent a year there as a teenager, then came back a few months ago," Nick jumped in. "That's where I found him." Nick was obviously the peacemaker.

Zack watched as Nick riffled through his thoughts as if searching for anything he could say to win him over. The fact was, nothing they said would win him over. He knew exactly what they were after, and it wasn't brotherly love.

Cody and Nick Dalton had shown up at Zack's Atlanta high-rise the evening before, cornering him on his way out of the building. It had taken only one look to know who they were. They bore features strangely similar to his.

Same hair. Same eyes. Same . . . *everything*.

They'd claimed to be his brothers, one year younger than his thirty-three. And he couldn't deny the truth. He had brothers, yes. He'd discovered the fact ten years ago.

Adopted into a loving family as a baby, Zack had met his biological mother exactly once. And once had been enough. Pam Dalton had lived in squalor, just outside of Nashville. He'd learned all he needed to know about her *and* his two brothers at that meeting. Now, the only questions remaining were, how much money did they want?

And when would they get around to asking for it?

He balanced his fork on the edge of his gold-trimmed plate, concentrating to keep his expression blank. They didn't need to know that their appearance had thrown him. He'd written them off after his meeting with their biological mother. That's where they would remain.

His heart thumped hard against his ribs.

Only . . . why, then, did they claim to have found each other only three months ago? That was contradictory to what Pam had said.

Which would mean . . .

He settled his hands together on the table in front of him, fingertips touching, and didn't allow himself to venture what that would mean. Instead, he systematically ran through the facts.

Fact: All three of them had been separated at an early age.

Their story matched his. He'd hired a private investigator ten years before, who'd reported back that Zack had not only been given away as a baby, but so had Cody, at the age of two—only he'd ended up a ward of the state. Nick had remained with Pam.

Fact: Their father had died years ago in a bar fight. That matched the info he had, as well.

Fact: Pam was dead.

This was a new one. Apparently she'd succumbed to a failing system due to longtime drug and alcohol abuse, merely one week before Nick had supposedly discovered he had brothers and sought out Cody.

Zack could buy organ failure as the cause of death. She'd certainly been well on her way to that fate when he'd met her. She'd shown up high as a kite before proceeding to down more whiskey in the thirty minutes they'd talked than he would wish for in a month. She'd also been the nastiest piece of trash he'd ever had the displeasure of meeting. Barb had been equally unimpressed.

He loosened his jaw after realizing that thinking of his ex-fiancée had made him grind his teeth together. She hadn't mattered in years, and she certainly didn't now. She was simply a lesson learned.

As had been Pam.

What Zack *wasn't* buying from Cody and Nick's story was that they'd only recently met. And that they'd never known *he* existed. That did *not* match his facts.

But then, that particular fact had come from Pam.

The strung-out, piece-of-shit drug addict who'd shown up to meet him only long enough to demand that he owed her money. She'd been running low on cash to feed her habit, apparently. Her claim was that she'd provided him with a good life by giving him away, thus he should repay her for that.

She'd skipped the part where his parents had handed over a hefty sum before she'd "given away" anything. They'd been more than happy to pay both the fees and Pam's medical and living expenses during the pregnancy. Everything had been handled legally through a private adoption.

However, as someone who'd been around for a while, Zack also knew that figures could be padded. Expenses faked.

He knew that Pam Dalton had made out like a bandit.

When guilt hadn't worked on him, she'd resorted to blackmail. She could have sued him for seeking her out without her granting permission.

But she was his birth mother. He'd had to know.

Thus, blackmail had worked. But only once. He'd also forced her to sign the waiver indicating she'd given permission to seek her out.

Probably he shouldn't have written the check, but he'd been more interested in getting him and Barb away from her at that moment. He'd heard enough. But when she'd seen that the amount on the check was only half of what she'd demanded, she'd started spitting like an alley cat. She'd let him know his brothers would be coming to collect as well.

Only, he'd given all he was going to. He would not bow to more threats. There was no way those drugged-out hillbillies would get another cent out of him.

Instead, he'd gotten the hell out of there and had never looked back.

Until now.

He stared across the table at the identical faces so similar to his, at the matching dark hair, both men waiting for him to speak. Now his past had shown back up. Claiming they wanted to get to know him.

Pam had been a piece of work, many times over. But had she lied about his brothers?

And if she had, did he care?

He was pretty sure he didn't. He had his work, his mother.

He had a life that didn't include Podunk, USA.

As far as he could tell, he didn't need anything else. Least of all two men who were most likely looking to scam him.

"Surely you two don't think there would be any reason I would want to visit," he finally made himself speak. His mouth had gone dry, but he refused to reach for his water glass. If they wanted to pretend they hadn't come here with their hands out, he would go along with their ruse.

Yet he didn't believe them for a minute.

"I'm not seeking long-lost family," he continued, "and I don't need to see the backwoods of America to know that Atlanta is where I belong."

Nick's brown eyes never left Zack's, but disgust now pulled at his mouth.

Zack needed time to think. To figure things out.

To not be staring into eyes that looked so much like his own.

He peered at them with disdain for two more seconds before lifting his hand to a passing waiter. What he *didn't* need was to be ambushed into something that would bring on false hope. He'd had enough of that in his lifetime. "Check, please."

He was done there.

Chapter One

In closing . . .

Zack turned his notes over and straightened in his seat. He didn't need to run through his closing argument one last time—he had this. He was ready to go.

In minutes, the case would be wrapped up, and Avery Butler would be a verdict away from free.

He took in his surroundings as he waited for the judge to return to the bench. The two-hundred-year-old courtroom was packed, as it had been for the last three weeks. Only this time there was an added buzz of excitement that filled the room. It spread out, climbing the high walls until it hovered like a thick cloud of chatter in the air above them.

An excited cloud.

The entire case was down to two arguments. Then it would be in the jurors' hands.

What they didn't know was that he was about to wipe the floor with the prosecutor.

He was about to make partner.

Cecil Lansing, founding partner of Lansing, Lansing, and Smythe, and longtime friend of the Winston family, sat beside him. Cecil had never given Zack an inch he didn't deserve, but they both knew that when he handed this case over with the bow he was about to tie on top of it, he would deserve everything he'd get.

A rectangle of light beamed onto the aisle of the gallery as the doors at the back of the room swung quietly inward. Two dark-haired boys tiptoed in. They weren't twins, but they looked so much alike they could be.

Which made Zack think of the two men who'd shown up in his life two months ago. Men who'd refused to exit his mind no matter how many times he'd tried to shove them out.

He had never expected to meet his brothers.

And he certainly hadn't expected them to leave without asking for a handout.

No one wants you. Not me. Not your brothers. Don't you think they'd let you know if they did? They only want your money.

Zack ripped his biological mother's words from his head and refocused on the boys now heading up the carpeted aisle. Behind them came a well-dressed but somber-eyed young mother. Her gaze was locked on the man to Zack's right. The tension on her face added a good ten years to her overall appearance.

She was Mr. Butler's administrative assistant. And those were his boys.

The three of them squeezed onto the pew directly behind his client's wife.

Mr. Butler had likely treated his mistress and sons as callously over the years as he'd treated everyone else. With little to no regard for their personal well-being.

At least he was only on trial at this time for the mistreatment of his employees.

"Mr. Winston?"

Zack jerked around, realizing the judge had returned. He sat peering over his bifocals at him. "Problem?" the judge asked.

Closing arguments. *Shit.* It was time.

Only . . . *fuck*. He looked down at the table before him, his speech gone from his mind. He couldn't pull out one thing he'd intended to say. His palms grew clammy as he glanced at the jury box. Then the prosecutor.

He took in Butler's two boys again, and suddenly imagined his brothers when they'd been younger. According to the most recent PI he'd hired, their story had been true. They'd both grown up like him, thinking they were only children.

Yet after all this time, they'd managed to find each other and form a relationship.

And now they said they wanted one with him. *Not* his money.

But could they be trusted?

Clearly Pam Dalton had lied with everything she'd told him. From what Zack's guy had found out, Nick hadn't even seen his mother since he was eighteen.

Cody hadn't seen her since he'd been two.

All of this had wound in and out of Zack's head for the last two months. His adoptive mother hadn't helped the situation. The minute she'd learned that Nick and Cody had come to Atlanta, she'd chewed him up and spit him out for the way he'd sent them away.

When he'd gotten the report back from the investigator, he'd been afraid his mother would call them up herself.

Yet he didn't need brothers in his life. No matter what his mother thought. He was a grown man. Putting his neck on the line for a half-assed relationship that would be pulled out from under him at the first bump was not what he was looking for.

Plus, they already had each other.

"Mr. Winston?"

Notes. There were notes he could read from.

He reached for them, his fingers seeming to have gone numb, and watched as one of the papers fluttered silently to the floor. Then Cecil Lansing put his hand down on top of Zack's.

As if he were having an out-of-body experience, Zack saw his boss nod to a colleague sitting at the opposite end of the table. The colleague stood. And then he proceeded to give Zack's closing argument.

Son of a bitch.

This was *his* case.

His partnership.

Now flushed down the fucking toilet.

Fury built inside him as he sat there doing nothing. He had never floundered like that before. For anything. Not through college, law school. Not even as a kid.

Yet one glance at a pair of young brothers with dark hair and he'd frozen. *Pathetic.*

Cecil slid a yellow legal pad across the heavy oak table, leaving it in front of Zack, while never taking his eyes from the proceedings before them.

Zack looked down. On the paper was one line of text, written in a heavy, bold scrawl.

See me in my office.

His hands curled into fists. He did not need the trouble he'd just bought himself. They wouldn't offer a partnership to someone who couldn't close out his case.

As he sat there, watching his colleague finish the work Zack had put months of time and effort into, he also had to be honest with himself. This wasn't the first mistake he'd made in the last couple of months. Cecil was aware of that.

It was merely the largest.

Sugar Springs had never looked so green.

That was the thought running through Holly Marshall's mind as she passed the WELCOME TO SUGAR SPRINGS sign for the small

East Tennessee town. She'd been gone to Chicago for six weeks, and at times it had felt as if all she'd seen had been metal and glass. And people moving fast.

Everyone had always been in a hurry.

It had also been stifling there.

Granted, it had been an unseasonably warm May all around, but mugginess had seemed to seep into every corner. The tower her cousin lived in, no matter how hard they'd run the air, had remained just this side of oppressive, and every time Holly had stepped from Megan's building, heat had risen up from the concrete to close around her. She'd felt sticky and damp all the time.

She rolled her window down now, letting the warm air flow in to mix with the cooler stream blowing from the car vents. It was hot here too, and though also on the muggy side, Holly knew it wouldn't be the same. Not like in Chicago.

There were no skyscrapers. Nothing to block out the purity of nature.

She hadn't realized how much she'd missed that, but she was most definitely looking forward to stepping foot on her family's land. She wanted to breathe the air in. To enjoy the picture the Smoky Mountains made rising up from the other side of the river.

She also just wanted to chill. Her stress level had climbed to an all-time high.

She'd honestly thought she'd love everything about the city. It had been her plan to live there for years. As well as to find success there.

Both dreams had been shot down. Brutally.

Bert Wheeler, the clerk at the pharmacy, lifted his hand in a wave as she entered the town square. Bert was sitting on a bench in front of the store, his white hair its normal puffy mess on top of his head. It was late Saturday afternoon, and though there were still people buzzing about, Bert was not letting that impact his relaxed state. He was on his break.

He always took breaks on the outside bench. It was easier to people watch.

Holly waved through her passenger-side window and gave him a wide smile. It was good to see Bert.

And the diner, and the cupcake store. Also the statue in the middle of the square. Something about the lone man standing there, tall and proud, always comforted her. As if the founding father was welcoming her home.

Even though she hadn't actually planned to come back home.

Now she never intended to leave.

Having both her dreams *and* her pride crushed into tiny shards could do that to a person.

She forced herself to keep smiling through the thought as she glanced over at the consignment store before exiting the square. At least she still had that.

Unless she gave *it* up too.

At this point she wasn't sure what she should do. After weeks of being told she was a nobody, that she couldn't possibly have a product worthy of their uppity stores, her confidence had failed.

There were a few miles remaining between her and her parents' bed-and-breakfast so she reached for her iPod and pressed play. Katy Perry belted out "Firework" through her speakers, and Holly once again felt a real smile reach her face. She cranked up the volume and pushed the gas pedal harder.

She might be coming home with her tail tucked between her legs, but she refused to allow that to keep her down. What she needed was a new plan. A new goal.

One that included remaining in Sugar Springs.

Only, there wasn't so much to offer here.

She sighed. There was the diner. The B&B. And the horse tour and river-rafting company.

Her family owned all three businesses—with rental cabins being added on the property this summer—and over the years she'd become a professional drifter between each. Whichever location needed her to fill in, she showed up to. Most of her time was spent at the diner. She and her four older brothers owned it, with Brian managing the majority of the day-to-day operation.

At thirty-six, Brian was eleven years older than her, and though there were two brothers in between, they'd always been close. He'd taught her the ropes of the restaurant business during her teen years. Back when her granny and pa had still been alive and running the place.

Brian was another thing she'd missed more than she'd expected. Though she'd never admit that to him.

What she hadn't missed was her nonexistent place in her family. As the only girl, and with eight years between her and her youngest brother, Sean, she'd never really been taken seriously. Instead, she'd just been the little sister.

If she needed something, one of her brothers did it for her.

If she came up with a new idea, it had probably already been tried.

If she stood out in the middle of the road naked and screeching at the top of her lungs, one of her family members simply patted her on the head and told her to stop being silly.

It was frustrating. She was somebody too. She had dreams and aspirations just like everyone else.

She knew her family loved her, but sometimes she needed more. Sometimes, she needed them to see that she was her own person. She had a purpose.

Only . . . she couldn't show them that because she'd failed and she was back.

Again, she let out a grumpy sigh and slumped in her seat. Sometimes life sure had a way of knocking the wind out of a person.

A couple more waves were exchanged as she sped down the road. One little old lady who was sweeping her front sidewalk even stopped and shook her finger at Holly in censure for how fast she was going. This made Holly grin once more. No one had bothered paying attention to how fast she'd driven in Chicago. The finger wagging was a pleasant welcome home.

She turned into the long drive leading to the house she'd grown up in, and took in the two-story white structure with the wraparound porch. It called to her. The porch sported rockers and overflowing pots of greenery, along with swings and hanging baskets. It was one of the most comforting sights she'd seen in weeks.

After her brothers had moved out, their parents had added on to the house and had opened the bed-and-breakfast. Her mom loved running it, and Holly loved living in her old room. It gave her the chance to chat with tourists every day. She liked talking to people.

Which was why she'd thought she would love a bigger city.

She parked, but instead of dragging her suitcase from the backseat of her SUV, or even getting out of the car, she took a moment to simply breathe. Life was what it was. She knew that. And she had a position here in her family. Clearly she wasn't yet meant for more. Which sucked. But at least she did have this.

Taking another deep breath, she stepped from her car and slammed the door. Then she bounded up the front steps. She was suddenly anxious to get inside.

The moment she stepped through the front door, though, she came to an abrupt halt. Her parents' luggage sat there as if waiting to be whisked away. And she knew her parents hadn't been anywhere recently. They'd been here taking care of the B&B.

No one was around, but she could hear voices coming from the direction of the kitchen. She glanced up the stairs, then around the door into the living room. Both were empty. She reached for one of the suitcases, grunting when she picked it up. The thing was loaded down.

"Holly!"

Holly dropped the suitcase and took hurried steps forward. "Hi, Mom," she said with a gush of emotion. It really was great to be home.

She let her mother pull her into a much-needed hug.

When she found it necessary to lick her wounds, it was always nice to have her mom around for comfort. Over her mother's shoulder, she saw her oldest brother, Patrick; his wife, Jillian; and Brian all come out of the kitchen. Patrick's three boys came running up from the basement. They tumbled into the hallway in a loud clatter, the oldest two shoving each other in a race to be first, and were followed by Holly's dad, her brother Rodney, and Rodney's wife and daughter, Erika and Kyndall.

Holly pulled back from her mother in shock. "What's everyone doing here?" she asked. Everyone but Sean. But Sean lived in South Carolina.

Sylvia Marshall pointed toward the dining room. "It's a welcome home party."

Love and longing swelled inside Holly. She hadn't expected that. She stepped farther into the house and peeked into the room to her right. There was even a WELCOME HOME banner strung above the large table.

Then everyone took turns hugging her.

"This is so nice." She wiped a stray tear from the corner of one eye as her niece hugged her tight around the waist.

"I missed you, Aunt Holly," Kyndall whispered.

"I missed you too, sweetie." Holly stroked her hand over her niece's straight hair and caught Brian's wink. She gave him one in return. It was nice to know she'd been missed. It went a long way toward soothing the heartbreak of disappointment.

Then it was Brian's turn to give her a hug. Instead, he locked his arm around her neck and knuckled the top of her head. "Good to have you home, sis. I'm tired of handling everything by myself."

Holly's smile faltered. She knew he was just joking, trying to lighten the mood, but she couldn't help it. She didn't want to be missed simply because she hadn't been around to fit into whichever job was needed.

"And I'm more than ready to hand back over the books," Patrick tossed out as he came forward from the pack. Holly did the books for the horse and rafting tours.

She forced a curve back to her lips. "Surely you guys missed me for more than that."

"I did," Kyndall said. She'd remained by Holly's side, and was currently tracing the tip of a finger over one of the appliqué daisies Holly had stitched to her maxi dress. Kyndall was ten and reminded Holly of herself more than anyone else in the family.

"Thank you, Kyndall." Holly gave the girl's cheek a kiss. "I missed you the most."

Kyndall's smile could have lit the room. "Will you put eye shadow on me?" She bit her lip with excitement. "Mom wouldn't do it the whole time you were gone."

Holly tapped one of Kyndall's bare eyelids and winked, knowing her metallic gold shadow flashed with the move. "I'll fix you up to match me just as soon as we party."

Kyndall giggled, and everyone moved into the dining room, where her mother had a massive spread of appetizers and desserts waiting. Holly knew it wasn't solely for her. Maybe the intent was for her, but with guests coming and going at all hours of the day, they couldn't have snacks out without including extras for them. But she didn't mind. The gesture was nice.

"We were hoping to do a welcome back dinner at Patrick's," her mother began as she grabbed a plate and passed it to Holly, "but you came home a couple days later than we anticipated."

Holly wasn't sure what that had to do with anything. Saturday nights were the norm for family dinners. They could just as easily be having dinner tonight. She took the plate and plucked one of her mom's chocolate petits fours from the serving tray, but before popping it into her mouth, reminded them, "Until a couple days ago, I didn't even plan to come home. Remember?"

That wasn't entirely true. She'd seen the writing on the wall weeks ago. She'd just delayed informing anyone of her imminent return. Especially given that they didn't know what she'd gone to Chicago to do. They'd thought she'd had some kind of wild hair she needed to work out. Sow some oats or something.

They had no idea she'd actually been chasing her dream.

She shoved the dessert in her mouth, all in one bite, to keep from feeling sorry for herself.

"Oh, Holly." Her mother patted Holly's bulging cheek as Holly chewed the sugary treat. Cramming too much food in her mouth was one of the habits that drove her mother crazy. "Of course we knew you'd be back," Sylvia cooed. "You aren't cut out for a big city."

The muscles in Holly's throat closed, threatening to keep her from swallowing the treat. Apparently everyone had believed that about her. A little support would have been nice, though. Even if they hadn't known the full reason behind her trip.

"Well," she said when she had her mouth clear. "I'm back now." The words came out much more chipper than she felt.

"And it's a good thing," Patrick added. He grabbed a plate while his three sons, ages five to twelve, filed in behind him. All three boys were spitting images of their father, and they mimicked his actions, taking a sampling of every dish on the table. "Mom and Dad are leaving tonight," Patrick informed her. "Jilly and I were getting worried that we'd have to juggle both the tours and the guests' breakfasts if you didn't get back today."

Holly swiveled her head to the front door where the luggage sat. Her heart was suddenly thudding in her chest. "You're leaving?" She looked at her mom and dad. "Tonight?"

Hank Marshall nodded. "Just for a week. Your mom wanted an anniversary trip." He gave Sylvia a slow wink. "I'm taking her to a hot spring over in Arkansas. It's gonna be romantic."

Every Marshall child in the room groaned. No one wanted to hear about their parents' love life.

"But Mom," Holly began. She knew she sounded whiny. She couldn't help it. "I just got home."

"I know, sweetie, but you'll be here when we get back. And this is the best time. Before we get too busy with the Firefly Festival."

The annual Firefly Festival was in three weeks. Every room at the B&B, as well as at the hotels in town, would be booked for at least the week leading up to it, probably for longer. People came from far and wide to see the synchronous fireflies that were native only to the Smoky Mountains. The picture the tiny insects made, all glowing and dancing about together, turned a normal hillside into a magical fairyland. Children and adults alike walked away amazed.

To capitalize on the event, Sugar Springs made a day of it one Saturday each June when the fireflies should be at their peak. The whole town would take part in the festival, as would thousands of out-of-towners.

"So . . ." Holly started. She was exhausted from the drive, and now confused on top of it. She looked around at the faces watching her, then to her parents' bulging luggage. Gloom settled inside her. She hadn't wanted to be automatically thrust back into cleanup position. "I guess I'm in charge of breakfasts until you're back?" she finally asked.

She'd been hoping to have a few days to relax. To figure out what she wanted to do next.

"Right," her mom said. Her brown, football helmet–style haircut didn't move as she nodded her head. Her mother was the only brunette in the family. Everyone else was blond. "I also left a list of chores for the week," her mother added. "The paper's on the fridge."

When Holly only stared at her mother and still didn't fill her plate, Sylvia took it from her to do herself.

"What?" her mother asked as she piled sausage wontons and little bites of turtle cheesecake on the stoneware plate. "You know we have to be ready for the festival or the week will get out of control before it starts."

Exactly. And that's what she was good for. Handling a list of chores.

As everyone nibbled on the snacks, Holly became aware that not one of them had asked her how her trip had been. Of course, she had talked to each of them several times over the weeks, telling them about the fun she and Megan had hanging out together. She'd embellished a lot. She loved her cousin, but Holly had been there to work. Megan had had a busy schedule as well.

But still, it would be nice if someone asked something about the trip. Did you have a good time? What happened that you decided not to stay?

Maybe even, how was the freaking drive home?

It wasn't that they didn't care. They just sometimes . . . forgot. To look beyond the surface.

Or so it had always seemed.

She pulled in a deep breath and fought the urge to stomp her foot like a child.

Her mom handed her back the plate, now loaded down with food, and patted her cheek again. "And when we get back, I have a nice surprise for you."

Dread knotted in the pit of Holly's stomach when she saw Brian roll his eyes. "What surprise?" she asked carefully.

"Oh." Her mother waved away her words. "It can wait. Let's party right now."

"What surprise, Mom?"

Holly looked at Brian when her mother didn't immediately answer. His eyebrows waggled and the face that all the single women of Sugar Springs wanted to snuggle up to broke into a devilish grin. A dimple identical to hers flashed deep in one cheek. "Cheater Thompson's son is coming home," he said. "Mom has a date lined up for you."

Holly gawked at her brother before shifting her attention back to her mother. Her father beat a hasty retreat to the kitchen, and

Patrick, Rodney, and their spouses busied themselves with seating the kids. Her mother was on her own.

Cheater was the justice of the peace, as well as the owner of the local funeral home and a wedding chapel. He was a good guy. Really, he could do no wrong in the town's eyes. But he had earned his nickname. More than once. With each of his wives.

And the apple hadn't fallen far from the tree.

Only, his son had yet to let himself be captured with a ring. Instead of the nickname "Cheater Jr.," the minute he'd grown the first hair on his chest, he'd begun working on his own.

Hounddog.

Chances were good he'd someday follow in his father's footsteps, at which point he would become Hounddog *Cheater* Thompson.

"Mom, no." Holly shook her head. "I don't want to go out with Hounddog Thompson."

"Bobby's a good boy, sweetheart. All he needs is a good woman and he'll settle right down."

Bobby *was* a good guy. Or he had been the last time she'd seen him. But he was also a hound dog. "And what makes you think *I* need him?" she asked.

Her mother's green eyes turned to her then, and what Holly saw in them tightened the dread in her stomach. Her mother was sad. For her.

Holly gulped.

"You need someone, sweetheart," her mom said softly. "I'm just trying to help. I thought that now that you had Chicago out of your system, you might be ready to settle down."

Her mother thought she needed to settle down? A lump rose in her throat.

"What do you even know about him?" she managed to eke out, unsure what else to say. "Have you even seen him since he left?"

Hounddog had graduated the same year as Holly, and had blown out of town before the ink on his diploma was dry. They'd been friends as kids. He'd teased her in elementary school by pulling her hair on the bus every afternoon, but by their teens they'd hung out. When he hadn't been busy chasing a cheerleader, that was.

But still, it wasn't like Holly had kept in touch with him over the years.

And his nickname was still Hounddog. The people who *had* kept in touch with him had made that clear.

"I've talked to his mama," her mother said. "She works over at the Soapbox Laundry. She assures me he's ready for more."

More women, most likely.

Holly swallowed and looked at the rest of her family. They all wore the same kind of sad, poor-Holly look in their eyes. Was everyone thinking she was some pathetic loser and all she needed was a man to make her happy?

What about doing something with her life? Having a career? Why had *that* never occurred to them?

And then something occurred to her. Were they right?

Was that what she needed?

Her heart pounded behind her breastbone. She'd just been thinking she had to find something to do. She didn't want to be a part-time cook-slash-bookkeeper for the rest of her life. Not *only* that.

And she *had* been thinking that there was nothing really to do around here. Not anything she was qualified for, at least.

If she'd gotten a teaching degree, maybe. That was one of the true "professions" in town. Other than doctor or vet, but she was sorely underqualified for that. Plus, she preferred something a bit more creative, even if her trip to Chicago had proved she didn't have what it took.

She thought about how she wasn't getting any younger, and figured she needed to be more settled. Responsible. She could drive out of town to work at the casket factory, she supposed.

Only . . . she didn't want to work at the casket factory.

And she didn't want to go back to school so she could teach.

Was marriage and babies it, then? All she had to look forward to?

Her chest tightened, but the thought wasn't as sour as she might have imagined. She did want to get married at some point. And yeah, she wanted babies. Several of them.

Was it time?

Her breaths grew shallow as she took in each member of her family again, including her dad, who now stood in the doorway between the kitchen and dining room. He wore the same woe-is-Holly look as the rest of them.

She didn't want them to think that marriage and babies was *all* she could do.

But then . . . she thought about the number of times she'd had the door slammed in her face in Chicago.

Maybe it *was* all she could do.

If she could even do that.

It wasn't as if her dance card had been full the last few years. The men of Sugar Springs saw her more as a buddy than a potential mate. Which was her own fault. She'd acted like their buddy. The cute little Marshall girl.

Could she change it?

Did she want to?

With an inaudible groan, she lowered her eyes and dug into her food. She didn't know what she wanted.

But she was pretty sure it wasn't Hounddog Thompson.

Chapter Two

As of right now, you're on vacation.

Zack tightened his fingers around the steering wheel and pushed down on the gas pedal as he replayed his boss's words from Friday afternoon. Cecil hadn't even let him stick around for the verdict. He'd kicked him out of the office the minute they'd recessed.

You've been somewhere else for months. Whatever is going on with you, we don't need it here. Fix it.

Zack had tried to argue.

He wasn't somewhere else. He was right there. He'd just had a bad day.

But that was bull and they'd both known it. In his eight years at the firm, he hadn't had a bad day. And he hadn't made a mistake. Until recently. Cecil was a good enough friend to call him out on his issues before it became a major deal. As if being unable to give closing arguments wasn't a major deal. Thank goodness his colleague had stepped in. With him, at least they'd still managed to win the case.

Zack took a curve too fast, gripping both hands tight on the wheel as he fought to keep from losing control. Killing himself in the middle of nowhere wouldn't solve his problems. Then again, he wasn't sure going to Sugar Springs would solve them either.

The low-slung convertible headed into yet another twisting curve, and Zack gritted his teeth in focus, this time tapping on his brakes instead of risking going out the wrong side of the curve. There was zero chance of getting any good speed going on the tiny two-lane, as the majority of the three-and-a-half-hour trip north had been.

On a day when he wanted to go fast, it frustrated the hell out of him that he had to crawl.

He rounded yet another bend in the road, and his head swiveled to the left. Really? It was Memorial Day, for Christ's sake. That made the third house he'd seen strung end-to-end with Christmas lights. He supposed the fact that the lights weren't on was supposed to mean they didn't exist. Or who knew, maybe come darkness, they would all shine bright.

He shook his head in disgust and returned his sights to the cracked asphalt in front of him. He couldn't believe what a backwoods place this town was.

Or that it was his destination.

But his mother had made a good point. As had Cecil. He supposed.

Zack needed to deal with his issues.

With no chance of getting back into the office for the next two weeks, and given that he had brothers and that little fact wouldn't be going away, he supposed he might as well deal with it.

He *supposed* he could spend the next couple of weeks in a town of less than six hundred if that meant he could get back to work. Back to making partner.

He wasn't looking for relationships to come of this trip. In fact, just the opposite. He'd meant it when he'd told them that he had no interest. That hadn't changed. They'd spent their whole lives never knowing each other. He couldn't imagine it would turn into long-lost brotherly love at this point.

Yet he could no longer ignore the fact that it had impacted him. His closing argument. His job. His chances at making *partner*, for crying out loud.

He'd stick around Sugar Springs long enough for everyone to get their curiosities answered. He'd show his mother that he'd put in a good-faith effort at "getting to know" them. Then he'd put the situation behind him for good.

He took another curve and pushed the gas pedal to zoom up the slight rise. He'd topped the hill and headed back down when he caught sight of the next house. It was a single-wide trailer with a rickety do-it-yourself front porch, and hanging off all sides of the porch—as if someone thought they were decorations—were wash-tubs. Gray and dusty old-timey metal tubs, some rusted, some big, some small. It looked like something that belonged on *Duck Dynasty*.

The car hit a dip in the road and he jerked back around, only to see that he was no longer actually on the road. He'd missed a curve.

And he was headed straight for a massive oak sitting in the middle of a handful of gravestones.

He stomped on the brakes and the car swerved. It slid through the grass at an angle, but he did manage to come to a stop before he hit the tree. Barely. Unfortunately, one of the stones wasn't so lucky. Nor was his airbag. He'd knocked a concrete marker out of the ground and his car now sat at an angle on top of it. His front tire no longer touched the ground. And a deflated airbag hung limply from his steering wheel.

A slight breeze whispered through the air of the open top, mixing with the acrid smell from the deployed bag and tickling against his neck and cheeks. He sat there fuming, taking in his surroundings. There were tiny red-, white-and-blue flags stuck in the ground at each of the plots. Beside the flags were small bundles of similarly colored flowers. They were all fresh.

This was not a forgotten family plot out in the middle of nowhere. And he was parked right smack in the middle of it.

Fantastic entrance, Winston. What else can you fuck up this week?

He forced himself to loosen his jaw, and turned off the engine. He wouldn't be getting the car out of there on his own. If he hadn't already ripped something vital out, trying to back off of the stone would surely do it.

Before he could pull his phone out to call for a wrecker, a squawking honk sounded in his ear. He snapped his gaze around. To the left of his car stood two Canadian geese. Clearly agitated. With an enormous, sable-colored horse hovering behind them. The horse slung its dark head and snorted, showing its teeth. Zack stilled.

What the hell kind of place had he landed in?

And then his eyes hit on a leg dangling down the side of the beast. His gaze shot up.

He took in the woman sitting on the horse. Thick, blonde hair parted down the middle, with braids hanging over each shoulder, and a face that was smooth and creamy. Bright-red lips and dark-ringed eyes drew his attention, and silver eye shadow glittered from her eyelids. She was dressed to match the flowers he'd just run over with his car.

She had on a sleeveless white button-down knotted at the waist, the buttons straining to hold the material closed over her breasts, and a pair of cutoff jeans covered in white stars. The shorts looked as if they would be showing about half her ass, except for the cherry-red leggings—also adorned with the pattern of stars—that ran to just below her knees. At the bottom of those legs were the oddest shoes to be wearing on a horse. Black patent leather with a buckle closure and wide chunky heels. Green and purple fringe circled around the backs.

He eyed the shoes for a moment longer, thinking they seemed more like something that should be worn on stage. By a transvestite, perhaps. Then he forced his eyes back up and over her outfit, lingering at the rounded curve of her butt, and having the random thought that she wasn't at all like the women he dated.

First, they'd never be caught dead in an outfit like that. They wore designer, or they wore nothing at all.

Second, they didn't have nearly the curves this woman did.

And "woman" was a stretch. He couldn't tell her age, but she looked younger than her body shape might imply.

He forced his gaze to continue up until he once again landed on her face. She was frowning at him.

"You ran over my granny," she said.

Of course this would be her land. Why couldn't he have made it to the bed-and-breakfast without incident? It couldn't be more than a couple miles down the road.

He opened his door to step out, intending to gain the upper hand by standing tall and using his courtroom voice. Instead, his foot sunk into mud.

"And your car is straddling a dip in the land," she added. "It rained last night."

He held on to his temper—but just barely—and stretched his other leg two feet away until he hit drier ground. He pulled his mud-covered foot out behind him.

His shoulders drew in tight at the sucking sound as his shoe popped free of the sticky mud, and when he finally stood, with only the barest amount of dignity remaining, he removed his sunglasses and peered up at the rider as if he had every right to be there. His chest rose and fell with a frustrated breath, and he ignored the airbag dust now sprinkled over the front of his suit. He shouldn't have come.

"As I'm sure you can guess," he began, "I missed a turn in the road." *On a road in such poor shape it should be illegal to travel on,* he added silently, and wondered if he should sue the city for the pitiful state of the asphalt. Or maybe he should sue the moron with the washtub ornamentation on his "porch."

He motioned behind him to the marker buried beneath his car. "I'll cover the repair as soon as I get my car towed. I'll leave you my card."

She eyed him from her seven-foot perch. If he were to guess, he'd say she was unimpressed. But then, he did have mud covering one of his Salvatore Ferragamos. It wasn't a good look.

He watched as her green eyes blinked and then she shifted her gaze to his car. The top was down, and there wasn't a thing to be found on the inside—other than the new layering of fine dust. The rest was spotless. It was as if he were seeing it himself for the first time.

Funny. He'd never thought himself quite as sterile as his car might imply. No-nonsense and to the point, yes. He didn't tolerate less than the best, either in work or play. But not necessarily cold and empty.

But if he were her . . .

"I'll give you a ride," she said. Her voice bore no emotion. She scooted forward on the saddle, leaving about half a foot of empty space behind her. "You won't get a tow truck out here today."

He eyed the horse. "I don't think so." He was not climbing onto the back of a horse. Especially not in a twenty-five-hundred-dollar suit. "I'll call my assistant. I'm sure she can locate someone."

His assistant had taken the two weeks off since he was banned from the building, but he knew she'd help him out. She'd be glad to. He pulled his phone from his pocket.

"Not in Sugar Springs she won't," the woman told him. "It's a holiday."

The geese squawked at him again as if reiterating her point, and he sighed. He was quickly losing patience. "And emergencies don't happen in Sugar Springs during holidays? Surely there are trucks on standby."

Who lived in a place like this?

She shrugged a slim shoulder. Her whole demeanor was one of casual unconcern. "Emergencies happen," she said, "but then there's always someone around to help." She patted the neck of the horse. "Like Misty here. She'd be glad to carry you up to the house."

Up to what house?

He wasn't sure he wanted to know.

Ignoring her, he turned back to his phone. He was not getting on that horse.

27

Holly Marshall watched the man for five more seconds before she directed Misty to turn. Her first impressions were rarely wrong, and her instincts told her this guy was an ass. So, fine. He could walk to the house.

She may have to deal with him when—*if*—he ever arrived at her parents' bed-and-breakfast, but she certainly didn't have to deal with him now.

What a jerk. He reminded her of every boutique owner she'd met during her stint in Chicago. If they hadn't been looking down their noses at her or talking about her behind her back, they'd insulted her directly to her face.

She hadn't needed their rudeness, and she didn't need his. She had better things to do with her time.

Before she, Misty, and the geese could get more than a few feet away, she heard the man curse. She couldn't help the smile. Arrogant pricks deserved to be put in their place.

She fought the urge to nudge Misty to go faster.

"Do you not get a cell signal out here?" he finally growled out.

Laughter would only make it worse. She stopped the horse and peered back over her shoulder, giving him the same loathing perusal he'd given her. "I don't *need* a cell signal out here, sugar."

She was tired and frustrated, having worked too many hours the last two days at the B&B and then fixing the mess Patrick had made of the books. She wasn't in the mood to deal with a jerk of a man who thought he was better than her simply because he saw himself as higher class.

Even if he was smoking hot in a black pin-striped suit.

With mud up to one ankle.

Plus, she knew who he was. Therefore, she already knew he was an ass. But what she didn't know was what he was doing there.

The name on the register she'd checked that morning was listed as "Z. Winston," with an Atlanta number. When she'd first seen it, she'd wondered if it would really be him. Cody and Nick had told her about their brother, and about how he'd treated them when they'd gone to Atlanta. Zack Winston had been less than receptive to their brotherly overtures.

So a fancy, fast car with Georgia plates and a lawyer type in a pricey suit—who just happened to look like Nick and Cody Dalton—could only be one person.

The thought crossed her mind to leave him standing in the middle of the mud and let him find his own way out. He *had* knocked over her granny's tombstone after all. And right after she'd put fresh flowers on the grave. He didn't really deserve her help.

But then again, she hadn't been raised that way. It wouldn't hurt her to help him out. So she tilted her head and gave him a polite smile. She was, after all, representing her parents' business.

"Misty still has a spot open," she pointed out. "All you have to do is climb up."

When he looked at the horse and his face lost some of its color, she almost felt bad for the guy. Was he afraid of horses? But then she remembered the way his lip had turned up when he'd looked at her shoes. He'd judged her and found her lacking.

Therefore, he didn't get her sympathy.

She did, however, hold out hope that he was in Sugar Springs for good reasons. Maybe her friends would get that chance to get to know their brother, after all.

"I do have work to do," she calmly informed him. She had too much still ahead of her to be out here waiting all day for him to make up his mind. She held her hand out in his direction. "Either climb aboard or prepare to walk."

His jaw worked back and forth. He'd put his sunglasses back on and she couldn't see his eyes anymore. Which was fine with her. They were dark brown like his brothers'. The color actually looked good on *them*. On Zack it just looked . . .

She growled under her breath. On him it looked good, as well. Dang it.

And she didn't want to think about someone like him looking good. Though he did. Even in his pricey, probably hand-tailored suit.

He looked like the best thing to come along in years.

Her mother's sad eyes darted through her mind, along with her telling Holly that she needed a man.

But she didn't need this one!

She'd had enough of people like him to last her a lifetime. She turned Misty to go once more, letting anger from her recent trip resurface. She'd tossed away her dream because of assholes like him, and she was still a little raw about it.

Hell, she hadn't even managed to get in the door of each gallery to *explore* her dream.

She'd gotten nowhere.

She'd been made fun of simply for being who she was. As if there were nothing more to her than where she came from and how she talked.

It wasn't fair. She was a good person.

And she had a hell of a lot of talent.

"Where are you proposing to take me on that thing?" he asked with an amazing amount of bluster. "I would still need a lift to the B&B where I've rented a room. It's the Marshall place. Do you know it?"

A sigh pushed up and out of her lungs as she turned back to him. "You're on Marshall property, Mr. Winston. You're here." At his arched brow over her use of his name, she merely continued. "We just need to go about one mile down the road and you'll see the house."

"Oh."

And then the fast-talking lawyer seemed to have no words left to say.

He looked at the rolling acres surrounding them, then back to his car and at her family's plots. Then he shook his head and mumbled something under his breath. He reached into his car to grab his keys from the ignition.

As he did, he forgot about the soft ground and stepped forward. His other foot sank in the mud. A snicker of laughter escaped Holly before she could clamp her lips together to stop it.

He mumbled again—this time allowing Holly to catch the word *two-bit*—as he raised the convertible top and locked the car up tight. When he turned back, Holly patted the spot behind her and wiggled her brows up and down in teasing enticement. For some reason, she was suddenly anxious to see the suit on her horse.

Only, when he put his foot in the stirrup and swung up behind her, she had a sudden change of heart. Holy moly, he was big. And his body felt like it was about two hundred degrees.

And it touched her *everywhere*.

She swallowed the nerves that sprang to life as he put a hand on either side of her waist.

When she didn't immediately spur Misty into action, he gritted out, "Can we go?"

Oh, hell yeah.

Because the last thing she wanted to do was spend more time than she had to with this guy on the back of her horse.

"My pleasure," she murmured.

She kicked the side of the horse, and when she had Misty moving, she tossed a quick glance back over her shoulder. With everything she had in her, she gave him a welcome she knew her mama would be proud of. Even if it was completely forced on her part.

"Welcome to Sugar Springs, Mr. Winston. I do hope your stay will be an enjoyable one."

Chapter Three

"Where the hell is he?"

Holly played with the straw in her Diet Coke as she peered across the booth at Cody. It was Wednesday afternoon, and they were at the diner.

Zack hadn't been seen since Monday night.

"I have no idea," she confessed.

"Why is he here?"

"Again . . ." At this point she felt bad that she'd called the brothers in the first place, which she'd done the instant she'd gotten Zack settled in at the house. She'd honestly thought Zack would be contacting them. "I have no idea. Jerry picked him up Monday night. I haven't heard from him since."

But his Benz was gone from the middle of the field. And her granny's headstone had already been fixed.

Jerry Whitlow was the local tow-truck driver. Holly had been shocked when she'd heard the low growl of the flatbed outside her bedroom window late Monday, and even more so when she'd peeked out to see Zack climbing into the passenger seat beside him.

She supposed Zack had been right. He *could* get people out on a holiday. Even in Sugar Springs. "Maybe he's somewhere getting his car fixed," she added. Though why he hadn't gotten a rental and come back while the work was being done, she didn't know.

She just hoped he *did* come back.

If not, he was one cruel person. And though she had no doubt he was a jerk and a pompous ass, she hadn't sensed cruelty.

Cody drenched his fries in ketchup as he quietly worked through his thoughts. They were good friends. Had been since almost the moment he'd arrived in town. But even so, she had no idea what to say to make this better.

"I'm sorry, Cody. I thought he would call. I thought . . ."

That his being here would be a good thing, she finished silently. She'd let her optimism assume the best. Instead, Zack's arrival was blowing up in her friends' faces. Hurting them one more time.

"It's not your fault," Cody assured her. He reached across the table and squeezed her hand. "He's playing some kind of game."

"Well, it's a ridiculous game."

"Yeah." He chuckled without humor. "But then, he was pretty ridiculous when we met him."

He held out a fry, asking if she wanted one, but she shook her head. She wasn't in the mood to eat. She also wasn't in the mood to think about Zack. But darned if he hadn't been poking in and out of her head over the last two days.

Not just wondering when he would get around to hunting up his brothers, but also thinking about what it had been like when he'd been sitting behind her on the horse. His body had outlined every last inch of her backside.

If it hadn't been him back there, it would have been nice.

Clearly it had been too long for her when she kept thinking about all the places the heat from his body had slid into instead of thinking what a jerk he was for not calling his brothers.

Places that she didn't need to be heating up.

Especially by him.

She slumped in her seat, humiliated by her own thoughts, and stretched her feet to the bench across from her. Then she sulked.

Cody eyed her as if able to read her thoughts. The very idea made her cheeks burn. Then he angled his neck and took in her feet. He gave a quick nod of approval.

"Cute," he said.

Holly tapped the toes of her University of Tennessee orange sneakers together and gave him a languid smile. The shoes had come with white laces, but she'd changed them out for bright green. They looked like little pumpkins with the green on top. "I found these in Chicago the last day I was there. I love them."

She loved all shoes. As long as they were cute and eye-catching. And more often than not, they didn't match her outfit. It was silly, but doing something that made no sense made her feel special. Noticed.

"So how was Chicago?" Cody asked.

Changing the subject from Zack was probably best.

Changing it to Chicago wasn't.

She lifted a shoulder. What could she say? She'd hated it. They'd hated her. She was a failure. "It was fine."

Cody eyed her again, this time as if not believing her despondent words, but instead of pressing her for answers he returned to his burger and fries.

They both grew silent and she took the moment to look around at the simple decor of the dining room. Since she'd been busy at the house the last few days, she had yet to return to working at the diner, but just being there now was already beginning to ease her stress. The place always had that effect on her.

Wood-block tables and booths filled the room, with the occasional mismatched chair. The chairs were a hangover from her grandparents' days. Vintage, vinyl-topped stools lined the counter in front of the grill window. And large, unpaned windows took up the space along the front of the building. The windows overlooked the square.

All of it was easy. Comfortable.

It felt like home.

A couple regulars were sitting at one of the tables, hanging on past the lunch hour, and gave her a welcoming chin nudge as her gaze passed over them. She returned the greeting with a wink and blew them a kiss. She'd seen several people in passing since coming home. They'd all waved as if glad to see her back, some pointing out that she'd been missed in the diner. But there had yet to be a chance to really talk to anyone. Being out today was nice.

Cody was one of the two local veterinarians, and regularly slipped over for a late lunch. When she was around, she often took a break and joined him. Today she was there because he'd called. It was good to see him again.

She looked at him then, at his dark hair and eyes and his hard jaw. And she thought about how much Zack looked like his brothers. Even the anger lurking in Zack's brown depths she'd seen in Cody's plenty of times. When he'd first returned to town, he'd been much harder than he was today.

That didn't mean Zack wouldn't bring that back out of him.

She suspected very much that he would.

Cody caught her looking and lifted a brow in question as he shoved another fry in his mouth. She just shook her head. "Nothing," she mumbled.

No doubt he was merely biding his time before he forced her to talk about Chicago. She'd left Sugar Springs too excited about the trip, spouting that if things went well she would be moving there for good. He had to be wondering what happened. She appreciated him giving her an out for the moment. She needed a few more minutes to gather her thoughts.

The bell on the outer door dinged and Holly looked up to see Lee Ann London enter the restaurant. Lee Ann was Cody's fiancée.

She'd once worked mornings at the diner, but now focused full-time on her photography and on raising her and Cody's teenage daughters.

Lee Ann spotted them and headed their way. As she did, Beatrice Grayson slipped in behind her, a quick blur of gray hair and feet too fast for an eighty-year-old.

Ms. Grayson ran her gaze over Cody sitting with Holly, then to Lee Ann, before shifting her attention to the remainder of the guests in the diner. She'd seen her share of living, and was currently considered the town mouth. If there was a secret, she knew about it.

If she didn't, she made it up.

She took a seat at a nearby table as Lee Ann neared their booth.

"I heard a rumor that you were back." Lee Ann gave Holly a hug. "Your mama and daddy must be glad to have you home." She slid in beside Cody, kissing him on the cheek, and Holly lowered her feet so they weren't stuck between the two lovebirds.

"They seemed pleased," Holly confirmed. "Got me working at the B&B already."

"Ah." Lee Ann nodded. "That's right, they were going out of town for the week. When did you get in?"

"Saturday afternoon."

"I was just asking her how it went," Cody added. He studied her with narrowed eyes. "She's quieter than usual today," he added. "I think Chicago changed her."

His words surprised her. She didn't think anyone would notice. She focused on her drink as she sucked at the straw.

"So you finally blowing out of this place for good then?" Cody pressed. "Just come back to pack more bags?"

Holly swallowed the liquid and looked up at the two friendly faces waiting to hear her plans. There was true caring etched in both of them. She appreciated that. She'd missed that.

"Nope." Holly shook her head and grabbed a fry off Cody's plate. Tears suddenly threatened, but she held them off. "Everyone was right. I'm a Sugar Springs girl." The whole town had told her that for years. "I'm not cut out for the big city. I believe it now."

Lee Ann's gaze turned warm with concern. Her mouth lost its smile. "What happened?"

Holly shrugged. "Just didn't work out. I don't belong there." She looked away from the concerned eyes of her friends and chewed on the inside corner of her lip.

She'd long said she'd outgrown Sugar Springs. And she knew she was the only one in the town who believed it. She was only twenty-five. Her life stretched out before her. She'd thought there was more out there for her.

Yet here she was, back at home like a whipped puppy.

She watched a couple more people enter the diner and take a seat: Jerry, the driver of the wrecker who'd picked Zack up, and Tucker Brown, the sixth-grade math teacher. The two had been friends for years. Jerry was weathered and rough around the edges, and Tucker had perfectly trimmed hay-colored hair and looked like he belonged in a tweed sport coat holding a pipe. He was one of the most serious people she'd ever met, and he and Jerry were two of the most mismatched people in the county. Yet their friendship had held over the years.

She turned her head back to her friends. Lee Ann and Cody had a friendship similar to Jerry and Tucker's. They'd been through a lot together, but even stupid mistakes and years apart hadn't broken the bond they held. Holly wanted something like that for herself.

If she were the wallowing sort, she might let her lack of direction in life get her down. Might let the fact that she had no one to share her secrets with bother her. Instead, she refused. After thinking about her mother's words over the last few days, she'd decided that her mom was onto something. She needed a man.

And Holly had done a lot of mulling over her possibilities.

She licked her lips and pasted on a smile, ready to present her new plan. If she couldn't have her dream, she'd make a new one. "I changed my mind," she announced proudly. She lowered her voice and leaned into the table to whisper when she caught sight of Ms. Grayson angling her head in their direction. "Instead of moving to a bigger place, I'm staying here. I'm getting married and having babies."

Cody choked on his drink. Lee Ann wasn't much better. Only, she had no liquid in her mouth. She simply choked.

"To who?" Cody and Lee Ann asked at the same time.

That was the problem.

She glanced to the other side of the room where the two men had sat down, and eyed Tucker. She'd had a bit of a crush on him for years. But then, only because he was cute. In a scholarly kind of way. Stiff shirts did it for her, apparently.

Everything else about him, though . . . she feared would bore her to tears.

But she had to start somewhere.

Out of the corner of her eye she saw Lee Ann follow her gaze.

"Really?" Lee Ann asked. Her voice held more than a bit of unease. "You're finally going to go for it with him?" Lee Ann had been aware of Holly's semi-crush.

"Who?" Cody was clueless.

Holly nodded slowly, more than a little hesitant. If she had to choose someone in Sugar Springs, Tucker was a decent catch. He had a good job, with nice health benefits. The school system was one of the best places to work when it came to benefits. Plus, summers off. That would be good for having kids. Plenty of time with them. They could take family vacations.

All in all, he would make a good choice for a husband.

He might be a bit on the stiff side, but she figured they could balance each other out.

She looked back at Lee Ann, realizing she was less than enthused at the thought. But it wasn't like Sugar Springs was a hotbed of potential husband material. Not material that hadn't already been caught up and taken. "I heard he broke up with Teresa while I was gone," she said.

"He did." Lee Ann nodded.

Tucker had been dating the fourth-grade teacher who'd moved into town last year. Apparently it had ended with the school year.

"Who?" Cody asked again.

Both women shot him an annoyed look, then Lee Ann nodded her head in the direction of Tucker. Men could be so obtuse.

Cody finally got a clue that the man of their conversation was in the room. He scanned the area twice, landing on each person in the dining room, before going back to Tucker. He narrowed his eyes on the other man, before bringing his head around to Holly. "No," he said without preamble.

"Why not?" she asked. As if Cody's no would stop her if Tucker was who she wanted. "He's cute." And she liked a man who looked good in a sport coat. Or a suit.

Zack Winston materialized in her mind, standing beside her horse in his mud-covered shoes. She fought a smile.

"He's too . . ." Cody paused.

"What?" Holly asked.

He glanced at Lee Ann as if to get her to help him out, but Holly reached over the table and grabbed his wrist. She squeezed until he looked at her.

"What?" she asked, her voice harsh. "You don't think I can get him?"

"Of course you can get him." His look of incredulity eased her mind. "The question is," Cody added, "why would you want to?"

She turned loose of him and sat back with a thunk. "Why wouldn't I want to? He's respectable. He has a good family. He's a total catch."

"He's boring as shit," Cody stated bluntly. "Has he ever looked at your shoes?"

Holly snapped her mouth shut. She'd once explained to Cody that her shoes were an indicator of her first impressions about people.

"What group does he fall into?" Cody persisted when she didn't answer.

"I don't—"

"What group?" Cody asked. "He's probably too mannered to turn his nose up at them."

Like Zack had, she thought. She'd seethed for the last two days over the snotty way Zack had looked at her shoes. They'd been perfectly good shoes. Vintage Mary Janes. And the fringe had been fun. She'd added that herself.

"And I can't see him *liking* them," Cody went on. Lee Ann simply watched the two of them without saying a word. "He probably isn't amused by them," Cody continued. "I'm not sure I've ever seen 'the Professor' amused by much of anything."

"I've seen him laugh at plenty of things," Holly blurted. Which wasn't really true. She had seen him laugh once. He'd been doing a spot for a local tourism ad, but his laughter had been so forced that it hadn't made the final cut.

"So that leaves only one group," Cody finished. He tilted his head and looked down his nose at her. "He's never even noticed them."

"Not everyone has to notice my shoes," she pointed out. She didn't know why they were talking about her and her shoes when she'd come there to talk about Cody and Zack.

Cody just stared at her. He knew that if people didn't notice her shoes, it was worse than people thinking her odd or off her rocker. She used to think ignoring them was worse than sneering at them too. Until Monday.

"You've never explained the shoe thing to me," Lee Ann said. "I thought it was just you."

"It *is* just me," Holly stressed. "I like shoes. And I like to be different."

"And she makes snap decisions about people based on their reaction to them."

Holly made a face at him. "That's only one factor."

"It's what you used to decide about me. And you claim to hold a ninety-nine percent accuracy record."

"I *do* hold a ninety-nine percent accuracy record." She couldn't remember the last time she'd been wrong about her first impression of someone. Rarely was she wrong about anything when it came to people. She watched them. Made studied observations.

"What was your first impression of *him*?" Cody asked. He glanced across the room to Tucker as he said it. Tucker was, as always, sitting straight and looking serious. He was explaining something to Jerry while Jerry watched the TV hanging in the corner.

"I've known Tucker my whole life," Holly hedged. "There wasn't a first impression. Or if there was, it happened when I was a kid and I don't remember."

They weren't the same age, but they'd been in high school together. He was a couple years older than her. She also remembered her first impression of him. The word *dweeb* came to mind.

He hadn't been cute then. He'd been awkward and hadn't yet filled out into his body. But he had been as boring as he was today.

She had a vision of the two of them sitting in a house together, years from now. Tucker would be telling her all about his day at work; their children would be politely listening—maybe one or two of them would be engrossed in a book . . .

And all her fun shoes would be tucked away in a box in the attic. *Great.*

She couldn't go out with Tucker. Cody was right. The man had never even noticed her shoes. She didn't want to think about finding herself long-term with a man who couldn't be bothered to look at her from head to toe, much less not appreciate her stellar collection of footwear.

Fine. She silently seethed. But she needed someone.

She thought about Zack sitting straight and stiff on the back of her horse.

No!

No matter how cute he'd been in his awkwardness, she didn't need him. For one thing, he wouldn't be sticking around. He was big city. She most decidedly was not.

Secondly, he'd looked down his nose at her.

And he'd hated her shoes.

Cody's cell rang.

"Yeah," he said, putting it to his ear. He listened a minute and then mouthed, "It's Nick" to Lee Ann. A line creased his brow, and he turned to peer out the large window by their table. Holly and Lee Ann followed his movement. "Now?" he asked into the phone.

Holly couldn't hear the reply, but whatever was happening, she got the impression it was supposed to be happening now. The fingers of Cody's free hand began to tap on the tabletop.

All was quiet outside, with the statue of the town's founding father standing tall in the middle of the square. Banners announcing the upcoming Firefly Festival flanked him on every side. It was high tourist season, but most people had either headed into the mountains or taken to the river today. Only a few nonlocals could be seen going in and out of the different shops. A couple stood outside Cakes-a-GoGo with cupcakes in one hand and pieces of paper in the other. Probably the tourist brochures that could be found stocked at each business.

A slight breeze rattled the trees spaced out along the sidewalks.

And then a low-sitting sports car came purring down the street.

It gleamed in the sunlight, and Holly's body heated at the sight. There was just something about a hot car.

And a hotter man.

She caught Cody's groan and glanced at him in time to see the quick flash of anger harden his face.

"I'll call you back," he bit out, then hung up the phone.

Ms. Grayson chose that moment to set aside the tea she'd been drinking and stood to leave. Holly blew out a breath of relief as the older lady made it to the door. It was best not to have the biggest gossip in town hanging around for the first sighting of Zack.

Especially since it would be too easy to see whom he was related to.

"That's him," Jerry said from the other side of the room. He pointed to the window. "The man I took to Knoxville Monday night. Picked him up out at the Marshall place. He paid me a week's salary to cancel my plans for the night and load up that fancy car of his. I drove them both to a dealer."

So that's where he'd been.

And how he'd gotten Jerry to get off his couch on a holiday.

"Who in the world is he?" This came from Janice, one of the waitresses who worked the morning and lunch shifts. She was in her forties and had lived in Sugar Springs her whole life. Her husband had hit a rough patch lately, leaving her with the need to pick up extra shifts to support them and their two teenage sons.

Holly and Lee Ann looked at Cody. The minute someone saw the men together, it would be clear.

The room grew quiet as the car passed outside the diner window and everyone got a good look. Zack's profile could easily be Cody's or Nick's—even with the sunglasses. The only difference was that he sat straighter and his hair was shorter and a shade or two lighter. Also, he had on yet another suit.

It would likely take a lot to get Cody or Nick in a suit.

Then all eyes in the diner turned to Cody.

They didn't even know he had a second brother, but Holly suspected they'd just figured it out.

"He looks just like you," Janice declared. She made her way over to their table.

"I knew he looked like someone." Jerry joined them. He shook his finger in the air as he spoke, and Holly couldn't help but notice that the backs of his fingers had an excessive amount of hair on them. It was kind of gross. "I just couldn't place him," Jerry finished.

Since Jerry had come over, Tucker wandered their way as well. He gazed out the window as Holly peered up at him. He really was a good-looking man. Clean-shaven, seemingly no wayward hair on unsuspecting body parts. She'd do fine to get him. Except for the fact she'd have to be around him day in and day out.

She shuddered at the thought.

So much for bachelor number one on her list.

"He's my brother," Cody finally admitted. A soft gasp came from the small crowd. Then the Benz disappeared down the street.

"He's a year older than us," Cody added. "Thirty-three." He glanced back out the window and Holly watched his jaw grow tense. "He was given away for adoption at birth. We found him in Atlanta earlier this year."

"Well, I never," Janice whispered.

Tucker looked down then. He glanced around the table, giving a slight nod when his gaze landed on Holly, but that was it. No gleam in his eye. No mooning look on his face.

Yeah . . . the man wasn't for her.

Maybe Jerry?

She almost snorted her Diet Coke up her nose at the thought. Jerry wouldn't have the first clue what to do with her. But she'd give him points. He had noticed her shoes in the past.

The group of them chatted about Zack for several minutes longer, Cody explaining in brief detail how his older brother had wanted nothing to do with them. His words were spoken pleasantly with an air of unconcern, but she and he were good enough friends that she felt the longing for more beneath their surface. He and Nick had gone to Atlanta hoping to have a relationship with the brother neither of them had known existed. They'd both come back hurt.

She glanced at Lee Ann, and the two women exchanged knowing looks. It bothered Cody, having Zack show up like this. Not knowing his intent. And most likely, not knowing what he himself wanted to happen. No doubt Nick would feel the same.

The unannounced arrival suddenly made Holly angry on behalf of her friends. It also irritated her that Zack had arrived nearly forty-eight hours earlier, yet hadn't made so much as a phone call to either of them.

When Cody finished talking, everyone returned to their tables with a gleam burning in their eyes. News would now spread, and Zack would have a town full of enemies before he ever even spoke to anyone.

Though she still thought the guy was a jerk, it almost made Holly feel bad for him. Gossip here could be brutal.

As the talk died down, her gaze once again turned to Tucker. He was the only one without his cell out to call or text the gossip on to the next person. Probably not because he was such a good, upstanding guy as much as because he had no one to text. Definitely off her list of potential mates.

That didn't mean she couldn't still look for someone, though. She just had to be resourceful.

She returned her attention to her table and gave a solid nod. She was going to do this. "I'll have someone by the time of your wedding," she proclaimed.

Shock hit Lee Ann's face, and she and Cody both looked at Tucker. "Him?" Lee Ann asked. Dread now filled her voice.

Holly shook her head. "No. But someone."

Lee Ann's eyes narrowed as she studied Holly. "As in . . . a date to our wedding?"

"As in *have*," Holly stated calmly. The words sounded more secure than she felt, but she was going to give it her best. "Someone I'm interested in a long-lasting relationship with. I'm not playing around anymore. I've got to do more than wait tables and work at the B&B when Mom and Dad are out of town. So I'm catching a man. And then I'm going to set my own wedding date."

"But our wedding is in—"

"I know when your wedding is," she cut in.

They were getting married on July Fourth and had invited the whole town. It would be a casual affair to go along with the annual fireworks show. Everyone was looking forward to it.

"But . . ." Lee Ann's words died off.

Holly gave her a tight smile. She had less than six weeks to find the man of her dreams.

And then what?

She glanced out the window again, and this time her eyes landed on the consignment store on the far corner. She'd sold several of her creations in the store over the last couple of years. Nothing special, but people seemed to like them. A few tourists had even gone home with one. Maybe she could continue doing that, as well. It would be better than nothing.

Supplemental income for the marriage.

A hand touched hers and she turned back to the table.

"Let me know if you need any help," Lee Ann said. "We'll get you whoever you want."

Holly smiled and nodded. That was the problem. There wasn't anyone she wanted.

She just wanted to have a purpose.

Chapter Four

Late Thursday morning, Zack emerged from his room, hoping it was sufficiently late enough that everyone else in the house would be gone. He'd figured out there were six rooms on the second floor, including his, and five of them were currently booked.

As he headed toward the stairs, he noted that the house was blessedly silent. Perfect. He wasn't in the mood to make small talk. Now he simply had to locate food, get a few more hours of work done, then figure out what to do next.

He hadn't spent much time at the house at this point. He'd gotten back into town yesterday after getting his car repaired, and had then taken the afternoon to drive around, familiarizing himself with the area. Afterward he'd headed into the mountains. Mostly to avoid the fact that he should be finding and talking to his brothers, yet had no real idea how to go about that. Especially since it had been he who had caused things to be so unpleasant between them the first time they'd met.

But also, it had occurred to him that it had been years since he'd done something so simple as take a relaxed drive to nowhere. In fact, he couldn't remember ever doing it.

It often seemed he'd been head down, barreling toward perfection his whole life.

So he'd blown through a tank of gas, had picked up a sandwich and fruit for dinner from a roadside grocery, and hadn't returned to the bed-and-breakfast until well past dark. He'd run into a couple guests on the way up to his room, but other than that, he'd slipped in unnoticed.

And he hadn't seen Holly Marshall again.

Which was fine. She was annoying.

He'd been uncomfortable relying on her for a ride Monday to begin with. As a rule, he didn't ask people for help. Especially not smart-mouthed, irritating women.

Who'd been laughing at him since the minute he'd stepped from his car.

But to have to do it on a horse?

A low point in his life had surely occurred.

He'd been even more uncomfortable because he'd been pressed up close to her body. He couldn't remember the last time that much warm, soft flesh had fit itself to his. Not without a few bones sticking out here and there.

But his thighs had snugged around hers, her curvy bottom had pressed against his groin, and he'd prayed like hell the whole trip back that she was at least twenty-one.

The mirror at the base of the stairs caught his attention and he stopped to study it. He'd come in and out of the house so fast since arriving that he'd missed noticing the beauty of the piece. At first glance it was nothing special. Just a mirror inside what looked to be an overlarge copper tray. The copper was pounded, and the color matched the wood flooring that ran the length of the hallway and up the stairs. It perfectly fit the room. As if it had been made for the space.

But looking at it now, he picked up on the intricate nuances around the perimeter of the glass. There were individual shards in a mosaic style framing each side, each piece a tiny mirror in itself. They were set at angles to pick up the light around the room and cast it back out. It gave the appearance that the outer rim of the mirror was glowing.

He stepped closer, looking to see if there was a company name printed anywhere. Something like this would be great in his office.

"Good morning, Mr. Winston."

He jumped back as if caught somewhere he shouldn't be, and spun to face the woman in the hall. Holly Marshall.

Today her golden hair was in a high ponytail on the top of her head, making her look about eighteen—*again*—but unlike Monday, her makeup was at a minimum. If he wasn't mistaken, though, her eyelashes were blue. Her lips matched her shorts.

Which was another pair that barely covered her rear.

Only today, she didn't have leggings on underneath. He found himself wanting her to walk away from him just so he could see if her cheeks were indeed slipping out the bottom of the material.

The shorts were bright pink, the T-shirt she wore white and snug with a pink crown stretched across the front, and he couldn't help it, but he slid his gaze the rest of the way down her body. Her legs were bare and tapered down from her thighs, and her feet wore high-top canvas sneakers with brown patches set against a tan color. They reminded him of giraffes.

"Morning, Miss Marshall," he returned, bringing his gaze back up to hers.

She eyed him from under long lashes, her face expressionless, providing no hint of what she thought of him. Which was fine. He didn't care what she thought. He was there for a place to stay. He didn't need to be friends with the innkeeper.

And he certainly didn't need to think about how cute she was in her pink shorts.

Her gaze slipped past him to land on the mirror at his back as if checking to make sure he hadn't left any fingerprints anywhere on it. When it returned, her green eyes trapped his. They were the color of grass. Bright green like the blades before the first cut of the season.

She held up a phone, her expression stoic. "Your mother's on the phone. She's worried about you."

His whole body went rigid. Was she freaking kidding him? Then he caught a hint of a smile touching her pink lips. She might be going for serious, but inside she was laughing at him again.

Irritation and embarrassment mixed as he pressed his lips together and stepped forward. He loved his mother. A lot. But he had a cell phone, for Christ's sake. She needed to use it.

He took the handset from Holly, and she spun around and headed down the hall.

His eyes dropped to her ass.

The shorts were not indecent. Unfortunately. But that didn't keep him from imagining what the naked curve of her rear would look like. Or feel like.

Not that he would be attempting to feel it at all. Holly Marshall was small town. She was curvy and round and plush. And she had a smart mouth on her.

She was not his type.

Plus, he'd seen her sitting with one of his brothers at the local diner as he'd driven through town yesterday. He wasn't sure which brother, since they looked alike, but he'd been unable to miss seeing Holly with him. The fact that they'd been having lunch together implied they were friends.

And if he didn't want to make matters worse, he probably shouldn't have a quickie with his brother's friend.

He turned his back to the doorway she'd retreated through, and brought the phone to his ear. "Hello, Mom."

Holly stood just inside the kitchen, blatantly eavesdropping. She couldn't believe Zack's mother had called him at the house. At first, Holly had gone instantly to "worry." There must be an emergency.

But then she'd learned that "Mom" simply wanted to check in on her son. He apparently hadn't been answering his cell that morning.

The whole incident put the haughty, polished, designer-suit-and-shoes man in a new light. As did the gentle tone she heard coming from him now.

She pulled the bowl of batter from the fridge and heated the griddle as she kept an ear to the conversation going on in the hall. She heard the phrases "Got back late last night," "A drive through the park," and "I'll find them, that's what I came here for," and she couldn't help but assume Mom was grilling him on his actions.

Though Zack had done everything he could Monday to ignore Holly's attempts to be polite as they'd ridden to the house, she'd already begun to sense that he wasn't as hard as he came across. He had the power suit going, the fast car. The big job. He'd also perfected the ability to make it clear he thought himself better than this town and everyone in it.

Yet . . . she'd sensed something about him. It had felt like a vulnerability that lay just beneath the surface.

There had been a couple times when she'd been talking to him when he hadn't looked her in the eyes. She hadn't thought it boredom or indifference so much—though it easily could've been. Instead, it had felt more like . . . shame.

Which hadn't made a lot of sense either.

But as she continued to listen to his conversation now, she had to wonder if he wasn't ashamed of the way he'd treated Nick and Cody before. Based on his capitulatory mutterings in the hall, she also had the sense that Mom might have given him more than an earful about the subject over the last two months.

"My cell next time, Mom," she heard him say. Then he sighed. "Yeah, sorry. I had it on silent. I'm supposed to be relaxing while I'm here, right?"

She suspected that was sarcasm. She doubted the guy ever relaxed.

Silence followed as he listened.

"I don't know when." He blew out a breath. "I know. Soon."

Pause.

"Me too, Mom. I'll talk to you Sunday."

He went silent and she glanced over her shoulder.

When he stepped to the door, her breath caught. He didn't have on a suit jacket today, but still sported a white, starched button-down and a pair of black slacks. And as she'd noticed out in the hallway, he didn't need the jacket to emit power.

Or sex appeal.

His dark eyes wore a haunted look as he held up the phone and put a question on his face. She motioned to the base hanging on the wall.

"How's Mom?" she asked as he turned away to replace the receiver. She let her mouth curve into a grin when his shoulders went stiff. It was simply cute that his mother had been worried about him.

"My mother is fine." His tone had her biting her lip to keep from laughing as he faced her, his eyes thin slits. "I let her know it's not appropriate to call the house phone," he said.

Holly shrugged. "I don't mind. She can call every day if she wants. I told her that before you came down."

A cold look whipped across his face, and just like that, she made another snap decision. He might be judgmental about her shoes—and yeah, she'd caught him frowning at them *again* that morning—but overall, she preferred being happy. Optimistic. She liked to find the good in people. And when the good wasn't obvious, she enjoyed helping to uncover it.

Though Zack might well deserve it from his brothers, she wouldn't hold him in disregard for something he'd done two months ago. Especially now that he was here, seemingly to right his wrongs.

Plus, Cody and Nick had walked in on him unannounced. That would be enough to throw anyone off their game.

He'd hurt her friends, yeah, but she could help him fix that.

It would make Nick and Cody happy in return. A total win-win.

She held up her spatula, plans already taking shape in her mind. "Pancakes?"

Zack's mouth watered at the thought of hot pancakes drizzled in warm maple syrup. He hadn't had a real breakfast in years. Weekdays, his mornings consisted of coffee and whatever pastry his assistant picked up in the first-floor coffee shop. Saturdays, he often didn't come out of his apartment until well past breakfast—unless he was going into the office, which, again, earned him a pastry. Sundays, he skipped the meal altogether in anticipation of the large lunch he knew would be forthcoming.

"No need," he said. Letting the cute blonde cook him breakfast didn't seem like a good idea. "I'll go into town."

He needed to spend time in public anyway. Maybe he would run into one of his brothers.

She turned fully to face him and propped one hand on a hip. Her breasts jiggled with the movement and he had a new appreciation for cotton T-shirts. "Breakfast comes with the room, sugar. My mama will be back to take over next week, and she'll have my hide if she finds out I haven't been treating you right. I won't take no for an answer."

He eyed her from his spot by the door, telling himself to be adamant. He wasn't a sucker for a sexy Southern drawl, and he wouldn't be swayed by one.

Yet his mother had just spent ten minutes reminding him to enjoy himself while he was here. Make it a vacation, she kept saying. Relax. Do things you haven't done in years—as well as talk to your brothers.

Pancakes would be one of those things.

As would a cute blonde.

He reminded himself that he preferred tall, lithe brunettes. Women who knew the score, and who were more than happy to leave his bed first thing in the morning. Most certainly not mouthy ones.

Who laughed at him because his mother called to check on him.

He needed to get out of this room. He was about to tell her no again, when she pointed at the table against the side wall.

"Sit," she said. "We have things to discuss."

No, they didn't. Yet he found himself moving to the other side of the four-person table.

She turned back to cooking, and he ignored her to take in the room. He hadn't been in here yet, but like the rest of the house, it was stylish and roomy. Sunlight flooded the space through the wide windows, and suncatchers hanging in the middle of the glass sent a spray of color in every direction.

Warm wood cabinets and stainless-steel appliances covered the two largest walls. A three-by-five-foot whiteboard hung on the wall to his left, with a week's worth of breakfast menus written out in perfect penmanship. And the wood-block table he sat at took up the last of the space. The table matched the one he'd seen in the adjoining dining room, only it was a third of the size.

Holly remained at the stove, her back to him, the shape of her body outlined in pink and white. When she reached above her to one of the cabinets, her shirt rode up to reveal a thin strip of skin before flaring out to her rounded hips. He'd had both his hands right there as the two of them had ridden to the house on her horse. He'd wanted to slide his palms down over her warm curves.

He wanted to now, as well.

She glanced at him. "Do you want something in your pancakes? Chocolate chips? Blueberries?"

He frowned, thoughts of touching her forgotten. "Why would I want anything in my pancakes?"

She didn't reply, just rolled her eyes as if his mere presence disgusted her.

He let another minute go by before he began feeling silly for sitting there and allowing her to wait on him. "Can I help?" he finally asked.

Not that he knew how to do anything in the kitchen. Other than pour coffee.

Once again, she eyed him. "Do you cook?" she asked.

"No."

She gave him a quick smile. A dimple appeared in one cheek, and the sight sent a twitch straight to his groin. "Honest," she murmured. She said the word in a way that made him want to sit up straighter and puff out his chest. As if being honest was important to her.

"There's juice in the fridge and coffee in the pot." She nodded her head to the opposite counter, where a white insulated carafe sat. "You can pour some for both of us."

"You're eating too?" He wasn't used to women actually eating. And certainly not a stack of pancakes.

"Absolutely. I missed breakfast this morning because I was waiting on everyone else."

She returned her attention to the stove, and they worked together in silence as she finished their meal. Then she turned with two stacks of fluffy deliciousness in her hands and her cheeks pink from the heat, and he paused in the middle of the room to simply stare at her. She looked so . . .

"How old are you?" he blurted out.

He really had to stop his perverted old-man thoughts if she wasn't even of drinking age.

She smirked. "Old enough. It's the lack of makeup. I look like a kid when I don't wear much."

The ponytail on the top of her head didn't help. Nor the short shorts. But he wasn't about to point out either because he liked them both. He also liked her innocent cuteness. It was refreshing.

She set the plates on the table and grabbed a small pitcher of syrup. Next was a platter of sausages from the oven. Berries and whipped cream followed.

Finally, they sat. She doused her chocolate-chip-filled pancakes with syrup before dropping a handful of raspberries on top and adding a four-second squirt of whipped cream. Then she held the can out to him. "Try it," she said.

"I like them plain."

She made a face at him. "Of course you do. Boring."

He wasn't boring.

She cut off a hunk of her pancakes and slid it into her mouth. He watched until it disappeared. Then he noticed that his breathing had hitched up a notch.

His phone rang, jerking him out of his thoughts. Thank the heavens.

"Excuse me," he muttered as he pulled the device from his pocket. It was rude to answer while at the table, but he needed a moment of escape.

He needed to quit thinking about sitting Holly on the kitchen counter and stepping between her legs.

When he saw who the caller was, though, he didn't answer. She was the reason his phone had been muted when his mother had called earlier. Shelley hadn't taken "we're done" well.

Not that he'd ever given the impression it was more than sex, nor had she expressed the desire to have more. She just wanted the *sex*. Along with more of his cash spent showing her a good time.

"Not answering it?" Holly asked.

"Nope." He shook his head and slid the phone onto the table.

Holly leaned forward until she could see the screen, and her brows went up. "Shelley," she murmured. Her green gaze turned to his. "She one of your women?"

As she'd leaned forward, the underside of her breasts had pressed against her forearm where it rested on the table, pushing them up, and the neck of her T-shirt had gaped. He'd been given one hell of a view. Which he was no longer looking at because she was now looking at him.

But they were still there. Creamy and plump.

Just inches from him.

"What do you know about my women?" he managed to get out.

He knew his women didn't have breasts like that.

She sat back then, and his breath slid from between his lips. He hadn't realized he'd been holding it.

"Nick said the morning they came looking for you, some hoity-toity woman was leaving your place. Apparently you two hadn't been in long?"

She left the sentence as a question. It was none of her business, yet he found he wanted to defend himself. Not that there was a defense. He often went out on Friday nights—which is why Shelley was calling now, because he'd cancelled their date last weekend—and yeah, he and his dates had been known to stay out until dawn.

Then the women left shortly thereafter.

What could he say to make it sound better than it was?

The better question was, why did he want to?

When he chose not to answer, Holly tilted her head to the side and he could see her thoughts churning. She suddenly looked older than eighteen, and his lust rocketed off again. This time not because she was a walking wet dream, but because she looked like an intelligent woman. One who would appreciate more than a good time or simply being showered with money.

That shouldn't turn him on so much.

"Eat." She wiped the intrigued look from her eyes and pointed her fork at his plate. He had yet to take a bite.

He poured syrup over his food and dug in. Then quickly followed the bite with, "*Damn.*" He looked up. "These are delicious."

She laughed lightly, the heavy mood from the moment before lifted, and he became mesmerized yet again. Not only by the sound, but by the unguarded happiness radiating from her. He rarely felt that happy. That unrestrained. How did she do it?

Did she not have worries? Regrets?

"They're my specialty, Mr. Winston." She squirted another dollop of cream on her food and snuck a quick squirt onto his before he could stop her. "I learned from the best. My granny. The woman whose final resting place you desecrated the other day."

"Zack," he mumbled with his mouth full of sweet bread and spicy sausage. He swallowed. "Just . . . Zack." He preferred to keep Mr. Winston in the courtroom. "And I fixed the marker already."

Her green eyes watched him until he found himself looking down and breaking contact first. It felt too intimate to be sitting there with her.

And he didn't do intimate.

"You fixed it yourself?" she asked. He could tell she expected the answer to be no.

He peered up from his plate, wanting to see her reaction when he told her that yes, in fact, he had done the work himself. He'd caused the damage; he'd taken care of it. It was a quality his dad had instilled in him early on.

"I had a rental Tuesday while I waited on my car to be repaired," he explained. "And time on my hands. So I bought cement and tools." He shrugged. "I fixed it."

The surprise in her eyes made him smile. The awe made his chest squeeze. No one other than his mother ever looked at him that way anymore.

"You're here to fix things with your brothers, right?" she asked.

And the moment was lost.

He lowered his gaze to his plate again and scooped up another bite. "Fix things" was a bit unrealistic. He was there to settle things. To . . . *meet* them. To not be an ass.

"Did your mom make you come?"

Laughter was back in her eyes now.

"My mother doesn't *make me* do anything, Miss Marshall." And she hadn't. She'd merely strongly suggested it.

"Holly," she said softly. The world slowed down a beat as her name slid between them.

"Holly," he repeated.

The green of her eyes deepened, but her expression didn't change.

"Answer the questions, Zack," she said. "Your brothers?"

He nodded. Yes, he was there to fix things with his brothers. As soon as he could figure out where to start.

"And your mother? She sent you?"

"She . . ." Was he really on the verge of telling this woman that his mother was the reason he was there? Most of the reason. There was also his boss.

And if he were to be honest, he'd admit that he'd been thinking about coming well before either had pushed the point. Now that he knew the truth . . .

"You said we had things to talk about." He changed the subject. He was not discussing his mother, his screwed-up job, or his brothers with her.

"We are talking," she replied.

"And now we're finished." He scooped up the last of his breakfast, washed it down with juice, and stood.

"I know where you can run into your brothers," she said before he could leave the room. She stared up at him from her seat. Her expression was blank, but he could read in her eyes that she had guessed what he'd been thinking.

He had no idea where to start. Or *how* to start.

He'd actually hoped that once his siblings knew he was in town, they'd make the first move. Again. Which was immature on his part, but he was more than slightly resentful for having to be there in the first place.

He would have been fine going the rest of his life without meeting them.

Only . . .

He felt his pulse thump in the side of his neck as he remembered his desire as a kid to have a brother.

He'd had great parents. His dad had been a doctor, and his mother adored him. He'd been given all the material possessions he'd ever asked for, and even more love. Yet he'd constantly felt alone in the world. A brother would have fixed that.

A brother would have made the years at school less—

"We have a movie in the park every Thursday night," she said. "Your brothers will be there."

"No," he said immediately. "I don't do movies in the park." Who had time for something so frivolous?

"Why not?"

"Because I'm too busy." There was work to be done. He might be on vacation, but that didn't mean his clients could wait. There were court appearances waiting for him. Depositions. Preparation was key. He wanted to show his boss, show the firm that he would not mess up again. He was going to be all business.

One blonde eyebrow lifted high on her forehead. She didn't audibly point out the obvious, but he heard it loud and clear.

He was there for *some* reason. He'd booked a room for two weeks.

If it wasn't to get to know his brothers, then what?

But a movie? In a park?

He swallowed. It was too . . . *country*.

Holly simply watched him as he worked through his thoughts, the expression on her face patient. Though he could spend all the time he wanted on his cases, it wouldn't change the facts. He wasn't in town to work.

He shook his head. He still wasn't going to a movie in the park. "It's not my style."

If he went, he'd have to approach Nick and Cody in front of everyone. There would be no secrets. No . . . hiding. There would also probably be people listening in, eavesdropping on everything that was said. He didn't need to be fodder for the town gossip any more than he assumed driving across the county line had already made him.

He shoved his fists into his pockets. He wasn't going.

When Holly still didn't say anything, merely eyeing him from her side of the table, he felt a muscle in his jaw twitch. She had to realize what a bad idea it was.

He didn't fit in there. No one would want him showing up for a cozy community event.

She just kept silently waiting.

He sighed. "I'm making no promises."

A flicker of a smile crossed her face. "The park's two blocks down Church Street," she informed him as if he'd asked for directions. Then she softly added, "I could meet you there."

Like he needed someone to hold his hand.

He took in her green eyes again, and he saw no judgment on her part. Simply the willingness to help. He didn't understand. He was nothing to her.

"Why would you help me?" he asked. His words came out gruff.

She was the one to break contact that time. She stood from the table and took their plates to the sink. After a few seconds, she turned back to him. She gripped the edge of the counter in her hands behind her. "I know what it's like to be lost in the middle of the crowd," she said. The words were spoken softly, but they seemed to be weighted down with meaning.

He couldn't imagine someone like her ever being lost in the crowd.

"You're friends with them?" he asked. He couldn't believe he would even consider the idea. Yet he was.

She nodded. Her look was solemn. "Good friends. You hurt them before."

He knew that. He'd seen it in their matching eyes when he'd tossed the bills on the table and rose to leave. But the other thing he'd seen was that the two of them were close. Even only knowing each other for a few months, they'd developed a bond. Zack didn't see himself fitting inside of it.

"I treated them poorly that night," he admitted. "That's why I'm here. To make it right."

But he still didn't see himself going to a movie in the park.

"I'll see you there, then?" she asked. There was something in her eyes other than the hope that he would show up, but he couldn't quite pinpoint it. It looked lonely. Maybe a little sad.

He might have to disappoint her. "I'll think about it."

She nodded again. A soft smile settled on her face. Just slightly, but something about it eased the knot in his gut.

He turned and left the room before he allowed himself to think too much about that smile, or what it did to him.

Or the woman who came with it.

Chapter Five

K yndall, honey, those shoes are just darling." Holly rose from the blanket where she sat waiting for the movie to start as her niece skipped across the grass. Kyndall had come with her mother, who'd stopped several blankets over to talk with friends.

"Where's your dad?" Holly squeezed her niece's hands as she fawned over the girl's lime-green flip-flops.

"He was just getting home when we were ready to leave." Kyndall flipped her hair over her shoulder as if she were years older. Polish that matched her shoes flashed in the waning early evening light. "He had a hard day. People getting into areas they weren't supposed to or something." Rodney and Erika lived in the national park due to his job as a forest ranger. "So Mom and I came without him."

Knowing her brother, he probably appreciated the quiet night. He worked hard, and he loved his wife and child, but he often preferred his recliner and a quiet house to just about everything else. The fact that he'd come over for her welcome-home party had meant a lot.

Holly and Kyndall turned to one of the two handmade quilts spread out on the ground, and as they sat, Holly glanced around, looking for her nephews. She'd come into town with Patrick and his family, and had offered to watch the boys until the movie started so their parents could enjoy a few minutes of grown-up time having dinner across the street. Zander, as the oldest, had taken Chance and Jason to the concession stand.

She caught sight of them weaving their way back through the crowd, then did a quick scan for Zack.

No sign of him yet. She hoped he would come.

She hadn't been able to forget the look in his eyes when she'd brought up his brothers that morning. He'd seemed powerless. As if he hadn't a clue where to start. But she had sensed that he wanted to.

As she perused the area, she set Zack on the back burner and returned to her recent resolution to find a man. If there was one to be found, he would probably be there tonight. Outdoor movies had become a town tradition over the years, starting when Holly had been only a kid. A theater wasn't feasible with the town's small population, but showing old movies on a big screen was.

Each Thursday between Memorial Day and Labor Day, most members of the community could be found right there, sitting on a blanket or in a lawn chair, with family and friends. Tourists loved it too. A couple of entrepreneurial locals had cashed in on this fact by renting out blankets and chairs.

The night was so popular, even the single guys came out.

Mostly in the hope that they'd get lucky with the single ladies.

Holly had a few of those guys in mind as potential dates, and looked around for them now. Keith Justice was nice. He was a volunteer firefighter and worked for Nick at his construction company. Keith had been married before, but he didn't have any kids. From everything Holly had heard, he'd been a good husband. It just hadn't worked out.

Then there was Sandy Brown. Sandy gave her a wink when her gaze landed on him.

He wasn't a bad guy, but his brother Bubba drove her nuts. The guy thought he was a comedian, but mostly he was just a jerk. And a pervert.

Sandy could be on the if-all-else-fails list.

As she took in the other varied faces in the crowd, the families, the people who were obviously on dates, she noticed that more than one man gave her an odd look. It was a bit longer than a casual glance, but not exactly showing interest either. Just . . . odd.

Then there were two guys who went so far as to blatantly check her out, one shooting her a somewhat lecherous smile when he finished. It made her skin itch as if she'd developed a bad case of the hives.

Most of the guys looking her way she knew, but a couple nonlocals were also in the mix.

She was beginning to get a very strange feeling about tonight.

Miley Rogers got her attention a few blankets away by tilting her head subtly to the side as if motioning to something. Miley was the daughter of Jean, who worked over at Sam's Foodmart, and had been a freshman in high school when Holly had been a senior. They'd been in the art club together.

Miley tilted her head again, the end of her cute bob swinging out from her face, and Holly followed the movement with her eyes. Johnny "Apple Pie" Simmons was giving her a wolfish grin.

What in the devil was going on?

Feeling more than a little uncomfortable now, she turned away from the crowd. As she did, she unobtrusively checked her outfit to make sure nothing was wrong. She'd worn a cute yellow-and-white checked sundress tonight and her ruby-red slippers. Everything appeared zipped and buttoned, with no inappropriate body parts hanging out.

Maybe her makeup was smeared.

She peeked around once more as she dug out her mirror, and yes, men were still watching her. This time she got a couple more smiles.

The guys were cute so she smiled back.

Ignoring the attention again, she quickly checked her face. All seemed fine. She turned and focused on Kyndall, asking what the girl had been up to the last few days, but found it difficult to keep her mind on the conversation. She kept wondering what was going on that she wasn't aware of. She hadn't been in town during the day today. Had she missed some important piece of gossip?

Was it about her?

"So then Mom said that if I saved up my allowance, she'd take me to the craft store," Kyndall rattled. "I want to make things like you do."

Pride filled Holly's chest at the same time a fist carved a hole deep inside her stomach. She loved that Kyndall wanted to be like her. She just worried about her niece dreaming too big.

At the same time, it killed Holly to think that she'd had to scale back her own plans.

"What kind of things do you want to make?" she asked Kyndall.

"Something unique," the girl said with clear determination. "I don't want to be like everyone else. Maybe flowerpots with rhinestones on them or something."

"Flowerpots with rhinestones sounds nice." The last thing Holly would ever do was discourage the need to be different. "I'm sure whatever you do, it'll be beautiful."

Kyndall wrapped her arm around Holly's waist suddenly, and leaned her head on Holly's shoulder. "I really did miss you while you were gone, Aunt Holly. I'm glad you're back."

Holly's throat grew tight. She'd really missed her niece too.

And her brothers, her sisters-in-law, and even her rowdy nephews. She'd missed the whole darned town.

She just wished she'd gotten the opportunity to prove herself. At least once. Her disappointment over the way things had turned out was thick enough to suffocate her.

"I'm glad to be home," she told Kyndall. The words didn't just sound right, they felt right. She *was* glad to be home.

Yes, she'd wanted to be a success in Chicago. She'd believed she could make a name for herself. Instead, she'd not only been called a small-town hick—she'd been laughed out of the city.

At least here, everyone loved her.

Case in point, a clump of people passed by and yelled out to her, tossing out friendly waves. The men in the crowd studied her as if weighing their options.

"How does everyone know you?" Kyndall asked.

Erika joined them at that moment, dropping her purse to the quilt. "Duh, because Holly's the best." She winked. "Plus, she's a Marshall. Everyone knows all the Marshalls."

"Does that mean they know you too?" Kyndall asked her mom. She scooted over so Erika could sit between them.

"They do. But mostly they know your dad." She tapped her daughter on the tip of her nose. "They know you too."

Holly smiled at the closeness between the two of them, then swallowed her tongue when her sister-in-law turned to her and said, "So tell me about you getting married."

Kyndall gasped. "You're getting married?" Her shocked words rang through the park.

This brought the heads of pretty much everyone in their vicinity around to look at Holly. Bubba Brown waggled his eyebrows suggestively at her.

"Sheesh," Holly mumbled. She brought a hand up to shield her from view of the crowd. "No. Where did you hear that?"

Had her mother said something? But then, her mother only *thought* she needed a man. She didn't know Holly was in the market.

Erika motioned to her friends. "Katy told me. It's all over town that you're on the hunt."

"How in the world . . ."

Holly's words stopped as her gaze landed on Cody and Lee Ann a few rows up. Lee Ann had glanced back at her with the shouted question. Her brows were drawn in tight. Had she told everyone? Had Cody?

That didn't feel right. Her friends wouldn't do that to her.

But then . . .

Holly's heart pounded with embarrassment. Who had done this?

Before she could think to ask any more questions, Erika jabbed her in the side. "Oh my." She moaned the words.

"What now?" Holly whispered, terrified to look.

Erika was staring off into the distance as if in shock. With Holly's luck, someone had probably shown up with a bribe, thinking he could buy her. Good thing her mom and dad weren't there. They'd form a line to accept bids.

Yes, Holly wanted a man. But she hadn't wanted to be paraded through town as if she were a prime side of beef.

She had *some* pride, after all.

"I'd heard a rumor that he was in town," Erika whispered. Relief immediately gushed through Holly. She knew who that someone would be.

Aside from the apparent rumors of her desire for nuptials, Zack had also been the talk of the town. Ever since he'd driven through the square the day before.

Everyone now knew that he was Cody and Nick's brother. They knew that the twins had gone to Atlanta to meet him. And they knew that he'd wanted nothing to do with them. The facts had been gathered, and the community had banded together in support of their own.

They disliked Zack on principle.

Holly turned her head in the same direction the rest of the people around her were now slowly turning. At least they were no longer staring at her.

Standing just past the ticket booth was Zack.

He was wearing black slacks again, but he'd shed the white dress shirt for a light-gray pullover. It fit snug to his body, and Holly knew that if all the women around her weren't busy whispering their indignation to their neighbor, they would be turning gooey inside. Just like Holly.

She raised a hand and waved it in the air without letting herself think about what she was doing, or what kind of additional attention she would be directing at herself. She'd told Zack she'd help him out. She'd been the one to suggest the movie.

She couldn't just sit there and hide.

He didn't immediately see her, so she stood, keeping her arm in the air. She felt, as well as saw, heads once again swivel her way. Of course, they probably assumed she was flagging him down as a potential suitor.

"What are you doing?" Erika whispered, while Kyndall followed with, "Oh my gawd. He's so hot."

Yes, he was. And her ten-year-old niece shouldn't be so aware of that fact.

Tall, sculpted, and too hot to be standing in the middle of the park looking like a lost little boy. He did this thing with his hair, styling it slightly forward and lifted at the front, that made her want to muss it up. Then she wanted to nibble on his neck, just beneath his jawline.

She blinked the thought away. He was not her type. Too big city. Too temporary.

But he did look tasty.

He finally saw her and turned in her direction. He didn't speak to anyone as he made his way through the crowd. And he didn't look anywhere but at her. The intensity of his gaze was enough to take her breath away.

If she were in the market for a high-class player, she'd make a move on him in a heartbeat.

Not that she really thought she could get anywhere. She suspected his type wasn't a small-town girl who cared more about being comfortable and having fun than she did about style and etiquette. Probably he dated money. And women who could keep it casual.

She didn't particularly like casual.

Though he was just about enough to sway her that way.

"Who's that?" Zander now stood at her side. Like his dad, he would be tall. He'd had a growth spurt within the last month and had outgrown Holly's five-foot-five inches while she'd been out of town.

"That's someone who doesn't belong here." This came from Patrick. He and Jillian had returned from dinner.

"What are you talking about?" Holly asked. "Zack has every right to be here."

She turned back to watching the man in question as she spoke. His gaze was still glued to her.

"He's a jerk, Hol. I know you heard about the way he treated his brothers."

"And I know you know better than to judge someone before meeting them for yourself." She broke eye contact with Zack and turned to her family.

"Hey, Jillian," Holly greeted her sister-in-law. Jillian gave her a smile, and Holly didn't miss the *ohmygod* look in her eyes when she checked out Zack. Because the man was *oh. My. God.*

"I heard about him too," Zander said. "Uncle Brian said he was staying at Mema and Pop's house."

Good to know her family was gossiping about one of their guests. "At the bed-and-breakfast, yes," Holly said. She nodded as she spoke. "He has a room rented for two weeks."

"Uncle Brian also said he was a jerk," Zander added.

"He is not a jerk," Holly said softly. She glanced back at Zack—he was within ten feet of her now, and her blood raced through her veins. She was pretty sure he wasn't a jerk. "And you're both going to behave," she added in a whisper. "He's a guest. You know Mema will kick your behinds if she comes home to find out someone didn't treat her guests right."

Zack made it to her side and she smiled winningly up at him, hoping to make him feel relaxed and welcomed. What she got for her effort was an expressionless face and blank eyes.

Her insides wilted.

It didn't help any when she caught snickers from several women who'd seen her blinding smile. She could guess what they were thinking. She couldn't make it in the big city, thus she couldn't handle a big-city guy. Not that she wanted to.

But they were probably right.

"Zack," she said, pushing her self-pity aside. Just because she'd failed in Chicago didn't mean she was a failure as a person. She had plenty to offer. To the right person. She motioned for Zack to step closer, ignored the stares still pointed their way, and tried to keep her voice pleasant. "Please meet some of my family."

She introduced Jillian and Patrick, the latter giving him a hard stare. Then Zander, who looked at his father first, and gave Zack the same glare. And then Erika, whose jaw had come unhinged and was hanging about half-open. She murmured an unintelligible hello.

Next were Chance and Jason. The younger boys couldn't care less about the man who had joined them.

And then she introduced Kyndall.

When Zack turned his gaze on the ten-year-old, Holly watched Kyndall suck in a breath and hold her stomach in tight. She smiled brightly, as if glowing in the light that was Zack.

Zack nodded a hello to each of them, but he held on tight to his politeness. Everywhere around them were whispers and stares. Enough that Holly almost turned and glared at all of them. They were better than this. There was no need to be so rude.

Before anyone could utter another word, the movie flickered to life.

Holly let out a sigh of relief.

"Let's sit, Patrick," Jillian said matter-of-factly. She tugged on his arm to make her point. "We're in people's way."

Patrick shot Zack one last hard look, then planted the same expression on Holly. Holly merely gave him a smirk. She didn't know what her brother's problem was, but he needed to rein it in.

"Would you like to sit with us?" Holly asked Zack.

"I thought we were going to . . ." His words ran out as he refocused on her. The coldness was gone from his gaze now, replaced by a hint of a pleading look.

He was there to meet his brothers. For her to help him break the ice. Not to be the center of attention in the middle of everyone.

"We will," she murmured. As she spoke, she reached out and touched his forearm. His skin was hot, and the muscles beneath tight. She had the urge to linger, but didn't let herself. It didn't seem the brightest of ideas to feel him up in front of everyone. Especially not without his permission.

"Let's sit first," she urged. "They know you're here. They had to have seen you come in. We'll let them adjust to that before we go over."

His dark-brown gaze studied hers as if trying to decide if he could trust her. Finally, he gave a small nod and looked down at the quilt.

"There's a spot here," Kyndall piped up. She patted the narrow area between her and her mom and blinked wide eyes up at Zack. The poor girl. Even at ten, she was experiencing what a good-looking man could do to a woman.

"I think he'll be more comfortable beside me," Holly told her niece.

Erika scooted over to close the gap between her and her daughter, and they all sat. The boys and their parents took the second quilt.

The movie started and everyone quieted. Holly glanced around the crowd again, noticing that people were still watching. The men were watching her, the women Zack. The single women no longer had the "I know you're evil" look in their eyes, either. They now read more like, "Call me up, hot stuff. I'll treat you right."

Holly puffed her cheeks and let out a breath. She'd been hoping not to cause too big of a scene when she took Zack over to his brothers, but with the whole town watching them both, that wasn't likely to happen.

"What's wrong?" Zack asked by her ear.

She startled. She hadn't realized he was that close. His breath smelled like mint.

"Nothing," she whispered. She wasn't about to tell him that she was beginning to think his coming there tonight might be a mistake. Not when he'd actually taken that first step. She turned back to the movie and settled in to watch, keeping one eye on the Dalton brothers as she did. Nick and his fiancée had joined Cody and Lee Ann on the blanket, along with one of Cody's twin thirteen-year-old daughters.

The other girl, Kendra, was sitting on another quilt with a boy her age. Holly couldn't help but smile every time she caught Kendra scooting an inch closer to her "date." Lee Ann shot her daughter a pointed look, and the girl crossed her arms over her chest and pouted. But she didn't scoot back over.

"Look three blankets in front of us and five blankets to our left." Holly leaned in and spoke softly to Zack. He hadn't loosened up at all since he'd gotten there. Since she couldn't concentrate on the movie anyway, she might as well try to get him to relax. "That girl with the really terrified-looking boy." She described what she wanted Zack to see.

"What about her?"

"That's one of your nieces."

Out of the corner of her eye, Holly saw his body still. He looked at Kendra. And then she swore that his hands began to shake. She had the urge to reach over and hold them, but wouldn't that give everyone something to talk about?

"They're going to love you," she said instead.

He shot her a look. "You have zero reason to believe that."

"The one with that boy will love you for sure."

"What makes you say that?"

"Because she likes to drive her parents crazy. The minute she figures out that Cody is still angry with you, she'll be your best pal."

Dark eyes captured hers. "He told you he's still angry?"

"He didn't have to," she said gently. She'd seen it in his body language when Zack had driven down the street.

Behind Zack, she saw Ms. Grayson rise from a lawn chair and head to the concession stand, and Holly suddenly knew where the rumors about her had come from. The stinking busybody had been in the diner while Holly had been talking about finding a man.

Served Holly right. She knew better than to discuss such things in public.

Didn't make her any happier about it, though.

She jumped to her feet. She had a thing or two to say to Ms. Grayson. "I'll be right back," she whispered down to Zack. Then she was off.

Zack watched Holly race through the darkening night, seemingly in a rush to get to the concession stand, and he was suddenly in a similar hurry not to be sitting there with everyone sneaking glances at him.

He'd gone out earlier today, hoping to run into Nick or Cody, but at each business he'd entered, conversation had come to a standstill. Requests had been met with stilted replies and knowing looks. Not to mention, he'd found only one spot in the whole town with Wi-Fi.

It was near impossible to get any work done when he couldn't hit the Internet. He'd pulled his phone out to use as a hotspot in the diner, but had learned there that Internet access was considered "spotty" everywhere.

Perfect.

He was stuck in nowhere Tennessee, where cell and Internet access could come and go at any moment, and everyone who lived there seemed to have an aversion to outsiders.

And he had orders not to leave until he made peace with his brothers.

Which yeah, he wanted to do. A semi-civil conversation shouldn't be that hard. He was a lawyer, after all. He spoke for a living.

Yet approaching them wouldn't be easy. Especially knowing they were still mad at him.

He didn't know why Holly's comment had surprised him. Of course they would still be upset. He'd treated them as if they were nothing. And he'd done even less to fix it.

But hearing it spoken out loud had affected him.

He rose from his spot on the blanket, only to feel the gazes of Erika and Kyndall follow him up. He jerked a thumb toward the direction Holly had headed. "I'll help her carry the popcorn."

A minute later he stopped dead at the step up to the platform of the concession stand. It was a concrete structure that appeared to be multipurpose. Concession stand for movie nights, and if the sign above was a correct indication, it was also an info stop for tourists during the day.

But what stopped him was seeing Holly in the glow from the lights . . . now surrounded by a gaggle of men.

She stood there in her yellow-and-white dress. It hit her just above the knees, nipped in at her waist, and except for the one-inch-wide straps, left her shoulders bare. The material clung at just the right places, outlining everything a man would want highlighted.

She was gorgeous.

Added to it, she had her hair down tonight. All that gold flowing to the middle of her back perfectly capped off her look. The only thing that could be classified as even remotely wrong was that she once again had on too much makeup. She still looked good. But she looked like she was trying too hard.

And she didn't need to try hard.

Her freshness was her beauty.

Though the effort did seem to be paying off as the men pushed in harder, closing around her. Each one seemed to be fighting for position to be near her. One even carried a shoebox with a ribbon tied around it. As if he intended to present it to her as a gift.

What in the world was wrong with these people?

Holly glanced around when she was bumped from the side, unease lacing her eyes, and a basic instinct kicked in inside of Zack.

He had to help her. Before he could take a step forward, though, he was shoved to the side and almost knocked to the ground.

"Out of the way," a teenager said as he moved up on the step in front of Zack.

Zack bit down on the words he wanted to spit out at the kid. It wasn't so much the rudeness that bothered him—though that was bad enough—but that he'd been in town for three days, and in that short span of time, he'd felt more like he was back in high school, junior high even, than he had in years.

He was being talked about, shoved out of the way as if he were no one, and looked down upon. The instant he made some sort of amends with his brothers, he would be out of there.

Holly snagged his attention again, but this time because of her laugh. It was pinched and tight. He didn't wait around for someone else to shove him out of the way. This time he did the moving.

He stepped into the group, and reached his arm through the rowdy men until he wrapped his fingers around Holly's elbow. She whirled around as if ready to fight. When she saw it was him, relief softened her eyes. Seeing that reaction gave Zack a high he hadn't felt in years.

"Come on," he mouthed.

She nodded, and he tugged her through the men until she popped free.

"Sorry, guys," he said. He pulled her to his side. Her body fit securely against his, though she felt more fragile than she came across. "She's with me tonight."

More than one groan echoed around them, and then the guy with the shoebox stepped forward. He thrust the box at Holly.

"I heard you like shoes," he said. He had no hair on the top of his head, and at both sides of the bald patch the coarse hair pointed straight out. He looked like he had wings.

Zack peered down at Holly's confused expression before deciding not to wait for her reaction. She didn't need this guy. He shoved the box out of the way. "Get out of here," Zack growled.

The man puffed out his chest as if he thought he would fight for the right. The right to what, Zack wasn't sure. Maul a woman in the middle of a crowd?

Zack made it clear with one look that the man wasn't getting anywhere near Holly. With a weak dip of his eyes, the guy mumbled under his breath, then left along with the rest of the group. Holly turned her face up to Zack's. Her cheeks were rosy and flushed.

He wanted to kiss her.

"Do you attract the crazies every time you step out?" he asked. Kissing her would not be a good idea.

She shook her head, and a slight smile returned. Her face lost its strain. "I'm going to *kill* Ms. Grayson," she whispered.

He had no idea what she was talking about or who Ms. Grayson was, but before he could ask, Holly slid her hand down to his and pulled him to the far side of the building. They ended up in the shadows where the movie screen wasn't visible, and, amazingly, no one followed.

"*Oh. My. God,*" she whispered as they stopped. Mixed in with the words was slight laughter. The woman was laughing at almost being trampled to death. She turned loose of his hand and dropped back against the building. She rested her head on the concrete wall and sucked in a deep breath of air, and her chest lifted with the movement. She exhaled and her chest deflated.

"What was that about?" he asked. He nodded toward the front of the building.

Her eyes met his. "About me getting married."

"Pardon?" His stomach rolled. He had not seen that coming. "You're getting married?"

Not that there was a reason she *shouldn't* get married. He just hadn't pictured her as "taken."

Or maybe he didn't want to picture her taken.

He wanted to picture her naked and sweaty and sliding over his body. With his palms molding her every curve.

She nodded, wiped the back of her hand across her brow, then seemed to realize which way her head was moving and switched to the negative.

"Which is it?" he asked. "And please tell me you don't really have your eye on the guy with the shoes."

Laughter sprang up from her then, and this time it was more than a chuckle. The sound was so pure and happy that he couldn't help but join in with a smile.

"It is him, isn't it?" He took a step closer. "You like a balding man who'll bring you shoes."

She laughed more. Just what he'd wanted to hear. It was far better than the *holy shit* look he'd seen written in her eyes only moments before.

"Probably they were cheap gold lamé with some gaudy bauble on top," he suggested.

"Hey." She stopped laughing and turned her head in the direction they'd come. "You think?"

He groaned. She had to be kidding him.

"Maybe I should hunt him down."

He recalled her shoes from the day he'd met her. Then the giraffe shoes she'd had on that morning. He glanced down at her feet now. It was too dark to see, but he'd taken notice of them earlier. She should be in a movie carrying a dog and spouting how there was no place like home.

The woman had serious issues when it came to shoes.

"You can't have him," Zack said. He didn't know why he sounded so possessive. He leaned in closer. "I already scared him off."

For good, he hoped.

Her bottom lip came out in a fake pout and he caught himself smiling at her again.

"I like it when you smile," she told him.

His mouth flattened.

"Ah, come on," she pleaded. She poked at the corner of his mouth. "Don't turn back into Grumpy Zack so soon."

"I'm not grumpy," he grumbled. He grabbed her finger and pulled her hand to his side.

She laughed again and pushed at his chest, moving him back out of her space. He released her hand. "You're totally grumpy," she stated. "But that's okay. It works with my master plan."

She had him more than a bit confused. And more than a bit turned on. She was still leaning back against the building, looking hot and lush, and about half spread out for him, and he couldn't remember ever wanting to touch someone so badly.

He gulped.

"What master plan?" He needed to quit thinking about her like that. They were alone. In the dark.

He could have her mouth under his in mere seconds.

"To help you," she said.

He shook his head. "I don't need help."

She grew still as she watched him. They both knew he wouldn't be there tonight if he hadn't come for help.

Didn't mean he *needed* it. Maybe the truth was that he just wanted to be around Holly.

Which reminded him . . . "About this marriage thing," he said. Best to keep in mind that she wasn't his type. He certainly didn't need to get tangled up with someone looking for a ring. Been there, done that. It wasn't happening again.

She waved her hand in the air between them as if the decision was of no consequence. "I recently spent some time in Chicago, where I decided that the big city wasn't my style. So I came home. Now I'm looking to get married."

He just stared at her. She was off her rocker.

"So yeah." She chuckled again. The sound struck him as forced. "I'm looking for a man. You know, husband, babies. The works. Only, I wasn't aware the whole county had been brought into my plans."

"Yet clearly they are." He paused. "Why did you go to Chicago?"

Her eyes grew shrewd. "To visit my cousin. And now I'm going to kill Ms. Grayson."

He wanted to know what had been in Chicago. "And Ms. Grayson is?"

"The source of most gossip," Holly explained. "She was in the diner yesterday when I was explaining my plan to Cody and Lee Ann. I should have known the woman was eavesdropping," she muttered, shaking her head. "But anyway, she pretty much knows all, and her goal in life is to be the first one to share it."

"So she helped you out, then?" he asked. He didn't understand a goal of getting married.

He understood getting married. It worked for some people. A few even made it seem nice.

But it didn't come before a career.

For others, it didn't come at all.

What he didn't understand, though, was how a person could want *only* marriage. Didn't she have ambitions outside of a ring on her finger?

"I don't know about that," she said now. "She threw a wrench in things. I wanted to be a bit more selective, you know? But I can make this work. Might be easier anyway. Obviously I have candidates to choose from."

"Obviously." He didn't like it. Not one bit. "Thanks to Ms. Grayson."

"Right. Seriously, if you ever need to know anything, she's your woman. Only, she missed out on the big news about you."

His eye began to twitch. "What big news about me?"

"About how Cody and Nick came to see you in Atlanta, and how you told them to take a hike. She ran out of the diner right before we got to that."

Things were beginning to become clear. "That's why everyone in town seems to hate me? Not just because I'm not from around here?"

"Honey, look around. Half the people here tonight aren't from around here. We love tourists." She shrugged. "They're our livelihood. We just don't love you."

Ouch. "Because I was rude to my brothers?"

"Right."

Having an entire town backing a person was a completely foreign thing to him.

And he wasn't sure he disapproved.

That was something he'd have to think about later.

"Will they ever get over it?" he asked. Strangely, he wanted them to. Which made no sense. Since when did he care what people thought?

She gave another shrug. "If Cody and Nick get over it."

Which *was* why he was here. With frustration, he shoved a hand through his hair. He had to make things right. They hadn't deserved the treatment he'd doled out that night. He'd had his facts wrong.

"We should get you over to your brothers," she said, as if reading his thoughts. She pushed off the wall and turned to leave. When he didn't follow, she stopped. "Don't you want to?"

Of course he wanted to. Otherwise he'd be doing something more productive. Like staying in and working.

But now that the moment had arrived, he found he'd rather get back in his car and go for another long drive.

"Come on." Her voice softened. She held out a hand to him, and he didn't let himself think about the fact that it looked like a life raft in the middle of a stormy ocean.

He took it and squeezed. He nodded. "Lead the way."

Might as well get it over with. His mother would call again tomorrow to check on things anyway. This would give him something to report.

Holly's adrenaline ramped back up as she took hold of Zack's warm hand. Time to find his brothers. She led him through the crowd, yet every time someone stared at their clasped hands, the irritation inside her inched up another degree.

She loved Sugar Springs, but sometimes people were simply too judgmental.

There was also the fact that they were making assumptions when they should be minding their own business. They had been told she was here to find a man. She had Zack's hand in hers, ergo she must want him.

Okay, that wasn't so much of a stretch. She did want him. Who wouldn't? He was hot.

And he'd just come to her rescue.

Only, all that marriage talk had drawn the fear of God right across his face. Yep, he was not for her. He didn't have to tell her that for her to know it.

When the two of them got to Cody and Nick's quilt, she stopped beside them, and found herself at a sudden loss for words. *Crap.* She hadn't really thought this through.

Nick looked up. And then his gaze went to her and Zack's hands. She turned Zack loose.

"Down in front," someone shouted out behind them.

With a frustrated sigh, Holly squatted. When Zack didn't follow her down, she looked up. He was staring at his brothers, his face etched in stone.

She turned back to Nick. Then Cody. Oh yeah, she hadn't been wrong. They were still mad. Both of them had their gazes locked on Zack, and it wasn't welcome they were dishing out. The three of them looked like dogs primed for a fight.

Okay, maybe this hadn't been the best way to reunite the brothers.

"Zack is staying out at the house," she began, adding a happy lift to her voice. "And I thought—"

Cody's dark eyes tracked to hers. His anger was clear. "So, what? He's your best friend now?"

"No," she stammered.

"Or is he more?"

Fury shot through her. "Of course not. I just offered to—"

"You're interrupting our night," Cody bit out. "I think you both should leave."

Holly's mouth hung open as she looked at Cody in shock. He'd never been so rude to her. She swallowed her nerves and shifted her gaze to Nick. He was the more sensible one. Were they really just going to push Zack away like that?

The man had come up here to find them.

Nick watched the silent man at her side before turning to Holly. He nodded. "Best go, Hol."

Pain for Zack filled her.

She knew her friends had been hurt by him, but they were good guys. She hadn't expected this kind of reaction. Before she could say anything else, Zack was ten feet away, and didn't look to be stopping anytime soon.

"What's wrong with you two?" she snapped out at the brothers. "You're better people than that."

Then she was gone, racing after Zack as best she could in pumps.

She caught up with him right before he exited the park. "Wait," she called out.

He paused, then turned his head slowly as if surprised to see her behind him. She expected the people around them to shush her, but no, they merely watched the two of them as if they were the show instead of the movie.

Her breath came in gasps. "You can't just run out."

"I can do whatever I want." He glared. "And I will. I'm leaving."

She grabbed the back of his shirt when he whirled around. "Take me with you," she begged.

"Why?"

"I . . ." Her breath came out hard. She'd just wanted to help him. Instead, she'd caused him pain. As well as his brothers.

"I can't stay here," she finally said. "Everyone is watching me, and now I've caused a scene. Please," she pleaded, "I came here with Patrick. I don't want to wait for the movie to end to leave. You and I are going to the same place. Take me with you."

He stared hard at her, his nostrils flaring and his jaw locked tight. Then he shook his head and she let out a small groan. But he surprised her when he said, "Get your purse. I'll pull the car around."

In a flash, she'd zipped back through the crowd, grabbed her bag, and explained that she had a ride home. She was waiting by the ticket booth when the sexy, silver convertible eased to her side.

When she didn't immediately get in, the window slid down.

She leaned her head in the opening, feeling like Julia Roberts in *Pretty Woman*, only *her* dress covered her far better. And she wasn't a hooker. "Any chance you'd let me drive?" she suggested lamely.

Of course there was no chance he'd let her drive. But it sure would make the night end better if she could get behind that wheel.

"Did you want a ride or not?" His tone was not friendly.

"Fine," she grumbled. She pouted and opened the door. "But you'll at least put the top down, right?"

Dark eyes cut to hers. "We're only five minutes from the house."

"So? That's five minutes of the wind blowing through my hair." The man sure was hateful when he'd had his feelings hurt.

They had a stare-off, and when he broke contact and pressed a button on the dash, she didn't hold back the grin.

"Don't smile," he warned. "You didn't win. I'm just not in the mood to argue over something so trivial."

But she had won. She'd made him crack.

And they both knew it.

Chapter Six

Holly pointed out the next turn, and as if they'd been taking drives together for years, Zack didn't protest. He simply took the right. They'd left the park together, and though he'd had every intention of dumping her at the house before he headed out to clear his head—possibly to point his car south and return to Atlanta tonight—he'd made the first turn when she'd softly commanded, "Turn here."

They'd wound around a couple of curves, made a few more rights, a few lefts, and, if he wasn't mistaken, they'd been leaving Sugar Springs behind. Only, the last couple of twists seemed as if they were now heading back.

"There," she said. Her finger pointed out a small opening in the trees. He could barely make it out in the dark.

"That isn't a road," he said.

"It's a road. It's just not paved."

"I've already had my car fixed once this week. I don't particularly want to do it again."

The corners of her mouth tilted up in the glow from the dash, and he darn near wrecked at the sweet expression. Then it occurred to him that she was laughing at him. Again. It seemed to be a habit of hers.

"It was your neighbor's fault," he mumbled. He turned where she'd directed.

They both fell silent as he pulled the car to the edge of the riverbank and stopped. The lights of Sugar Springs could be seen off in the distance.

The town was tiny and didn't emit a great deal of light, but it was clear where the park sat. Equally clear was the movie screen. It was only a rectangular speck from this distance, but if they had powerful binoculars, they could watch it from this very spot.

"Where are we?" he asked.

"The other side of the river from our property."

She reached over and turned his car off, and both silence and darkness shrouded them. He closed his eyes and listened, and could hear the river down below. It slipped smoothly and continuously over the rocks of the riverbed. The sound reminded him of the water feature his dad had installed in the backyard as a fiftieth anniversary present for his mom.

"What was my neighbor's fault?" she asked softly beside him.

He opened his eyes and rolled his head on his headrest until he looked at her. She'd slumped down in her seat and had her face tilted to the sky. The stars were out and bright. He slumped down as well and took up the same position.

"That I wrecked my car," he answered.

"How so?"

"I got caught up staring at the . . . *ornamentation* on the front porch."

Her throaty laughter hit him in the gut and spread out through his limbs. It cradled him as if he'd pulled a fuzzy glove over his entire body. He enjoyed hearing her laugh. The sound fit her.

She was one of the happiest people he'd ever met. A person like that should have a great laugh.

"Judy has collected washtubs for years," she explained. "She used to have them stacked in their living room, and the story goes that it was about to cause a divorce. Her husband finally told her, 'It's me or the washtubs.'" She chuckled softly again. "Judy informed him that he was mistaken, of course. Said he wasn't going anywhere. But that she *would* compromise. If he'd build her a porch."

"The thing looked like it was about to fall down."

"My guess is it eventually will. Her husband isn't much of a do-it-yourselfer."

That was the truth.

A light flickered on across the river. It wasn't right against the bank, but close enough that it had to be on Marshall property.

"What's that?" he asked.

"The main house. The floodlights out back."

He'd noticed a couple of employees who worked in the afternoons. Probably it was one of them, staying late.

"When are your parents returning?" He didn't know why he asked. It didn't matter. But the quiet surrounding them made him want to talk. And he didn't particularly want to talk about the fact that he'd apparently come to Sugar Springs for no reason.

His brothers didn't want him in their lives.

"They'll be back on Sunday."

"Does that mean she'll be cooking pancakes for me next week instead of you?"

Easy laughter stroked over him again. "She is a better cook than me."

"But your pancakes changed my world," he teased.

In actuality, with a single breakfast that morning, *she* had changed his world. At least bent it a little. He'd spent so much time running from meeting to meeting, client to client, that it had been years since he'd so much as considered sitting down to start the day. Or having a simple conversation while doing it.

Or discovering the beginnings of a friendship.

He felt her shift on her seat to face him. When she didn't say anything, he finally glanced her way. There was a soft, understanding look on her face. It made it hard not to lean over and brush his lips across hers. *Only* brush their lips together.

Which left him with a question.

He didn't romance women. He didn't seduce them. It was simple with him. If he and a woman wanted each other, he took her to bed. Yet as he studied the details of Holly's face, he had the strongest urge to be gentle with her. He found himself wanting her to like him. Wanting her to want him.

He pushed the inane thoughts from his mind. He'd written off "normal" relationships years ago. They didn't work for him. Yet he couldn't completely leave it alone just yet. "You're different than most women." He spoke quietly.

The twist of her mouth wasn't a smile. "Tell me about it."

She turned back to the river and he felt the loss as if the sun had blinked out.

"That's a good thing," he told her. When she didn't reply, he picked up her hand and turned it over in his. Her fingers were soft beneath the slide of his thumb. "Always being the same is boring."

He thought of the women he dated. Each and every one of them was the same.

Holly closed her eyes. "But being me doesn't get me noticed."

He kept the laugh in as he peeked in the dark down to the floorboard. Her shoes were bright red tonight. With sequins. He didn't know how that couldn't be noticed. "How do you figure?"

Her face tilted higher toward the sky, and against the backdrop of the blue night, he detected sadness tugging at her features. She should never be sad.

"I'm everyone's pal." She grimaced. "Not girlfriend material."

"Could have fooled me. You had your pick of guys tonight."

She gave him a droll look. "And how many of them do you suppose were there looking for marriage, as opposed to hoping for a quick roll in the hay?"

He was a man. He knew the answer to that. "But they noticed you."

"Because someone told them to."

"That's not true."

She snorted. "That's entirely true. If Ms. Grayson hadn't run her mouth about what she'd overheard, I could have sat there tonight without a stitch of clothes on, and still not had anyone look at me."

He would have looked at her. In fact, he wanted to look at her right now. Without a stitch of clothes on.

"Why do you want to get married?" he asked. *Focus*, he told himself. Do not think of her naked. Do not suggest what she'd just pointed out men too often did.

"I told you why."

"You told me you'd decided the big city wasn't for you so you were going to get married."

"Right."

Zack squeezed her hand where it still rested in his and her eyes lifted. "That doesn't make sense," he whispered. "You should marry because you find the right person. Because you find . . ." he paused, thinking about the past and wondering if he still believed in what he was about to say.

But he knew that deep down, even if he never found it himself, he did.

He wanted to believe in that kind of life.

"Because you find love," he finished. "You should be living your life *until* love comes along. Not trying to force it."

She gave him a strange look. "Wouldn't expect something so flowery to come from you."

"Yeah, well." Neither would he before he'd said it. "My parents set a good example."

"Yet it's one you don't plan to follow?"

He eyed her. "Not everyone is cut out for love. Doesn't mean I don't believe it exists."

Her eyes were still narrowed. "Why aren't you cut out for it?"

"We're not talking about me. Why are you looking so hard for it?"

"I'm not. I'm living my life, just like you said."

"Really? What are you doing, then?" As far as he'd seen, she cooked breakfast in the mornings and had lunch with her friends. "Do you have a career? Are you looking for one? Or is marriage it?"

She went silent, and for a beat he felt bad. He hadn't meant to come across as judgmental. Not everyone had the need for goals and high expectations. "I'm sor—"

"For your information, my family owns several businesses here in town." Her words were tight. Filled with hurt. "I help out with whichever one needs me that day. If my parents were in town right now, I'd be spending most days at the diner," she said. Her voice cracked and she finished by tilting her nose in the air. "That's career enough for me."

Only, it didn't sound like it was. It sounded like something was broken inside of her.

He shouldn't push. It wasn't his business. Yet he opened his mouth anyway. "But surely you want more?"

The sadness returned for a brief second before her features once again grew taut. It felt like he was missing something.

Her jaw twitched before she spoke, and then she surprised him by showing no anger.

"Look around, Zack." Resignation leaked from her. She shook her head. "Sugar Springs isn't a hotbed of jobs. I could apply to be manager of Sam's Foodmart, I suppose. I heard Bill will be retiring soon. But how's that any better than working at the diner?"

"And marriage and babies is better?" He couldn't seem to stop himself. Because he couldn't picture her as simply a wife and mother.

Not that there was anything wrong with that. His own mother was a wife and mother. He would swear in court that she'd been born for it. But Holly . . .

It just felt like she was meant for more.

It took a few seconds for her to answer, but she finally nodded. Her gaze held his as she said, "Marriage and babies is what I want."

He didn't know whether to believe her or not. But she did look convincing.

"Okay." He would let it go. Whoever got her would be a lucky man. "Just don't go for the weird shoe guy."

"The weird shoe guy was the only one with potential."

His jaw very nearly fell to his lap. "How do you figure?"

Her eyes rounded. "Hello? He brought me shoes."

"Yeah." He nodded. *"He brought you shoes."*

She smiled just the tiniest amount. It still held a fair amount of sadness, but at least her mood was looking up.

"You're weird," he grumbled. "But thanks for your help earlier."

"My help with what? Pissing off your brothers even more than you managed to do by yourself?"

Yep. That's about what they'd accomplished. He simply shrugged.

"We've got to fix that, you know?" She let out a sad-sounding sigh. "That was not the way tonight was supposed to go."

"Don't worry about it. They have each other. They don't need a third." He didn't want to think about the fact that that bothered him way more than it should. "I just dread having to tell my mother that I struck out."

Finally, she laughed again, and he felt better when her dimple made an appearance.

"Your mother did send you up here, didn't she?"

He tried to look serious. "I came because I wanted to."

"Liar."

Three seconds passed before he lost the straight face. He couldn't help it; he laughed with her. "My mother threatened to hire someone to club me over the head and haul me up here if I didn't do it myself."

Holly's laughter grew louder, and he found himself leaning slightly over to her side. She drew him in the same way her pancakes made his mouth water. It was nice talking to someone who wasn't looking to beat him in the courtroom or step on him on their way to the top. She just wanted to enjoy her life.

"I can't help it that I'm a grown man and my mother is still overprotective," he explained. "But you're going to have to stop laughing at me." He didn't mean it. He was already thinking of stories he could tell that would get her going again.

"Not going to happen." She swiped at her eyes. He'd brought her to giggling tears. He smiled at her in the dark. She studied him, her mouth curved with ease, her eyes glistening with unshed tears. "I like your mother," she said. "I think it's cute that she worries about you."

"Ouch." Cute? He put one hand to his heart and shook his head in disgust. "Nothing about me is cute."

"Oh, I don't know."

She sat up straighter now, putting a bit of distance between them as she looked him over. "You seem to have this aversion to being casual, which is charmingly cute."

He had no idea what she was talking about. "How do you mean?"

"Ever heard of jeans?"

Ah, yes. He had picked up on the fact that he'd been the only one there tonight not in jeans. Except for the women who'd worn dresses.

"That's one you might have to get used to," he admitted. The fact was, he didn't own any. He hadn't since high school. "What else?"

Normally he wouldn't ask someone to pick him apart, but he liked to hear her talk.

"You have this stern, hard look," she said. "You like to scare people with it, but I think it's cute too."

He brought out that stern, hard look, adding in a lifted brow and a dangerous tilt to his head. "This is not cute. This is scary."

Giggles filled the car. "Only for people who don't look past it."

"Ah. You don't believe the look is real?"

She shook her head.

"Then what do you see behind it?" He found that he really wanted to know. Because most of the time it *was* fake. But he'd never had anyone point that out to him.

Her smile dropped, and she lifted one hand to draw a finger lightly down his cheek. The touch sent a jolt through him. She didn't say anything at first. Just deliberated. Her eyes moved over every inch of his face, and he found himself growing uncomfortably warm under her scrutiny.

Then she let her hand drop back to her lap.

"I see a lot of the same thing I see when I look in the mirror."

Even though he'd asked the question, he suddenly didn't want to go serious. "You see bright lipstick and too much eye makeup?"

"Hey," she said, "what's wrong with my makeup?"

"You hide behind it."

He didn't know where that had come from, but he knew the words were true. "You barely had any on this morning," he told her, "and I couldn't look away from you. I was seeing *you.*"

The tip of her tongue appeared a second before she pulled her top lip between her teeth.

"That's what you need to do to get a man's attention," he said. "You're pretty *with* the makeup, but sometimes less is more. Tone it down and the men around here won't know what hit them."

She shook her head. "You don't know what you're talking about. I look like a kid without the makeup. And anyway, you don't even like my shoes."

"What?" Her subject change gave him whiplash.

"Every day you make a face when you see my shoes."

"They don't match your clothes."

"I know."

"So you're not color-blind?"

She laughed again, and they both leaned their heads back against their headrests, faces toward each other. "No," she said, still chuckling. "I see colors perfectly. I just want to . . ."

When she trailed off, he thought about what he knew about her. She was the youngest. He'd seen that in a family photo hanging in the house. And she was the only girl.

She was content to live in Sugar Springs, yet she didn't seem especially happy with her options.

She didn't have a real career, and didn't appear to be chasing one. She merely filled in.

And then he got it. She was fading into the background.

"You want to be seen," he stated. "Stand out from the crowd."

Eyes that he knew to be green stared at him across the space. She didn't blink. "I just want people to see *me*," she whispered. "Instead of the little Marshall girl."

He nodded. He could understand that. He'd been Dr. Winston's son throughout his early years. It wasn't the same as with her, but even then, he'd begun to resent that he was seen as the good doctor's son instead of his own person.

"So you wear weird shoes to get noticed?" he asked.

"They aren't weird."

He didn't reply. Because yes, they were weird. But they fit her. Perfectly.

"I'm right about the makeup, though." His voice came out more gentle than he'd intended, but he couldn't help it. He was picturing her as she'd been that morning. Fresh-faced. And those shorts. "Trust me."

His gaze dipped to her lips. The red that had been bright earlier had faded, and he found himself once again wanting to close the distance to touch them.

Instead of following his urge, he dragged his eyes back up. She was watching him. He wondered if she'd been able to read the lust in his eyes. Hopefully it was too dark. He didn't want her to know that he was attracted to her.

He'd rather have her as a friend. He didn't have enough of those.

"I see loneliness," she whispered.

"When?"

"When I look at you." She brought her hand up again, and caressed her fingers over his cheek. "The same thing I see when I look in the mirror each morning. Loneliness."

His chin lifted.

He wasn't lonely. He could get any woman he wanted. Hadn't Shelley been calling him just that morning? He had colleagues who would do dinner, drinks, golf. Whenever he tossed out the suggestion. No, she had it wrong.

He shook his head. "You're seeing the wrong thing there, sweetheart."

"I don't think so."

"Well." He returned to sitting forward in his seat and looking out over the water. "I'm telling you, you're wrong. I'm perfectly happy. I don't need anyone."

A picture of him as a kid flashed to mind. Maybe he *had* been lonely at one point, but he wasn't now.

"I'm fine," he repeated.

She remained silent until he looked at her. It was as if her mere presence had pulled his face around to hers. When their eyes met, there was sadness in hers. "You need to start by apologizing," she said.

He understood that she was talking about Cody and Nick. "I know."

He should have called them up weeks ago and done just that.

"My mother isn't the only reason I'm here," he confessed.

She watched him, and he knew that she got it. He'd wanted to know about his brothers too. He'd wanted to see if there *was* a place in their world for him. If they really wanted to let him in.

Even though he was terrified the answer would be no.

"Your father too?" she asked with a teasing smile. "Did he threaten to club you over the head as well?" She was giving him the chance to back off the fact he'd just revealed. That he was vulnerable.

He shook his head. "My father passed away three years ago."

She sucked in a breath. "I'm sorry, Zack. I didn't know."

"It's okay." He reached for her hand again, and she slipped her fingers between his. "I miss him, but Mom and I are doing well." The fact was, he'd looked up to his father his whole life, and with him gone, there was a hole left in Zack's heart. His mother wasn't any better. "He went out the way he would have wanted. On the golf course. A stroke and he was simply gone."

Holly squeezed his hand in hers and they sat in silence.

"We'll start in the morning," she said after several minutes. "Only, one brother at a time this time. Nick first. He'll be the easier one."

Zack didn't think anything about this was going to be easy. But he did want to get to know his brothers. And he did owe them an apology.

He nodded. "Sounds like a plan."

Chapter Seven

Holly paused at the stove as she felt Zack enter the room behind her. She'd gotten up early that morning to see to the chores, then she'd readied the quad for them. She was taking him to the cabins being built on her family's property. Nick was contracted for the job, and she wanted to get there the fun way.

She turned, as she had the day before, to find Zack once again standing in the doorway. And just like yesterday, her breath caught. The man was way too handsome. And he darn near took up the full space of the doorway.

"Breakfast?" she asked. Her voice had a nervous croak to it, and she was quickly reminded of the way he'd looked at her the night before. He'd made her feel nervous then too.

It had been a brief glance, but his gaze had lingered on her mouth, and she'd had the very real thought that he'd been about to kiss her.

Which would have been a mistake. She didn't do casual. He was leaving in two weeks.

These things she had to keep in mind.

But his look most certainly had made her wonder what his kiss would be like.

His gaze flickered over her now, and she found herself standing there as if on display. She was wearing her normal summer, around-the-house attire of shorts and a T-shirt. Royal blue was the color scheme for the day. But this time, she'd paired it with work boots that came up above her ankles. The boots were purple and studded, and the tongue was done in a cow pattern.

Poking out the top of them were retro tube socks with gold horizontal stripes circling just below her knees.

"Nice boots," Zack said. He didn't even try to hold back the sarcasm.

She smirked. "Nice pants."

His pants weren't the standard dress pants of the last few days, but he still looked like he belonged in the middle of a roomful of suits instead of a construction site. Navy chinos and a short-sleeve button-down were not what he needed to show up wearing if he wanted to connect with his brother.

Plus . . . construction site. Duh.

Turning her back to him, she flipped the pancakes. She also used the moment to *not* look at Zack. Because she was finding that every time she looked at him, she got a little further away from remembering he wasn't her type.

"You'll need jeans today," she told him. "You have time to change before your breakfast is ready."

He didn't reply for a few seconds, and then he admitted, "I didn't bring jeans."

She felt him step up behind her as much as heard him, and then he peered over her shoulder. She held her breath. He kept getting in her space like that. It made things inside her all fluttery.

"You aren't seriously thinking of serving me pancakes with chocolate chips in them, are you?"

God, he smelled good. What kind of soap did the man use, anyway?

She drew a deep breath in through her nose, just to tease herself with the expensive smell, before pointing out the whiteboard on the opposite wall. "I could stick with my mother's plan and serve you eggs and grits if you prefer."

He made a face. "Grits?" He said the word as if she'd just asked him to eat raw liver for breakfast.

"It's what everyone else got."

"Why would you serve that to people?"

"Because we're in the South, sweetie. And because people like grits." She waved her spatula at him. "So choose. Grits or pancakes?"

He glanced at the stove. "And I have to have them with something in them?"

"They aren't *something*, they're chocolate chips. They're good."

"Why would you ruin a perfectly good pancake with chocolate chips?"

"Because they're fun."

He went silent. His dark gaze once again studied her, this time concentrating on her face and hair. She had her hair pulled back in a French braid running down the middle of her back, and she'd worn less makeup today. Only a hint of lip gloss, and just a brush of mascara. But not because of what he'd said last night about being unable to look away from her when she wore less.

She just didn't need it today. After she dropped him at the cabins, she planned to put in a few hours of work.

Makeup wasn't needed when she intended to spend the day by herself.

"You look nice today." His words were easy. Her knees went weak. What the hell was wrong with her?

They'd had a good time after they left the park last night. But that was all. They'd talked. They were becoming friends. She liked him.

But not *liked* him.

He was Cody and Nick's brother, for crying out loud.

Her friends who were now ticked at her for springing Zack on them to begin with.

Getting weak-kneed over the man was out of the question.

"Thank you," she murmured. "You do too. But I still think you're wrong about the makeup. Less is not always more." And she had no idea why he thought she hid behind it. She had nothing to hide *from*.

"No, I'm not."

She pointed a finger at him. "I'll prove it," she declared.

His gaze narrowed on her, and she stood there in front of him as if on trial. She wanted to know what he was thinking when he looked at her. Did he really have a hard time looking away?

The thought did more for her cardiovascular system than a jog into town and back.

"What did you have in mind?" he finally asked.

She had to rewind the conversation in her mind to remember what she'd even said. Oh yes, makeup. She intended to prove him wrong. "I'll pick the perfect time, and I'll wear even more than I normally do." She gave him a haughty look. "And you'll admit you're wrong."

"But I'm not wrong."

The man did not lack in confidence.

She held out a hand. "Deal, or not?"

"What are we playing for?"

She ran a couple of ideas through her mind, tossing out the more lewd ones, and then smiled. "Pancakes." Before he could respond, she added, "You'll eat them however I serve them."

He grew silent, as if giving serious contemplation to the terms. "And if I win?" he asked.

Excitement winged its way through her at the thought of the prizes he might request if he won. None of which were appropriate between friends.

"What do you want?" she asked. Her voice dropped to a near whisper.

He once again took his time deciding. As he did, his gaze skimmed over her body. When it landed on her feet, she grew nervous. Surely he wouldn't suggest she wear shoes that made sense to him. She liked the shoes she wore.

His gaze traveled back up. She wet her lips when he lingered briefly on her mouth. He made her too antsy. At long last, his eyes once again met hers. The seriousness in them took her by surprise.

"If I win," he started, "then you consider chasing something other than marriage."

The back room of her studio came to mind. Then Chicago.

Then the crush of failure.

But she knew she would win this bet, so it didn't matter. She closed her fingers around his outstretched hand. "Deal."

They didn't shake their hands up and down. They just stood there. Palm to palm. She could feel the rougher toughness of his fingers against her smoother, softer skin. It wasn't a calloused kind of rough. Just a manly rough. And big.

His hand was very big.

Her mind hit the gutter.

"Today I want pancakes without chocolate chips," he said. It wasn't a demand. Exactly. It was more of a plea. In a no-nonsense, I'm-in-charge-here sort of way.

Her chest moved up and down with her breaths, and they stared at each other. Once again she was reminded of last night. They'd had a staring match over him putting the convertible top down when they'd left the park. She'd won that round, but something told her that had been rare. She didn't think she could take this match.

Looking away, she grunted in frustration. "Fine," she muttered.

He laughed softly beside her. The sound feathered over her ear and slid down her neck.

"But I'm going to find you a pair of jeans to wear," she tacked on.

His laughter shut off.

She peeked at him. "There are some clothes of Sean's here. My youngest brother. He leaves a few things for when he comes home."

"I'm not wearing someone else's clothes."

"You can't wear those," she pointed out. "I'm taking you to the cabins your brother is building. It's messy out there. Plus, I thought if things go well, you could hang out with him for a while." She jabbed her spatula toward his pants. "You can't stay there all day looking like that."

Twenty minutes later, Zack was in another man's jeans and someone else's work boots.

He was on the back of a four-wheeler, his fingers digging into Holly's sides as if he were a scared little girl, and they were blasting across the green fields of Marshall property.

At least he'd gotten pancakes without chocolate chips in them.

But still. What the hell was happening to his life?

Normally he'd be on his third or fourth meeting of the day. He'd be seeking out a case that would win him a partnership. And he'd be readying for lunch with someone who could get him somewhere.

Instead, he was laughing in the wind as if he hadn't a care in the world.

Holly continued to amaze him. When she'd turned around that morning and he'd first caught sight of her, he'd known that the rest of his two weeks there were going to be a challenge.

"Why do we have to ride out there on this thing?" he shouted over the roar of the motor.

He wasn't sure she'd heard him until she leaned back into his chest and tilted her chin up. She angled in his direction. "Because I like it."

And that was enough.

With her still pressed to him, he fought the urge to slide his hands from her sides on around to her front. Her body was just soft enough, and he found it a struggle to remember the type of women he normally spent time with.

She straightened in the seat and he silently groaned at the loss of her touch.

Instead of focusing on the woman who was quickly becoming an addiction, he took in their surroundings. She was flying through a heavily wooded area now, though they seemed to be sticking to a well-worn path. The occasional glimpse of the river and mountains to their left kept pulling his gaze. It was beautiful out here.

If the sound of the engine and the rushing wind wasn't filling his head, he suspected it would be near silent.

Suddenly, Holly lifted slightly off the seat. His brain registered what she was doing a millisecond before the tire of the quad hit a rut. Mud splattered up on his jeans, a small clump making it all the way to his cheek, and Zack moaned out loud as he bounced hard on the seat. He barely kept from reaching to cup himself to shield his testicles from more torture. If his fingers weren't clenched so tightly around Holly, he probably would have.

She settled back on the seat and let up on the gas. Slightly. Leaning back again, she shouted, "Sorry about that. I don't normally have someone with me and didn't think to warn you."

"And you normally drive like this?"

She burst out laughing. "Of course. What's the point of having something fun if you don't have fun with it? If you'd let me get behind the wheel of your car last night, I would have driven it like this too."

"You just killed any future opportunity to drive it," he shouted back.

She laughed again. "You need to take more risks," she yelled out. "Anyone ever tell you that?"

"I'm not sure where the word *need* comes from in that sentence, but I assure you I'm fine the way I am."

Except for one thing. He was wrapped around a woman he couldn't have, yet growing more and more certain he wanted. Holly was not the type to settle for a fling, and he had a career to get back to in Atlanta. He had no business touching her, but he couldn't help himself.

He slid one hand to her front and flattened his palm on her stomach.

When she didn't say anything else, merely sat up straighter and pulled slightly away, he leaned forward and followed her. He didn't stop until he once again had his front pressed to her back. He put his mouth to her ear. "Tell me again why we had to come out on this thing instead of taking a car?"

He felt her back move against his chest as if her breathing had grown heavier.

"Because this is more fun." She slowed again to take a tight path through a tiny part in the trees. He followed her lead, ducking his head in sync with hers.

"We could have gone over to the stables and saddled a couple of horses," she suggested. "That would have been fun too."

The memory of climbing up on the horse with her was not a pleasant one. He hadn't been that out of control of his own destiny in years.

"If those were my only two options," he began, "this is much preferred." Plus, he was actually enjoying himself. Not that he was ready to admit it.

She hadn't kicked the speed back up, so he took the time to enjoy the scenery. They were still in the trees, but the density was fast becoming sparser. He could see more glimpses of the river, and even picked out a small log cabin sitting alone against the riverbed. It looked to be only large enough to contain two or three rooms, and the roof rose up from the front and then stopped a few feet down the back. The side facing the river was at least half a floor higher.

"You should come with me tomorrow," she told him as she slowed more, this time gently bumping them through a rut. The tire spun in the mud and he held tight as she shifted their weight and freed them.

"If it involves this particular vehicle, I'm going to go ahead and say no."

"Spoilsport." She laughed with the word and pointed out a flock of birds sunning in the middle of a meadow off to their right. "I promise it will be something that can be done via my car." She shot him an evil grin. "Or yours."

"What is it?" He was not letting her behind the wheel of his car.

"We're going to go buy you some jeans."

Not having to wear someone else's clothes appealed to him.

And if he would be spending more time with Holly—which he fervently hoped he would be doing—then he would need something other than the clothes he'd brought.

"I could get down with that," he said.

He slid his other arm around her and held her snug against him. He even caught himself smiling for no apparent reason. It was turning out to be a fun morning. All of that might change the minute she got him to the cabins. Probably Nick would still have no interest in seeing him. But the fresh air and Holly's happy spirit made the thought of trying again less depressing.

He even managed a small hope that his apology would be well received.

They came out of the woods and nature's beauty burst out around them.

"Wow," he murmured. The river glistened in the sunlight, and everywhere he looked was green. Grass, trees, mountains. Even moss-covered rocks.

"Right?" she asked. She pulled the quad to a stop and turned it off. "I love this place. I come out here all the time."

They both climbed off, his movements slower than hers due to the fact that his testicles felt more like they'd been vibrating directly on the engine than on the padded seat.

When he finally made it to her side, they stood watching the soothing waters with the Smokies as the backdrop. It looked like a good place to fish.

As if he knew anything about fishing.

She pointed to a small area across the river where there were no trees. "That's where we were last night."

He didn't say anything. Just stood with his hands on his hips, soaking it all in. It was a nice moment, and he was glad she'd brought him here. If he were to imagine a spot where he might like to escape the craziness of life on occasion, something like this might come to mind.

When he looked around, he found Holly watching him.

"What do you think?" she asked.

He didn't have to think. "It sure beats Atlanta traffic."

She nodded. "I know. I couldn't get over the constant noise in Chicago. And the sheer number of cars. Everywhere."

"You never did tell me what you were really doing up there."

"I told you . . ." She shrugged and turned away. "I went to see my cousin."

She stuck with her story, but he got the impression it was a lie. At most, a partial truth. Which only made him want to know more. Instead of pushing, he continued his examination of the area around them. He could push later.

"What's that?" He pointed to the log cabin he'd seen through the trees.

Holly followed the line of his outstretched arm to land on the building. A look of sadness once again crossed her face. It twisted at his heart. And it made him *definitely* want to know more.

"It's my place," she finally answered.

He raised a brow, shocked.

She shrugged. "It was an old house that had been on the property since before I was born. I had my dad and brothers fix it up for me a few years ago."

"Yet you stay at the main house. Or is that just when your parents are out of town?"

"I stay at the house most of the time, yes."

She started walking back to the quad as if the conversation was over.

"Wait," he said. He didn't know what question to ask first, but it was clear she didn't want to talk about it. Whatever *it* was. Before he could string together the right words to get an answer, a familiar honking sound ripped through the air.

He cringed at the squawk as two geese sauntered out of the woods and headed toward them.

"What is up with those geese?" he asked. They'd been beside his car that first day.

"They're mine too," Holly said. She pulled a pack of crackers from the front pocket of her shorts and tossed some in the direction of the animals. They honked as if in thanks.

"You have pet geese?"

"It's more like I'm their pet. They chose to stay a couple of years ago. I just gave them names."

"You named the geese?"

"Sure. Wouldn't you hate to live somewhere and have everyone just call you 'man'?"

Her back was to him as she tossed more crackers on the ground, and he simply stared at her. He had no words.

"You are one of the strangest women I've ever met," he finally managed to mutter.

She nodded. "I know."

He followed her to the quad and climbed onto the back of the seat, moving gingerly as he slung a leg over the cushion. "What are their names?" he asked.

Green eyes that he could look at for hours turned to him. In them was a mixture of sadness, teasing, and contentedness. She was the most interesting person who'd ever come into his life.

"Snow White and the Huntsman," she said.

It took a couple seconds to come up out of her eyes and figure out she was talking about the geese. She'd named them after a movie. All he could do was shake his head.

And fight the urge to pull her close.

"Why don't you stay out here?" he asked.

She started the machine. "Because I get lonely."

Like she'd accused him of being last night. He peered back at the building and could see how someone like her wouldn't like it out here. She needed people around her. She needed liveliness and laughter.

But then, why had she gotten her brothers to fix it up if she didn't intend to live there?

With the question still rolling through his head, the motor revved and he reached for her waist.

Looked like answers would have to wait. It was time to go find his brother.

Chapter Eight

Holly eased the quad into the construction site, keeping an eye out for Nick. This time she'd done better than spring Zack on him unaware. One of the first things she'd done that morning had been to call both brothers and apologize. She should have warned them last night that Zack might show up.

Nick had seemed okay with things, but Cody was harder to convince. In the end, both men had agreed that since Zack was in town, they supposed they could talk to him.

She'd lined up Nick for today.

Cody would be Monday. He had other things going on over the weekend and had refused to change them.

When she cut the motor, she saw a familiar dark head appear in the doorway of one of the cabins. No words were exchanged, but with the pounding and power tools going on around them, they wouldn't have been able to hear each other from this distance anyway.

"This is it," Zack muttered. His breath tickled her ear. He'd been holding onto her tight since right before they'd stopped near her studio. He'd resumed the position when they'd climbed back on, and he hadn't let go since.

As before, one arm circled her waist, his big hand splayed against her stomach, and his chest pressed to her back. It had made focusing on the drive more difficult than usual.

She wasn't accustomed to a man being so close. Especially one who seemed to be made of heat and steel. She'd told herself the whole way out that it *wasn't* pure, unadulterated attraction she was feeling. Just that he was a good-looking man. She'd feel that way with any good-looking man smooshed up against her.

Also, he smelled simply divine.

He shifted back when Nick headed in their direction, breaking their connection, and his palms slid to her sides. But he didn't let go.

She turned her head to peek at him. He had a smear of dirt on his cheek. "You okay?"

His eyes shifted from Nick to hers, and she felt for a second as if a live wire were connecting the two of them. He nodded.

"You told him we were coming?" he asked.

"I did."

Nerves vibrated inside her. She very much wanted the brothers to get along. Nick and Cody had no reason to believe it yet, but Zack was a good guy. She'd seen this more than once.

And he needed them in his life.

She'd seen that also.

Whether he wanted to admit it or not, he was lonely. He might love his mother, and he might have had a good life up until now, but he was missing something.

She also thought the twins could stand a third brother in their lives. They'd bonded quickly with each other, and that had only grown stronger over the last months. But they *had* gone to Atlanta looking for Zack. They'd wanted to know him.

Just because they'd had their feelings hurt didn't mean that desire had gone away.

"Want me to stay?" she asked.

"You're leaving?" Panicked eyes widened before her.

She gave him a gentle smile, and she would swear the simple act loosened his stiff shoulders. "You boys don't need me hanging around. Nick said he'd bring you back."

Zack didn't say anything for a few seconds. His fingers tensed where they remained at her sides. "How do you know I can be of any help out here? I might just be in the way."

"You fixed my granny's grave, didn't you?"

"Doesn't mean I can do more."

She pried his fingers from her waist before Nick reached them. "Then I guess you get to be the inferior one and let your little brother show you how it's done."

He gave her his "scary" look that she could so see through. She supposed being called inferior didn't sit well with him. Instead of saying anything, she simply blew him a kiss and gave him an innocent grin.

"Zack." Nick held out his hand when he reached their side.

Zack nodded in greeting. Holly watched him swallow. The man was a tangle of nerves. Finally, he seemed to remember protocol and stuck out his hand.

"Nick," he started in his uppity, lawyerly voice. "Nice to . . ." He trailed off, and she could feel his chest expand with the breath he drew in. "I apologize about before." His words were less clipped. "In Atlanta. You two caught me off guard."

His free hand inched back to Holly's waist, and she pressed her palm over the tips of his fingers where they gripped her. Not because he was hurting her, but because she wanted him to know she was there for him.

"I shouldn't have been so rude," he finished.

Nick eyed him, and then gave a nod. "I showed up on Cody's doorstep without warning too. We spent the evening getting drunk. Having a brother show up out of the blue is tough. We should have called."

The air went out of Zack's chest, and Holly silently cheered. This might just work.

"And I shouldn't have let two months go by without a word."

Oh, that was so the right thing to say. She could see it on Nick's face. He was the peacemaker of the family. But he was also the ring-leader. He'd been the one to bring the brothers together in the first place.

He probably wanted this more than any of them.

"Maybe we should start over," Nick said then. "Spend the day out here. Let's see how it goes."

She glanced at Zack when he didn't immediately respond. *This is it*, she wanted to shout at him. *Get off the quad and say yes.*

But what she saw when she looked at him choked her up. His eyes held timid hope. He had not been expecting Nick's easy acceptance.

She had.

Though Cody might be a really good guy, he was the cautious one. He'd been hurt a lot in his life. Without him here for this meet-ing, Nick would open the door wider. He would give Zack more of a chance.

Zack's hand was still at her waist and she gave it a squeeze.

He glanced at her, and she read his thanks. Then he looked back at Nick. "Thank you. I'd like that."

He climbed off the vehicle, and the two men stood somewhat awkwardly together. She needed to get out of there. She felt as if she'd been dropped in the middle of a moment where she didn't belong. She imagined it would be similar to walking in on a couple holding their baby for the first time.

Only, these two were grown men. And neither was likely to hold each other.

She revved the motor. "You'll bring him back?" she asked Nick.

Two sets of identical—gorgeous—eyes turned to her. Man, she'd like to see pictures of their biological parents. The pair might have been worthless human beings, but they had passed along some good-looking genes to their sons.

"We got this," Nick said.

She glanced at Zack to be sure, and her heart fluttered at the warm look he gave her. He really did appreciate her help.

"Don't kill yourself heading back," he said.

She nodded, and he stepped out of the way with Nick. He'd sounded like her brothers with his statement. As if he cared if something happened to her.

It was nice.

Holly roared off, and Zack was left standing there, watching the thick braid of her hair flap in the wind. He owed her for easing the way with Nick today, though, granted, he'd only been there a couple of minutes. He supposed things could change.

Not to mention, he still had to come clean about why he'd been such a son of a bitch in Atlanta. They deserved to know.

He turned to Nick. The first thing he noticed was that the pleasant look was gone. In its place was the same hardness from the previous night.

Damn. And he'd just let his ride head off.

"Don't hurt her." Nick's words were clipped.

"Excuse me?"

"I saw the way you looked at her. Don't hurt her."

Ah. The glare was about Holly. Zack nodded. "No intention of it."

"Intentions can be shot to hell. Especially with a pretty girl around. You might be my brother, but I'll kick your ass if you break her heart."

"Man." Zack held his hands up in front of him. "We're just friends."

"Friends who left the park together last night."

"Yeah," he said, beginning to take offense. "Friends who left the park together. Stay out of it."

An evil slash lifted one side of Nick's mouth. "Cody cares about her more than I do. Think you can take us both?"

He thought he'd get his ass whipped if even one of them took him on.

Though Zack wasn't a lightweight, his brothers easily had twenty pounds each on him. Of muscle. As well as a couple of inches in height.

"We're just friends," he repeated. He found it reassuring that Holly had people watching her back.

"Keep it that way."

The hardness cleared and Nick changed before Zack's eyes. He didn't become friendly, exactly. But he no longer seemed ready to take Zack out either.

"You only here to apologize?" Nick asked.

Meaning . . . do you want to know us?

He did.

Zack hadn't fully realized it until that very moment, but he wanted to get to know them. He'd missed too many years already.

"The apology is just the beginning," he explained. "I'd like to actually get to know my brothers."

That had been far easier to say than he'd imagined.

"I should also tell you that I met our birth mother ten years ago," he added.

Nick's matching eyes locked on Zack's. His voice went flat. "You met Pam?"

"I did."

"Where?"

"A run-down bar outside Nashville."

"She sober enough to know who she was talking to?"

Sounded like Nick wasn't blind to what the woman had been. "She was sober enough to extort me for a good chunk of money."

"Are you kidding me?" Anger heated Nick's words. "You gave her money? You know she either drank it or snorted it."

"I know. But I'd tracked her down—which wasn't exactly legal. She'd never signed the release. I couldn't risk her filing suit because I looked her up." He still wasn't proud that he'd handed a junkie a pile of cash. "Heard what I needed to hear, got her signature on the form, and then I got the hell out."

There was so much he left unsaid. Nick seemed to get it. He studied Zack quietly for several seconds, his gaze never wavering. Then he slowly nodded.

"What else did she tell you?" he asked.

Anger suddenly fueled Zack. He'd had every intention of looking his brothers up ten years ago. Before he'd met Pam. The worthless piece of shit had taken that from him.

"When I didn't come off the full amount she wanted, she made it clear the two of you would do her bidding. Said to watch my back. She also implied you were drinking buddies."

"*Sonofabitch*," Nick growled. And then he got it. "You thought we came to Atlanta for money?"

"It took a while, but yeah. I have a lot of money. I assumed you wanted some of it."

"What changed your mind?"

"Private investigator. Confirmed you didn't actually meet Cody until last year and that you were both respectable business owners. That went against everything Pam had said."

Nick shook his head. Disgust covered his features. "Why would you ever believe something a strung-out drunk told you?"

Because after meeting her, he'd been afraid to hope for more.

Zack had sought Pam out ten years before, naively believing he would mean something to her. He hadn't been looking to build a relationship so much as to have a few questions answered. To find out what his biological family was like.

The PI had warned him not to expect much. He'd seen the woman in action himself, and had already deduced the type of person she was. At least that hadn't been a surprise. But for a guy who'd grown up always wondering, always imagining that he meant something to the woman who'd given him life, it had been near impossible to keep from hoping.

How did he explain that to Nick? Nick *had* grown up with her. Nick knew better.

And after meeting her himself, Zack hadn't wanted another reminder of what his genes were. He didn't need to see his two strung-out brothers to be reminded of what low-class stock he came from.

"I'm not sure what I can say," he finally answered. "It is what it is. I believed her."

"You didn't want to risk having junkies hanging around?"

He took his brother full on. "Would you?"

He knew the answer. Nick had grown up with the woman, and he hadn't spoken to her for fourteen years before she died. Clearly he'd wanted that distance himself.

"I suspect you already know the answer to that," Nick acknowledged.

"I suspect I do."

Both men grew quiet, drifting in their own thoughts, until Nick finally asked, "You good now? Don't think we're out to scam you?"

"I wouldn't be here if I did."

He nodded. "Good enough." Then Nick reached out to slap Zack on the back, and the tension of the last few moments evaporated. Just like that, they were ready to move on. "You have any idea how to hold a hammer?"

A tight chuckle escaped Zack. He still had Cody to get past, but this might just turn out okay.

"I can hold my own," he assured Nick.

"Then let's do this."

The log cabin sat quiet and closed up as Holly straddled the idling four-wheeler. The building was small, but big enough for her purposes. It held one bedroom and a combo living room and kitchen, with an eat-in area large enough to be her work space. It was a home, just as she'd implied to Zack when he'd asked earlier. Only, it was so much more.

It was *her* place.

It wasn't her parents', and it wasn't her brothers'. It was hers.

And it used to hold her dreams.

Now she wasn't sure what it held.

Her heart sat heavy in her chest, as she wondered what she should do next. She climbed from the vehicle and made her way up onto the small porch that spanned the length of the house. A couple rockers sat there, where she sometimes worked out a design in her head or sketched it in a notepad.

There was also a small table she'd confiscated from her parents' basement. It had ring stains from years of glasses of lemonade sitting on it during the sluggish heat of summer. She ran a hand over the back of one of the rockers. They were painted a glossy white, and were just as inviting now as they had been the last time she'd been out here. Seven weeks ago.

She'd driven her SUV here that afternoon, making use of the one-lane dirt road that led only to her cabin. Excitement had flooded her at the new direction her life was about to take. She'd loaded up as many of her original pieces as she could fit in the back without risking damage.

Then she'd headed north.

And last weekend she'd come home with all of them once again packed away and loaded in the back. They were still there now.

She hadn't even bothered to unload them.

But she knew she couldn't ignore the task forever. She had to decide if she was going to accept that this was truly it for her, and be happy with just a hobby . . . or if she would quit for good.

She unlocked the front door and pushed it open.

Sunlight streaked through the oversized floor-to-ceiling windows on the opposite wall that looked out toward the mountains.

The light angled off the many mirrors hanging on every available space in the living room.

The mirrors in this room were the ones she'd refurbished. They were the ones Holly would eventually take to the consignment store.

But it was what was in the bedroom that she was most proud of. Or had been.

She walked slowly through the room, her eyes roving over each and every design. There were large antique mirrors all the way down to small, handheld ones. For each of them, she'd touched up the mirror itself, if needed, and had then added embellishments. Some she'd removed from their original holders and had put into something new.

Like the one that hung at the base of the stairs at the B&B. She'd rescued that mirror from a fake brass frame like those that were once seen in any number of homes throughout the country, and had found and cleaned the copper tray she'd seated it in.

Then she'd gone to work on what she enjoyed most. The perimeter of that mirror was one of her favorites. She liked the mosaic work. The fine detail it took to get it just right. But she also liked creating new designs from scratch.

She made her way through the room to the adjoining kitchen, noting that, as she'd left it, every surface was covered with containers holding glass, beads, slate . . . whatever item she'd run across that could be repurposed for her mirrors. Of course, there was a layer of dust covering everything now, as well.

Then there were the sheets of mirror waiting to be cut and styled into the more artistic works, like those she'd taken to Chicago. No one in Sugar Springs had ever seen any of those.

They were her babies.

The ones she lost hours of her days creating. They were also the ones she'd been fearful to share with others. She hadn't wanted anyone to laugh at what she thought was unique and original.

Because what would she have left if she found out they were nothing special?

She let out a shaky breath. She'd have exactly what she had now. Nothing.

She was just the little Marshall girl; she might as well accept it. The boys' baby sister.

Whatever she'd needed all her life, all she'd had to do was ask. If her parents didn't give it to her, her brothers had.

But no one had ever asked *her* what she really wanted.

The back of her nose burned as she stood at the windows and looked out over the water. She loved this house. And she would love to live here all the time. Though she did get lonely. Just as she'd told Zack. She preferred being around people.

But there was something about this space being so "her" that made it special.

She picked up a notebook where she'd made several sketches, and flipped through the pages. Some she'd already created, and some she still wanted to.

Pain pressed into her chest at the thought of giving this up. This was her thing. It had taken a long time to find it, but she had. And she loved it. She'd never had anything that was truly hers before.

And she didn't want to give it up.

She looked around and saw nothing but beauty surrounding her. She shook her head and set her jaw. There was no reason she had to.

Screw those highbrow people she'd met in Chicago. They didn't control her. They did not choose her destiny.

And she wasn't giving this up.

Even if her more intricate pieces never went anywhere but this house, she could still enjoy creating them. And she could still enjoy working with the ones that she did take into town to sell.

People loved those.

In fact . . . She went to the kitchen cabinets and riffled through the extra-large space that most people would use as a pantry. She found what she wanted, a triangular mirror she'd picked up at a rummage sale in the spring, and nodded her head as her vision for the piece came to her.

She knew just what she wanted to do.

She put the mirror on the sturdy workbench in the eat-in area of the kitchen, and pulled several containers from the shelves running along the wall. She would finish this piece and take it into town next week. That would make her feel back to normal.

And she'd put her trip north completely out of her mind. It had been a mistake to go in the first place.

It had shown her one thing, though. She belonged *here*.

Chapter Nine

You sure you want to do this?" Zack halted outside the door to the Bungalow and eyed his brother.

He and Nick had spent the day together working on the cabins, and though the hours had passed with them getting along well enough, Zack found it difficult to imagine the man honestly wanted to continue their time together into the evening.

Or that he wanted to do it so publicly. He had to know what everyone thought of Zack.

"Got to show off my big brother," Nick replied. The words sounded sincere.

Zack eyed Nick. "This could be your downfall. You might be ostracized."

"You don't give them enough credit." Nick pulled the door open and country music pounded out. The bar was packed. "They protect their own, yeah, but I'm one of their own now. They'll see that I'm good with you, and will cut you some slack."

"What about Cody?" Zack stepped inside the building. His nerves pulled tight at the base of his spine, keeping him from taking more than a couple steps forward. "He might take issue with you spending the evening with me."

Cody had declined to come out with them tonight. Which hadn't surprised Zack.

"Cody will be fine," Nick assured him. "He doesn't trust easily. Years of rejection will do that to a person."

Sounded like Zack and Cody had some things in common.

Nick perked up at the sight of a blonde in the corner, and waved. "That's my fiancée, Joanie," he explained. He nudged Zack to move, and the two of them headed across the room. As they did, conversation came to a halt. The music continued blasting from the speakers, but no one danced.

Every single pair of eyes was focused on them.

"It's all good," Nick said, while giving a smile of greeting to the people they passed. "Stop looking as if you're ready to snap someone's head off and it'll help."

Zack forced a more pleasant expression to his face and thought about Holly. She would have called him out on his scowl too. She probably would have laughed in his face and told him he wasn't nearly as scary as he thought.

He wondered where she was tonight. After working with Nick all day, he'd been dropped at the house, but she'd been nowhere to be found. Zack had considered staying in for the evening and working, yet that had held little appeal. Truth be told, he'd wanted to come out with Nick. Hell, he'd wanted to come out with Holly.

She was probably out on a hot date, though.

So instead of hanging at the house as if he had no life, he'd showered and changed into the least dressy clothes he'd brought with him. He was still overdressed.

"Zack." Joanie Bigbee smiled warmly up at him as they reached the table. Nick had talked about her a lot during the day. She owned the local cupcake store, and apparently had go-go boots and short skirts that brought his brother to his knees. The man was a goner.

She also had blue-tipped hair, and her eyes said that she was not only intelligent, but that she knew how to hold her ground. If he wasn't mistaken, they also said that she'd rip him apart if he hurt her fiancé again. He liked her on the spot.

"It's a pleasure to meet you," he said. He expected her to offer a handshake. Instead she stood and reached across the table, wrapping both arms around his neck in a warm embrace. This made conversation around them start again. The noise level quickly returned to normal.

"Sit," she urged when she pulled away.

Before doing as she asked, he made a quick sweep of the room. Most people were still watching, but no one seemed ready to do anything about him being there. From what he knew about small towns, he'd expected someone to offer to kick his ass just for walking in the door.

"Take a seat, man." Nick pushed him to the empty bench before sliding in next to Joanie.

The number of firsts Zack had experienced in the last two days kept piling up. Why not add spending an evening at a honky-tonk to the mix? He often went out on Friday nights anyway. Usually with some babe who was more interested in his money than his wit. But this was fine.

Actually, his first impression of the relaxed atmosphere was favorable. There were pool tables in the back, a dance floor in the middle of everything, and tables scattered all around. Most seats were full, and the dance floor was filled to capacity. Everyone looked to be thoroughly enjoying themselves. It didn't seem to be a bad place to hang out.

"So tell me about working with Nick." Joanie stretched a hand across the table and rested it on his. The motion made him feel included. "I hear he can be a real slave driver," she said.

Before Zack could answer, a woman slid onto the bench seat beside him.

"Hey darlin'," she drawled. Her perfume was strong but not off-putting, and her cleavage was expansive. And it was right up in his face. She gave him a wide, inviting smile.

"Gina," Joanie groaned at the newcomer. Nick simply chuckled under his breath. "Could you not give us five minutes before you pounced?" Joanie asked.

"In five minutes, honey, any number of women could snap him up," Gina replied. She gave Zack a lidded look and pouted her lips suggestively. "I sure do love you Dalton boys."

He stuck out his hand. "Winston, actually. Zack."

She took his hand in hers and petted the back of it. "Dalton, Winston. Either works for me. As long as they come as good-looking as you. I'm Gina Gregory. I'm single, looking, and I know how to give a man a good time."

He didn't quite know how to take her.

Actually, he did. He could probably take her in the bar's restroom in about two minutes flat.

"Nice to meet you, Gina." He preferred a woman in his bed.

Also, he didn't think he preferred her. He glanced over Gina's shoulder toward the door, wishing Holly were there.

No Holly, but he did see a couple of the guys who'd been coming on to her the night before. At least she wasn't out with them. Shoe man wasn't in the group, though.

The thought of her spending the evening with him put a sour taste in Zack's mouth. That guy had been weird.

"Gina was one of the first to welcome me to town," Nick explained, pulling Zack's attention back to the table. A waitress stopped by and they each ordered a beer, then Nick picked his story back up. "We had one lovely evening together, her and me."

Gina snorted in disgust. "You used me."

"I—"

"Used her," Joanie finished for her fiancé. She looked at Zack. "Nick wanted me, and I didn't want to be caught. So he took Gina out to make me jealous."

"It worked," Nick muttered.

"Except someone at this table got used," Gina fired back. The words were said in a joking manner, but Zack sensed residual hurt riding below the surface. "I was looking good that night too. And I didn't even get kissed. I just got to him too late, is all," she explained to Zack. "He'd already seen Joanie. Like your other brother, apparently you boys take one look and you fall head over heels."

Gina propped an elbow on the table and shifted on the seat to face him, putting her breasts even more on display. "I'm making sure you see *me* first."

Zack's eyes widened at her words and he moved his gaze from her chest up to her eyes. "I'm just here for one more week," he explained.

"Yeah. That's another thing you all say. You boys show up, thinking you're going to leave again. But you don't." She shrugged as if she had him figured out. "So I'm claiming you as mine."

Across the table, Nick coughed a laugh behind his hand. More like a guffaw. What in the hell was Zack supposed to do about this? He'd been out of his element ever since he'd driven across the county line four days ago.

"I . . . uh . . ." At his faltering, he reminded himself that he was a respected lawyer and that he knew how to speak to a person. "I think you'll find things different this time around," he managed to get out. "I am leaving. I have a job in Atlanta."

One he was ready to get back to. One more brother to go, and he could go home.

"We'll see." She eyed him from beneath fake lashes and carefully applied eyeliner. She was a good-looking woman, and any other night he might take her up on her offer.

The offer of sex only. Which was blatant.

Even if she did imply that she wanted more.

The beers arrived and he grasped for one as if he hadn't had a drop of liquid in a week.

Gina scooted closer, going for full-body contact. Everything about her was soft. Which wasn't so bad.

But instead of being turned on, he thought about being wrapped around Holly on the back of the four-wheeler that morning. She'd been soft too. And she'd fit perfectly between his legs.

She'd also smelled like sunshine.

"How about a dance, big guy?" Gina purred up at him. "You look like you could twirl a girl around the floor."

He shot a desperate look across the table to find Joanie suddenly interested in something in her purse, while Nick was completely focused on his phone.

Those two were no help at all.

"Come on." Gina grabbed his arm and pulled. "Let's leave these two to themselves."

Unsure what else he could do, Zack went. It wasn't like he had any better offers.

The minute they stepped onto the floor, the music turned slow and Gina looked up at him with a sexy pout. He chuckled lightly. At least she wasn't playing games. She made her intentions clear. He pulled her into his arms and wondered if someone like her wasn't what he needed for the night.

"How are you enjoying our little town?" Gina asked as she snuggled closer and wrapped her arms around his neck. They began to move.

Normally when he danced it was at an elaborate charity event or a gala that either his date or his firm had talked him into. Sometimes an upscale bar. Everything at those places was proper and classy.

But there was nothing proper or classy about what was going on around them tonight.

There wasn't a couple on the floor who wasn't grinding against each other—or looking like they wanted to be.

He brought his attention back to Gina, and damned if he didn't catch himself doing a bit of grinding of his own. She had the kind of body that made it hard not to. "To tell you the truth . . ." he said, trying to refocus his attention. He didn't want to give her the impression this was going anywhere. And really, he wasn't the grinding-in-public type. "I get the feeling I'm high on the list of discussion points the last few days."

"You got that one right, darlin'." She laughed and her chest bounced up and down against his. The move made him more uncomfortable than turned on. "They're also talking about your car. That's one hot ride."

Again, he thought about Holly. She liked his car too. He'd like to see her hair loose and blowing around her face the way it would if he took her out on the open road.

"I bought it for myself earlier this year," he said.

"Were you celebrating something?"

He had been, but he didn't want to share that with Gina. "Just always wanted one," he said. Which wasn't a lie.

"Well, it sure is enough to turn a girl on."

She moved closer as she spoke, and his leg ended up between hers. The move was unintentional—by him—and made him begin to sweat. He caught sight of Nick and Joanie watching him from their table. When he shot his brother a look of help, Nick merely lifted his beer in salute.

And then Zack shifted his gaze to the door.

He couldn't say what had made him look. He hadn't seen it open, and most certainly hadn't been able to hear it open. It was just . . . as if he'd known.

Holly stood there, the door swinging silently closed behind her.

She had not taken his suggestion of wearing less makeup to heart. In fact, he would say that tonight she was enacting her revenge on his words. And hell if she wasn't winning.

What she'd done was manage to turn the head of every man in the room.

Her eyes were painted with black and gray. They were dark and sexy, and they said she knew how to do bad, bad things to a man. Her skin had taken on a dewy, soft look, as well. And her lips curled in a heavy glistening pout.

Ringlets of curls cascaded down her back, making him think of Goldilocks. Only she didn't look so sweet. One side was pulled behind her ear and pinned in place, and he had the craziest urge to go over there and mess it up.

He wanted to jam his hands in her curls and pull her mouth to his.

With pleasure, he trailed his gaze down the rest of her.

She wore a silver halter dress that wrapped tight around her torso. It cinched at her waist before circling up around her neck. The skirt flared out to end just above the knee. The whole thing gave her a Marilyn Monroe feel.

And she shimmered each time she moved.

Zack swallowed.

Her figure was just as impressive an hourglass as Gina's, but not nearly as much skin was showing. At least not in the front—though with that halter top, one small move and it could be.

He lowered his eyes over her legs until he reached her feet. Hot-pink boots that had stilts for heels and laced up the front. The boots reached halfway up her calves and had a row of tiny matching bows running up the backs. The shoes glittered as much as the dress did.

She looked like a pinup girl, just waiting her turn to step in front of the camera and slip out of her clothes.

He lost his footing and trampled on Gina's toes.

He grimaced. "Sorry about that."

"That's okay, hon," Gina soothed. She'd laid her cheek against his chest as they'd moved, and she lifted her head now, going for her own pinup look. But he only caught it out of the corner of his eye.

Because he was looking at Holly again.

Two men had already approached her to dance, and she hadn't gotten five feet into the building. She wowed them with a sultry smile, and said something that sent them on their way. Then she was looking at him.

He gave her a pointed look up and down and a tilt of his head. Touché, he silently said. The girl had had a point to make, and she'd done a damned good job of doing it. She was smoking hot, makeup and shoes and all.

Looked like he'd be eating some jacked-up pancakes soon.

Which he was suddenly looking forward to.

"You've got to be kidding me," Gina said in front of him. She'd stopped dancing and was staring up at him.

"What?" He glanced down at her before going back to Holly.

Gina grabbed his jaw and pulled his face around to hers. "Holly? Really?"

"What do you mean?"

"I swear, you Dalton—*Winston*—boys. You saw *her* first, didn't you?"

He was thoroughly confused. "First what?"

He glanced at Holly again. She was eyeing Gina.

"I heard about how you came to town. You ran over her granny's gravestone and she gave you a ride to her house. I thought the rumors about her leaving the movie with you last night weren't true. Thought you'd just given her a ride home. But there was more to it, wasn't there? You're just like your brothers. You saw her first and you fell like a dying man."

"I didn't fall." What was she talking about?

And then he got it.

"You mean *for* her?" he asked. "No." He shook his head. "I haven't fallen for her." He didn't fall for people. Not anymore. "Holly's just my friend."

Though at the moment, he wouldn't mind if she was more. He wanted to see how that dress unfastened.

"I don't know how I've managed to miss each of you," Gina muttered in disgust, disentangling her limbs from his. "I'm always one step behind."

With her words, she huffed out a sigh, and she was gone.

He was left standing in the middle of the dance floor to a crooning tune about lost love, and being bumped on all sides by couples who needed to get a room. Holly lifted a brow at his predicament, and then her lips turned up in a gorgeous smile. She was laughing at him yet again.

He held out his hand. Surely she wouldn't leave him standing there like that.

She didn't hesitate. She gave a nod, and then she slithered her way through the thickening crowd of gyrating people until she was standing in front of him. She was much taller in her heels. Her mouth was almost lined up with his.

"I see Gina found you," Holly raised her voice to be heard. Her mouth was an interesting shade of red tonight. Deep, berry red. It made the words *juicy* and *ripe* dance through his mind.

He nodded and held up his hands for hers. "It took all of about two seconds. I take it that's common?"

"New man in town? And he's hot? That's got Gina written all over it." When she skipped his hands and wrapped her arms around his neck instead, desire coursed through him for the first time that night.

She thought he was hot? He did not need to know that.

He didn't let himself look down into the vee of her dress, though Lord God, it was the hardest thing he'd ever not done.

"Did you have a good time with Nick today?" she asked. She'd leaned into him and put her mouth close to his ear so she could be heard. Her cheek brushed against his, and he caught her scent again. Sunshine. Fresh and bright and hot.

He turned his mouth to her ear. "I did. Thanks for your help."

He was insanely turned on, but he was pretty sure she was feeling nothing. She was simply snuggling with him because that was what everyone else was doing. And because it was easier to be heard that way.

"No problem," she replied. "I'm glad to see that it worked out."

He kept his hands at the sides of her waist, fighting the urge to slide his leg between her thighs. *Now* he wanted to grind up against someone.

"I couldn't find you when I got home," he said. "I met Nick here after I cleaned up. Thought you might want to come with me."

"I was busy all afternoon. Just got back."

He couldn't help but wonder what she'd been so busy doing.

They got bumped, and he slid his hand to the back of her waist to keep her steady. His palm landed on warm, bare skin, and he squeezed his eyes shut in mental anguish. Dancing with her might just give him cardiac arrest.

When he opened his eyes, an angry glare caught his attention from across the room. The man was standing on the platform where the pool tables were, a woman draped on his side, and he was locked in on Zack as if he intended to make it his life's mission to remove him from the premises.

Apparently not everyone was so welcoming after all.

But then he recognized the guy from a picture in the Marshall home.

"I think one of your brothers is giving me a dirty look," he said into Holly's ear.

"Which one?" She pulled her head back.

"I have no idea."

When Zack nodded to his left, Holly followed with her eyes. "Oh, that's just Brian."

"Okay. And why do you suppose Brian is looking like he wants to rip my head off?"

She giggled, and when *her* breasts moved up and down against his chest, he barely held back a groan.

"Probably because I'm all snuggled up to you." And then she snuggled closer. "He thinks he's my protector."

He wasn't the only one. Zack remembered Nick's words from earlier that day.

"Holly," he said carefully. His teeth scraped against each other. "You do know what all that snuggling does to a man, right?" She was young, but surely not that young.

She laughed again.

Her breasts jiggled again.

She tilted her head back and when her eyes met his, her smile was so bright and pure that he wanted to figure out a way to be that happy himself.

"But we're just friends," she said.

Her words caused a little flip in his heart.

"I'm also a man." He put a couple of inches between their bodies. "And though I'd take on your brother if that's what it came to, I'm going to need you to dial it back a notch."

"But this is how you were dancing with Gina," she teased. She wiggled up to him again, and her hip brushed over his growing erection. She didn't seem to notice. "Was she getting you all hot and bothered too?"

He lost his ability to pretend she wasn't turning him on, and let the heat coursing through him fill his eyes. "Gina was doing nothing like this to me," he admitted.

Holly quit wiggling then, and she flicked her gaze over his face. It felt like he was being scrutinized by one of his law professors on the eve of a big exam.

"I really am turning you on?"

"Sweetheart." He had the desperate urge to press her hard into his groin. To hold her there until she invited him back to her bed. But he was more of a gentleman than that. At least with her. "You're a very good-looking woman. I'm a warm-blooded male. And you're rubbing every last one of your curves against my body. Yes. I'm really turned on."

"Oh." Her mouth formed a small *O* and her eyes shifted away from his. "I'm sorry."

"No need to be sorry. Just be aware."

"I didn't mean to . . ." She trailed off and looked pained. "I thought maybe I'd make a few men jealous tonight. Shake out the ones who could be serious and the ones who aren't."

Cold water . . . meet a raging hard-on.

He'd suspected she wasn't into him, but to have it so bluntly explained was harsh. And it wasn't like he'd even planned to do anything about it.

But damn.

"I can assure you," he promised, "that every man in here right now is jealous."

Holly stared at the hard angles of Zack's face. He was attracted to her.

A lot.

Which should not excite her nearly as much as it did, but hot diggity, Zack Winston wanted her.

He was a successful, intelligent, extremely sexy man, and she would have never guessed she could turn him on to the extent that he implied.

Implied was the wrong word.

She saw it in his eyes. Felt it in his touch. He was most definitely ratcheted up a notch. Or three.

And damned if she didn't want to crank him up a little higher.

They danced quietly for a few more minutes as she pondered this turn of events. Yeah, he wasn't the man for her. She knew that. But that didn't mean she couldn't sample a bit of the wrong man, did it? Especially when the wrong man got her all hot and bothered.

After silent deliberation, she decided to play with fire. What were a few singed fingers? You only lived once.

"What if I tell you that I'm turned on too?" She tilted her head back to look up at him.

His brown eyes seemed almost black as he peered down at her.

His hand at her back burned her like a brand, and when his fingers curled into her bare skin, just the slightest amount, her nipples tingled to life. Then he glanced at her lips.

She didn't breathe. Was he going to kiss her? Right there? With everyone watching?

Talk about hot!

But then he pulled his gaze from her mouth. "Then I'd have to point out that I'm the wrong man for you," he murmured in a way-too-sexy, bedroom kind of voice. "I'm not looking for a wife."

The air went out of her chest. Honor was so overrated. "I got that, Romeo. You flash that sign around like a neon light."

He nodded. "So it doesn't matter that there's attraction. It's just chemistry."

"And touching body parts."

"Right." His hand shifted on her back. "Touching parts. Which we should probably stop doing."

"Because we're not right for each other."

"Exactly."

Only they didn't stop.

He glanced over her shoulder before coming back to her. "And because I don't want your brother thinking he needs to try to kick my ass. I'm not wearing my fighting clothes tonight."

Strained laughter slipped from her, releasing some of the pent-up tension. Not all of it, for sure. Because duh, she *was* still in Zack's arms.

She peeked over her shoulder at her brother. He was still watching them. Very carefully. She made a childish face at him, but did decide to put a bit more distance between her and Zack. Because Brian *might* just decide to kick his ass.

"I promise I won't let him," she said.

Incredulity flashed back at her. "First you laugh at me at every turn, and now I'm supposed to let you protect me from your brother? Uh-uh." He shook his head. His hand still burned at her back, palm flat and every finger splayed out, and she still wanted to take his clothes off and lick him all over. "If he wants a fight, I'll give him one. I can't have you making me look like a girl."

The idea of Zack fighting her brother over her made her grin. Her brothers had intimidated many a man over the years—not that she'd ever considered dating near the number they'd flashed their big-brother glares at—but there'd never been an instance in which the mere idea of seeing a man fight gave her the instant hots.

She could get into watching Zack throw a fist for her.

She could get into a lot of things with Zack.

Which they'd just said they wouldn't do. Because it was just chemistry. And because they were friends.

With the reminder, she decided he had a point. She didn't need to sleep with her friend. Knowing her, she'd do something stupid like fall for him. And then he'd break her heart.

She released him. Bodies still moved around them, and a country tune still saturated the air. She felt like they were the only two people in the room. "So how about that bet?" she asked. Time to lighten the mood. She held her arms out at her sides so he could take in her appearance. "Ready to admit I won?"

He checked her out from head to toe. As he did, she grew warm on the inside. *Warmer.*

She knew she looked good tonight. That had been the plan.

Just as they hadn't seen her mirrors, rarely did anyone in Sugar Springs see her put this much true effort into her looks. For some reason, the thought of dressing up around the guys she'd been pals with her whole life never felt right. And it often embarrassed her.

But if she was going to catch one—and she was actually on the fence about that at the moment—then maybe she should start putting in the effort.

"That dress is killer," Zack said.

"And the makeup?"

He studied her intently, and she found herself wishing she'd worn even more. Maybe he did have a point. Maybe she hid behind the makeup. She certainly wanted to hide from his scrutiny now.

"The makeup has every man in here wanting to take you to bed and not come up for air for a week."

Including him? She had to wonder.

"You owe me pancakes," she said. The music chose that minute to stop, and her words sounded overloud in the confined space. The people around them turned to watch.

Zack didn't take his eyes off hers. "I owe you pancakes," he agreed.

She licked her lips. It was time to get away. "I'm going to . . . uh . . ." She flailed her hand out to her side, before finishing lamely, "Find someone else to dance with."

He nodded.

She stepped back. They remained in the middle of the crowd as the music once again started up, neither of them moving away, and she wondered if he'd say something else. Like . . . *Don't go. Stay here and dance with me.*

She wanted him to.

But he didn't.

Instead he motioned with his head to the bar. "There's a guy over there who's been watching you since you came in. Dark hair. Looks respectable. My guess is he's after more than a night or two."

Her heart pounded in her chest. Really? He was directing her to another man? Okay, fine. Good idea. She needed another man. One who'd stick around for longer than two weeks. She followed his gaze and then gave an approving nod.

"That's Keith Justice. He's actually at the top of my list of possibilities."

A muscle twitched in Zack's jaw.

"Go dance with him," he said. He gave her a casual wink. "Be sure to snuggle up to him like you did me. He'll like it."

Chapter Ten

Go dance with him? Be sure to snuggle up to him?
What the hell was wrong with him?

Holly had been in his arms last night—*wanting him*—and he'd sent her to another man.

When had he lost his balls?

Zack growled under his breath as he stepped from the men's clothing store nestled in between the pharmacy and the Welcome Center. Two dark-haired boys loped along on the sidewalk in front of him, pretending they were riding horses, and he squinted into the bright midday sun. He pulled his sunglasses from the top of his head and took in the lazy Saturday morning.

People were flowing from store to store, yet no one seemed to be in any huge hurry. Just coming and going, packages tucked under their arms. Many had kids by their sides. Others were with friends, maybe family, and were talking as much as they seemed to be shopping.

He didn't understand the total laid-back style here.

That had bothered him at first. A person didn't get anywhere in life if they didn't work hard. Didn't go fast. Yet the residents here seemed happy, seemed to be enjoying themselves. That made him wonder if there might be another way to play it. Possibly there wasn't always someplace to be.

He would add that to his list of things to think about later. Along with the small-town bonding to throw support behind a person, how hot Holly had looked in her silver dress when she'd strolled into the Bungalow the night before, and the fact that he could have taken her to bed if only he hadn't decided to grow a conscience.

Yeah. Things there were definitely causing him more than a second thought or two.

He looked across the square to where he could see a crowd through the diner windows. Sugar Springs had another, more upscale restaurant; a couple smaller ones he'd seen while out driving around; and of course, the Bungalow, which he'd understood was a calmer, more toned-down place in the daylight hours. But the diner seemed to be the hub of the town. There was currently a line of people out the door waiting to be seated for lunch.

A banner for the upcoming Firefly Festival flapped in the breeze off to his right, making him wonder what that would be like. It also made him think of his mom.

She'd been from a town similar to this—though Zack had never been there himself. Her family had been gone before he'd come along, and she and his dad had already been settled in Atlanta for a couple decades. There had never been a need to visit his mother's hometown.

Yet he'd heard her talk about small-town festivals for years. She'd even dragged him to a couple in his younger days, but he had only vague memories. His dad hadn't been a fan so his mother had eventually quit suggesting them.

Zack would be gone before Sugar Springs had their festival, but he could come back. Maybe bring his mother. She would like that.

Thinking about his mother, the festival, and how he really should be spending his Saturday morning working instead of shopping, he turned to head two stores down to where he'd left Holly. He saw the boys again. This time they were heading toward the street.

The younger one ducked between two cars parked end-to-front, giggling with all the freedom that young boys felt, and the other followed.

Zack lifted a hand. "Hey!" he yelled out. He took a step in their direction. "You're—"

He didn't get another word out before two large arms reached in from nowhere and swooped the boys up. Zack sagged in relief as the man pulled the boys back just as a truck rolled past.

"Whoa." The man held the boys off the ground, each of them tucked under an arm as if they were footballs. "You two better watch where you're going. If that truck would've hit you, you'd be flatter than a flitter."

The man set the boys down, and they took off in the other direction.

Zack watched as a woman rushed from inside a nearby store. Her eyes were wide and panicked as she caught the two boys up by their collars. She stooped to hug them close, and tears streamed down her cheeks.

Then she proceeded to chew her boys' ears off for running away from her.

The chastising made Zack smile. It reminded him of his mother again. He'd gotten into his own amount of mischief as a boy. She'd never veered from sounding exactly like that woman.

"Did either of you bother telling Mr. Bert thank you for saving your lives?" the mother asked her sons.

Contrite faces and stiff backs turned to the older man who'd walked over to them.

"Thank you, Mr. Bert," they chorused.

Bert rubbed them each on the top of their heads. "No problem, boys. That's part of the job. I watch out for the rambunctious ones out on the sidewalks."

"Hey," a female voice yelled out.

Zack looked around to find Joanie waving from the other side of the street as she jumped from her cupcake van and headed to her store. He waved back. He'd had a really good time with them last night, leaving only after they'd closed down the place.

Holly had disappeared a couple hours before that—after dancing with half the men in town. Too many of whom had merely been trying to get into her pants.

He had to give her credit, though. She seemed to be able to pick out the players easily enough. They hadn't gotten more than one lukewarm dance, and some not even that. He had noticed a couple of men, though, who'd seemed legitimately wowed with her.

One was the guy who'd been hanging out by the bar. Keith something. The one Zack had told her to snuggle up to. What an idiot. And yeah, she'd snuggled.

Keith had seemed to enjoy it.

Thankfully, Holly had moved on to dance with others, before finally leaving alone. Zack wasn't sure how he would have handled watching her leave with a guy.

It was something he didn't want to think too hard about.

He neared the consignment store, peeking in the front windows as he went. Holly had dragged him out early that morning, only to drive them all over the back roads of Sugar Springs. They'd been stopping at yard sales, of all things. He'd never been to a yard sale in his life. Yet he'd found himself humorously entertained. Then she'd wanted to pick through more junk at the consignment store.

He found her inside now, digging through a pile of picture frames on one of the tables. An older lady was standing at her side.

"Good morning," he was greeted as he stepped through the door.

He took off his sunglasses and nodded at the clerk. The place was crammed full of clothes, knickknacks, appliances. Everything he could imagine. Including people. They were everywhere.

Then his eyes landed on the walls above the shelving.

Decorative mirrors of all shapes and sizes hung in every available space.

Some were antique, some newer, but the thing that was the same about all of them was the creativity that made each and every one unique.

"Interested in a mirror, sir?" the clerk asked brightly. She was about twenty, with a head full of red hair. "We have quite the selection. It's one of the things we're known for. We even have out-of-towners drive in just to see them."

"I'm here with . . ." When he spoke, Holly looked up from the table where she stood and her eyes met his. Her mouth curved up at the corners. His did the same. "Her," he finished.

His lungs felt as if they were holding too much air.

"Ah," the clerk said. "I should have recognized you, Mr. Winston." She nodded politely. "Please let me know if you need any help."

Holly hadn't looked away from him while the woman at her side continued to rattle on. Her cheeks had a cute pink hue to them today, and her face was washed clean of makeup. She was like a breath of fresh air that kept hitting him in the face.

"Monday night?" the older lady asked as Zack approached. "I'll set it up. Something nice. How about Talbot's?"

Holly's lips inched further up. She shifted her focus to the woman, politeness radiating from her. "That sounds lovely, Ms. Francis. But how about you have Tony call me? He and I can set something up if we decide we both want to go out."

Ah, a date.

With *Tony*.

Whoever Tony was.

Ms. Francis beamed. "I'll do that, sweetheart. And he wants to, trust me. I've already talked to him about it. I even gave him money to take you out. He'll treat you right."

Zack held back a laugh at the look on Holly's face. Apparently she didn't want to date someone who needed his mother to both give him money to take a girl out *and* get his dates for him. He couldn't say he blamed her.

Ms. Francis finally noticed him, and scrutinized him up and down. The verdict seemed to be that she found him lacking because her nose turned up and she gave a little *hmph*.

Then she patted Holly's arm, shined another bright smile her way, and trotted off.

Holly watched her go, that polite little smile still on her lips, before turning to him.

"Got a hot date?" he asked.

She rolled her eyes. "If only I could get away with giving out a fake number. But I'd get caught." She motioned to the bag he held in his hands. "Did you find jeans?"

He held the bag up. "Two pairs in my size."

The jeans weren't the brand he'd choose if he were shopping in Atlanta, but with it being years since he'd worn *any*, he figured there was little need in being picky now.

"We could have gotten you more if you weren't so particular."

By more, she meant that he could have bought some "used" from one of the yard sales they'd stopped at. Several pairs had been available. She'd worked that angle until he'd finally convinced her it simply wasn't going to happen. He preferred having his boys where he knew no other boys had been.

"Are you cleaning the store of their junk?" he asked.

He'd been amazed at the number of items she'd bought as they'd made their way from sale to sale that morning. At first he'd assumed she was just being polite, not wanting to leave empty-handed.

But as they'd loaded up her backseat after each stop, he'd begun to see a pattern. And strangely, that pattern reminded him of the mirrors hanging on the walls.

She'd been gathering items she could reuse.

And suddenly the mirrors made sense.

They were so beautifully unique. Just like her. Just like the mirror at the house. He stepped up beside her and almost bent forward to kiss her when she tilted her head up to his.

"Did you create all the mirrors in here?" he asked.

Her brows shot up. And just as quickly, she propped a hand on her hip. She cocked her head at an angle. "Who outed me? Who have you been talking to?"

"No one. They're just so . . . you."

"Really?" She studied him quietly. He began to think she wasn't going to say more when she finally admitted, "It's a hobby of mine."

He took in the sheer number of items hanging on the walls. At the uniqueness in every piece. As he did, he saw three different people pointing out mirrors they wanted, asking a clerk to get them down. "Looks like more than a hobby to me."

Her eyes dimmed a little and she refocused on the pictures she was digging through.

"Nope," she said lightly. "Just a hobby. I do it in my spare time. Just like everything else." Her last sentence was finished on a mumble, and he had the impression he'd just uncovered another clue to figuring out Holly Marshall.

She may act like she was perfectly fine doing nothing substantial with her life, but she didn't really like it. This he could understand. He'd been struggling with her lack of desire to have more, but if she just hadn't found it yet, then that was different.

"You ever thought about getting out of here?" he found himself asking.

Her green eyes took a quick peek at him. "You ready to leave?"

"I can stay *here* as long as you want." He began rummaging through the items she'd already looked at, not seeing anything in his hands. "But I'm not talking about leaving the store. I meant Sugar Springs."

She didn't respond so he continued. "You complained about the lack of career potential." He shrugged. "Maybe you could find whatever you're looking for somewhere else. It doesn't have to be as big as Chicago. Just . . . more than here."

She put down the frame in her hand, and calm, grass-green eyes turned to him. The look sent chills down his spine.

"Don't you dare judge me," she said in careful, slow words. "I'm happy here. And I love who I am. I don't need you to—"

"Hey," he cut in. "No. I'm not judging. I'm sorry. I just . . ." He shook his head and took her hand in his. "I see sadness in you every once in a while. And for someone who's so optimistic ninety-nine point nine percent of the time, I don't like that sadness. I just wanted to help."

"You're wrong. I'm not sad. And I don't want anything but Sugar Springs. Even if my family wasn't here, *they* are my family." She'd pulled her hand from his and swung her arm toward the windows as she said "they," as if including the whole town. "They love me exactly as I am."

Clearly he'd hit a sore spot. "I didn't mean to upset you."

"We can't all be big-time lawyers, Mr. Winston. But that doesn't mean I'm not happy."

"Hey," he said again. He kept his tone soft and calm. "I'm not Mr. Winston, remember? I'm Zack. We're friends. And I'm sorry I hurt your feelings. I made a mistake. I apologize."

He wished he knew what kind of mess he'd just stepped into.

She pulled a deep breath in and held it before slowly letting it out. The sadness was back. "I'm sorry," she muttered. "You hit a button."

"I saw that." He bumped her shoulder with his in a friendly manner. "Want to talk about it?"

"No."

The word was final. He could feel her pulling in on herself. He didn't like that.

"How about lunch then?" he suggested. "My treat. Let's go into Gatlinburg and grab a bite, then find something fun to do. We'll take my car. I'll even drive fast." He winked.

He thought the enticement of his car might make her smile again. He even expected she'd ask to drive it.

But it didn't. And she didn't.

She shook her head. "I have things I need to do this afternoon. We can grab something at the deli on the way back."

And before he could protest, she'd gathered up her items and headed for the register. He was left standing there, staring after her. Wondering exactly what he'd just done.

When she turned, ready to leave, he took the bags from her hands. "Sure I can't change your mind?" he asked as they walked to the door.

She cut her eyes to him.

"Sorry about that back there," she said. "I shouldn't have gotten upset over nothing. I know you were just trying to help."

"I'd still like to." He held the door for her and she stepped out.

"I really do have things to do this afternoon. But a drive into Gatlinburg would be fun. Especially if *I* was driving your car." There was the Holly he knew. "Tomorrow?" she asked.

He stopped dead on the street as she went on ahead of him. He'd just realized something.

He liked her. *Really* liked her.

It had bothered him seeing her so upset. It still bothered him. He wanted to fix it, and he wanted to make sure all she ever did was smile.

Since when did he let himself care enough to have such thoughts?

She was getting under his skin, and that wasn't allowed. *That* led to him wanting things he'd written off years ago.

Maybe it was simply the friendship thing. Friendship with a woman was new for him. People cared about their friends, right? That was natural.

Only, it felt like more than because she was a friend.

Which make him twitchy.

"You okay?" she asked. She'd reached her car and turned back to see him ten feet behind.

He nodded. He had to be okay. Because he couldn't fall for her.

She had every intention of living the rest of her life in Sugar Springs.

Also, there was the fact that a relationship would get in the way of his career. Possibly he could see himself somewhere down the road having something. A live-in girlfriend maybe. But not now. Right now he had to make partner.

That came first.

Pulling himself out of his thoughts, he nodded. "Yeah, fine. Just thinking."

"So, tomorrow then?" she asked. "Gatlinburg?"

He reached her car. "Sorry, I have somewhere to go tomorrow."

Without thinking about the fact that they'd been storing everything in her backseat all day, he lifted the back door of the SUV to put away her purchases.

"Don't." She reached out to close it, but the packages tucked inside caught his eye.

"What are these?" he asked. He kept his hand clamped on the door when she tried to close it.

She had numerous wrapped items, all flat, each protected between sheets of Styrofoam.

"Nothing. Here, give me the bags. That's why I've been putting everything in the backseat. Because it's full back here."

He handed off her bags, and when she reached to close the door again, he still didn't let her. Instead, he picked up the top item. It was heavy in his hands.

"Don't," she begged.

The untaped bubble wrap slipped from one corner before he could put it back down. Curious, he propped the item on his thigh and tugged at the wrapping on the opposite corner. It was a mirror.

Holly let out a soft groan.

This mirror wasn't at all like the ones inside the store.

Those all had standard shapes. Squares, rectangles, circles. He'd even seen a couple octagons and some triangles. But they'd each been a single shape with a unique frame.

The mirror in his hand had no frame. And it wasn't just a rectangle. There was a rectangle in the middle, but then there were five- to ten-inch shards of mirror overlapping, and strategically placed around the outside. The shards themselves made up the frame.

It wasn't just a mirror. It was art.

And it was stunning.

"What is this?" he asked.

He suspected he knew.

She shoved her bags in the car and didn't make eye contact. "Just some things I picked up in Chicago."

He set the piece down, carefully propping it against the car so he could pick up the next.

She groaned again.

This one looked like it was in an antique silver frame. The inside—the "mirror" part—was a rectangular shape running vertically with the corners rounded and bulged out slightly from the main shape. Yet the frame was what he couldn't take his eyes off of.

At first glance it looked like scrolled silver. Lots of detail, lots of cutouts. It would be beautiful if that's all it was.

But it wasn't silver. It was a mirror also. Each detail looked to have been painstakingly cut, and then there were etchings along the edges that gave the whole thing a 3-D look.

It was spectacular.

"Oh, my God," breathed out someone beside him. "Is that for sale? I'll buy it."

He and Holly looked around at the person who'd spoken. A woman who'd just come from the consignment store.

"I saw the other mirrors inside, and there were several I wanted," the lady went on. "But we're just up for the weekend, and my whole family is with me. I don't really have room in the car to get a mirror back to Alabama safely. But this . . ."

She held her hands out in front of her as if wanting to hold it. "This is so amazing I'll pay to have it shipped. Or I'll make one of my boys walk home just so I can put it in his seat," she added with a laugh. "The teenage one. It'll be nice without him in the car." She reached out her hands again. "Can I look at it?"

Zack turned to Holly. Her face had taken on a pinched, wary look, but when Zack raised his brows at her, she slowly nodded. He handed the mirror over to the lady.

"It's exquisite," she whispered. Her head tilted at an angle as she studied the intricacies of the edges. "Did you make this?"

Holly didn't answer. Instead, she just stood there. Silent.

The woman angled her head in the opposite direction and studied the other side. When she didn't say anything else, Holly finally asked, "Did you really want to buy it?"

Zack watched her. He'd never seen her look so unsure about anything, but that was definitely the look she was wearing now. Why would she have her doubts about anyone wanting to buy this piece?

"Absolutely," the woman said. She handed it back to Zack. "Just tell me how much and I'll take it."

Holly's jaw dropped open.

The two women quickly negotiated a steep, yet in Zack's opinion, very fair price, and the woman walked off, still staring at the piece in awe.

Then someone else stopped and bought the mirror Zack had propped against the side of the car. When she left, he turned to Holly and gave her a pointed look. "You are such a liar."

She continued to look dumbfounded over what had just happened. "How so?"

"You did not pick these up in Chicago."

Her eyes locked with his. This time he saw fear.

What could possibly scare her about selling these?

"Can we just go?" she asked.

He nodded and closed the hatchback, then went around to the passenger side and climbed in.

At least she wasn't the only one confused. He had no idea what was going on either.

And something told him she wasn't about to fill him in.

Chapter Eleven

The smack of the bell echoed a ding from the order window. "Table fourteen up," Holly shouted out. She went back to the grill and started on the next order.

Her parents had returned home the day before, so Holly wasn't needed at the house anymore. Thus, she'd gotten up early and come into the diner. It felt good to be back. Also, it took her mind off what had happened on the street in front of the consignment store two days ago.

And the call she'd gotten from her cousin yesterday afternoon.

Someone in Chicago loved one of her mirrors.

Holly had let Megan pick one out as a gift for letting her stay there, and Saturday night Megan had thrown a party. One of her guests had fallen in love with Holly's mirror. The guest said she knew someone who knew someone.

Supposedly those someones would be talking this week.

Six weeks Holly had spent up there, and she couldn't even get in the door. No one would so much as look at her pieces because they couldn't get past *her*. She was small town. A no one.

They wouldn't give her a chance.

She'd been laughed at by more than one snotty bitch.

"Table two needs two stacks with bacon."

Holly nodded at Janice's request and grabbed the tub of batter as her mind returned to Saturday morning out on the sidewalk.

Two total strangers had bought her mirrors out of the back of her car. For a lot of money.

How had that happened?

She looked up through the order window and out the front of the restaurant as she replayed it in her mind. She'd been embarrassed when Zack had lifted the first mirror in his hands. She hadn't wanted anyone to see those. They meant too much to her.

And then . . . without even trying, she'd sold two pieces.

It made her wonder about the others.

Had it been a fluke?

She could see the consignment store from here. It was closed up now, but would soon open for the day. Should she take some of her originals in there?

People didn't normally go to the consignment store looking to pay hundreds for a single item, though. It could hurt business as much as help it.

Her gaze landed on the storefront sitting empty on the other side of the square. At one point she'd thought Nick might rent it as an office for his construction company. Joanie had mentioned a while back that he was trying to decide whether he needed a physical location or not. It would be a great spot for him.

But now she wondered if it might not also be a great spot for someone else.

Like her.

And her mirrors.

She'd never considered doing that before, but after what had happened Saturday, the thought had poked around in her head all weekend.

"Three full houses for number six," another waitress chimed out. The cook who'd replaced Holly when she'd gone to Chicago went to work on the order, and Holly returned to finishing up the pancakes for number two.

If she opened a store, she wouldn't get to work in here anymore.

Or maybe she could still work mornings here and open the store later in the day.

But she would need time to create her mirrors, as well. And how could she do that if she had a business to run?

Brian came in the back door, his blond hair ruffled from the wind, looking relaxed and happy. As if he'd already had a great morning. Probably it had to do with whatever woman he'd spent the night with. Rarely did he find himself sleeping alone.

She shook her head in amazement. Without Ms. Grayson running around town telling everyone she was hard up for a husband, she couldn't get a man to notice her. Yet Brian got all the women looking his way.

She flipped the bacon and pulled the pancakes off the grill while Brian shot her a look.

"You back?" he asked.

"Not back," she said. She wasn't sure why she said it. Likely she'd be in the diner every morning from here on out. "Just wanted to make sure people don't forget me."

Brian popped her with his apron. "No chance of that, brat. Good to have you back."

"Special request from the front," Janice called out, and Holly ignored her brother to return to the job. They had a counter that ran across the front. Mostly it was used for people wanting milkshakes later in the day, but when the place was packed, diners sat there too.

She looked up from the grill and her gaze landed on Zack. She smiled. She was glad to see him.

His returning grin gave her heart palpitations.

He hadn't been around yesterday except for his quick stop in the dining room to grab a scone on his way out the door. He'd left before seven and hadn't returned until well after she'd gone to her bedroom for the night.

And yeah, she'd been listening.

He hadn't said where he was going, but if she were to guess, she'd say to see a woman. He was a virile man, after all. There wasn't much to offer someone like him in Sugar Springs.

Of course, he could have had Gina.

But then, as far as she knew, he had. Possibly Friday and Saturday night both. And hell, maybe that's who he'd been with all day yesterday.

He'd said Gina had done nothing for him while they'd been dancing, but that didn't mean she'd given up easily. Plus, Zack had come home well after midnight Friday night. Then he'd gone out again Saturday night.

Not that it mattered. He could do what he wanted.

She could have had her own date anyway. She thought about the two men who'd called her up Saturday afternoon. Yeah, she could have had a date. Or two. But both those men had been looking for only one thing.

She'd danced with each of them at the Bungalow the night before, and had quickly determined that their interest had nothing at all to do with long-term. Unless long-term meant staying until morning.

And she wasn't even sure either would do that.

No, she wasn't looking to get laid. That wasn't what she was about. But it would be nice to have a good man.

She'd also like to give Ms. Grayson a piece of her mind. The old busybody had scurried away the other night before Holly had managed to catch up with her. She still owed her a good talking-to.

Pushing thoughts of old ladies and horny men aside, Holly held up the tub of pancake batter to Zack. He was there to see her. And he'd lost their bet. "You here to pay up?"

God, he'd missed her.

He'd gone only one day without seeing her, yet it had seemed like the longest day of his life. Which was silly and overdramatic. And he didn't get silly and overdramatic.

But the fact was, being around Holly made Zack's day better.

Now he needed to get her out from behind the grill so he could see what kind of shoes she had on.

"Only if you join me," he taunted.

Today her hair was twisted into some sort of braid on the top of her head with a ponytail coming out the middle of it. It reminded him of Barbara Eden in the old reruns of *I Dream of Jeannie*. Holly didn't have on the little hat or scarf the character had worn, and there was glittery silver on her eyelids that he didn't remember Jeannie having, but there was what appeared to be a strand of pearls twined through the braid. From her ears hung tiny pink tassels.

And dipped low in the front was some sort of pink shirt he could only halfway make out.

He wanted to see more.

"You got it." She nodded and blinked her eyes at the same time and he burst out laughing.

"I knew you were going for an *I Dream of Jeannie* look."

She just grinned. The dimple that he loved appeared. "I was in the mood for something different today," she told him. "I thought about wearing my Jeannie costume that I wore for Halloween a few years back, but decided I didn't want to have my stomach exposed back here at the grill. That might be more painful than fun."

Good call, he thought, but bad for him. He wanted to see her stomach exposed.

Just like he wanted to touch her. And kiss her.

And spend the whole day with her.

Saturday had been fun, but it had ended way too soon. She'd refused to talk about her mirrors on the way back to the house, and the minute they'd returned she'd pulled the quad out of the shed and taken off.

He'd been surprised to find himself upset that she hadn't offered to take him with her.

He'd spent his free time catching up on work and checking in with his boss, then he'd taken Nick up on the offer of dinner. They'd driven into Pigeon Forge and had steaks, watched a baseball game, and drank a couple beers. It had been a good evening.

Things were going well with Nick. Now he had to make the same happen with Cody.

Which was where he was headed next.

He watched as Holly worked in the kitchen. She didn't appear quite as cheerful and happy as normal. She laughed and smiled with the other cook and with the waitresses as they placed orders at the window, and then elbowed her brother in the stomach when he walked up and said something behind her.

Brian bent down, holding his gut, and peered through the window at Zack. The look wasn't any more pleasant than it had been Friday night.

Zack stared back at the other man, daring him to say something.

Yeah, Zack wanted Holly. Didn't mean he was going to act on it.

Couldn't stop a man from wanting, either.

The stare-off continued until Holly looked up from the grill and caught them. She punched her brother in the arm.

Then she grabbed two plates, and disappeared from sight.

Energy flowed through Zack's veins. She was coming out to have breakfast with him. He could hardly wait to see what she'd done with his pancakes.

Or what shoes she had on.

"Sprinkles," she said with a flourish as she set the plate down in front of him.

His pancakes had different-colored dots in them with whipped topping piled high on top. More sprinkles covered all that. It looked disgusting.

"Sprinkles?" he asked in horror.

Her stack was the same. She settled on the stool next to him, then immediately stood on the rungs to reach over the counter and grab a small pitcher of syrup. As she leaned, he took in her head-to-ankle pink attire. The shirt was tight and cut low and her arms were left bare. The jeans hugged her tight. There was another tassel hanging from the belt around her waist, and he fought the urge to tug on it.

She plopped back down on her seat, and he blinked as cleavage bounced in front of him. Dang, but that was a good way to start the day.

"You need sprinkles in your life," she pronounced. She poured syrup over his breakfast before doing the same to hers. "I figured if anyone was going to give them to you, it would have to be me."

He stared down at the mess in front of him, trying to get her breasts out of his mind. "You ruined my pancakes."

"No I didn't, sugar. I made them happy."

He liked when she went all Southern and called him sugar. He felt a grin take hold, even though he didn't mean to. "Happy pancakes?" he asked.

She nodded. "Everyone needs happy pancakes once in a while."

What the hell was wrong with this woman? And why was he so turned on by the thought that she'd made him happy pancakes?

"Did you realize you're wearing rainbow-colored shoes with a pink outfit?" he asked.

Her face glowed. "You noticed my shoes?"

She swiveled on the stool and held her legs out in front of her. Wrapped around her feet were sandals that had a stripe for each color of the rainbow. They were atrocious with her outfit.

But they were so Holly.

"How could I help it?" he said. "They make as much sense with your outfit as this crap does on my pancakes."

He liked teasing her, and when she glared at him, he just laughed.

"You have no imagination at all," she accused.

She was wrong. He was imagining all sorts of things right now. Ignoring his thoughts, he grabbed his fork and dug in. But he did *not* let himself moan at the pleasure that erupted in his mouth. Damn, the woman could cook.

"You like them, don't you?" she teased.

He refused to answer. When he gave her an irritated look and shoved another bite in his mouth, she cackled with laughter. It made his day.

"Hey, Holly."

They both turned at the words. Keith—from the Bungalow—stood behind Holly, his hands clasped together in front of him. He wasn't much taller than Holly, but was a decent-enough-looking guy, Zack supposed. He had sandy-colored hair and was dressed in jeans, a pullover, and sneakers. Nothing special. Pretty much standard fare for Sugar Springs.

Just what Holly was looking for.

"Hey, Keith." Her eyes lit up. "Great to see you. I was just taking a break. Want to join us?"

The man looked hesitant for a second, eyeing Zack as if sizing him up, but then Holly patted the stool beside her and her breasts jiggled in her shirt. Keith sat.

Zack's good mood vanished.

"What was so funny?" Keith asked.

"Zack just got his first happy pancakes."

Jealousy flared when Keith looked around her to see what Zack was eating. Zack didn't want Keith in on happy pancakes.

When the other man's eyes lingered on the creamy skin of Holly's breasts for the second time, Zack almost came up off the stool. He wanted to toss the man out the door.

But what Keith looked at wasn't his business. Especially not if Holly liked him.

"Looks good," Keith replied. The look in his eyes implied he wasn't merely talking about the breakfast. "What's a guy have to do to get him a plate of those?"

Holly turned her grin on Keith. "I can cook you some."

"Let your brother do it." The words came out brusque, but Zack didn't care. He didn't want her to leave. And he certainly didn't want her cooking happy pancakes for someone else. When she looked at him in confusion, he added, "Yours will get cold if you don't eat them."

My God, he was fighting over pancakes.

And cleavage.

He should have let her go to the back. Then Keith wouldn't still be eyeing her breasts.

"It's okay," she said. She gave an awkward laugh. "I can have happy pancakes anytime. In fact . . ." She pushed her plate over to Keith, and Zack's mood scraped the ground. "You can have mine," she practically cooed. "I haven't taken a bite of them yet."

"You don't mind?" the other man asked.

"Not at all." She looked at him as if he had something she wanted.

Zack's fingers tightened around his fork, and he lost his appetite. Catching Brian's smirk from the grill did nothing to help. The brother approved of Keith, then? Or did he simply approve of him more than Zack?

Didn't matter, he supposed. Keith was better for her.

Zack pulled out his wallet. "What do I owe?" His tone was rude, but he couldn't make himself care.

"You're leaving?" She turned her head back to him, and he felt like he was a paddle in a Ping-Pong game. On the losing side.

"I'm meeting Cody at the clinic."

"Oh. Good." Her brightness dimmed as she glanced at his plate. "But I'm sorry you didn't like the pancakes."

Now he just felt bad. "I loved them." He softened his tone. "I just need to go."

Keith eyed him from the other side of Holly. Zack ignored the man. "How much?" he asked again.

"Nothing," she said. She put a hand on his arm. "Are you okay?"

He flicked another look at Keith. "Fine."

"Will you let me know how it goes?"

The concern on her face made him stop as he straightened from the stool. He peered down at her, wishing he could have finished his happy pancakes with only her by his side. Wishing he were a different kind of guy and could go for it with her. "You bet."

Holly watched Zack walk away. He'd worn a pair of his new jeans today and he looked really good in them. So good, she noticed she wasn't the only one watching him leave. The man had a nice butt.

And he was heading to meet Cody. Nerves filled her at the thought of him meeting with his brother alone. She wanted to go with him. She'd like to hold his hand and help him through it. Though he would probably scoff at the suggestion. He still thought he didn't need any help.

She wondered why he'd run off so fast, and then remembered Keith sitting on the other side of her. She supposed that was it. He was giving her privacy.

Which was nice.

Though she wasn't really in the mood to charm Keith. She was in the mood to be with Zack. She'd wanted to have breakfast with him. To ask about his weekend. Even to tell him about the call from her cousin.

Good grief.

Her breath stuck in the back of her throat as she realized what was going on. No, no, no. She barely kept from shaking her head back and forth in a panic. She could not be falling for Zack Winston. He was leaving. *This weekend.*

She would not let herself care about him.

Plus, there was Keith. He obviously had interest, or he wouldn't have sought her out. And she did like him.

He was cute and nice, and he had a great butt too. She'd checked it out Friday night.

Might as well take advantage of the situation presented to her and see where it went.

She swiveled back around and flashed him her most winning smile. It occurred to her as she did that he may not appreciate her all-over-pink I-love-Jeannie look. But then, if he didn't, it was best to find that out now. Because she didn't want a man who didn't appreciate all she brought to the table.

And sometimes, she brought Jeannie.

Especially after a weekend of sitting around wondering if Zack was off with another woman.

She'd wanted to be happy that morning, and her outfit had brightened her day.

Keith had eaten only a few bites of his pancakes; mostly he was watching her. His eyes were soft and blue, and they seemed to be smiling gently. It put her at ease.

"I had a good time dancing with you Friday night," he said. He sounded nervous.

"Me too." She nibbled at the corner of her lip. God, she hated the dance of dating. She should have never let her mother's words get to her. She was fine without a man.

Only, yeah, she did want one. In the grand scheme of things, she wanted a husband by her side and babies running around the yard. She wanted a normal, traditional little life. So why not go for it now? Especially since Ms. Grayson had already helped her out.

She held in a sigh. It would be easier to go along at this point than it would be to stop, anyway.

"I looked for you Saturday night," Keith said. "Was hoping to see you again."

"I didn't feel like going out." She'd still been in a bit of a funk over what had happened with her mirrors out on the street. Plus, she hadn't been in the mood to fight off the grabby hands of men who thought she was just looking for some action.

"I heard Travis asked you out."

The words shocked her. "He did." She nodded. Since she'd turned him down, she wouldn't have expected Travis to mention asking her out.

"I also heard you didn't go. I was hoping that means I'm not too late." He stopped talking and gave a slight shrug. "Listen, I hate this. Dating, I mean." He shook his head, then started again. "I hate the *uncertainty* of it. The fear."

"Dating scares you?"

He laughed lightly. "Believe it or not, asking a girl out terrifies me."

"But you've been married before."

"Yeah, and I thought that meant I'd never have to ask anyone out again."

She understood thinking your life would go in one direction, only to find out you had no real clue what you were doing.

He put his fork down and leaned in, his eyes earnest. "Don't get me wrong, I love the dating part. I love spending time with a woman, getting to know her. I just hate the dance of it all. You know?"

Exactly what she'd been thinking. Maybe there *was* potential here. She could feel a flicker of hope flame to life.

"Ask me out," she said in a rush. She wouldn't find a husband by sitting at home every night. "There's nothing to fear here."

His bottom lip was fuller than the top, and when he smiled, she felt a little something stir inside her. It wasn't exactly a roaring flame.

Not like what had stirred when she'd been in Zack's arms Friday night. But it was definitely a stir.

And she loved stirs.

He nodded, and reached for her hand. "I'd love to ask you out for tonight. Or tomorrow. But I just found out Nick has me heading out of town most of the week for a job. I leave as soon as I finish here. I can run back over Wednesday night, though. I won't be too far away. How about we drive over to Pigeon Forge for dinner and a show?"

As if he'd overheard the offer, her brother was now shooting dirty looks at Keith. She ignored him. Basically, if a man spoke to her, he got the look. But Keith was sweet. And she thought it was cute that he got nervous asking her out.

If her family had to pick someone for her, she had a feeling Keith would sail through with flying colors.

"I'd love to," she assured him. She squeezed his hand under hers.

And she almost convinced herself she'd like to go out with him as much as she wanted to spend time with Zack.

Chapter Twelve

Fourteen steps from the road to the front door.

That was what weighed on Zack's mind as he faced the front door of the Sugar Springs Veterinary Clinic. He'd parked his car, stepped to the sidewalk, and then counted.

And now he had to go in.

He stared at the oak door, not bothering to peer through the frosted panes to the inside. Cody knew he was coming today. Holly had set it up, and Nick had confirmed it Saturday night. But what the hell should he say to him?

Nick had also been helpful with that.

Don't push. Don't be an ass. And don't act like the fact that they were brothers didn't matter.

Not that he'd planned to do any of those things. But given that his walls went up when he was uncomfortable—and both Nick and Cody had already experienced this—Zack supposed it was good advice.

His mother had given her own advice the day before. *Be nice.* As well as asked him about a million questions about his trip.

She'd wanted to know what all he'd done since he'd been there, what he and Nick had done, what they'd said, and if they were getting along. But she'd also asked about the town and the people. She'd specifically narrowed in on Holly.

She'd apparently let her imagination run wild while she'd been sitting home alone. She thought Holly sounded exactly like the type of girl he needed.

He'd reminded her that first, he didn't need a girl—a woman. And second, he had a career to get back to.

She'd waved away his concerns and asked about the festival he'd also mentioned.

And he'd been right. She wanted him to bring her.

He'd made no promises. He had to get back to work next week, and then he'd see if he had time to make it up for the weekend. Or if there would even be a place to stay.

The door opened in front of him, and a curly-haired woman stared out from behind round glasses. The gray of her hair reminded him of the color of battleships.

"Did you need something?" she asked. Her mouth was pursed so tight that tiny lines sloped up to the edges of her lips. "We don't allow no solicitors in here."

"I'm not a solicitor, ma'am." It irritated him to call this woman ma'am, but his mother *had* taught him manners once upon a time. Even if he didn't always use them.

She looked him up and down. "I know you're not. But I'm not sure we take what you're selling either."

Looked like Cody had his security team on hand.

"Cody knows I'm coming," he told the woman as politely as he could manage.

"He know you were just going to stand on the front porch?"

There was something about the people of this town. They either annoyed the piss out of him . . . or they annoyed the piss out of him.

Yet somehow, most of them grew on him.

This one didn't.

He gave the woman his scary look and asked, "Can I come in?"

She returned her own scary look. "I reckon," she said. "It's an office building. Not my front door."

With her words, she turned and disappeared back inside. The door closed in front of him and he rubbed his hands down the sides of his legs. Then he looked down at the jeans he wasn't yet accustomed to.

He'd picked up several more pairs yesterday. Along with work boots, loafers, a pair of sturdy gloves, and a few polo shirts. He'd even tossed in a couple T-shirts on his shopping spree, thinking they would be more appropriate in the event he ended up helping Nick again.

The work hadn't been bad. He wouldn't want to do it all the time, but he hadn't been involved in any kind of construction since before he'd started law school. He and his dad used to handle random projects around the house for his mom. She'd preferred things done by them instead of hiring outside help.

Didn't mean she'd always gotten her way, but when time had allowed, he and his dad had done just that. Until Zack had become too busy. Then it had all been left to his dad.

He saw the woman from inside giving him the evil eye again so he wrapped his fingers around the doorknob and pushed open the door.

The smell of dogs, cats, antiseptic, and Pine-Sol hit his nose at once.

None of them were overwhelming, but mixed together, they stung the senses.

"I let Cody know you're here," the woman snipped out. She'd moved to sit behind the reception desk, and her nose was stuck in the air as if *he* were the thing that smelled funky in the room.

"Thanks," he said, but she was already ignoring him.

Zack roamed the small room, not in the mood to sit. No one else was there other than him and the grizzly bear behind the counter, but he did hear the occasional bark from the back.

The waiting room held six armchairs, a small rustic bench that looked to serve as a seat, a basket of magazines, and a fake plant perched on a coffee table. There were a handful of posters on the walls. They all advertised different services or products the office offered.

A creak sounded behind him and he turned. Cody stood in the doorway. His expression was not welcoming. But at least he was there.

Zack could see so much of himself in the face looking back at him that it set him on edge.

The man was guarded. He was careful. And he had walls.

"I couldn't get him to sit down," the old lady said.

Zack eyed her again. He tried his scary look once more. The old bat hadn't even suggested he sit. Her nose went back in the air.

"That's okay, Ms. G.," Cody said. "Thanks for letting me know he was here. And thanks for covering this morning. Amy should be in any minute."

Cody met Zack's eyes again, and without knowing anything else about his brother, Zack knew that this was the one he wanted to know most. They were the two who had been discarded by their biological mother.

"Come on back," Cody said.

He turned and Zack caught the door before it closed. Ms. G. sniffed.

He followed Cody down the hall, made a right, and followed down another.

Cody poked his head into a large utilitarian room. "I'll be in the office, Keri."

"Sure thing." The woman's white lab coat had KERI WRIGHT stitched across the chest. She met Zack's eyes and gave him a friendly, easy smile. "Nice to meet you, Mr. Winston," she said. Her hands were full with a golden retriever, so she gave him a nod. "I'm the other owner of this office. Thanks to your brother buying in, I get to see my six-month-old baby on a regular basis."

Zack nodded in return, appreciating the welcome. "Call me Zack," he offered. "And nice to meet you too."

Cody had stepped on down the hall, and now stood at the entrance to an office. A bored look was pasted on his face, so Zack moved into the room without another delay. Cody closed the door, and the space was suddenly, deafeningly quiet.

"So," Cody started. He moved to the other side of the desk and looked as uncomfortable as Zack felt. "You wanted to talk."

The room was sparse on decorations. There was a shelf full of reference manuals, a couple of filing cabinets, and a handful of pictures. There was also a black, long-haired cat parked in the middle of Cody's desk.

"I did," Zack said. It went against everything he believed when there was a confrontation brewing, but he pulled out a chair and took a seat first. He could not come into this in a challenging manner. Looking up at his brother now, he added, "I would like to apologize for my attitude and rude behavior when you and Nick came to Atlanta."

None of the stiffness left Cody's shoulders. Nor did he sit. "Words are easy," he said.

Zack counted to five. It would be *easier* to get up and leave. He wasn't a man who made a habit of begging. Then he reminded himself that this was important. They were blood. And that mattered. He also pictured his mother's pleading eyes as she'd encouraged him to come here.

And her threatening to hire a man with a big stick.

The memory helped him force his own posture to relax. "Not for me, they're not," he said. "Not apologies, anyway. I can count on one hand the number of times I've admitted I was wrong in my life. Counting this one. And I'd still have a finger left over."

"That's supposed to make me think you're a stand-up guy? Because you think you're never wrong?"

"How many times have you admitted *you're* wrong?"

A muscle spasmed in Cody's jaw a second before he yanked out his own chair and sat. Zack almost smiled. He could recognize his own arrogance in Cody. He'd pegged him right. The man didn't make a habit of apologizing either.

"Nick thinks I should give you a second chance," Cody said. "I don't see why. We tried to get to know you before. You made your opinion clear." He shrugged. "Open-and-shut case to me. Why bother now?"

"You also ambushed me. I'm sure you know what that's like. Walking out your door to find a brother?"

Nick had filled him in on how he and Cody had met. He'd shown up on Cody's doorstep and knocked. Cody hadn't taken it well.

"How about walking out to find two of them?" Zack finished.

"I didn't shove my money down his throat," Cody defended. "Nor did I tell him to take a hike."

Yeah, Zack had done the money thing too. He'd chosen the priciest restaurant he could get into on short notice, then had tossed down a few hundreds as he'd left the meal early. It hadn't been one of his prouder moments.

"You're clearly a better person than I am," he said. "That doesn't mean I don't deserve a second chance."

"Maybe I don't believe in second chances?"

Cody was just being bullheaded now. This town liked to talk. Even without Nick, he'd easily learned that Cody's fiancée had given him the biggest second chance anyone deserved. If she hadn't, Cody wouldn't be there now. And he wouldn't be getting to know his daughters.

Zack merely lifted a brow.

"*Fuck*," Cody grumbled. "Damned town. Everyone tells every fucking thing they know here. Ms. G. is probably standing outside the door right now. I wouldn't doubt she has a notepad and pen in hand, just so she can relate our conversation verbatim."

A shuffling sound came from the hallway and then a thump. Then the sound of footsteps hurrying in the opposite direction. Both men looked at the door.

Zack burst out laughing. Cody merely shook his head.

"Why I ever suggested to that woman that she fill in when our receptionist needed a morning off, I'll never know. She is the bane of my existence."

"I hear she's sweet on you," Zack added. He'd just put two and two together and figured out that Ms. G was, in fact, the town gossip. Nick had mentioned that she had a fondness for their brother.

Cody's dark eyes turned stormy. Yet at the same time, Zack saw bluster.

"Don't let anyone fool you," Cody muttered. "She's sweet on gossip. That's all. She's a cranky old biddy."

"I reckon I'm not, Cody Dalton," the sharp voice came through the door. She rapped on the wood three short times. "I'm a nice woman. I bake you pies."

The two of them looked at each other, and this time they both burst out laughing. The ice between them was slowly beginning to thaw. They decided to go for a walk. Away from Ms. G.

Ten minutes later, they ended up in front of a charming two-story house. There was a basketball hoop with a concrete pad in the yard to its left, flowers of all colors overflowing from containers lining the porch, and a Great Dane slapping his tail in greeting where he lay on the top step.

It was a cozy place.

It made Zack think of his childhood. His parents had provided a good home. There had been love. Family.

A closeness he was only now starting to recognize that he was missing.

Cody stood in the middle of the road in front of the house, and he shoved his hands in his pockets. "I did get a second chance. A big one. It turned my life around." He eyed Zack.

He didn't say he would grant Zack another chance, but Zack felt it being considered.

He nudged his chin at the house. "Your place?"

"Lee Ann's," Cody said. "As well as the girls'. I won't move in until we're married." He shot Zack a look. "You know I have twin daughters, right? Teenagers?"

Zack nodded.

"They're terrific." The man softened. "My life wouldn't be right without them."

"Probably wouldn't be nearly as stressful either."

Cody chuckled. "You got that right. Kendra has a different boyfriend every other week. I can't believe how many kids I want to beat with a stick just for looking at my girl. Candy is all about basketball. She doesn't have time for boys yet. Thank God."

Together they turned and headed the way they'd come. They neared the back of the clinic, and Zack saw Ms. G. now on the porch of the house across the street. He looked at Cody.

"She lives there." He pointed to the stairs leading to the apartment behind the office. "I live here. She knows every flippin' move I make." He lifted his mouth in a wry smile. "But she does make good pies."

Zack held out his hand, reminding himself of Nick's words. *Don't push it.* He'd go around the side of the building instead of through it. They'd had a good talk, and things were moving forward. That was enough for today.

"How about dinner?" Cody asked. He shook Zack's hand in return. "Lee Ann will have my hide if I don't ask. The girls want to meet you, as well as Lee Ann's mother." He nodded toward his neighbor. "But be warned. She's as bad as that one."

Zack pictured sitting at a dining room table with five people, all staring at him, trying to decide if they wanted to let him into their lives. With one of them apparently looking for juicy gossip to spread.

Not the way he'd imagined his life heading two weeks ago.

But the funny thing was, he was already looking forward to it.

And then it occurred to him for the first time that he wasn't just getting two brothers. He was also getting two sisters-in-law and two nieces. Which meant that his mother would see it as two sons, two daughters, and two granddaughters.

He would definitely have to bring her up to meet them.

But first, he had to fix this. His and Cody's relationship. He had to make *them* okay.

He nodded. "Name the day."

"Friday night. I'll invite Nick and Joanie too. Bring Holly if you want." When Zack just looked at him, Cody added, "Tale is you're becoming friends. Thought you might be more comfortable with her there."

He would be. He would love to have her there.

"There's also rumor you're more than friends," Cody pointed out. He didn't sound pleased by the thought.

"That why you suggested I bring her? So you can check that one out for yourself?"

Cody didn't answer, which was answer enough. If Zack hurt Holly, his brothers would take him down.

"Friday," Zack said. "I'll see you then."

He left his brother and headed around the side of the building, contemplating asking Holly. She'd come with him, he was sure. She liked to go out. And she kept saying she wanted to help.

He just didn't want it to feel like a date.

Because then he might act like it was a date.

He came close to walking into a diminutive, older man when he rounded the corner of the building, barely managing to pull himself up short in time.

"Excuse me," Zack spoke first. His hands went up in front of him.

"My fault," the man said. "I apologize. I was going too fast, afraid I'd letcha git away."

Zack lifted a brow. "You were looking for me?"

The man nodded. "Ms. Grayson called. She knew I was looking for ya." He stopped and shook his head, the sagging skin under his chin moving back and forth. "Let me start over." He thrust his hand out. "I'm Waldon Martin. I live out at the edge of the county. My property backs up to Old Man Wilson's."

Zack pumped the man's hand, noting the grip wasn't terribly strong, and didn't let his confusion show. "Nice to meet you, Mr. Martin. Is there something I can do for you?"

"Oh," the man groaned out as if in agony. "That old man. I'll tell ya, he drives me and the missus crazy. We had this property dispute. Only, the missus and I paid to have the land surveyed. Wilson wouldn't do it, he's a cheapskate. Anyways, we were right with the lines, so we called a guy to put up a fence. Wilson's dog keeps terrorizing our ducks, you see. That's when our problems began. The man's dog keeps grabbing our ducks up by the necks and carrying them around as if they're chew toys." Mr. Martin took a breath before finishing with, "Worries my Carol to death."

Zack merely nodded. That had been a lot of words in a short amount of time. He waited to see how the duck-dog story turned out. Right now, it didn't look so good for the ducks.

"So anyways, every time we get the fence people out, there's Wilson standing on *our* property with a shotgun. He won't let the men put up the fence."

"I see." Sounded like Old Man Wilson was a pain in the ass. "Did you call the sheriff?"

The man's shoulders sagged. "His son *is* the sheriff, Mr. Winston. Now don't get me wrong, the boy makes a fine sheriff. He does a good job. He just ain't gonna throw his own daddy in jail, if you know what I mean."

Zack thought he did know what he meant. The law was the law, until it came to your kin. Got it. "Okay," he said. "I can see that being a problem. So then what happens next?"

"That's why I'm out huntin' you. We need us a lawyer."

"And there isn't one in town?"

The bony shoulders slumped even more. "His other son is the lawyer."

Zack couldn't help it. He laughed.

"I know," Mr. Martin grumbled. "The man could come over and piss on our front porch every day if he wanted to, and all we could do is clean it up. He wasn't like this years ago. The guy used to be a decent person. But now he's sad and lonely, and he's turned into nothing but a grumpy old Gus."

A grumpy old Gus? Zack smiled again. The quirks of this place were starting to grow on him.

"So what can I do for you, Mr. Martin? I'm afraid I won't be a lot of help since I practice law in Georgia."

Weariness passed through Mr. Martin's features. His faded eyes latched onto Zack's. "Couldn't you just pretend? I'm worried for Carol. I'm afraid she'll have a heart attack out there yelling at those dadgummed dogs. And the poor ducks—one's eventually gonna git killed."

He pictured Holly and her two geese, and then imagined her fifty years down the road trying to chase off a dog who thought her geese were toys. He wouldn't want to see her stressing herself out either.

"I know somebody, Mr. Martin." It probably wouldn't take more than a letter to scare Wilson into backing off. Especially if his lawyer son thought he'd have to face Zack's friend in court. "He's a big name up in Knoxville. You get me the address for Mr. Wilson, and I'll have my friend send a letter. How's that?"

"You think that'll do it? Get him to back off?"

"If it doesn't, I'll go have a talk with him myself."

Relief washed over the man's face, and happiness slid quietly into Zack's heart. He could help this person out. Really help out someone who deserved it. Not just someone with a wad of cash in his wallet.

Zack liked the feeling.

Waldon Martin grabbed Zack's hand then, and gave it a hearty shake. "I thank you. And my missus thanks you. I'll get that information right out to the B&B. You just let me know what we owe you."

"No charge, Mr. Martin. I'm happy to do it."

Mr. Martin looked as if he'd just been handed a gold brick, then he shook Zack's hand again.

Zack took his time making his way back to his car. As he did, he took in the little town he'd temporarily landed in. At first glance it hadn't looked like much, but every day he found something new to love about the place. He was beginning to see why his mother had often talked about the town she'd grown up in. People took care of people here. It was nice.

Chapter Thirteen

A nd lastly, don't forget to pick up more cards on your way out. We got a new batch in just this morning."

Holly sat in the back row of the library meeting room as Trina Evans wrapped up that week's Firefly Festival committee meeting. Trina held up a handful of rack cards. The cards showcased highlights from past festivals, and were easy to hand out to tourists who passed through town. Business owners had been distributing them for two months now.

"We've got only ten more days to bring in a record-breaking crowd this year, people." Trina's hand rocketed straight into the air, and her head did a little cheerleader-type bob. Her three-carat diamond wedding set flashed on her French manicure–tipped finger. "So let's get out there!"

She was far too excited, in Holly's opinion. Trina and her husband, Paul, owned Talbot's restaurant. Talbot's was known for their chicken and dumplings and their cheesy bread appetizer. Trina was known for volunteering for every committee that had ever existed in Sugar Springs.

As well as being head cheerleader when she'd been in school.

Holly had trouble concentrating on committee business today. She was more focused on tonight's upcoming date with Keith.

Nerves had destroyed any attempt at breakfast, and lunch hadn't been much better. Not so much because it was Keith, but because she hadn't gone out with *anyone* in quite a while. And because she felt added pressure.

This date needed to go somewhere.

Holly eyed Ms. Grayson, who sat straight-backed on a front-row metal fold-up chair, her gaze glued to Trina. Ms. Grayson, the danged lady, was the reason for the nerves. Everyone now knew Holly was looking for a man.

Everyone!

She'd been reminded of it each day. If it wasn't another guy calling her up and offering to "buy her a drink"—with the implied roll in the sheets thrown in—it was a mother stopping her on the street, professing the charms of her son . . . whom she just knew would be the perfect man for Holly.

Yeah?

Then why wasn't said perfect man there in front of her himself instead of letting Mommy do it for him?

Holly fought to keep from rolling her eyes as she recalled yet another woman who'd rattled her ear off at the diner that very morning.

No. She did not want to go out with a man who couldn't be bothered to show a bit of interest himself. What was so hard about that?

And so far, Keith had been it.

Thus the nerves. What if this date turned out to be a disaster?

Keith was a good guy, and she had no reason to believe she would do anything to tank the evening, but what if they didn't click? What if she couldn't manage to find one single man she wanted to be with when the entire population of Sugar Springs knew she was on the hunt?

Would there be a second chance for her or would this be it?

She squinted at her gray-haired nemesis as she thought forward to years down the road. Would *she* be the town spinster? Maybe take up Ms. Grayson's own hobby?

It wasn't like Holly couldn't be a busybody herself if she wanted to.

Especially if she continued hanging out at the diner every day. She ran into practically everyone who lived in Sugar Springs over the course of a week. If there was gossip to gather, the diner was the place for it. And yeah, she already knew most everything that ever happened. She just didn't run around sharing it as fast as she possibly could.

"And don't forget that I need to see the parking committee as soon as we wrap up," Trina continued, as perky as ever. "We've had a second bus donated to be used to ferry visitors between the Monroe farm and the festival, so we'll also need a few people to handle that. Any volunteers?"

Trina's smile and eyes went wide at the same time, both inclusive of everyone in the room, and Holly's stomach chose that moment to let out a loud growl. Trina paused. She glanced in Holly's direction, a perplexed expression slipping over her perfectly composed face.

Holly's stomach growled again.

Jesse Beckman from three rows up snickered under his breath, his shoulders moving with the action. Jesse was only twenty-three, but he was a decorated war hero, the little brother of a friend of hers, and smoking hot in a stocky, weightlifter kind of way.

He'd just recently come back to town from a tour in Afghanistan, and she'd seen him for the first time in months Friday night. She'd danced with him at the Bungalow. It had been a very nice dance.

Her stomach growled yet again, and she blushed to the bottom of her feet. Obviously, she would need to eat something before Keith picked her up.

She eyed the loaded-down table in the corner. The snack committee provided homemade goodies at each meeting. This week had been her mother's turn.

And yes, Trina was also on the snack committee. As well as the parking committee.

She headed up both.

"Well," Trina murmured at the front of the room. She sounded as if she'd lost her train of thought. Jesse turned in his seat, the rickety metal creaking under the movement, and his eyes landed on Holly.

Again, Holly blushed.

He didn't look away.

His eyes were dark. Not as dark as Zack's, but close. And his whole body was taut and muscled. He was a lean, mean, killing machine.

A bead of sweat came to life between her breasts and she wondered if Jamie would mind terribly if she dated the little brother they'd once teased mercilessly. It wasn't like they were in high school anymore. Plus, who knew if things with Keith would even work out? If they didn't, Jesse could quite possibly be a nice alternative.

Assuming he had any interest outside of a dance.

And that his interest wasn't purely bedroom related.

Given the fact he was barely twenty-three and had been out of the country for months, most likely he was only looking for fun.

"Everyone please thank Mrs. Marshall for the snacks today," Trina wrapped up. All eyes except Jesse's shifted to Holly's mother. The corner of Jesse's mouth turned up. "We'll meet next Wednesday for any final details." Trina clapped her hands together as if she would break into shouting, "Go team!"

Jesse only smiled wider.

Holly shook her head, gave him a "What's with her?" roll of her eyes, and rose to head to the snack station. At least she knew the food would be edible today.

"I swear, Holly Beth," her mother whispered in Holly's ear as she reached the table before anyone else, "eat a pinwheel or something. I've never heard such as all that noise you were making back there."

Holly did not let herself roll her eyes at her mother. Her mother hated that.

She did, however, cram an entire ham-and-cheese pinwheel in her mouth.

"Holly!" her mother whispered in disgust. Holly grinned around her food, even going so far as to chew with her mouth open.

"She ain't never gonna find her a man that way."

Holly whirled to find Ms. Grayson now standing at her other side. Her face was pinched in the same disgusted way as Holly's mother's, as the older lady also stared at Holly's bulging cheeks.

"I taught her better than that, Beatrice," Sylvia Marshall said. She reached across Holly and patted the older lady's forearm. "But you know how she can be."

"Oh, I know. I done helped her out with gettin' dates, and has she even gone out one time?" Ms. Grayson shook her head back and forth. "Nary a once. And I know for a fact she's had some calls. Even had a good handful of men to choose from at the movies last week. Yet she went and drove away with that out-of-towner instead."

Ms. Grayson clucked, only to be joined by Holly's mother.

Holly quickly chewed and swallowed her food, then shook her finger in Ms. Grayson's wrinkled face. "You . . ." She didn't know what she wanted to say.

Except she did. Only, her mother was still standing there—as were others who were gathering around the table—and Holly couldn't bring herself to chew out the older woman in front of everyone.

Instead, she leaned into Ms. Grayson and whispered harshly, "You had no right. And you even told them that I like shoes?" She pictured the men gathered around her at the concession stand Thursday night. "What was that about? Ray Taylor *brought* me a pair that night," she said, aghast. She might have told Zack that Ray had been the best option in the pack, but in truth, she'd been horrified. Who brought a girl a pair of shoes to try to win a date? "What did you do? Tell them that I could be bought?"

Ms. Grayson's nose lifted. "I just told them what I heard. You said that's how you choose men."

It was not how she chose men.

"If you're going to eavesdrop, old woman, get your facts straight."

Holly's mother shot her an evil glare at the "old woman" comment as Holly's voice inched a notch higher, and Holly pressed her lips together. She stood straight. But good grief, the *old woman* had butted in where she hadn't been invited.

And it was causing more than a bit of grief!

"You'll thank me when you find you a man," Ms. Grayson proclaimed in a sniff. Several people at the table laughed behind their hands, not even trying to pretend they weren't listening in, and Holly once again turned bright red.

Ms. Grayson grabbed a paper plate and began daintily picking up an assortment of finger foods as if she wasn't in the middle of an argument. "And when you do," she continued smugly, "I'll expect an invite, asking me to be front and center at the wedding."

"You won't ever be invited to my wedding," Holly growled out.

"Holly Beth!" her mother chastised.

For crying out loud.

Holly grabbed another pinwheel and, looking straight at her mother, shoved it fully in her mouth. Then she turned, intending to stalk out of the room, but there was Jesse Beckman smiling naughtily at her.

While she had her mouth not only full, but bulging.

Lovely.

"Hi, Jesse," she mumbled around the food. Might as well add to the bad impression by talking while eating.

"Now he'd be a fine possibility," Ms. Grayson mumbled behind her.

"I'd say so," Holly's mother chimed in.

Holly wanted to die on the spot.

Jesse's low chuckle and heated, male scent reached her at the same time, and she had the thought that it might just turn out to be Keith

Justice's very lucky night. She wasn't a loose girl by nature, but a woman could only handle so much frustration in her life before she sought out some relief. If it wasn't a busybody sticking her nose where it didn't belong or a mother who had never bothered to notice that Holly had grown up, it was a hot guy giving her an "I want your body" look.

Zack came to mind.

She wanted to give him an "I want your body" look.

"You leaving?" Jesse asked.

Holly nodded.

He motioned to the door with his head. "Mind if I walk you out?"

She had the manners to cover her mouth with her hand this time. "Just let me get my purse," she mumbled.

She quickly swallowed her food, shot her mother and Ms. Grayson a hard look when Ms. Grayson opened her mouth as if to say something to Jesse, then grabbed her purse and headed with her friend's little brother to the stairs that would take them up to the first floor of the library.

Jesse made a comment about the hobbies of the older women in town, and had Holly relaxed and laughing as they hit the top step. Her laughter died when she spotted Zack sitting at one of the small study tables, his laptop open as if he'd been working.

But instead of working, he had his arms crossed on the table in front of him, leaning forward, his weight on his elbows, and was giving the librarian the full power of his charm. Larissa Bailey seemed to be drowning in the attention.

Holly found her body growing tight with jealousy.

She hadn't seen Zack since Monday morning when he'd been in the diner for pancakes. She'd heard from Nick that Zack and Cody's meeting had gone fairly well. Even that a dinner party was set up for Friday night. But Zack hadn't told her himself. Instead, he'd either been working with Nick out at the construction site, or simply not around.

Or hanging out at the library.

Of course, she hadn't been around the house too much herself. She'd been spending a large amount of time in her studio. Getting back in the groove of working with her mirrors had been a good thing. She'd dropped off a new piece at the consignment store just that morning, and if work progressed the way she hoped, she'd have a new original finished within a week or two as well.

"So how about it?" Jesse asked, and Holly realized she'd completely tuned him out.

"I'm sorry." And dang, if she didn't grow heated with embarrassment again. She blamed the nerves on tonight's impending date. All her nerve endings seemed to be hanging out right at the edge of her skin today. "I must have zoned out."

Jesse glanced across the room to where Zack now had Larissa shyly smiling. The white-blonde was a really pretty woman, and Holly found herself more than a tad jealous at the attention. As she watched the two of them, Zack turned his head to her. He took in Jesse standing at her elbow.

Nothing was said, and barely any recognition showed on Zack's face, but electricity seemed to come to life in the room.

"I asked if I could take you out," Jesse said. His voice seemed to boom in the small room. "I actually came to the meeting today just to see you." He gave a little shrug, and now he was the one turning on the charm. And the boy had it in spades. It oozed from his pores.

He'd come there to see her?

That was different.

"I think we'd have fun hanging out together," he added when she just stared. "Thought we could go hang gliding if you feel adventurous."

Hang gliding? With Jesse?

Wow. She studied the super-cutie at her side with the dimple in his chin and the almost-buzzed cut. She supposed military guys had a need for adrenaline rushes. Not that she'd be against the idea. Hang gliding sounded like a blast.

She swallowed and peeked at Zack again, and saw his eyes locked on her. He was waiting to hear her answer too. She turned back to Jesse.

She wanted to say yes. But then . . .

"Surely you know I'm going out with Keith tonight," she stalled. The whole town knew she had a date tonight. Ms. Grayson even knew it, Holly was positive, though the pain in the ass had acted like she knew nothing of the sort.

"Sure." Jesse nodded. "But it's a first date, right? Why lock yourself in?" he asked. His voice was deep and seemed somehow able to reach inside her and pluck at her like a string. He took her hand in his and she almost giggled like a schoolgirl. This was her friend's little brother! And he was looking at her like he knew just the right way to strip a girl naked.

She didn't need to go out with Jesse because she suspected that if *he* didn't try to get in her panties, she might just show him the way.

If for no other reason than to *not* think about Zack. And the fact that that's exactly where she wanted *him* to be.

"I . . ."

"Come on," Jesse wheedled, good-naturedly. He gave her hand a squeeze as his mouth tilted on one side. "Sample the dating pool a bit. No need to be in a hurry, right?"

She laughed lightly. If only she really were the sampling kind.

She wanted to be.

She really, really wanted to be.

Because he was right. Why lock herself in to one man too fast?

She glanced at Zack again. Unless it was him.

The thought of going out with Zack and *then* going out with someone else? Ludicrous.

As was the thought of going out with Zack at all.

Hadn't he already made it clear what he would be interested in?

She gulped again. Nerves had her shying away from Jesse. She was suddenly feeling overwhelmed with all the added attention she'd been getting.

"Let me see how tonight goes, okay?"

Keith was tamer than Jesse. He was a better person to dip her toe into the dating waters with.

Jesse's eyes glowed at her with a mixture of understanding and interest. It was a potent look. It didn't come across as simply a man looking to score, but as someone who wanted to get to know her.

Which was exactly what she was looking for.

She almost groaned at the thought. Surely she would not have to thank Ms. Grayson when all of this was over.

"As long as you keep me in mind," Jesse murmured softly. He leaned in and brushed a quick kiss across Holly's cheek. "You were always my favorite of my sister's friends," he whispered.

Then he was gone through the outer library door, and Holly was left standing there, shocked at the direction her life was suddenly taking. She had a date tonight, another just waiting for her to say yes . . .

And a man eyeing her from fifteen feet away as if he'd take her in the storage room right that very moment if only she'd ask.

She pressed her eyes closed and prayed that she would enjoy her date with Keith tonight.

And that she would *not* think about Zack and storage rooms.

Chapter Fourteen

S he failed.

Holly most definitely *had* thought of Zack during her date with Keith last night.

She'd also thought of storage rooms.

A date that, all in all, had gone really well. Keith had been charming and funny, and he was just flat-out cute.

And he'd kissed her.

One good-night kiss as they'd sat in his pickup in front of the house.

It hadn't set off blasting fireworks or anything, but it had been pleasant. Given how long it had been since she'd been kissed, she'd take pleasant.

The only problem was, she'd thought about Zack while Keith's mouth had been on hers.

Not intentionally, but she hadn't been able to keep from wondering what a kiss from him would be like.

Would it be fireworks?

Better than Keith's?

Or maybe she was just being impatient. Probably with practice, she and Keith could reach fireworks.

At least sparklers.

She groaned under her breath as she parked the quad in the shed and stepped from the building. Should a person have to work for sparklers?

She stretched her neck and shoulders, working out the kinks from where she'd been hunched over her worktable all day, then pulled the ponytail from her hair and dug her fingers into her scalp. She was exhausted, drained, and all kinds of thrilled. Her new piece might just turn out to be her best work yet.

It had kept her busy late into the afternoon yet again.

"Where do you go on that thing all the time?"

She jumped, letting out a high-pitched squeak and pressing her hand to her racing heart. It was Zack. She'd stepped one foot up on the steps of the back deck, and hadn't seen him sitting in the far corner. He was stretched out on a lounge chair with a book in his hand, and he was wearing another yummy pair of jeans, a black pullover, and no shoes. For some reason, she couldn't look away from his bare feet.

The whole pose just seemed . . . erotic. As if he were stretched out naked instead of fully clothed.

Or maybe that was just how she wanted him to be.

She also wanted him to kiss her. Right then. Right there.

She wanted to see if there were fireworks.

Pulling her gaze away, she managed to finish climbing the steps, all while doing her best to remain casual. As if she hadn't been thinking about his mouth on hers since late last night.

Or days before that.

"You don't strike me as the lounge-around-and-read-a-book type," she said as she headed his way. The activity seemed too slow for him.

He held up the hardback. It was a copy of one of the latest best-selling thrillers. "Larissa recommended it. Figured since I'm supposed to be on vacation, I might as well give it a try."

That silly little jealousy thing reared its head again. The librarian's name sure slid easily off his tongue.

"Good for you," she muttered. She dropped into the chair next to his and stretched out her feet. She was bone tired. "I'd heard you were spotted at the library again today."

He lifted a brow. "You keeping tabs on me?"

She laughed tiredly. "Not intentionally. But gossip central seems to think it's their job to keep me informed of your comings and goings." The tension began to ease from her shoulders, and she closed her eyes. "And as usual, it got back to Linda Sue over at the salon, who told Gina, who called and passed it on to me."

"So if I want to know something, I could go to . . . Linda Sue? At the salon?"

"Right. Or Gina. That woman knows all too. Or wait about five minutes and it'll make it to me."

"What if I want to know how your date went?"

She lifted her eyelids. He'd set his book down and was watching her from under hooded eyes. He looked dangerous.

His jawline was hard, and his cheeks were rigid.

She licked her lips. "It went great," she said.

"He treat you right?" His gaze slid over her lips. "Was he a gentle-man?"

Was he trying to find out if they'd kissed?

Or more?

Her heart took off at a gallop as she sat there watching him, wondering why he wanted to know. Was he finding it as hard to ignore the chemistry between them as she was? Because she most definitely was.

Even knowing he wasn't the right man for her.

"He was a perfect gentleman," she finally answered. "We drove into Pigeon Forge and saw a show, and then he brought me home. I was in bed before midnight."

Ten seconds passed before Zack admitted, "I saw his truck pull up."

His voice dropped low, swirling over her like silky sheets sliding over her naked body.

"I was watching for you," he confessed.

Her mouth parted, but she didn't know what to say. His bedroom was in the back of the house, though there was a small study in the front of the second floor. He'd had to have been in there to watch for her.

But why?

"Didn't look like much of a kiss," he pointed out.

She tilted her head, wondering if he'd been jealous. Or was she just wishing for the moon? "If you saw it, then why did you ask?"

His mouth curved, the edges lifting slowly. "I wanted to see what you thought about it."

The look in his eyes was deliciously wicked. Apparently she hadn't given the impression she'd thought too much.

She narrowed her eyes at him. "We have another date planned for Friday night. I'm sure he was saving his best for then. You know, when he doesn't have to get up early for work the next day." She had no idea if Keith had to be at work Saturday morning or not, but she liked the way a muscle jerked in Zack's jaw at her words. "I'll be sure and report in after that date too. If you'd like."

If he could tease, so could she.

Though the last thing she was thinking about right then was Friday night's date. Or the kiss she might get from Keith.

Zack nodded. The twinkle in his eyes dimmed, but it didn't leave. "You be sure and do that," he said. "I want to hear all about it."

She couldn't breathe.

The air felt like it was being cut off in her throat.

They were playing a dangerous game here. Her body didn't understand that he was simply taunting her, and her heart was stupid enough that it could get confused.

She needed to walk away. Go think about Keith. Or maybe Jesse or one of the many other men who'd been calling. For the first time in her life, she had her pick.

Only, Holly increasingly found herself wanting to pick Zack.

"Stay away from hang gliding too," he said now. And yes, she was fairly certain that sounded like jealousy in his voice.

"What's wrong with hang gliding?"

His nostrils flared the tiniest amount. "It's not for you."

He was jealous. She would bet the money she'd made off her mirrors he was. But what did that mean? Anything?

"So where do you go on that thing?" he asked. His tone changed, lightening, as if to lift the mood. When she just looked at him, confused and still thinking about him and his mouth and the fact that he looked like one hell of a jealous man, he nudged his chin toward the steps. "The quad. You head out of here on it a lot. You left Saturday the minute we got back. Probably did Sunday too. Best I can tell, you have every day this week. Are you working on your mirrors?"

She had no idea how he'd figured that out.

"Where did *you* go Sunday?" she asked instead of answering him. If he could ask probing questions, she could too.

He didn't hesitate. "To see my mother. I have lunch with her every Sunday. Then I took her shopping. She helped me pick out my new casual clothes."

That was not the answer she'd been expecting. She gulped. It was a far cry from the booty call she'd imagined.

"The mirrors?" he asked. "Is that what you're doing?"

"What would even make you ask that?" No one ever asked her about the mirrors. Of course, no one but he knew about the custom ones she did, either.

"I looked in your car," he said. "You unloaded the back."

"So?"

"So, I don't see them in the house. You had to take them somewhere."

"They might be in my bedroom."

"Are they?"

She didn't answer.

"Or are they out at your house? At your place?" He used her words. As if he knew what it meant to her to have her own place. To be her own person.

She was suddenly wishing she had not chosen to sit down with him. She swung her legs to the side and pushed up to a sitting position. "I just remembered that I need to help Mom with something."

Zack sat up too. They faced each other. He put a hand to her arm and she stopped.

"Will you show me?" he asked.

Her gaze shot to his. "Show you what?"

"Where you work," he said. "Your mirrors."

She was shaking her head before he'd gotten the words out.

"Why not?"

"I don't show anybody," she whispered.

"Does anyone even know you make them? The ones that are works of art."

She'd never had anyone call something she made a work of art. She wanted to get up and walk away from him, but he knew something about her that no one else did. And he saw it as art.

That meant a lot.

He'd also figured out that this was a part of her she didn't share. Yet as she looked at him, she had the craziest urge to share it with him.

She finally shook her head. No. No one knew that she made them. She was too afraid to tell.

"Will you show me?" he asked again. His words were soft and stroked her like a caress, and she leaned forward on her seat. He made the same move, and they now sat face-to-face. There were only inches separating them.

"There's the movie tonight," she began.

"Let's skip it."

"But . . ."

"I go home this weekend," he said. "Show me."

She didn't want him to leave yet. "Your brothers," she paused. "You need to spend more time with them."

"We're having dinner together tomorrow night. They won't miss me today."

When she didn't answer, his hands slipped over hers and cupped them between his larger ones. "Show me, Holly. Spend the evening with me."

She wanted to show him.

And silly as it may be, she wanted to spend the evening with him.

And she liked what it felt like when he held her hands in his.

She nodded. Wouldn't be the first time she'd made a mistake.

Zack looked up from his seat in the living room when he heard a door close down the hall. Holly had agreed to take him to her cabin, but she'd wanted a shower first. Everyone else had left for the park, so it was just the two of them at the house.

She'd seemed exhausted when she'd come home earlier, and he'd told himself to leave her alone. She didn't need him butting into her life. She didn't need him hanging around, wanting things from her that she didn't want to give.

But with the clock ticking on his time there, and the fact that the longer he'd gone without seeing her, the more he'd realized he'd missed her, he hadn't been *able* to leave her alone. He'd gone out to the deck specifically to make sure he didn't miss her.

He'd had a couple of good days, spending part of them with Nick, and of course there was the dinner invite to Cody's coming up tomorrow night. Things seemed to be going well enough. But that had been dampened by the fact that he hadn't gotten to share the details with Holly.

And then last night.

Last night she'd been out with another man.

That had about driven him mad. All he'd been able to think about was wondering if the two of them were somewhere making love. If another man's hands were touching her the way Zack longed to do.

He couldn't have gone to bed if he'd wanted to.

Not without making sure Holly got home. With all her clothes intact.

When he went out to the deck, he'd intended to ask her to come to dinner with him the next night. Instead he'd learned she'd lined up a second date.

And if that date didn't work out, she had another man waiting in the wings.

Neither of those things sat well with him.

Thus he'd talked her into spending the evening with him tonight. Just him. Not him in the middle of the whole population of Sugar Springs.

Again, he should leave her the hell alone. But he couldn't.

Blonde hair was the first thing to catch his attention when she stepped back into the room. It was twisted into a loose braid of some sort, reaching to the middle of her back. A few strands floated softly around her face, and he closed his hands into fists with the desire to reach out and pull the strands free. He wanted to know what all that gold felt like.

Then he took in the rest of her.

Zero makeup and a ruffled, light-green shirt that was wispy and flowy. It buttoned up the front, leaving just a hint of cleavage, and made her look like a magical fairy. The jeans fit snug all the way down. On her feet were simple flip-flops. They didn't even stand out.

But her toes did.

Each toenail was painted a different color. They so loudly screamed *Holly* that he realized he would have been upset if nothing about her had been outside the norm. She was an out-of-the-norm kind of girl, and he was finding that he liked it. Very much.

He dragged his gaze back up her body, telling himself not to let her see what she did to him, but he wasn't sure he could hide it any longer. He wanted her. And he might just have to push the issue.

It would be selfish. Because he wouldn't get involved in anything that wasn't quick and easy. He'd learned that lesson before.

But at the moment, quick and easy with Holly was looking pretty damned good.

"You ready to go?" she asked. Her green eyes watched him carefully.

He nodded, but he didn't get up. God, she looked so young. She'd been right about the lack of makeup.

"You never did tell me how old you are," he pointed out.

Her dimple winked in her cheek and he got hard in a flash. She held out a hand. "Come on, old man. I'm twenty-five. You won't get thrown in jail if someone catches you with me tonight, I promise."

Twenty-five was still eight years younger than him. Not that he hadn't dated plenty of women eight years younger. They just normally looked their age.

He took the hand she was offering, and his fingers wrapped around hers. Her hands were strong, her fingers long. And he could no longer keep from imagining them on his body.

Things were almost out of control in his mind.

He let her pull him from his seat.

"We're taking your car," she informed him.

Right then, he would have let her drive his car.

She pulled free of his hand and shot him a wink. "But I want to go for a ride first. Can we do that?"

"We can do whatever you want," he promised.

Her eyes once again met his, and for a brief moment, he had the thought that she wanted what he wanted.

She was attracted to him. He knew that.

He couldn't miss it.

But did she want no strings attached?

"Then I want to go fast," she said. "So fast my laugh is swept away in the air before I can even hear it."

He didn't know about that, but he would give it his best shot.

All while attempting to figure out how to keep from trying to get in her pants once they got to her cabin.

Two hours later, after darkness had fully engulfed them and Holly knew that the rest of the town was engrossed in the movie being shown at the park, she looked across the seat of the car to Zack. She'd directed him through several back roads she suspected he hadn't known about, teasing him the whole time to be careful not to wreck.

He'd taken it well.

Very well.

In fact, he'd been overly accommodating. It had almost felt as if this were a date and he was trying to charm her. It still felt that way.

And she had been charmed.

Especially when he'd pulled into a small country grocery store they'd run across, and bought hot dogs, chips, and bottles of root beer for dinner. They were now parked at her favorite lookout in the mountains, and sat watching the stars and finishing up their meals. He was licking the tips of his fingers, swiping off crumbs from the pastry he'd picked up for dessert.

The whole night had been much better than dressing up and going to the park. They'd started off by taking the car out to a straight stretch of road, where he'd opened the thing up. The car could fly.

If she hadn't already been turned on, that would have done it for her. She was a sucker for a hot car.

And a hot man.

And going really fast.

Her body still hummed at the memory. "Thanks for taking me for a ride tonight." She smiled at him as she said it. It had been clear as they'd raced down the road that she wasn't the only one who enjoyed speed.

"Thank you for showing me where I could go fast," he replied. "I was beginning to think there were no such places around here."

She laughed easily. "Tease me with another ride and I might show you more."

Her words felt too much like she was offering something other than directions to an open road. His silence said he'd heard the same thing.

"Tell me about your mom," she requested, pushing the words out fast. She needed to change the subject. Rein it back in. She could not offer him more.

He would break her heart.

She lifted a knee to the seat and turned to face him. She liked looking at him. Especially because he was so different than he had been ten days ago.

He was relaxed now.

The angles of his face didn't scream stress and tension. They shouted sex and heat. And they made her want to climb into his lap and straddle him.

"My mother is great." He glanced at her as he spoke, and her subconscious whispered that he wanted her in his lap too. That he wanted her legs around him. "She was a stay-at-home mom," he continued. "She doted on Dad and me as if we were the most important things in her life."

"She sounds like a good person."

"She is. And she still dotes." He made a face. "And worries."

"And calls to check on you when you least want her to," Holly teased.

He lowered a hand and rested a loose fist on her knee. The move was casual. Familiar. And it made parts below her waist ache.

"I still can't believe she called the house," he said with an easy grin. "I'm thirty-three years old. I don't need my mother checking up on me."

Holly couldn't help but smile along with him. She had a secret she'd been waiting to share. Now was the perfect time. "Then I don't suppose I should tell you that she called again?"

Zack's expression went flat. "What?"

She nodded. "Earlier today. She got Mom, but I ended up talking to her too."

"Why in the world?"

It was too dark to tell, but she wondered if he might be blushing. She loved seeing him embarrassed. She also loved teasing him.

"What did she want?" he asked.

"She was checking on availability. Apparently she wants to visit."

He shook his head. "She knows I'm coming home this weekend."

Holly lifted a shoulder. She didn't let her disappointment in him leaving show. She liked having him around. "Mom let her know that we had a cancellation yesterday. There's now a room available for the next two weeks."

"She didn't reserve it, did she?"

"Not yet. But she did ask us if we'd call before we booked it. She said she's thinking about it."

His mother had also said that she'd called because she wanted to talk to Holly. Apparently Zack had mentioned her on Sunday when he'd been home, and Mrs. Winston wanted to check her out. Holly tried to decide if she should mention that or not. She'd like to know what had been said. And why he'd been talking about her to begin with.

In the end, she decided against it. It felt like a juicy secret and she wanted to hang on to it.

She hadn't been sure what part of the conversation had consisted of Mrs. Winston checking her out, though. They'd basically talked for twenty minutes about nothing. They'd laughed over Snow White and the Huntsman. Zack had told his mom that her geese didn't like him. Holly had assured the woman that wasn't true. Her pets liked everyone.

Then the conversation had turned to what she did for a living. Zack had mentioned the mirrors. As far as Holly had been able to tell, though, he hadn't mentioned the custom ones. His mother said that Zack made them sound so special and unique that she just had to have one. She would ask her son to pick one out and buy it for her.

And then they'd talked about the upcoming Firefly Festival. A lot.

Something told Holly they would be seeing Zack's mother next weekend, whether he wanted her to come or not.

"Do you really have lunch with her every Sunday?" Holly asked now. His fist was still on her knee, and she covered it with her hand.

Dark eyes flickered over her. "Unless I'm out of town for work."

"You must be a good son."

"No better than anyone else."

He wasn't giving himself enough credit. Holly's first impression of him had been wrong. She hated to admit it, as it messed up her ninety-nine percent accuracy rating—and Cody would enjoy giving her grief about it when he found out—but it had become clear in the past few days. Zack was an upstanding guy.

"Tell me about growing up," she urged. "What were you like as a kid? What made you want to be a lawyer?"

"You're asking a lot of questions tonight." His hand flattened under hers, and his fingers and palm now rested on her knee. She held her breath. The heat from each of his fingers touched her through her jeans.

She slowly let out the breath. She liked him way too much.

"I just like to know things," she said. She swallowed, thinking she'd like to know what his hands would feel like on her bare skin. "I like to learn. Asking questions is one of the best ways to find things out."

He didn't answer at first. Instead, his thumb moved in a tiny arc against her leg. She tried not to let it get to her.

Which was laughable. The man's breathing got to her.

Of course his thumb stroking her leg would.

"I was on the debate team in high school," he finally began to talk. She ignored his thumb and concentrated on his words. "I was the captain. My dad made the statement after one of my debates that I would make a good lawyer." He turned his hand over so that their palms touched. Her nipples beaded. "So now I'm a good lawyer," he finished.

She nodded. Good lawyer. Got it. She was losing focus fast. "What else?" she whispered. "What were you like before that? In elementary school. Junior high."

She could picture him in little dress pants and jackets. He would have stolen her heart.

His fingers closed over the fleshy part of her palm and held her hand trapped in his. "I was picked on, actually."

"What?" Her heart thundered at the admission.

He nodded. "No friends. Glasses. Boys called me a nerd. Girls giggled behind my back."

"Why?" The word came out as shock. "I can't imagine . . ."

She trailed off. She couldn't imagine everyone didn't want to either be him, or be with him. But she couldn't say that out loud. It might make her sound needy.

"I was smart. I was different. Adopted, you know. Not that that was such a weird thing, but something they could point out. And my mom likes to dote." The corners of his mouth slid into a sexy arc. "You've seen it. Can you imagine what it was like when I was ten?"

"Ah, geez," she whispered.

"But that was okay. I was special. Mom and Dad told me that from an early age. They chose *me* to adopt, and they wouldn't have had it any other way. So I loved her doting. I loved the attention." His thumb slipped between their hands and slid over the center of her palm, and the edge of his tongue briefly touched his bottom lip. "Only, I had no friends. And yes, I was lonely."

She'd accused him of being lonely the other night. "Are you still lonely?"

She was certain he wouldn't admit the truth.

The man made it a point to never miss Sunday lunch with his mother. He may play the loner card exceptionally well, but she was no longer buying it. He needed people in his life.

At least a few.

Ones who honestly cared about him.

She swallowed, her throat tight. Because she cared about him.

His hand moved once again, and this time his fingers ended up twined between hers. His eyes shifted to her mouth and she held her breath.

Then he lifted his gaze and he arched a brow. "Sometimes," he admitted. "But not tonight."

This was it. He was going to kiss her.

She was certain of it.

And she was going to let him.

His gaze once again swept over her lips. Her heart raced.

And then he untangled his hand from hers and started his car.

"I get the impression you're trying to delay taking me to your cabin," he teased.

Her entire body wept at the loss of the potential kiss. It was a fight not to physically cry at the calm, unconcerned tone of his voice.

Had he seriously not been thinking about kissing her? At all?

She had issues.

She needed to quit fixating on this man. Who would be leaving her in a matter of days.

Without expressing anything she really wanted to say, she directed Zack back to their property and pointed out the one-lane road that would take them to her cabin.

Zack exhaled silently as he pulled the car to a stop in front of Holly's log cabin. Everything went dark when he turned off the engine. The glow from the moon came into focus, as well as the sounds of the night.

The river not far from them, the mating songs of insects. He even heard rustling in the woods behind them.

Yet generally speaking it was quiet. Near silent. Including the woman by his side.

My God, he'd almost kissed her.

And if he had, he would have done more.

Right there in his car, he would have pulled her into his lap and done his very best to get her out of her clothes.

Holly was the last person he wanted to hurt, though.

So he'd reminded himself that she was looking for a husband. Not a one-night stand. And he'd started his car and driven away.

"Some reason we're not getting out?" Holly asked beside him.

He hadn't even looked in her direction.

Because he still wanted to stretch her out and feast on her body.

Forcing casualness to his voice, he gave her a teasing wink. "Just enjoying the quiet. We don't get nights like this in Atlanta."

"I'm sure that's the truth."

She shoved her door open and he followed suit. He couldn't help but watch as she moved ahead of him. She was mostly a silhouette in the dark, but the moon was almost full. It picked up on the pale skin of her cheeks and throat, making them glow in the night.

He could imagine his mouth tasting the very spots the moon landed on.

When he didn't move toward the house, she looked back. "You still want to see, don't you?"

The tentativeness in her voice kicked him into gear. His hesitancy was making her nervous. Fearful that her stuff wasn't good enough.

He'd seen that in her eyes Saturday morning, and he'd seen it again that afternoon. He'd asked her to show him her work, and she'd tried to run away. She was terrified she wasn't good enough.

"Absolutely," he said.

He caught up with her, and they stepped onto the porch together. When she paused before unlocking the door, he slid his hand down the inside of her arm and grasped her hand in his.

"You saw how fast those two sold the other day." His words were meant to soothe. To let her know how good she was. "I have no doubt we could have pulled the rest out and sold them just as quickly."

Her face turned to his. She was nothing but a shadow, but he knew it was fear radiating back at him. She didn't speak, and he was honestly humbled to be standing there beside her.

"Thank you for showing them to me," he added sincerely. "I know how scary it can be."

And he did. That's why he'd told her about being picked on as a kid. Sometimes, the vulnerabilities that have the power to hurt the most need to be addressed.

He had deep scars from his formative years, and he'd wanted her to understand that. He'd been through his own hurts. His own fears. And if she'd been paying attention, she would recognize that he still had plenty of them hanging around.

But for her, he was strong.

She made him that way.

She held up the key. "You do it," she whispered.

He nodded. He took the key from her hand, and because he couldn't help himself any longer, he leaned in and pressed his lips to her cheek. He lingered for only a second. "You're the most amazing person I know," he whispered.

Then he put distance between them and he slid the key into the lock.

Chapter Fifteen

With one flick of the switch, light filled the room from the front wall of the house to the back, and Zack found himself mesmerized by the work hanging around him.

He stood in the doorway feeling Holly inch in beside him, and took in the mirrors on every wall of the space. These weren't the ones she'd had in the back of her car. They were like the pieces hanging at the store.

But still. They were works of art themselves.

The creativity she held inside her was astounding.

He glanced down to where she stood beside him. Her hands were in front of her, nerves twisting her fingers tight.

"Where are the others?" he asked.

Pleading eyes turned up to him. "You can't just be satisfied seeing these?"

He shook his head and gave her a soft smile. She might give him a hard time about the mirrors, but he knew she would show him her best. He suspected she was anxious to. "Nope," he said. "Show me the goods, Marshall. I want to see it all."

His words could be taken in more than one way, and if the quick glaze that came over her eyes was anything to go by, she *had* taken them in more than one way.

She wanted him.

He wanted her.

What the hell was he supposed to do about that?

"Show me," he demanded. He grabbed her hand in his and ignored all those wants.

She licked her lips, glanced at his lips, and then nodded. "They're in the back."

With that, the two of them walked through the room together. There was a couch in the living room, as well as a flat-screen, a DVD player, and an oversize recliner. He could picture her taking a break from working and curling up in that recliner with a book, or maybe a glass of wine. The chair was large enough that he could fit in there with her.

They entered the connected kitchen.

Though there *was* a table in the room, it wasn't used for eating. Nor was any of the counter space used for normal kitchen jobs. Everywhere he looked, there were bins of items. Every color, shape, and size he could imagine.

And then his eyes landed on the piece on the table.

He took in the work before him. The mirror wasn't complete. Far from it. But already he could tell it would blow him away.

It was interlocking pieces. And if he wasn't mistaken, every piece would end up looking like a continuation of another. As if there were no beginning and no end. He'd seen pictures like that. Brainteasers. But never anything done in this fashion.

"You have unimaginable skill," he told her. She was brilliant at what she did.

"Thank you." Her words were not spoken timidly. As if in this house, surrounded by all that was her, she didn't doubt her skill.

When he looked up from the table, he took in one of the most dazzling sights he'd ever seen. Holly, fresh and pure and simple. Standing in the middle of the room, hundreds of mirrors glistening around her, each one standing out more than the next.

The contrast of the explosion of light and color next to Holly's simplicity was eye-catching. It was beautiful. As was Holly.

And then two small frames caught his eye. They were as original and unique as everything else in the house, but instead of holding mirrors, they held certificates.

"What are those?" he asked. He nodded in the direction of the frames.

They looked like . . .

"Diplomas." She didn't even turn to see what he meant. "One from the Art Institute of Pittsburgh, and the other an MBA from Columbus State University in Georgia."

He was at a loss for words.

Finally, he shook his brain loose—sort of—and asked, "You went to college? Twice?"

Dumb questions.

"Online," she said.

"Why?"

That had been the wrong thing to say. He knew it the second it was out of his mouth, and it was only confirmed by the tightening at the corners of hers.

"Why not?" she snapped out.

"I'm sorry," he said. Seemed he kept saying that with her. "I meant . . ."

He stopped talking and just looked at her. Her shoulders had pulled in a fraction, and she no longer looked tall and proud as she had just a moment ago. He'd done that to her.

"Hell, Holly. I don't know what I meant. It just caught me off guard. I had the impression you weren't interested in"—he motioned toward the diplomas—"that."

"Why?" The word was not confrontational, but merely sounded as if she really wanted to know. Why did he think she *wouldn't* want a college degree?

And he knew he was a snob.

Might as well be honest. He suspected she would call him on it if he wasn't.

"Because you work for your family, filling in wherever they ask, and you don't seem to want more. Because you're happy here. In a town that's so small a person could almost drive through it and miss it. None of that strikes me as overly ambitious." He honestly felt bad for his words. "So college never entered my mind."

He should have known there was more to her.

If he'd been paying attention at all, he would have seen it. Hadn't she told him she liked to learn new things? To know things?

But then why do nothing with it?

And then he replayed her words. Art Institute of Pittsburgh. MBA.

She *had* done something with it.

She'd sought her own path. She'd studied and learned, and she'd created something with originality and skill. And if he were to guess, he'd say she had a good head for business as well. She'd negotiated the sale of her two mirrors the other day with skill and finesse. He hadn't been in on that. He'd simply watched the interplay.

"When I graduated high school, my parents never once asked me what I wanted to do with my life," she told him now. "Nor did my brothers. I was eight years behind Sean, and everyone just assumed I would stick around and fill in where needed. Mostly they assumed I would be happy at the diner forever. It was as if I was nothing but the accidental little sister."

"They don't think of you that way." He'd met her parents. They were great people. They thought the world of Holly.

"Maybe not consciously, but I felt like an afterthought. It never occurred to them that I might want more."

"Why didn't you tell them?"

She shrugged and chewed on her lip, and he saw indecision return. She'd been afraid they wouldn't believe in her dreams.

"Show me the rest," he prompted.

She didn't hesitate. She moved to a door just to his left and put her hand on the knob. Her chest rose and fell with a steadying breath as she paused there. He could see her nerves. He could feel his own.

Whatever was behind that door was something she hadn't shown to anyone else.

With a twist of her wrist, the door opened.

The full-length windows from the back wall of the kitchen extended into the bedroom, and the moon seemed to hang just outside the glass. Blue light streaked in from outside, bouncing off the more intricate designs that hung on the walls. These were the pieces that had been in the back of her car.

The ones that were her core.

He could see that from where he stood. Everything she was had been poured into them. Originality, shine, and sparkle. They were breathtaking.

She flipped on the overhead lights, and he took a step inside.

There was a bed against the middle of one wall, with a small lamp and bedside table beside it. On another wall were a dresser and a closet door.

Everything else was mirrors.

"Why in the world are these here instead of in a gallery somewhere?"

For the first time since he'd met her, sadness dimmed her light.

And then he got it. His heart broke for her.

"This is why you went to Chicago," he said.

She nodded.

"What happened?"

She paused, just for a second. "I couldn't even get in the door," she said. "I went to top-of-the-line boutiques. Big names. I don't want to be lost on the shelves, I want my name front and center. So I shot big." Her voice tightened to the point that Zack reached for her. He wanted to hold her in his arms and take on her pain. She shook her head and took a step away. "They wouldn't even look at them," she whispered. "They assumed a local yokel like me wouldn't have anything worth looking at."

She jabbed a finger at her chest and said, "They sneered at me. Snickered and called me nobody."

Fury boiled inside Zack. They had no right.

"You don't need them," he said.

"I need someone!" she exclaimed so suddenly he was taken aback. Her voice rose higher. "As it is, these are going to remain hidden right here. I can't stop making them. They're my passion. I see new designs every time I close my eyes, and often when I don't. But I can't do anything with them."

"Why?"

His single word seemed to let the air out of her.

She blinked. Then she gave him a funny look. "Why what?"

"Why can't you do anything with them?"

She didn't answer for a few seconds, but then crossed her arms over her chest and said, "Because they aren't good enough."

Translation, she didn't think *she* was good enough.

Just like she thought her family didn't think she was good enough.

So many things suddenly made sense.

"That's why you hide behind the makeup. You're hiding your desire to be taken seriously."

Her face scrunched in confusion, but he could see he had her attention.

"You don't show people the real you," he said. "Because you fear you're not good enough."

"The shoes are the real me," she fought back. "I love them."

He nodded. "I didn't mention the shoes."

He loved the shoes too. And he did think they were the real her. They were vibrant and fun. They were happy.

But the makeup was a tool. It was a device meant to deceive.

"Why would you give up on yourself?" he asked quietly.

Panic flared in her eyes, and he had the sudden thought that he was looking in a mirror.

Only it was years ago.

He'd put it all on the line once himself. It hadn't ended well. But he remembered wanting more than what he had now.

More than work.

And then he realized what he'd done over the years. He'd given up on himself. Only, his *work* was his mode of deception. He hadn't hidden his desire for a career, but for a life. He was the opposite of Holly. Yet they were the same.

He thought about the fifty-plus years his parents had been together. They'd had something special. His dad had worked hard, yes. Always. But he'd made sure to be around for the important parts. They'd lived life instead of just rushing through it.

They'd been a family.

And now Zack couldn't help but wonder if he might have that someday too. If he even wanted it.

Or if it wasn't worth the risk.

He did know he wanted his brothers in his life. More than the superficial, give-me-a-call-once-a-year relationship he'd come here with the intention of seeking. They *were* his family, actually. Looked like he already had one.

And it would be surprisingly comforting to know he could count on them.

Work was important, sure. But for the first time, he saw the need for more.

He'd messed up two months ago. He'd shoved his brothers aside before taking the risk of letting them do the same to him. But the three of them were on a good path now. He wanted to build on that.

He *needed* to build on it. But did he want anything else?

He looked at Holly. She radiated fear standing there before him. It touched him.

She touched him.

Because he cared for her.

And if he squinted just a little, he could see growing something with her. Possibly. But he didn't know if he should even consider it.

She lived here. She wouldn't want to leave.

He wouldn't ask her to.

He pulled in a deep breath, letting it fill his lungs, though it did nothing to untangle the unease swirling inside him. No matter how much he might grow to care for Holly, that one small thing would be their downfall. She was small town. He was not.

But he *was* different than he had been two weeks ago. And he cared enough to help.

He reached for her hand. "You have an amazing talent," he began, letting sincerity show through his words. "Don't settle for less. If Chicago doesn't want you, there are other options. We can make this work."

Her eyes narrowed. "We?"

"I want to help." He wanted to right the world for her.

She watched him, seeming nervous and possibly scared. "How?" she asked.

Here was where he had to prove himself.

He had weeks of unused vacation remaining. And truth be told, there wasn't a case so important that he needed to return immediately. Nothing he couldn't handle from here if an issue came up.

He had brothers he was just beginning to get to know.

Nieces he had yet to meet.

And then there was Holly.

He rubbed his hands together. Work could wait. He could give his life two more weeks.

"I have a friend in Atlanta," he said now. "Let me take you to her. She'd love your work."

"No." Holly shook her head. "I tried that. I told you."

"So try again," he urged. He knew how scary it was to put your neck on the line. Sometimes the answer was no. Those times could change a person. He wasn't ready to let her give up on herself, though. "Come with me to Atlanta this weekend. We'll spend the night at my mom's and I'll take you to the gallery Monday morning."

"You'll be back at work Monday morning."

"I'm staying longer." It felt good to say it. It felt right.

It lifted a ton of pressure from his chest.

"I have more vacation time," he added. "The job can wait." When shock stared back at him, he gave a little shrug. Yeah, he couldn't believe he'd said that either. "I'll take that room you mentioned for the next couple weeks. I'll even bring my mom up, how's that? She'll love the town." He groaned as he realized the problem with that plan. "Only, I'll need to find her a room too."

"She can have mine," Holly stated. She nodded. "We've rented it before. Not often, but it can happen without too much trouble. I'll stay out here."

She glanced at the bed in the room. So did he.

Then he was thinking about her in that bed. And him in that bed with her.

And her kissing another man as he'd watched her do the night before.

His back teeth ground together. He had not liked that at all. And she planned to go out with the guy again tomorrow night.

"Come with me to Atlanta," he urged again.

"I don't want to meet your friend."

And *he* didn't want to leave her there all weekend to go out with Keith. Or whoever else happened along. "Then just come with me to pick up Mom. She likes you. She'd love to talk to you on the drive up."

That got her attention. He could tell by the light that showed up in her eyes.

"Come on," he begged. He reached for her hand and gave her the pleading look that he saved for special occasions. Like when he'd been younger and had wanted to get his way with his mother.

Holly let out a strangled laugh, and finally gave him a nod. She left her hand in his. "Okay, fine. I'll come. But only because I like your mother."

Fair enough. He wasn't above using whatever means he could get.

Then his eyes landed on the bed again, and he knew he was going to beg her for one more thing before they got out of there tonight. He couldn't help it.

He had to know.

"Holly." Her name came out in a low whisper. Was he really going to do this? It could change things.

His breaths grew heavier. He was still looking at the bed, and out of the corner of his eye he saw her head turn so that she was looking at the same. The energy in the room popped.

"What?" she asked cautiously.

He returned his gaze to hers and took her in. Her hair had come loose in the car during their drive, and she'd swept it back, twisting it high on her head. Tendrils trailed down around the sides of her face, while some stuck up, an unruly mess from the back.

Her eyes were wide. Her skin clear and a little flushed. As if her blood might be heated just the tiniest amount. Like his.

The fingertips of her free hand were shoved deep into the front pocket of her jeans.

She was going for casual, but he wasn't buying it. He let the pad of his thumb glide over the back of her hand, and like a caged animal, he wanted to roar when the move lit goose bumps up her arm. She was as aware of him as he was of her.

He could not walk out of there tonight without knowing what it was like to have his mouth on hers.

And if it was how he imagined . . . he would be in trouble.

He forced himself to look only into her eyes. He wanted her.

Like a dying man with only one last meal to choose, he wanted that meal to be Holly.

"Will you let me kiss you?" he asked.

Holly held her breath at Zack's words. Her heart pounded in her chest.

He was asking to kiss her.

Asking?

Not taking.

Not demanding.

He had to know she wouldn't say no if he merely leaned in.

Yet instead of closing the distance and taking what they both kept ignoring, he was insisting she admit that she craved his touch as much as he did.

She looked at his mouth. She did crave it. But what if she didn't want to stop with a kiss?

What if they *didn't* stop with a kiss?

"Tell me why you want to," she said instead. Where those words had come from, she had no idea. Her lips had already parted in anticipation, and her breath had long since left her lungs.

His brows lifted at the question.

Was he thinking she would just be this week's girl?

His eyes grew to near black as he stood in front of her. He still wore his jeans and black pullover. And he still looked like an erotic dream, only now standing upright. Especially with his hair mussed from the car ride, and his five-o'clock shadow scrubbing at his jaw.

She wanted to slide her palm over that jaw.

"Because I need to know," he stated simply.

She didn't have to ask. She got it.

She needed to know too.

Zack Winston was vanilla bean ice cream with whipped cream and sprinkles, all melting down over a thick, warm, chewy chocolate chip brownie.

And that was her favorite dessert.

The one she always had to try. Just to see if it could top her imagination.

She licked her lips. "One kiss?"

His nod came slow. "One kiss."

"But not because you're thinking it could be more?"

That little muscle spasm in his jaw went to work again. He shook his head. "I don't do more. Not the kind you're thinking of."

The kind that came from dating and ended with a ring.

That was what she'd been thinking of. But she knew better. Zack may give her "more," but it would be temporary and last for about one night.

The whole idea seemed a bit masochistic to her. What if it turned out really good?

"And then what?" Her words were spoken with intent. She was asking if he intended to take her to bed. She watched him contemplate the question. He glanced at the bed again, but only for a second, before returning his gaze to hers.

"Then I'll take you home."

She stared at him. He meant it. He really was just asking for a kiss.

That almost sounded safe.

Like it would keep her from doing something stupid such as stripping herself naked, then waking in the morning knowing she was heading over a cliff she couldn't come back from.

Because she didn't give herself easily to a man. Her feelings ran too deep.

Making love had to mean something.

But kissing . . .

She pulled her lip between her teeth and stared at his mouth. It was a wide slash in his broad face, and it looked hard and unyielding. And hot.

Kissing she could do.

She nodded and her voice came out as a whisper. "One kiss," she said. "And then we know."

But what they would do with the knowledge was what went left unsaid.

Zack took a step forward, putting him within inches, and she held her breath. Then he lifted his hand to her hair. His fingers fiddled with the clip at the back of her head until a pop broke the quiet. The plastic had snapped in two.

He cringed, and her hair tumbled around her neck.

"Sorry about that," he muttered.

"No problem." *Just do it!* "They were cheap anyway. I got them at—"

One large hand slipped into her hair, and her words stopped. Her face tilted up.

A breath slipped from her in a rush.

The smell of man permeated her nose, his scent exploding inside her, seeming to fill her from head to toe, and suddenly, all she could think about was the fact that she wanted so much more than a kiss from this man.

She wanted more than sex.

His face dipped and a moan sounded in the back of her throat.

Then his lips touched hers.

Neither of them moved. It was simply his lips on hers. Electricity zipped all the way to her toes.

Her nipples went hard, her breathing ragged, and Zack seemed as stiff as a board. She had the thought that he was giving her the chance to escape. As if she might change her mind.

Then his fingers slid along her jawline and dang if another tiny moan didn't slip out.

He angled his head and added pressure. Just a bit. It made a rushing sound ring through her ears. She nudged her chin forward.

Her lips clung to his as if desperate for more, and then she did something she would have sworn ten days ago she would never do to Zack Winston. She boldly ran her tongue across his bottom lip.

This time the moan came from him.

Then his tongue mimicked hers.

A shiver raced down the back of her neck.

"Zack," she whispered his name. Her body was so tight it was vibrating.

He pulled back. His dark gaze met hers. She saw so much desire there that her legs threatened to sit this one out.

"Do it," she whispered. She gripped her fingers into the front of his shirt as if that could keep her from falling. "Now."

He gave a nod and his mouth once again moved toward hers.

And then it landed.

This time, there was nothing timid about his moves. He didn't go slow, and he didn't give her a chance to run. He cupped the back of her head in both hands, and he slanted over her.

And he showed her how a man was supposed to kiss a woman.

His tongue parted her lips, stroking a heated path inside as he moved with purpose and just the right amount of pressure. She hung on for the ride. Her hands gripped at his biceps, the muscles under her fingers tight and hard. It made her yearn to lean into him and see what other parts might be tight and hard.

What she should *not* do, however, was climb him as if he were the very mountain peak at the top of her bucket list. Not for just one kiss.

But then he nibbled on her bottom lip, sucking it between his teeth, and her breasts declared the game unfair. They wanted in on the action. And they wanted in now.

A man should know better than to forget a woman's breasts.

She couldn't help herself. Call her easy—and maybe for Zack she would be—but she pushed forward until her chest crushed against his.

He stilled.

She groaned.

And then her better senses kicked into place.

She retreated, dropping her hands from his arms and breaking the kiss. Three steps backward and she bumped into the wall. She landed against a mirror and thumped her head against it. She stood there staring up at the ceiling, her breaths coming in gasps, trying desperately to figure out what to do next.

She'd darn near lost her mind with one single touch. A touch that hadn't even involved hands and had two layers of clothes between them.

What would it be like if they actually shed their clothes?

Her head moved back and forth as her vision blurred. *No.* No shedding of the clothes. She could not do that with Zack. She . . .

"I . . ." She closed her eyes. She didn't know what she wanted to say.

She pulled in a deep breath and blew it back out. One more, and she finally began to get herself back under control. Then she lowered her gaze and looked across the room to Zack.

He remained where he'd been. He seemed as shell-shocked as she, simply staring at her, his chest rising and falling, as if he, too, was at a loss for words.

With a shaky hand, she pushed her hair back from her face. The strands didn't stay put, slipping down to whisper against the slope of her neck. Damn, but that had been some kiss.

"I guess now we know," she finally got out. She knew that she was screwed.

No other kiss in her life had ever come close to that.

Zack nodded. "Now we know."

Holly swallowed.

"And now you have something to think about tomorrow night," he murmured.

When she looked at him in confusion, he flipped off the light switch and moved to the door. He held his hand out for her as if they'd done nothing more than step inside the room and take a look around.

Grasping his hand, she left alongside him. "What do you mean?" she asked. "Something to think about when?"

"At the end of your date."

Oh, crap. Keith. She had a second date with Keith tomorrow night.

And she certainly hadn't been thinking about *his* kisses while she'd been mouth to mouth with Zack.

Because the two would never come close to comparing.

Which meant . . . she groaned out loud. She'd just destroyed any potential with Keith. What would be the point of going out now? She didn't see him magically able to light that kind of flame.

Not after tonight.

Zack looked down at her as they moved through the room. The corners of his mouth rose in a resigned smile, and he gave her a little shrug. Yep. It had lived up to what both of them had expected.

Ridiculously hot.

And yeah, she was screwed. Dating other men had just gotten a hell of a lot harder.

They left the cabin and the warm night air touched her face. She was so hot and bothered that she considered running down to the river and dousing her head. Or maybe her whole body.

Snow White and the Huntsman chose that moment to appear, honking as if in agreement with the other thought running rampant in her head.

Yeah. She nodded at them as if they understood.

She was an idiot.

Zack pulled the car up to the front door of the B&B so Holly could get out.

She looked over at him as she reached for the handle. "You aren't coming in?"

"I need to run into town."

He needed to get the hell away from the woman by his side.

What had he been thinking kissing her like that? What had he been thinking kissing her at all?

Yeah . . . now they knew. *Hell.* He knew he would need a cold shower every night for the foreseeable future just to keep from knocking her door down and begging her to let him in.

Probably he should find a new place to stay. Maybe another town. Somewhere he wouldn't be tempted by that mouth and the glazed, soft look in her eyes. And those breasts!

He'd damn near forgotten his name when she'd pushed into him. The touch hadn't lasted long, but long enough to register that her breasts were soft and round, and so heavy against him that his palms still itched to hold them now.

Her nipples had been hard. They'd nudged against his chest and his mind had left his body.

One kiss was not supposed to mean body parts touching. He wasn't a saint.

And clearly not very bright.

One kiss.

He almost snorted at the absurdity of the idea. He'd known better.

And now he had to forget it.

Shit. He didn't know if forgetting was possible.

But it had to be. Because she was dangerous to his peace of mind. And his peace of mind was dependent on not letting any woman get to him. He knew how that would turn out.

"Okay then." Holly pushed the door open when he didn't give any more explanation, and slid a leg out. A gentleman would have gone around and opened the door for her.

But then, a gentleman wouldn't be having the thoughts he was.

As she stepped from his car, the top still down so he could see her clearly, he knew what he had to do. He had to back the fuck off.

Tonight had been a mistake.

Putting his mouth on her in the first place had been a mistake.

Not dragging her down to her bed had probably been the biggest mistake of all.

"I may not be around for the next few days," he said, reaching for excuses since his brain wasn't firing on all cylinders. "Need to catch up on some work. Plus, I'll be with Nick and Cody tomorrow night."

He stopped when lines marred her brow.

"What?" he asked.

"I should forget about Sunday, then? About going with you?"

Jesus. Sunday. With his mom.

Which reminded him of her and Keith. Whom he'd been trying to get her away from by talking her into going to Atlanta with him in the first place. She still had a date with Keith tomorrow night.

He closed his hand into a fist. "No," he said. "We'll go. I want you to."

Crap. What had he done? He looked up at her as he sat there. She wanted permanent, he chanted in his head. She wanted a good guy. A husband. Babies.

She didn't want him.

He wanted to make partner. And be in a big city.

He wanted a long, sweaty night with another round first thing in the morning.

"My mom will love it," he added. He was having trouble breathing. "Be ready to go by eight?"

"Fine."

She walked away from his car, and he sped off without a backward glance.

What he should do was go to the Bungalow and see if Gina was still offering. Maybe a night spent with another woman would wash the taste of Holly from his mouth.

He laughed out loud at the thought, the angry sound harsh in the whipping wind. There would be no washing the taste of Holly from his mouth. Not anytime soon. And the last thing he wanted was to spend the night with another woman.

But he did need to get his mind on something else. Otherwise, he would wind up outside Holly's door before the night was over.

If not Gina, surely there would be someone in town looking to do a little bump and grind.

Hell, he could even dance with Gina. He just didn't want to sleep with her.

Then he'd come back, take his cold shower, and not think about Holly.

Chapter Sixteen

H ow about that one?" Holly pointed through the passenger-side
window to the yard sale on the side of the road. "I'm certain I
see something there that I could use."

Zack cut his gaze to hers. He didn't pull over.

She frowned. "You're no fun when you have somewhere you
think you have to be."

It was Sunday morning and they were heading to Atlanta.
They'd taken her car so they would have room to bring his mother
back, and she'd let him drive. Mostly because she hadn't wanted to
do it herself. She preferred watching the sights around them to just
watching the road ahead.

But also because she'd wanted to be able to stare out the window
and ignore him if she felt like it. She'd heard from Linda Sue Friday
morning, Saturday morning, and again that morning. Apparently
Zack had been at the Bungalow each of the last three nights. He'd
been buying rounds, having a good old time, and rumor was that he
hadn't been shy about dancing with the ladies.

She had no idea if he'd gone home with any of the women, but
she wouldn't be surprised to find out he had. The thought twisted a

nasty, tight feeling in the pit of her stomach. She shouldn't let it bother her. Wasn't like Zack had ever offered anything more than a kiss.

As for her and her weekend, she'd cancelled her date with Keith and had gone to her room early. Because really, why go out? Compared to Zack, Keith's kiss had been brotherly.

He'd been disappointed, but when she'd declined to go out another night he'd asked if it had anything to do with Zack. He'd apparently been at the job site last week and had seen her bring Zack over on the four-wheeler.

Then there had been rumors milling about. After all, she and Zack had been seen together more than once. Both at the construction site and then again going to yard sales the next day. Thus they must be having an affair. She'd deflected questions whenever she was asked around town, but when Keith had brought Zack up, she'd gone quiet. She hadn't admitted he was to blame for her cancellation, but she certainly hadn't denied the suggestion either.

She'd also gotten a call from Tony of the my-mother-gave-me-money-to-take-you-out family over the weekend. He'd phoned her Saturday morning because he'd heard that she and Keith had broken up.

First, she and Keith hadn't been an item. They'd had one date. But no, she didn't want a date with Tony, either.

At this point, she wasn't sure she wanted a date with anyone. In fact, she was beginning to wish she hadn't gotten roped into the whole mess to begin with.

So instead of spending her Saturday night out on the town—or risking running into Zack and his many female admirers—she'd moved her stuff to the cabin, and had gone ahead and spent the night there.

"We're not supposed to be having fun today," Zack pointed out. And, as he hadn't all day, he didn't look at her when he spoke. "We have to be at Mom's in time for lunch."

She was beginning to wonder why she'd bothered to come. Since she'd gotten in the car, they'd barely spoken, she hadn't been able to get him to pull over to even one yard sale, and he was acting as if he wished she weren't there.

Even with the kiss that they were both now ignoring, she'd thought they could at least have a good time riding down together. It wasn't like they'd done anything more than kiss.

Of course, maybe the problem was whatever he'd been doing the last few nights. Or whomever.

Again, her stomach cramped up at the thought.

She sighed as they passed yet another yard sale and Zack didn't even give it a glance. *Fine.* The man had no spirit in him at all. She didn't want to deal with it. She settled back into her seat and closed her eyes. After moving into the cabin last night, she'd stayed up way too late watching a movie. Might as well catch up on her sleep.

When she awoke, a couple hours had passed and Zack was exiting off the interstate.

Holly sat up and looked around, but noticed that he was still careful not to glance her way. Enough was enough. If he'd slept with someone and didn't want to admit it to her, too bad. This silent treatment had to stop.

"Who was it?" She turned to him on the seat. "Gina? Melinda?"

Melinda O'Neil was heir to half the town's property, and often thought herself too good to go to the local hangouts. But rumor was that she'd been at the Bungalow the last couple of nights. Apparently Zack and his big-city dollars could bring her out.

Zack deigned to glance her way, but he didn't say anything.

"Or maybe you brought out the big guns and seduced Larissa Bailey out from behind the library desk?" Holly asked.

No one had ever seen Larissa go out on a date, but Holly figured if anyone could convince her, it would be Zack. And he had been seen in the library again yesterday morning.

"What are you talking about?" he asked. His words were loaded with frustration.

"Which one did you sleep with? Or was it all of them?"

His hand clenched around the steering wheel. "When, exactly, was I supposed to have slept with someone?"

"Last night. Friday night. Hell, probably Thursday night after you kissed me and then ran away."

He pulled off the road, taking the turn too sharp and locking the seat belt across her chest, then he steered the car into a small shopping center parking lot. Once parked, he turned off the engine and shifted on the seat to mimic her position. His jaw was clenched tight, and there was anger in his eyes.

What was *he* so upset about?

"I don't know what you've heard," he started, "but I wasn't the one not at the house last night."

"You were probably out till all hours. You were the two nights before." Yeah. She'd been awake, listening for him to come back.

"I was avoiding you," he bit out.

"By sleeping with everyone in Sugar Springs?"

He growled under his breath and reached for her hand. She jerked it back, not wanting to touch him, but he was relentless.

When he had her hand between the two of his, she became the one who didn't want to make eye contact. She couldn't believe he'd kissed her like that and had then gone straight to another woman's bed.

She shook her head back and forth as she felt tears burning behind her eyes. "Never mind," she murmured. She shouldn't have said anything about it.

She shouldn't have come.

"Holly." Zack's tone was solid and sure. He thought all he had to do was say her name and she'd fall under his spell.

She didn't look at him, so he reached one hand out and turned her face to his. When she met his eyes, she was ashamed because there were tears welling up in hers.

"I didn't sleep with anyone," he said gently. "I was staying away from you. Trying to let you live your life."

223

"Live my life?"

He sighed. "Date," he ground out. "I didn't want to be at the house to see you coming and going on dates with other men."

Funny, because she hadn't been.

"Why?" It wasn't like *he* had wanted her. Not for dating, anyway.

He shook his head as he stared at her. "You can be so silly sometimes."

"I'm not silly."

His hand cupped her cheek as she turned away, bringing her face back to his once again. "I was giving you space," he told her. "I wasn't off sleeping with anyone." His thumb slid under her eye and she realized he'd caught a tear as it had escaped.

"I didn't ask you for space."

"Sweetheart, if I hadn't given you space, I would have been in your bed Thursday night."

She gulped. And she would have let him.

She'd lain awake for hours listening for him to come to her door.

"But I didn't like it," he told her now. He shook his head again, and she could see the anger still riding hot inside him. "I don't like knowing that you're out with other men." His jaw clenched. "I know that isn't fair, but those are the facts. So I went out and I partied. I pretended I wasn't thinking of kissing you. Wanting to touch you." He leaned into her until she could smell the toothpaste from his breath. His eyes bored into hers. "And wanting to do a hell of a lot more than that."

The saliva had officially left her mouth.

He'd been avoiding her, so he could avoid her. So he wouldn't be tempted to get in her way.

Life was so ridiculously complicated sometimes.

She lifted a hand and pressed it to his where it covered her cheek. "Probably we shouldn't have kissed," she whispered.

A dry chuckle came from him, and he tilted his head until his forehead rested against hers. "Probably we shouldn't have."

"But just to let you know, I didn't actually go out with anyone the last two nights."

He lifted his head off hers. "What are you talking about? I know you had a date with Keith Friday night. If you hadn't, I would have taken you to Cody's with me."

He'd wanted her to go to dinner with him and his brothers? That knowledge probably made her happier than it should. She'd *wanted* to be there with him.

But she'd had a date.

"Didn't the rumors get back to you?" she asked. She gave a tight smile. "I cancelled."

"I haven't listened to rumors about you," he admitted. "Didn't want to hear them." His eyes narrowed. "Why did you cancel?"

She gave him a wry twist of her lips. "Seems you gave me something else to think about. With that knowledge, it seemed somewhat unfair to the man."

A smile broke the tension on his face, but was just as quickly swept away. "What about Tony?"

Her eyes went wide. "What about Tony?"

"I heard . . ." He paused and then wore a look of chagrin. "Okay, yes, I did hear that rumor. The moron wouldn't shut up at the bar last night."

She counted slowly to ten as she thought back on what she knew about Tony Francis. The guy didn't hold a steady-paying job, he sponged off his mother on a regular basis, and he'd once started a rumor that he'd hooked up with two models at the same time when there'd been a convention in town.

The man could not be trusted.

"What did Tony say, exactly?" she asked carefully.

The anger evaporated from Zack's eyes, to be replaced with a hint of a smile. "He said you two had snuck off to the old water mill the middle of Friday night, and that he was meeting you at your place late last night. He implied there would be a lot of condoms put to good use."

Her temperature soared. "Did you happen to see him at my place last night?"

A spark of anger returned to Zack. "I didn't see *you* at your place. Not at the bed-and-breakfast, anyway. I assumed you and Tony were at the cabin."

The cabin that she had only ever shown to Zack. Which he knew. She rolled her eyes. "And you call me silly."

"Hey. The man sounded like he knew what he was talking about."

"Do you think I would be with someone like him?"

And then Zack laughed. The sound was hearty and loud, and for the first time that day the both of them finally relaxed. He shook his head, still chuckling, and admitted that no, he didn't think she wanted to be with someone like Tony.

"The guy doesn't even have a job," she pointed out.

"I know. I'm sorry. Of course he's not what you're looking for." He'd shifted back to his side of the car, but still peered over at her. There was serious contemplation in his eyes. "I just wish it didn't bother me that you're 'looking' to begin with."

He was admitting that he was jealous. She got it. She was jealous too. And she wished Zack *was* the type who was looking.

What they didn't mention again was the kiss. Because yeah, maybe they shouldn't have done it, but given the choice, she knew she'd do it again.

"So we're good?" she asked.

He reached over and squeezed her knee. The touch felt intimate. "We're good."

Then he started the car and pulled back out on the road.

It took only ten more minutes before he stopped the vehicle at the front gate of a well-kept retirement neighborhood.

"Your mom lives here?" she asked. She'd pictured the woman living in the home where Zack had grown up. It made her sad to know she wouldn't get to see it. She'd been looking forward to exploring that part of his life. He may have acted like a jerk this morning, but she'd gotten to know him over the last two weeks. And grumpy or not, he was still her friend. She'd wanted to see the place that had helped shape him into the man he was today.

"She moved here after Dad died," he said. "After she broke her hip when she fell while trying to change a lightbulb," he added drily.

Ouch, Holly thought. That had probably hurt both of them. Mrs. Winston the physical pain, and Zack the mental. Holly knew how much he loved his mother. She suspected that now that their roles were reversing, he was likely returning some of that doting she'd doled out on him over the years.

"Is she okay now?"

"Physically she's good. It was a couple years ago. The healing process was long, but other than being a bit slower occasionally, she's fine. She has arthritis in the joint now that gives her problems on rainy days," he explained. He glanced at her as he passed through the gates. "She was supposed to wait until I got there that Sunday. I would have changed the bulb for her. Here she doesn't have to worry about things like that. I pay extra to make sure someone responds to her calls fast, including calls to change lightbulbs. She knows not to even *think* about trying to get up on a ladder."

Holly reached out and touched the hand he had resting on his leg. "It scared you?" she asked. "When she fell?"

He nodded. He turned his hand over and captured hers. "It shaved ten years off my life."

"How about not physically?"

"Huh?"

"You said physically she's okay. What about *not* physically?"

"Oh." His hand squeezed hers. "She misses Dad. She's gone downhill more over the last couple of years than I would have liked. She's sad sometimes. Aged a little." His thumb rubbed the side of her finger for a couple seconds before he added, "She gets lonely."

The emotion from Zack tugged at Holly's heart. She could understand. Her parents were crazy about each other, and she knew that if one went first, it would be heartbreaking for the other left behind.

She grew quiet, thinking, and they passed several streets before Zack turned onto a dead-end road. The neighborhood was nice. There was a social building in the center of things, well-maintained sidewalks throughout—with the occasional bench tossed in for those who needed to stop and catch their breaths—and the whole thing was gated. All the houses were single story and brick.

And high class.

"It's nice," she said.

"Mom missed the house a lot at first, but she really does like it here. She's made a number of friends. They keep her busier than she would have been at the house by herself."

"So she just sold it?"

His dark eyes glanced at her before he admitted, "I bought it."

Holly's jaw dropped.

"But I thought you lived in some ritzy penthouse?" That's what Cody and Nick had told her.

"I do. I've lived there for several years."

"Then why did you buy the house?"

He shrugged. "Just figured . . . I don't know. Maybe I'll want it someday."

He pulled into the driveway of one of the larger homes, but didn't turn off the car. Her heart thumped. He had a house. In case he wanted it someday. She stared at him. He was even less of a hard-ass than she'd given him credit for.

"It has a waterfall that Dad built for Mom there," he tacked on as if she'd asked him to explain himself. All she'd done was look at him. Which she was still doing. She smiled a little. He stared straight ahead, but she knew he could see her. So she smiled some more. He sighed. "Okay, fine," he grumbled. "I have a soft spot for the house I grew up in. Satisfied? We had a lot of memories there, and I wasn't ready to part with them yet."

Holly nodded. "I knew you were a softie when I first met you."

Of course, that was a total lie.

"Will you just forget it? I don't even live there."

"Does anybody?"

He shook his head. "I have it cleaned on a regular basis, and pay someone for upkeep." He paused before adding, "And I take Mom to visit a couple times a month."

Oh my god, he was killing her.

Too bad he had such issues with commitment. He would make someone a good husband someday.

"Why are you so against marriage?" she blurted out. "Family?"

His gaze shot to hers. It was a ballsy question. But one she wanted the answer to. Not so much because she wanted him to want her—though that wasn't so out of the question either—but because the more she got to know him, the more who he was didn't match who he claimed to be.

"I'm the job," he explained. "That's what's important to me."

"Your childhood home is important to you."

His knuckles whitened where he still had hold of the steering wheel. "Memories," he said. "You *live* in your childhood home. Surely you can understand the idea of that suddenly being gone. Out of your reach."

She slowly nodded. Yeah, she could understand. But it wasn't simply the memories that would disappear for her. It would be the idea of a home. A family. That's where the magic of her life happened.

"You didn't answer the question," she pointed out. "Why are you against marriage?"

His thumb tapped on the steering wheel for a good fifteen seconds.

"I have things I want to prove," he finally admitted. He didn't look at her as he spoke, and his words didn't come out hard. They were honest. "Success," he added. "Worth." He glanced at her and she saw a hint of the little boy he'd once been. "I want to make my mom proud."

A lump lodged in her throat.

She didn't point out that his happiness and his mother having grandchildren would quite possibly make the woman proud. Maybe she was off on her thinking. Maybe his mother *was* all about seeing him at the top of his game.

But she didn't think so.

She also didn't think he was going to give her anything else.

Turning to look at the house in front of them now, she took in the sprawling structure. "Is it just her living here?"

"Yeah." The word was dry with sarcasm. "She might have been okay to move, but she was not ready to give up her space. We had a large house. She refused to be stuck in what she called a 'box.'"

Holly liked her already. She wouldn't want to be stuck in a box either.

Though none of the houses they'd passed would Holly ever consider to be a box.

They got out and headed to the front door together, but it opened before they got to it. A lovely older lady with a stylish dark bob and kelly-green rimmed glasses stood there in greeting.

Zack had told Holly that his mom was seventy-five, and though her skin might have lost enough elasticity to look her age, she didn't carry herself that way. She was elegant. And she had class. Holly supposed that came from being a doctor's wife for fifty years.

"Holly." His mother said her name with such warmth that it caught Holly off guard. "When Zack told me that he was bringing you, I was thrilled. I've got a room all fixed up for you. I hope you'll love it. And I made you my chocolate cake." She took Holly's hands in hers, diamonds twinkling off three fingers, and squeezed. "You do like chocolate cake, don't you, dear?"

Holly nodded, laughing a little, and glanced at Zack. Did he not tell her that they weren't staying overnight? This was a day trip. "I wouldn't want to go through life not liking chocolate cake, Mrs. Winston. Thank you so much for having me."

"Ah." Mrs. Winston patted Holly on the cheek. "Such a sweet girl. Good manners and everything."

"Mom," Zack said in a warning tone.

His mother ignored him. "Call me Janet, dear. And I told Zackie you were the one for him. I knew it without even meeting you."

Holly's eyes went wide. The one for him?

Zack stepped in between them and took his mother's hand from Holly's. "That's enough. I told you she's just a friend. A good one."

He looked back at Holly as if to make sure she was okay, and she felt cared about. Truly. Not in a man-woman kind of way, but in friendship. She saw it in his eyes, and she knew that they did have something special. Even if they had kissed and almost ruined it.

Plus, he liked her mirrors. She'd seen that when she'd taken him to her house. He really had been impressed with them.

That had meant so much more to her than she'd known it would. So had showing him her work in the first place. She'd wanted to know what he thought.

"Your dad and I were friends too," his mother informed her son as they all made their way into the front room of the house. Holly noticed that the color of Janet's shoes perfectly matched her glasses. As did the scarf tied loosely around her neck. "Made the boring years after you left better," Janet added. She looked back at Holly and winked. "Trust me. *Better.*"

Holly couldn't help it. She laughed. This woman was the perfect person to be Zack's mother. Holly could just imagine her keeping him on his toes when he was little. Probably still did.

"I just love your shoes, by the way." Janet had stepped away from Zack and was now peering down at Holly's feet. "What size are they? Do you think they'll fit me?"

Holly knew she was going to love this woman. She stuck out one toe of her pink-and-black zigzag-patterned pumps. She'd toned down her style today. She had on cream slacks and a bright amethyst blouse. The shoes didn't even clash with her top. And she'd worn enough makeup to look her age, but nothing at all outrageous.

Her hair was secured in a large barrette at the base of her skull. She looked sophisticated.

Zack hadn't commented, so she'd assumed he'd approved.

"Mom," Zack butted in before Holly could slip off a shoe and pass it over. "You are not trying on Holly's shoes. You'll fall and break your neck."

"I don't need a man to tell me what shoes I can wear, dear. I've walked in heels much taller than those. Plenty of times."

"When was the last time?" he demanded.

His question made his mother give him an evil look, and Holly burst out laughing again.

Both of them turned to her. "What?" they asked in unison.

Holly motioned back and forth between them. "You have your mother's mean look. That's the scary look you keep trying on me. The one I think is cute."

His mother smiled with a mix of pride and fondness. "It is cute on him, isn't it?" Janet said. "Poor thing, he just can't pull it off."

Zack shook his head as if disgusted with both of them. "You two are made for each other." He turned and headed into the other room. "I'm going for the food. I'm starving."

Chapter Seventeen

With the meal finished, and her stomach more than full, Holly leaned back in her chair and eyed the piece of chocolate cake sitting on a plate in front of her. She'd forgotten to save room for dessert. No wonder Zack always came to his mom's for Sunday lunch. The woman was a terrific cook.

"Don't feel you have to eat that right now," Janet said, as if she could read her mind. "I just put it out in case you wanted it. You can always eat it later. We've got nowhere to be."

Again, Holly was reminded that Zack's mother thought they were spending the night. He must not have told her his plans had changed. He'd tried once again to convince Holly to bring her mirrors with them before they'd headed out that morning, but she'd steadfastly refused. She wasn't ready yet. Chicago had broken her spirit more than she'd realized.

She looked across the table to Zack, who wore a look of satisfaction with the meal that had to be close to what was on her own face. He also seemed to be happy.

Really, truly happy.

She'd seen him smile plenty of times over the last two weeks, and she'd seen him having a good time. But she wasn't sure she'd ever witnessed the contentment on his face that she did now.

It was heartwarming.

But still, the man had to tell his mother that they weren't staying. She kicked his shin under the table to get his attention.

"Ow." He sat up straight in his seat and shot her his scary look. She gave him a bored look back. Then she nodded her head toward his mom. "What?" he mouthed.

He must have replayed his mother's words in his mind because his eyes registered recognition. He faced his mother.

"I forgot to tell you, Mom, we won't be staying overnight after all. We can head back once the food settles."

"No, we can't." Janet shook her head and rose to clear the dishes. "I have to feed Mr. Dancer's cat tonight. I told him I would."

Holly jumped to her feet to help clear the table, and shot Zack a hard look. She didn't want to spend the night in his mom's house. That was too . . . personal. He made a face back at her.

"Can't we just feed him before we leave?" he raised his voice to be heard because his mother had disappeared into the kitchen already. Holly hurried in after her. They dumped the dishes, and headed back out.

"It's a her. Not a him," Janet explained, "and no, we can't just feed her before we leave. She eats at seven-thirty."

"She can eat at four."

"I won't do it. If she doesn't get her canned food at exactly seven-thirty, then she lets her irritation be known by leaving him a present on his bed." Janet shook her head. "I won't be the reason Mr. Dancer comes home from his great-granddaughter's first dance recital to find cat poop on his pillow. Plus, I already have Holly's room all made up."

"But she didn't bring clothes, Mom. Neither of us did. We need to go back tonight."

Janet gave an unconcerned shrug. "Then you can come back and get me tomorrow."

"Or I can leave you down here," he grumbled. "Forget Sugar Springs. You probably wouldn't like it anyway."

She turned to Holly. "I hope he's not this rude to your mother at her house, dear. I did teach him better manners. It was the lasagna. A thing to note for future reference. Pasta makes him grumpy."

Holly started to smile, then flattened the line of her mouth when she saw Zack's scowl.

"Mother," he said pointedly. As if the single word would control the situation.

It didn't.

"And I explained all of this to him on the phone," she continued to Holly. "He simply thinks he can always get his way. I don't know why. He hasn't gotten his way around me in thirty-three years. Except for that one time in the middle of his father's office party. I will admit, he did get his way that time. He was two." She made a face as if remembering a nasty event. "He had quite the temper."

"Mother," he tried again.

"I apologize that he didn't make the situation about today clear, but I would love if you'd reconsider and stay. There's a mall just fifteen minutes from here. I'm sure Zackie would be more than happy to buy you anything you need." She cut shrewd eyes to her son. "Since this *is* his fault."

The two Winstons had a stare-off, and Holly enjoyed the show. Looked like "Zackie" had learned his stubbornness from the best.

She was rooting for Mrs. Winston to win. Zack should have warned Holly that they would have to stay. He should have listened to his mother.

And though staying at his mom's house overnight did not make her completely comfortable, it wasn't as if she *couldn't* do it. She'd been working at the diner in the mornings, but not because she was needed so much as because she'd missed the people.

They still had the cook who'd replaced her, so there was no real need to hurry back.

Plus, she was enjoying watching mother and son interact. She could hardly wait to see how they did together in Sugar Springs.

Zack blinked first and Janet won the stare-off, and Holly made up her mind.

"That *would* give me time to enjoy my cake later, Janet. When I'm not so full. Thank you for the kind offer." She turned to Zack. "I'll be ready to go to the mall in fifteen minutes."

At seven forty-five that evening, they were back on the road. Only, they weren't heading to Sugar Springs. Zack had taken Holly shopping at the nearby mall, they'd all had an afternoon snack of cake—the rest of which was now securely packed up in the backseat—his mother had embarrassed him by dragging out photo albums, and Mr. Dancer's cat had been fed.

Then his mom had announced that she'd prefer to sleep in her old room before going to Sugar Springs. If Zack didn't mind.

At first he'd minded. A lot.

He hadn't had a woman at the house in ten years.

Plus, he knew what his mother was up to. Hadn't she already told Holly that she was perfect for him? He cringed at the memory of that. His mother had definitely butted in where she wasn't needed.

But then he'd seen the excitement in Holly's eyes at the idea of going to his house, and he'd been unable to say no. What guy wouldn't want to put that kind of look on a woman's face?

So off they'd gone. All packed into her SUV, and they were now approaching the home that held his life.

And he was having trouble *not* wanting her to be impressed.

The house sat in a suburb north of the city, and he couldn't help but glance at the passenger seat as they passed through the area. He hadn't grown up poor, that was for sure. If Holly had any doubts about that before, it would clear be now. The houses in this area were huge, the yards expansive, and the neighborhoods gated.

She wasn't saying a word, but her green eyes were taking everything in.

He found himself nervous as he waited to hear her opinion. It wasn't just the house that he'd grown up in. It was his house now. Not that he'd given thought to living there. Not consciously anyway. But the mere fact he'd kept it had to say something.

He didn't want to grow old alone.

Okay, yeah. He could admit that.

The thought of growing old alone bothered him. But he didn't know what that meant. Should he get a dog? Hire a live-in maid?

Or would he someday want to take a step back and reevaluate his life?

Holly turned her head to look at him, and gave him a soft smile. And an internal voice whispered, "Reevaluate."

When he finally made a turn into his neighborhood and slowed in front of the house, he watched her jaw go slack. The house was enormous.

"Is that three garages?" she asked.

Two four-car, and one two-car, to be exact.

"Dad liked cars," Zack replied. And then he felt pretentious. He'd never felt that way growing up because everyone in his school had been the same. But for an outsider, it must look like a lot.

"We also used to have two boats." His mother spoke up from the backseat as Zack turned into the long driveway. "At one point we had the two cars that Randolph and I drove every day, the two boats, Zackie's car,"—he cringed at the long-ago nickname—"and two classics. A 1936 DeSoto and a 1951 Chevy coupe. Oh, and the other car. The—"

"I'm sure Holly doesn't want to hear about Dad's hobbies, Mom." He glanced up in the mirror, trying to catch his mother's eye, but she ignored him. As usual.

"Sure I do." Holly turned to the backseat. His mother sat buckled tight in the middle of the bench seat. She had on her green coat, the one that matched her green glasses and green shoes, and Zack couldn't help the smile as he compared the two women. They both had their eccentricities, that was for sure. "I'd love to hear all about it," Holly told her now.

He didn't want his mother telling her about the car.

He reached the attached garage and shifted into park, stomping on the brake a little too hard and causing both women to jostle in their seats. "Let's get Mom inside."

Janet made a face at him. "He's a prickly one sometimes," she murmured. Then she looked at Holly. "Make him show you the car."

He planned to show her the car. He wanted to see her face when she saw it.

"You still have one of them?" Holly glanced at Zack.

"Yep." He opened his door and stepped out. She would just have to wait to find out more. "Which piece of luggage do you need for tonight, Mom?"

"All of them."

Zack stared in through the back window at his mother. "Really? You brought three bags. Couldn't you put everything you needed for one night in only one of them?"

She shook her head and unlatched her seat belt. "My toiletries are in the small one, my shoes for tomorrow in the Vera Wang, and my clothes in the garment bag."

He forced himself not to grit his teeth. He should have known. His father had grumbled about this exact habit of his mother's every time they'd gone on a trip. She always overpacked. And she did it in her own unique way. Zack used to think it was funny.

When his dad had been the one toting all the luggage.

Knowing she was heading to Sugar Springs for two weeks, his mother had packed up half of her closet. And now he got to drag it all inside. Twice. He shook his head and opened her door.

A woman never knew what she'd want to wear, she always said. *Better to be safe than sorry.*

Right.

Except his mother always wore the same color. How hard could it be to get "just the right look" when every outfit looked alike?

Love overshadowed his irritation as he stepped to the back of the car. He was glad she was still healthy enough to go with him. He wouldn't complain.

Plus, it would do no good if he did.

He grabbed Holly's and his bags from their shopping trip, as well as his mother's luggage, and slammed the door. When he picked everything up at the same time, he caught Holly watching him. She was wearing her impressed face.

He liked her impressed face.

"Lead the way, ladies."

They led, and he couldn't help but follow. And watch Holly's ass as he did.

They may have cleared the air between them and agreed that they shouldn't have kissed—but that didn't mean he didn't want to do it again.

Holly stood in the room Zack's mother had called the Display Room and took in everything around her. She'd expected priceless art.

She found popsicle stick art and lopsided pottery.

The popsicle art had lost a few sticks over the years, with dried glue leaving dark stains where it once had been held together.

From the looks of things, Janet Winston had kept every single thing her son had ever created for her. And then probably some he hadn't.

Her gaze fell on a crude crayon drawing of a stick figure with two large swoops hanging off its chest. The unsteadiness of the marks implied it had been done by a young child. Probably one who was just discovering that girls were different from boys. Janet had put it under glass in an eight-by-ten frame.

Footsteps sounded behind her. Zack had come into the room.

Her body woke up as he neared. "Your mom get settled in her room?" she asked.

It hadn't taken long after they'd come in for his mother to declare that she thought she'd turn in early. Holly suspected it had been merely a ploy to leave the two of them alone, but she wasn't about to complain. She liked being alone with Zack.

"She's in her room," he said. "Let's just hope she stays."

He stopped beside her and she looked over at him. Her mouth had watered at the sight of him hefting all that luggage earlier, and now she couldn't help but wonder how many more muscles were hiding under his clothes that she couldn't see.

Her gaze flitted down over his chest and she swallowed. Probably a lot.

This trip had not been a wise move.

Though it had pointed out one thing. He was way out of her league. There was nothing like driving up to a mansion of a house to make that clear.

"I see you've found my artwork," he said drily as he stared at the framed piece she'd been looking at. "Clearly I was a young Picasso."

She chuckled. "It is impressive," she confirmed. She tilted her head as she studied the blue stick figure in front of them. "Are those actually what they look like?"

"Good grief," he muttered. He stepped away from her. "Quit looking at it. I still can't believe she put that in here. She found it in my backpack in first grade, and no matter how much I begged, she wouldn't take it down."

"So you didn't draw it for *her*, then?"

One eyebrow lifted on his forehead and she laughed out loud. He joined her with a smile.

"Poor Zackie," she murmured.

"Oh, stop it." He groaned and scrubbed his hand down over his face. "My mother is a priceless piece of art all on her own. I can't believe she called me that all day."

He moved around the room now, taking in the different "art" sitting around. "This is the kind of stuff I was talking about before," he said. "She devoted a whole room to me in the house. What kid wouldn't feel special about that?"

Holly nodded. It would be impressive.

"Yet the one time I convinced a kid to come over, he took one look at this room and I became a laughingstock."

"Kids can be cruel."

"Yeah. They can be. I wanted to hate this room after that, but I knew that it was special. *I* was special. Who could hate something that made them feel that way?"

Exactly. It was clear his mother loved him dearly.

Holly felt bad thinking about him in elementary school, all the kids picking on him. She'd seen pictures of a younger Zack earlier in the day, and yeah, he'd been a little nerdy with his glasses and perfectly styled hair. And his sweater vests. But throw in kids talking about this room? *Poor Zackie.* He hadn't stood a chance.

"You planning to keep the display going forever?" she asked now.

When he just looked at her, she added, "It's your house. Yet it's still here."

He actually blushed. It was cute the way his ears turned pink. "My mother loves it. It'll be here as long as she's around."

And there went another piece of her heart.

Damn the man for being so sweet.

"So how many women have you brought here?" she asked. She needed to remember who he was. What kind of women he dated. "Wowed them with your great skills?"

He shoved his hands in his trousers. He'd dressed up today, same as her. Trousers and his light-gray pullover. His hair had lost a bit of its style, though. It looked as if he'd run his hands through it several times.

"One," he finally said.

She lifted her gaze to his. That was not what she'd been expecting to hear. "You don't bring them over on a daily basis to impress?"

His head angled with attitude. "I don't see women on a daily basis," he pointed out. "I work too damned hard for that."

"Weekly then?" She teased.

He grinned like the little boy he once had been. "I do see women on a weekly basis," he admitted. "Usually."

Jealousy was a nasty thing. It came with a sharp, jabby point.

She kept the smile on her face. "So you don't bring them here to show off your big house?" She waved her arm through the room. "Or your very own gallery?"

He shook his head and an odd expression passed over his face. "They're more the impressed-with-a-penthouse type."

Ah, yes. They would be.

"And ten years ago?" she asked. "I take it she wasn't the impressed-with-a-penthouse type? What happened then?"

"I didn't have my penthouse then. Come on." He held out his hand to her. "Enough talking. Let me show you the rest of the house."

So she took his hand and they left the room.

And he didn't explain ten years ago.

They wandered through room after room. Each one larger than the last, and each making her think of her little log cabin more. She felt like a fish out of water here. She only hoped she didn't come across that way.

It would break her heart if he looked at her as the shop owners in Chicago had.

Like she didn't belong.

They stopped in the enormous kitchen, and she took in the stainless steel stove with the six-burner top. It stood in the middle of the room and had a copper hood hanging over it. She got all tingly just thinking about standing there cooking on that monster.

"I sure would like to cook your mother pancakes on this thing tomorrow morning."

When he didn't reply, she glanced over at him. He was watching her.

"Does your mother not like pancakes?" she asked.

"She likes pancakes."

Holly nodded. "Okay, then how does she eat them? Is she as boring as you?"

His dark eyes burned on hers. She suspected he was fighting the urge to give her his scary look, so she smiled, giving him her best charm. He rolled his eyes. But he also smiled.

"She would be in heaven if you cooked her your happy pancakes," he finally admitted.

The charm disappeared and pure joy filled Holly's face. "Really? You'd let me cook those for her?"

"I suspect I couldn't stop you if I wanted to. But I want mine plain."

She made a face at him. "Just when I think you're loosening up, you go and ruin it."

She headed to the cabinets and started opening and closing doors. Each one held dishes, appliances, or nothing. Then she opened the refrigerator.

And then she remembered.

No one actually lived there.

"You have zero food in the house," she accused.

"Keeps the bugs out."

She sighed before holding out her hand. "Give me my keys. I'll run to the store and get what I need."

He shook his head and once again reached for her hand. "I have a better idea."

"But I need to go to the store."

"I'll take you to the store. I want to show you something first."

"Oh."

She hurried to keep up with his long strides as he pulled her along beside him. They left through the back door of the kitchen and headed across the yard.

"Where are we going?" she asked.

He nodded toward the farthest garage.

"Oh," she said again, only this time she drew the word out into two syllables. His mother had mentioned there was still a car here. Energy pumped through her at the thought that Zack intended to show it to her.

"You're going to show me the car, aren't you? What kind is it?" she asked. When he didn't answer, she added, "How old is it?"

Still no answer.

"What color? I'll bet it's blue. Or maybe white? Oh . . . how about cream?"

He just eyed her.

She grew quiet with a sigh, then focused on his hand still wrapped around hers. It was large and warm. And it totally engulfed her fingers. She'd been trying not to think of how many times he'd grabbed her hand today.

It had felt good.

Even though she couldn't let it mean anything.

"Will you let me drive it?" she asked. She made her voice as sweet as she was capable of.

Zack grunted and lengthened his strides.

Then they were at the door of the garage, and he took out his keys. A different look came over him as he slid the key into the lock. One she hadn't seen before.

It was a mix of anticipation and pure joy. Darkness had fallen while they'd been in the house, but a motion sensor light had flickered to life as they'd approached the garage. He looked at her now, and she caught a glint of excitement deep in his eyes.

Whatever was in this garage, Zack loved.

The door opened and he flipped on the lights. She stepped in beside him. And then she stopped.

"Oh. Wow," Holly whispered.

She could do nothing but stare at the car. She didn't have a clue what kind it was, but it was old, and gorgeous, and *ohmygod* sexy.

"It's a 1949 Buick Roadmaster Series 70 convertible coupe, royal maroon in color."

Zack turned to Holly. She was impressed.

As he'd wanted her to be.

"You still think my Mercedes is hot?" he added.

She slowly shook her head. "Not like this."

He laughed. That's what he'd expected. The car even turned *him* on.

"How long have you had this?" she asked. She moved forward a few feet as if drawn to it under a spell.

Ah, the big question.

"Do you mean how long have I had it *running*? Or how long has it been sitting in this garage?"

She whirled back around. "You didn't restore it?"

He nodded. Pride filled his chest, though he couldn't take all the credit.

Her eyes went hot, and she looked as if she might jump his bones right then and there.

He knew it wasn't directed at him so much as the car. It was a sexy-as-hell car. The long nose, curved lines, and sparkling chrome grill were enough on their own, but then there was the fact that it was a convertible. He'd left the top off when he'd taken it out the weekend before, and it sat gleaming under the fluorescent lights.

Holly clearly had a thing for convertibles.

And he had a thing for Holly.

"Want to go for a ride?" he asked.

Her eyes grew round. "Really?"

He nodded. Oh, yeah. Really. He couldn't wait to see her in it. "You need to get stuff from the grocery store, right?"

She looked back at the car as if not believing he would let her in it, so he closed the distance between them.

"There's only one condition," he spoke in a teasing whisper. He stood near to her now. Close enough to hear each breath she pulled in and out of her lungs. He rubbed a strand of her hair between his fingers. It was as silky as he remembered from when he'd slipped his hands behind her head the other day. When he'd kissed her.

"What's the condition?" She turned bright-green eyes up to his. She was breathing fast, as if he'd already kissed her senseless. Instead of just thinking about it.

"You have to take down your hair." He nudged his chin toward her hair. He didn't like the boring clip holding it behind her neck.

She gave him a questioning look.

"If we're riding with the top off of this baby, you're letting your hair blow in the wind."

Her dimple was back. "Deal."

She stuck out her hand, and he took it. He *did not* pull her into him as he wanted to. He'd had the thought several times throughout the day to suggest that they go on a date. That she should forget the other men. But that wasn't fair.

Not for her.

She was looking to settle down.

He was just looking to keep her away from other men. And to get her naked.

So he'd kept his desire to himself. And his lips off hers.

It hadn't been easy.

They both climbed into the car, but before he started it he simply let her have her look. She was like a puppy checking out a new place. She ran a finger over each of the buttons and dials in front of her, and popped open the glove compartment to check inside. She leaned across the seat to make a quick sweep of his side of the dash.

Then she turned, rising to her knees, and did a thorough check of the backseat. Her butt stuck in the air, and that, combined with her fingers sliding sensuously over the leather, caused him to tighten below his belt.

Watching Holly check out his car was the hottest thing he'd ever seen.

"You like it?" He grinned.

She moaned. "Oh man, I could so have sex in this car."

Her eyes jerked to his and she slapped a hand over her mouth. "I didn't mean . . ." she mumbled behind her hand.

He laughed out loud. She looked almost sick at her words. He reached for her hand, leaning into her as he did, and pulled it away from her mouth.

"I know what you meant." He winked. He also closed the distance and planted a tiny—innocent—kiss against her lips. "I feel the same way," he whispered.

"Oh wow, Zack." Her eyes were still burning with excitement as he pulled away, but he didn't think it had anything to do with him.

Suddenly he was jealous of his own car. Yes, the kiss had been tiny, but he'd thought she'd at least register it. At this point, he wouldn't be surprised if she didn't even know he was in the car with her.

"Where did you get this?" she asked. "And did you really restore it? How long did it take?"

He started laughing again. He couldn't maintain jealousy while she was so enthusiastic. And then it occurred to him that he'd laughed more in the last two weeks than he had in ten years.

Hell, he'd laughed more in one day than he had in ten years.

"My dad bought it when I was sixteen," he explained. "He'd restored the DeSoto before I came along, and then the Chevy when I was a kid. I'd sit out here for hours and watch him. He'd let me hand him tools, but mostly we were just together. Then I turned sixteen," he said, making a face with the words. Those had not been his best years.

"What happened?" she asked. "Though I can guess. I remember Sean when he turned sixteen. Or fifteen, maybe. I did my best to steer clear of him."

"Right. I wasn't the easiest to get along with, and since Dad was already in his sixties, I had less than no time for him. So he bought this beauty. It didn't run, it was old and rusted, and I hated it on sight. Even worse, I wanted nothing to do with helping him restore it."

"How could you hate it?" Again, she ran her hand along the dash and he had fantasies of that hand being somewhere else. "It's like a three-thousand-dollar pair of shoes."

"That doesn't match your clothes?" he teased.

"Exactly." She punched the word with life. "So that all you see are the shoes."

He paused as her words sunk in. Interesting. She was her shoes. And all she wanted was to be seen.

He once again reached for her hand. He brought it to his lap.

When she turned to him, he reiterated slowly, "I hated it . . . because I was sixteen."

She gave an understanding nod.

"He'd hoped it would bring us together, but it didn't. Not immediately. But during college I started helping him on weekends. Until the course load got too much to even come home."

"Dad never worked on it without me, though. He told me when he bought it that it was our car. If I didn't want to work on it *with* him, then it could just sit here."

"That must have killed him," she whispered. "Having this sitting here. You know he had to want to fix it up and take it out."

"Yeah," he agreed. "I get that now. At the time, all I got was that he'd bought a piece of crap instead of the car that I did want."

"What did you want?"

Embarrassment slid over him. "A silver Mercedes-Benz convertible."

Her brows shot up. "Looks like you got one."

"I did. But not until this year."

"Why this year? Surely you could have afforded one before."

It was his turn to run a hand over the beauty of the car. Every time he sat in it, it was as if he were talking to his dad. They'd gotten beyond their troubled years, but they'd never had the chance to finish the car together. He'd graduated college and gone on to law school. Then there had been the internship. Then the job.

And then his dad had died.

He brought Holly's palm to his mouth and pressed a light kiss to the center of it. "Because that's when I finished this car," he said.

Understanding dawned on her face. He'd known she would get it. He wouldn't allow himself to have his dream car until he'd gotten this one done.

"You had to finish it without him."

"Yeah."

"I'm sorry." The words were sincere. "I didn't know him, but he raised you, and I do know you. So I feel like I understand who he was. He would have been proud that you finished it."

Zack nodded. He knew his father would've been proud.

That's why he'd done it.

He'd always wanted to make his dad proud.

Her hand was still in his—and she still didn't seem to notice—so he nonchalantly turned it loose and faced the front. He hit the garage door opener, and gave Holly a wink.

"Ready to go for that ride?" Enough of the heavy stuff. He wanted to see that glorious blonde hair blowing in the wind.

She grinned, her eyes showing the happiness that was rooted deep inside her, and he took a step closer to figuring out what he wanted in his life.

Starting the car, he pulled out of the garage and smiled at the woman by his side.

It might just be her.

Chapter Eighteen

O rder's up!"
   The bell rang and Holly looked up from the front counter to make sure Janice had returned from her break. The Tuesday lunch crowd had been heavy with the influx of tourists as the city ramped up for the Firefly Festival, but had been thinning out over the last thirty minutes. Thus Holly had shifted from waiting tables to working on the new rubber "ducks" they'd had made for this year's games.

The Marshalls hosted the rubber duck races down the river, and were excited that their new products had finally arrived. Her sister-in-law, Jillian, had found a company to design and produce fifteen thousand firefly-shaped "rubber duck" toys.

Only three thousand more needed to be tagged with a number before they could be raced.

Thankfully, Holly had no problem with monotonous tasks. It gave her a chance to chat with the customers. Jean Rogers was currently parked on the other side of the counter from Holly. She'd come in about fifteen minutes before, ordered a strawberry milkshake, and had been filling Holly in on the changes to the grocery store's Firefly Festival booth ever since. Jean had worked at Sam's

Foodmart for years, and as she'd known the owner since she'd been a child, she'd always felt she had an "in" with the decision making.

"So I told him, we need to fancy up. Some new paint. Maybe even a flower arrangement on the counter. It'll pull the customers in."

Sam's Foodmart brought their booth out once a year, and this coming weekend was it. The grocery also housed a small deli; therefore, in sticking with the "if we can fry it in grease, we do" mentality of local festivals, Sam would sell Monte Cristo sandwiches and slices of hand-tossed pizzas from the booth. Thankfully, the pizza would not be fried. They'd once sold cupcakes as well, before Joanie had opened Cakes-a-GoGo. Now they ceded the baked goods to her.

"Anyway, Sam didn't take too well to my ideas." Mrs. Rogers made a perturbed face.

Holly nodded appropriately and picked up another firefly to mark with the next number.

"But I'm telling you it's a good one. You know Miley has loads of talent, what with her drawing since she was just a little girl and all." Mrs. Rogers had always been proud of her daughter's abilities. "So I snuck her the key to the shed, and I told her that Sam approved of changes, but that he wanted to be surprised come Saturday, you know? He'll thank me." Mrs. Rogers nodded. "Because my vision will put Sam on the map."

Sam was already on the map due to owning the only grocery store in town that would make party trays with pigs in a blanket. He was a regular entrepreneur.

"Have you seen it yet?" Holly asked. She remembered Miley from school, and though the girl did have talent, she'd also once believed in excessive vibrant colors. Holly had no idea if that theory remained.

"Oh, no." Mrs. Rogers shook her head. Her hair didn't move with the motion. "I thought it would be better if it was a surprise to me too. More exciting that way, don't you think?"

"Absolutely."

What Holly thought was that Jean Rogers was eventually going to give poor old Sam a heart attack with all her ideas. And if Miley had changed that boring white booth that Sam had refused to paint since he'd bought it secondhand twenty years ago, that heart attack might be coming sooner rather than later.

"So anyway." Mrs. Rogers put her hands in her lap and took on an air of innocence. "I heard things didn't work out with either Keith or Tony."

Irritation had Holly setting down her firefly. She and Zack hadn't gotten back into town until the middle of the afternoon yesterday, yet in the last twenty-four hours, Holly had heard no less than ten people comment on how things hadn't worked out with Tony and her.

"Things never started with me and Tony, Mrs. Rogers. And I only went out with Keith the once. It's just bad timing for us."

"I know, dear." Mrs. Rogers patted Holly's hand and made a tsking noise. "And it's good to see you're over it."

Holly picked up a firefly and rolled her lips together. Sometimes it was best to just ignore.

"That's why I wanted to stop by today. I have a nephew, you see—"

"No." Holly shook her head.

"But he's a good boy."

"I'm done. I'm off the market."

She wasn't off the market. She just didn't want anyone else shoving a man down her throat. Especially when all she could think about was Zack. She'd wait for him to go back to Atlanta, and then she'd start all over. In a Zack-free, no-kissing-experiment zone.

Of course, it wasn't like she'd ever forget that particular experiment.

"Oh?" Mrs. Rogers asked. She looked around as if the man who'd captured Holly's heart must be nearby. There was a family of five in the diner, all wearing Sugar Springs Firefly Festival T-shirts, a couple of painters who'd been knocked out of work for the afternoon due to a busted pipe flooding the house they were supposed to be painting, and a handful of teenagers who were talking more than drinking the milkshakes Holly had made for them thirty minutes before. "Who is it?" Mrs. Rogers asked.

"There isn't anyone, Mrs. Rogers," Holly assured the woman. "I'm just not interested. I didn't really mean to be dating in the first place."

Worn blue eyes looked at her in puzzlement. "I don't understand."

"I didn't think it through. I need to wait a while before getting serious."

"Oh." The word was spoken sadly that time. As if Mrs. Rogers had just given up hope and lumped Holly in the old-maid category. Terrific.

The outer door opened and Holly looked, if for no reason other than to look away from Mrs. Rogers. At the sight that greeted her, she set down her firefly.

"Oh my," she whispered.

Jean swiveled around on her seat. She had the same response.

As did probably every other female in the place.

Walking through the door had to be one of the best-looking men Sugar Springs had ever produced. Over six feet tall with tight, compact muscles, slicked-back brown hair, and eyes that were a crystal-clear blue. They drooped just a little on the outside edges, only enhancing his looks, and his jaw sported sexy, groomed stubble that screamed for a woman to trace her fingers over it.

He looked like Ryan Gosling, only with longer hair.

"That's . . ." Mrs. Rogers whispered, but her words seemed to get stuck.

"Bobby 'Hounddog' Thompson," Holly finished.

She wouldn't have recognized him if not for the mouth. His lips carried a hint of a pout. One that had been the object of many girls' affections during his high school days.

Hounddog turned toward the counter and when his eyes landed on her, they lit up.

"Holly." He drew the word out as if she were the sweetest-tasting honey he'd ever put to his lips. She blushed.

Holy moly, no one had told her that Hounddog had grown up to be *that*.

"Hey, Hounddog," she greeted him. She went for country sweet, but it came out low-throated hungry.

His smile was naughty and fast. "Now Holly, surely you've heard. I'm just Bobby now. I'm a changed man, darlin'. Didn't your mama tell you? I've put my wanderin' days behind me."

Her mama had told her that she'd lined Holly up for a date with this man.

And Holly had said no.

But . . . *damn*.

And then she remembered why she wouldn't date Hounddog Thompson. Because he would most likely *never* put his wanderin' days behind him.

He sure was pretty to look at, though.

"Holly here is looking for a man," Mrs. Rogers supplied.

"No!" Holly butted in. She turned wide eyes to the woman. "I just told you that I'm *not*."

"Is that right?" Hounddog chuckled. He granted Mrs. Rogers a smile, and danged if the woman didn't flutter her eyelashes at him.

"She was just telling me about the poor heartbreaks she suffered only last week," Mrs. Rogers added. She did that tsking thing again. "Two of them. Bless her heart."

Oh, for crying out loud.

"Mrs. Rogers." Holly enunciated carefully. This had to stop.

"I've got to run, dear." Mrs. Rogers reached over and patted Holly's hand, then blasted Hounddog with a sad smile. "Broken-hearted, I tell you. See if you can't help out, won't you?"

Hounddog promised he'd do his best, then turned to Holly as Mrs. Rogers scurried off. "Your mama told my mama that I could find you here."

Her mama needed to keep her mouth shut.

"What are you doing out looking for me, Bobby? My mama should have also relayed that I'm a busy woman." She held up a firefly in each hand. "Unless you've come to help me number these, I've got no time for the likes of you."

The smile that had once made many a teen girl swoon reappeared. It almost made Holly do the same. Hounddog most definitely was a good-looking man. Seems this town wasn't lacking in the good-looking man department quite as badly as she'd once thought.

First Jesse comes home, and now Hounddog.

"What if I offer to help?" Bobby suggested.

Holly shook her head. "I'm sure you've got better things to do."

"Nah." He reached over and snagged up a firefly. "Show me what to do. I'm waitin' for Dad to get done over at Doc Maples'. He had a tooth break this morning. Thought I'd drop by and say hi to the cutest blonde Sugar Springs High ever saw."

She snorted. They both knew she'd never been the cutest blonde. One of her brothers, maybe. But she and Hounddog had been friends once upon a time. She was glad he'd stopped by.

"Suit yourself." She handed over a Sharpie, and together, the two of them began working on the rubber toys. "It's good to see you, Hounddog."

The man gave her one of his panty-melting smiles and she just laughed.

The door opened again, and this time Zack and Janet walked in. He'd told Holly he would be introducing his mother to his brothers today. She hadn't realized he intended to do that here.

She shot him a welcoming smile. They'd had a good time in Atlanta. The car ride had been spectacular. Then she'd fixed him and Janet pancakes yesterday morning.

And thankfully—she supposed—no other kiss had been forthcoming.

There might have been the desire for one. On her part. Probably his too. But they hadn't acted on it. Very grown up of them.

Zack's gaze shifted to Bobby, sitting there with her fireflies in his big hands, and damned if she didn't blush again. She felt as if she'd just been caught out behind the bleachers . . . with someone *other* than her boyfriend. Instead of returning her smile, Zack merely lifted his brow, then led his mother to a booth.

Holly blew out a breath. Bobby followed her gaze to Zack. "Friend?" he asked.

"Yeah."

"More?"

She looked at Bobby. Was Zack more? *Yes.* Would she admit it? "No," she said.

Bobby shot her a disbelieving look but didn't call her out on the lie. He picked up another firefly. "So tell me what you've been up to since I left. Word is you spent some time away recently."

Before she could form an answer, her cell rang from inside her pocket. She pulled it out, expecting it to be her mother telling her that Hounddog was back in town. Instead, it was a number she didn't recognize. The area code was Chicago.

"I'll . . ." She had no idea who it could be. Her cousin, maybe? But it wasn't Megan's number. Holly glanced back at Bobby. "Be right back."

Bobby nodded, and Holly stepped into the kitchen to take the call.

"Ms. Marshall?" said an unknown female voice.

"Yes?"

It wasn't especially quiet in the back room, but it was more private. She stepped around the side wall until she stood behind the grill so she could look out over the dining room as she talked. Nick and Cody came in with Cody's daughters and headed to Zack's table.

Nervous excitement pounded in her for Zack. He was bringing his family together today. She wanted to go out there and be a part of it.

"Megan Dillard gave me your number," the woman said in her ear. "I hope that's okay."

Holly suddenly thought of the "someone" who'd seen her mirror at her cousin's house. And the someone that someone supposedly knew.

Was that who was on the phone?

"I suppose that depends on what you're calling for?" she replied cautiously.

A forced laugh sounded in her ear. It was like fingernails scraping down a chalkboard. "It's about your mirrors, Ms. Marshall. My name is Elizabeth Daughtry. I have a customer who attended a party at your cousin's apartment last week. She was very impressed with a piece of your work she saw there. I requested a viewing, and Ms. Dillard had me in her apartment this morning. I'd like to talk to you about seeing more."

All the blood rushed out of Holly's head. She had to put her hand onto the wall to keep from falling.

Someone wanted to see her work?

It became hard to breathe.

Rabid joy was the first thing to sweep through her, only to be followed just as quickly by anger. She couldn't help but wonder if the woman on the phone was one of the people who'd snubbed her last month.

She closed her eyes in an attempt to block the memory of her treatment inside one of the more ritzy boutiques. The owner had looked her up and down, peering over her nose at Holly as if her appearance alone were so repulsive that it might bring the woman's breakfast back up.

When Holly had ignored the visual barb and started on her sales pitch, the woman had literally laughed out loud.

"Surely you don't think you *could make anything our customers would want?"*

She'd continued to snicker, made another rude comment—that time concerning Holly's apparent low-class vocabulary—then had waved over the security guard with one sweep of a long, witch-like finger.

The woman had been a first-class bitch.

All because Holly didn't dress and speak rich enough for her.

"Can I ask the name of your store, Ms. Daughtry?" Holly held her breath.

As the woman rattled in her ear, she watched Zack. He was watching her.

He was talking to his mother, but his eyes were on her. One eyebrow lifted in question as if to ask if she was okay. She nodded. She was fine. And the store Ms. Daughtry worked for was *not* one of the ones Holly had visited. It was even more upscale than what she'd targeted.

The fact that this woman wanted to see her work made her almost ill.

Holly looked out the front windows to the still-empty storefront across the street. She'd given the idea of opening her own place a bit of thought since she'd sold those first two mirrors, and now with the uppity voice chirping in her ear, Holly couldn't help but wonder if she should give it more. Couldn't help but wonder if she could make a go of it.

Chicago would be better, though. More clients, more money. She could *be* someone.

And it wasn't like she'd have to live there to do it.

That had been her original plan, but after her brief experience, there was no way she'd move there now.

But sell mirrors there? She nodded to herself. She just might do that. Even to a snooty bitch.

She made arrangements with Ms. Daughtry to send a digital portfolio within the next two days, and got off the phone.

"You okay?" Brian asked from the grill.

"Huh?" She barely gave him a glance. She needed to get home and pick out the pieces she wanted to showcase, as well as set up a spot to photograph them. Then she'd need a piece of black velvet for the backdrop. And a camera. She didn't even have a decent camera.

"The phone call," Brian said. "Everything okay? You look like you've seen a ghost."

She nodded. Then she shook her head. "No. No ghost. I'm fine. I just . . ." She glanced around, wondering if there was anything else she absolutely had to do before she left. "I need to go. I think. Can you box up the fireflies? I'll finish them tomorrow."

"Sure." Her brother nodded. He watched her carefully, as if he feared she might flip out and start screaming obscenities at the customers. "Anything wrong?" He pointed to the phone.

"No. I just . . ." Oh, my God. Someone wanted to see her work. Her hands began to shake. She looked out the order window and found Zack again. She wanted to tell him about the call. And then she wanted to go home and get busy. "You got a camera I could borrow, Brian?"

"Sure. You need it today?"

"Yeah."

"I'm here for another thirty minutes. I'll bring it to you. You going to be at the house?"

She had moved to grab her purse from the office, and as she came out, she saw the concern on her brother's face. They all gave her grief about men, and they'd picked on her all her life for one thing or another, but they also loved her. And she'd excluded them from something that was a vital part of who she was.

They thought her mirrors were a hobby.

They had no idea they were her life.

It was time to change that.

"Can you bring it out to the cabin?" she asked. "Maybe even hang around a couple hours? I could use some help."

"Sure." There was no delay in the response. He was her brother. Her family. He'd be there for her. She wasn't sure why she'd ever doubted that.

He'd probably even go to Chicago and punch all the snotty people in the face if she asked him to.

"Thanks," she said. Then she stood on tiptoe and kissed him on the cheek.

She headed out through the dining room, hoping to get a minute alone with Zack. She wanted to tell him about the call. Yet as she stepped through the door, she saw that his mother and brothers were hitting it off. She didn't want to interrupt.

And then Hounddog smiled at her.

She got a little tickle in her stomach. That boy was dangerous with that smile.

"Important call?" he asked.

She looked down at the phone still clutched in her hand. "Yeah, actually. Sorry, Bobby, I've got to run. Can we catch up later?"

"Sure thing." He rose and gave her a hug. While he had her close, he planted a friendly kiss on her cheek. "Real good to see you, Holly."

"You too."

Zack looked up from the table while Holly stood in the circle of Bobby's arms. The planes of his face hardened.

"Can I walk you out?" Bobby asked.

She shot one more peek at Zack. He looked to be stewing. Jealous. But he had no right.

"Absolutely."

Without a glance back, she turned and walked out the door with Bobby "Hounddog" Thompson. All the while hoping Zack was watching. And that it stuck in his craw to see her with another man.

Zack sat at the table, his fingers tight around his water glass, while Holly left the building with the man who'd just kissed her. That made three times in less than one week he'd had to watch another guy put his lips on her.

She'd been laughing with this one as Zack had come in. Not a polite, friendly laugh. The kind filled with true I'm-happy-to-be-around-you, I-couldn't-stop-myself-if-I-tried bursting joy.

The kind that weakened Zack every time he saw it.

That was what he liked best about Holly. She always found a way to be happy. She could have her feet completely ripped out from under her, and she'd find a way to roll over and start dancing.

He wanted that.

He wanted Holly.

Zack had also noticed that the guy she'd left with wasn't hard on the eyes. Which he suspected she'd been well aware of herself. She certainly wasn't blind. It made him wonder where they were heading off to.

And what that call had been about.

She'd looked shell-shocked as she'd stood talking on the phone. She'd sought him out with her gaze, and ridiculously, he'd expected her to come out from the back and tell him all about it.

Instead, she'd hugged another man and left without looking back.

Zack's temperature rose. Jealousy was such a bitch.

He dragged his attention back to the extra-large booth where he sat. His mother, brothers, and nieces were having a good time. His mom had immediately fallen for the two men who looked so much like him. And truth be told, they acted a lot like him too. Zack found it interesting that genetics played as big a role in what shaped a person as the environment they grew up in.

But even more importantly, she was head over heels for Candy and Kendra.

If the girls lived in the same city as his mother, he suspected Janet's long-time love of doting would reappear in full force.

"And what grade will you two be in?" his mom asked.

Candy sat up straight, as if to make herself look older than she was. She was tall and thin, and with her dark eyes and matching smile, looked strangely almost as much like him as his brothers did.

"Eighth grade, Mrs. Winston. I'm on the basketball team. First string next year."

"And I'm one of the top cheerleaders," Kendra piped in. She swished her long brown hair back over her shoulders and preened from between her uncle and sister.

Candy slid her sister a look as if to point out that "one of the top cheerleaders" didn't quite compare to first string of the basketball team.

"I also have a boyfriend," Kendra tacked on.

"Oh my," his mother murmured. "Is it serious?"

Both Candy and Cody guffawed as if the idea wasn't possible. Kendra rolled her eyes.

"It's just as serious as I want it to be, Mrs. Winston. I'm not looking to settle down yet."

"Well, that's certainly a good thing." His mother reached across the table to pat both girls on the arm. "And please, feel free to call me Janet. Or even Grandma, if you want."

Guilt cracked Zack's chest open. His mother wanted grandchildren and he was doing nothing to give them to her.

He had no intention of giving them to her.

Only . . .

He looked at the door again where Holly had left the building, and let the idea float through his mind. *Could* he be someone else? The kind to provide grandchildren?

The girls entertained his mother for a few more minutes, telling her about their school and fun things she might want to do while she was in town, while Zack just took it all in. His brothers and nieces both seemed to be as taken with his mother as she was with them.

Of course, he'd expected nothing less.

He was the only one who'd ever not been civil in the group. But they were getting over that. He and Cody had come a long way since their first encounter. Dinner at Lee Ann's Friday night had been great. It had gone much easier than he'd anticipated. In fact, being around Cody had grown almost as easy as hanging with Nick.

"Maybe we should invite Joanie and Lee Ann too," his mom said now, in response to an invitation to take her over to the national park to give her the flavor of the Smokies. "I'd feel bad taking you away from them. Plus, I want to meet them too. I'm sure they're wonderful people."

Though Zack was included in the outing, it felt almost like he was on the outside looking in. He knew that was unfair. His mother loved family, and she'd wanted more than one son. Her attaching herself to his brothers and nieces now only made sense.

But still. He couldn't help but feel like his brothers were swooping in to steal his mom.

Or his mom was choosing them.

They did have kids, after all. And soon-to-be wives that his mother was already looking forward to meeting.

The jealousy running through him over his mother irritated him as much as watching Holly leave the restaurant with another man. He had to get this under control.

"How about the Firefly Festival?" Nick pointed out. "We'll all meet up there. Joanie will be working the morning shift, but she has someone who'll take over in the afternoon."

"I'm on it," Cody said. "The girls want to arrive early so we'll stake out a place."

Kendra and Candy nodded exuberantly, and then Kendra looked at him. "You'll be there too, right?"

His heart seized up. "Absolutely." A mutter was all he could manage.

Kendra gave him an easy smile, and his heart took off again, this time at a gallop.

Zack watched his mother's face glow as she sat across from the four of them. She was in love with her new extended family, and she'd barely even scratched the surface. The next thing Zack knew, she'd be inviting them all to Atlanta and cooking them a big meal.

"One other thing," Cody said as he looked over at Zack. "I've been meaning to bring this up. Now seems like the perfect time."

Zack had no clue what Cody was about to say, but did notice that the girls began to twitch on the seat as if they couldn't sit still. Smiles fought their way to their lips.

"My wedding is in a little over three weeks," Cody said. "I'd love it if you'd stand up with me."

Zack's mother sucked in a sharp breath. "Oh, Zackie. You always did want brothers."

He shot his mother a look. No need telling all his secrets. And quit calling him Zackie!

Cody and Nick both gave him smug looks. "So we weren't the only ones?" Nick teased.

Shit. Leave it to his mother to put him on the spot. But the truth was that, no, they hadn't been the only ones to want brothers. And he suddenly didn't see the harm in admitting it.

He shrugged. "Brothers would have been nice."

"Yeah." Cody nodded. His gaze went serious as it locked onto Zack's. "Real nice."

The moment felt heavy. The three of them had missed out on a lot together because of one selfish, inconsiderate person, but at least they *had* managed to find each other before it was too late.

"It's actually not so bad now," Zack grudgingly admitted. Nick smiled. Cody nodded.

And one more chink clicked closed.

"What do you say, then?" Cody asked again. "Be in my wedding?"

Candy and Kendra both nodded with excitement. This was big.

Cody had talked about the upcoming nuptials, and Zack had assumed he'd be welcome to come up for the event. But honestly, it had never occurred to him that he might be invited to participate.

The invitation meant a lot.

Then he glanced at his mother and a petty thought crept maliciously into his mind. Was it because of her? Did the invitation have more to do with wanting her there than him? The offer *hadn't* come until after she'd shown up.

But he refused to let himself think like that.

"It would be an honor," Cody urged.

"Having you stand there with us would make me proud too," Nick chimed in.

"Zackie," his mother cooed.

His brothers chuckled and his nieces pleaded. "Please," they chimed out together.

It wasn't like he was going to say no. This was what he wanted. He wanted to be in his brothers' lives. He wanted to be in his nieces' lives. He wanted relationships. And all four of them were offering that.

He nodded, an unusual warmth spreading through him, seeming to wrap around him and hold him tight. "I'd love to," he confessed.

His mother closed an arm around his waist and pressed a kiss to his bicep. "I'm so happy for you," she whispered.

"And you'll be there too, of course?" Cody asked Janet.

"I wouldn't miss it for the world."

A knot of tension grabbed hold in Zack's shoulders at Cody's words. But again, Zack shoved it aside. This wasn't about his brothers and his mother. It was about him and his brothers. His mother just happened to be part of the package deal.

Talk continued around the table. About the wedding, Lee Ann's color scheme, and how the whole event would be incorporated into the community activities. They also talked more about the weekend's upcoming festival. As they did, Zack watched the comings and goings around him.

He recognized several people whom he saw almost every day. Even spotted a few he'd never spoken with but could pick out as locals. As opposed to the many tourists who'd begun to file into town over the last two days.

Walking outside on the sidewalk was Mr. Martin, the man with the chew-toy ducks. Zack wondered if the letter his friend had sent to Mr. Martin's neighbor had settled the dispute.

Conversation wrapped up and Nick looked at his watch. "Got to get back," he said. "I may own the company, but the biggest part of my workforce is me."

That was a lie. Dalton Construction may have only been around for a few months, but Nick was building quite the business. Already he employed a good handful of people, and things seemed to only be growing.

His brothers and nieces said their good-byes, including hugs for his mother, and then were gone.

Left in their place was Mr. Martin. He stood beside the table, holding a home-baked pie.

"I know it ain't right to bring a pie in the diner," he said. The man's accent was heavy with Southern drawl. "What with them selling desserts in here an' all. But I needed to get this to ya."

He handed the pie over.

Zack knew he must look as stumped as he felt. "Why would you bring me a pie, Mr. Martin?"

"Because you helped me out. The missus baked it up this morning. I do appreciate your help." Then Mr. Martin stuck out his hand for Zack to shake. Zack shifted the pie to his other hand and shook the older gentleman's.

"There was no need," Zack started, thinking again about the differences in how he lived and how it was here, as well as the differences in what he'd expected, and what he'd found. The place was quaint. It was charming. "But I can't say I don't like a good pie."

Mr. Martin nodded. "And that letter worked, right nice. The fence went up today."

"Good," Zack said with enthusiasm. "I'm glad it didn't have to come to anything more."

After introducing the man to his mother and telling her about Mr. Martin's less-than-friendly neighbor, Zack watched him turn and shuffle back out the door. One of the waitresses gave Zack the evil eye as if it were a sin to have someone else's pie in the diner, so he slid it to the back of the table. The baked peaches smelled heavenly, but he'd wait until they got back to the house before tearing into it.

"Well, isn't that just the perfect thing," his mother said in wonder. "Being paid with a peach pie."

Zack chuckled lightly. If only his boss could see him now. Accepting baked goods as payment. "I can't say that I was expecting payment." He glanced at the pie. "But I also won't say no to homemade pie."

His mother's nose inched up. "As long as you don't forget that it's my pies you like the best."

Zack grinned at his mother. Seemed he wasn't the only one who could have a jealous streak. "You haven't made me a pie in a while, Mom. Better get on that."

He was teasing, but her eyes turned serious.

She grasped his hands in hers. "You're different here, Zackie. You aren't as hard."

Her words made him think about the fact that he should be in the office working. He *should* be hard. He feared if he stuck around here much longer he might lose his edge. Yet he couldn't bring himself to leave just yet.

They'd get through the festival, and then he'd give his mom one more week.

But then he had to get back to work.

Of course, that meant he'd have to leave Holly too.

"I like it," his mother added to her previous words. "A softer Zack is a good thing." She gave him a gentle smile. "Tell me about you and Holly."

There was no him and Holly.

And given that he was just thinking about getting back to Atlanta and getting his hard-ass going, there couldn't be a him and Holly. Even if he wanted it, she didn't belong there. She was much too soft.

She was the personification of this town.

"There's nothing between me and Holly, Mom. We're friends."

His mother studied him quietly. Then she patted the back of his hand where she still held it in hers. "I think there might be more to it than that," she said. "You seem happy when you're around her."

He was happy. Being around her made him feel good.

He nodded. "I am."

"Then quit pretending it's nothing. She might be just what you need."

"I don't need anything."

"Everyone needs something." She patted his cheek. "Everyone needs some*one*. Don't let the perfect person pass you up because you're afraid to get your heart broken."

He wasn't afraid. Didn't he already know what it felt like?

"She's just a friend," he reiterated.

She didn't take her eyes off his for several seconds. Then she tilted her head and gave him "the look." "Neither you nor I are stupid enough to believe that."

Chapter Nineteen

Holly heard a car approaching as she folded the piece of black velvet she'd used for her impromptu photo shoot. She'd spent the last three hours with Brian, getting her best work captured for her portfolio.

Her brother had been incredible.

First, he'd been floored by Holly's skill. He'd hugged her close as if letting her know that he was proud of her. She also thought he was finally catching on to the fact that when no one had been looking, she'd grown up. She wasn't just the baby sister anymore. She had dreams and aspirations of her own. And somehow, she was going to catch them.

Secondly, Brian had turned serious and had gotten down to work. He'd even cancelled an early date he had lined up with some girl from the next county over. She'd been a first date. His cancelling at the last minute had *not* made a good impression.

That thought made her smile. It also gave her a warm fuzzy.

She stepped to the window at the sound of a car door closing, not surprised to see it was Zack. Who else would be coming out to the cabin? Until today, she'd never even invited her brother there.

She peeked into a mirror to check her appearance. Her hair was wild in a quick topknot where she'd pulled it up earlier, her shirt was tugged out of her shorts on one side, and her cheeks were flushed from hanging mirrors back on the walls.

She looked like crap. But she didn't care. She was riding on a high from the photo shoot.

She slung the velvet around her neck, and walked to the door.

When she pulled it open, Zack stood there, his eyes intense.

"I didn't like it," he said.

"Excuse me?" She stepped back to let him in. As he walked past her, he eyed the velvet wrapped around her neck.

"The guy," he said. "I didn't like the guy."

"What guy?"

"At the diner."

Oh. She almost smiled. He'd gotten jealous again. Over Bobby this time. "Why not?" She closed the door, and when she turned back, he was right there. So big in her small space.

And she couldn't help but think about what had happened the last time he'd been there.

Or what else she'd wanted to happen.

He gave an unconcerned shrug and took a step forward. He backed her to the door. "Because he's not right for you."

If she'd been drinking at that moment, she'd have spit the liquid out with her laughter. "You think? His nickname is 'Hounddog.' Trust me, I know he's not right for me."

"You liked him though."

It was hard not to like Bobby. "What makes you say that?"

"The way you smiled at him." His hands grabbed the edges of the velvet and he lightly tugged. She took a small step forward. "The way you laughed with him," he added.

They were so close his breath brushed across her cheek.

"I like to laugh," she whispered.

He nodded. "I like it when you laugh. Especially with me."

"You weren't there."

He tugged again. Their toes touched. "I'm here now."

The words were spoken softly, but they seemed to usher tension into the room as if a gate had been lifted over a dam. It slapped at her legs at first. Threatening to pull her under. Then it rose, closing in around her body until it pushed against her, cutting off her air.

Until all she could see was Zack.

All she could feel was Zack.

She gulped.

"What are you doing here, Zack?" She sounded panicked. Hell, she felt panicked. He was acting like he was going to kiss her again. "I don't want to play games."

She *did* want to play games.

She just didn't want to get hurt when the game ended.

"I can't stay away," he admitted.

His nostrils flared as he inhaled, seeming to pull her scent inside him, and then he leaned forward, shifting at the last second and burying his face in her hair. Her heart missed a beat at the longing moan that came from him.

She wanted him to kiss her.

She let out a shaky breath.

"Zack?" she begged. Her lips parted. She didn't know if she was begging him to kiss her, or for him to stop.

"I can't stay away," he said again, more slowly this time.

He shifted, leaning back so that his eyes were on hers. "I don't know what this is, and I'm not promising anything," he began. "But I can't sit by and watch you with other men."

Fear filled her at the same time as a kernel of hope flared to life.

The fear won. "How about if I promise not to date anyone until you go home?"

He shook his head slowly. "I think you should date me *until* I go home."

Well, that put it bluntly. He really was promising nothing. A week and a half of bliss. Nothing more.

Wasn't like she was finding bliss anywhere else.

And didn't a girl deserve a taste of bliss once in a while?

She swallowed. He was going to break her heart.

"Can I have some time to think about it?" she asked. She wasn't asking for time to consider going out with him so much as she was asking time to consider what would happen *if* she went out with him. They would end up in bed together. She needed to give that clear thought when her nether regions weren't weeping at the pure joy of having all that testosterone nearby.

He nodded. The move was slow and deliberate, as if he was thinking that it might be wise for him to take that time as well. "You can have two days."

Then he twisted his hands, and the velvet at her neck wrapped around his fists.

And his mouth met hers.

Holly opened under him the instant his lips touched down, and Zack sank into the lusciousness of her mouth.

The tip of her tongue stroked against his. Tentative, but seeking. Wanting.

He wanted to.

He wanted everything about her he could possibly get.

Not tonight, though. Not everything. Tonight would just be this. A kiss. A stroke.

A touch.

Enough to leave her looking forward to the next time. To make sure he stayed topmost in her mind. Because yeah, there was going to be a next time. There would be as many next times as he could get.

He'd taken his mother back to the house earlier, and he'd no more than set foot inside the foyer than he'd known he'd been kidding himself. Holly was not just a friend. They'd crossed that border days ago.

Thinking he could ignore this had been wrong. He had to see where it went.

He lifted both hands, the velvet still wrapped around his palms, and cupped the sides of her face. The tips of his fingers slid into the silkiness of all that glorious hair, and he was reminded of her pure joy Sunday night as they'd raced through the streets of Atlanta.

If he were the romantic type, he'd think he'd fallen a little bit in love with her that night.

Everything about her had been so alive. Electric.

Her joy had vibrated through his car until it filled his heart. He'd wanted to freeze the moment so he could hold on to it forever.

He lifted his mouth from hers and stared down through lust-heavy eyes at the plump, red lips he'd been feasting on. Her eyelids fluttered beneath him. Finally they opened enough to reveal the same desire he himself felt. She was beautiful.

She could be his.

That was a staggering realization. Along with the fact that he'd almost let this get away.

"Thursday night," he whispered. He dragged his thumb over her bottom lip and her chin lifted with the action, moving along with him. He dipped his head once more.

When they parted a second time, he pulled a groan away with him.

"I'm taking you to the movies," he told her. "Thursday night. On a date."

Her eyes began to clear. "A date?"

He nodded. And then fear hit his chest and radiated out. He didn't date. He hooked up. He had understandings.

But with Holly, he wasn't sure he had anything. Not anything he could control.

That was the worst part.

Then again, maybe it was the best part. It sure as hell left him breathless.

However it turned out, he had to let himself see. He had to know.

Placing one last kiss against her lips, this one barely a graze, he then dropped one on the tip of her nose and stepped away. As he did, he unraveled the velvet from around his hands and smoothed the material back into place.

"What's with the velvet?" he asked. If he didn't know she was as turned on as him, his breathless voice would be embarrassing.

"Oh!" Her ardor disappeared in an instant. "I was going to tell you about that earlier. I got a call today. From Chicago." She bit her lip as if to try to keep the smile from getting away from her.

"About the mirrors?" From the looks of her, it had to be. And good news at that.

"Yeah."

"I thought you never showed them to anyone."

"I didn't, but I gave one to my cousin. She had a party and a guest saw it. The guest is a client of a specialized boutique. It was a store I hadn't tried," she explained. "Even more upscale than I was shooting for. Anyway, the manager got a look at it today, and she asked to see more."

His breath caught. "Are you going back up there?"

"No. But I've spent the last few hours taking pictures to send to her. Brian helped me."

So that's why he'd met her brother on the road into her place.

"You showed him the mirrors?"

She grinned wide once again. "I did."

"And?"

"And he loved them." Her tone held such awe that he once again wanted to kiss her. He wanted to share in that feeling. "I think he was proud of me," she said shyly.

"Of course he was proud of you." He took her hand and gave it a squeeze. "You're amazing. And he's your brother. Brothers are proud of their siblings."

Zack realized that was true. Even if a person had just met his siblings.

Everything he'd learned about Nick and Cody in the last two weeks had sealed his fate. He couldn't walk away from them. Ever. They were blood. He'd been wrong to think that didn't matter.

He'd been wrong about *them*.

He would make sure they remained a part of his life. Though it would be scary, he would even consider having them down to his place. Or maybe he would have everyone out to the house. The one he'd grown up in. He could show them his car. His mother would cook. She would love it.

He wondered if Holly might come down too.

"What happens next?" he asked.

"I'll e-mail the file to her tonight." Her eyes burned with a renewed energy mixed with nervous anticipation. "And then I wait. She said she'd let me know something soon."

He couldn't hold back. He wrapped his arms around her and pulled her to him. "I am so happy for you," he murmured into her hair. "She's going to love them."

"I hope so." Her arms hadn't gone around him, but her hands clutched at the front of his shirt. She was pressed up tight against his chest. "But I'm nervous," she whispered into his throat.

He pulled back. Just enough to look down at her. At the worry etching her face. Then he put his lips to the spot right between her brows. She let out a sigh and he felt her melt into him. He *was* falling for her. Hard.

And he was going to let himself do it.

He wanted this woman in his life.

Lessons had been learned long ago, but they were hard to remember when he was wrapped around Holly.

"Let me send them to my friend," he suggested. He released her. "You have the file already made. It wouldn't hurt to have more than one person take a look at it, would it? Maybe you could get into both locations."

It surprised him when she immediately said, "Yes."

"Just like that?" he asked.

She nodded. "I was already thinking that," she said. "Hoping you might want to."

"Wow," he murmured. The belief she suddenly had in herself was very sexy. "Where did this come from?"

"I've never been afraid to be different. To put myself out there," she told him. "Except when it came to my mirrors. But that never felt good and I'm tired of it. I guess showing them to Brian helped me to see that. I'll be bringing the rest of the family out too. I want them all to see what I'm capable of. What I want." Her dimple showed up with her smile. "What I'm going to accomplish."

He couldn't have been happier if she'd just stripped naked and climbed onto his lap.

Well, not much.

"I'm so proud of you," he told her.

She nodded and her entire face glowed. "I'm proud of me too. Thank you, Zack." She lifted a hand and caressed his cheek. "You helped me get here. I owe you everything."

He brought her hand to his mouth and put his lips to the center of her palm. "You don't owe me anything." He folded her fingers down over his. But he might just owe her.

Chapter Twenty

T hanks for choosing to stay with us, and I hope you have a wonderful vacation." Holly smiled at the guests she'd just checked in, and handed over the rack card for the Firefly Festival. The couple was from Virginia, come down solely for the festival. "Your room is right at the top of the stairs on the left, the Magnolia Room. Also, there's a movie in the park tonight. Everyone comes out for it. I hope to see you there."

"Perfect," the wife murmured.

Holly handed over a map showing parking for the festival, and explained how to get to each lot. When the couple moved up the stairs, she took a quick peek at her watch. It was date night, and here she was, sitting in the middle of her parents' bed-and-breakfast instead of at her cabin primping for Zack.

Which made her think of the lack of primping she'd done for Keith.

She'd looked nice for Keith. She just hadn't gone out of her way to really stand out.

For Zack, she wanted to stand out.

For Zack, she wanted to be the only thing he saw tonight.

The front door opened and she fitted another smile to her face, expecting it to be the final guests they were expecting. Instead it was the man who hadn't been further than a minute from her thoughts since he'd walked into her cabin Tuesday afternoon and declared he couldn't stay away.

Hallelujah for small miracles, because she didn't want him to stay away.

Yeah, it was stupid. She was already half in love with the guy. She didn't need to fall the rest of the way just to watch him walk out of her life.

But how could she not say yes? To whatever he wanted?

He saw her sitting at the corner desk and stopped, and the look that came over his face turned her into complete and utter mush. His smile was slow. It said he'd been thinking bad, bad things when it came to her. And the heat in his eyes could singe anything it came into contact with.

Lord knew she was singed.

He wore dusty boots, his jeans hadn't fared much better, and the navy T-shirt he had on clung to his chest and shoulders as if it was damp with sweat. Either he'd been working with Nick again, or he'd turned into some kind of caveman overnight.

She liked the look.

They hadn't seen each other since Tuesday afternoon. She'd been keeping busy at the studio working on a couple new designs. If word came from either Chicago or Atlanta that there was interest, she wanted to have something fresh and new ready to go.

She'd also been working so hard just to avoid Zack.

Because she didn't think she could be around him and "avoid" him any longer. Not after the way he'd reeled her in Tuesday afternoon. He'd barely kissed her when he'd been at her house, yet he'd made a very lasting impression.

The kind of impression that let her know his next kiss would come with more. She was ready for that. She'd thought long and hard about it the last couple of days, and yes, she wanted it. She wanted Zack.

Her heart pounded so hard behind her breastbone just from thinking about it, that she wouldn't have been surprised to look down and see her shirt moving in sync with her pulse.

"Hi," she said. She swallowed around a dry throat.

He gave a single nod. "Hi."

Then his gaze drank her in from head to toe as if he hadn't seen her in months. "I didn't expect to see you here."

She hadn't expected to be here. "Mom called." She forced herself to breathe normally. No sense letting him know she was this turned on merely by looking at him. "She needed me to handle check-ins while she ran into Pigeon Forge. There's a sale on patio furniture. Apparently some of the chairs need replacing."

Mundane chitchat was about all she had available right then. As well as a spiked temperature and increasingly damp panties. If she played her cards right, she was going to have sex tonight. And then she was going to have sex as often as possible for the next ten days.

"I thought you were working at your studio?" Zack asked. He moved farther into the room, his body honed and tight, and his movements not wasting an ounce of energy. He didn't come close enough to touch, though.

She wanted to touch.

She gave a little shrug. "Duty called."

Being here annoyed her for the simple fact that she'd explained to her mother yesterday morning that she was working on something important she wanted to show the entire family this weekend. Yet her mom had decided she needed to go shopping, and here Holly sat. *Not* working on her mirrors.

Not being important enough that *her* plans mattered.

"Don't worry, though. I'll be ready in time to leave," she began. "You just won't have to go out to my place to pick me up. I'll change here."

He nodded again. He kept looking at her like she was dinner and he hadn't eaten in days.

Her phone let out a short buzz and vibrated on the desk, and she jumped, pulling her attention away from Zack. She hurriedly reached for it. She had an e-mail.

As she pressed the button, her hands began to shake.

"Is it them?" Zack asked. He stepped closer now, leaning over the desk to peer at her phone.

Holly scanned her inbox, her eyes searching for more than was there, then she let out a pent-up breath. "No." Her shoulders slumped. "When I sent the portfolio Tuesday night, she said I'd hear something in a couple days." She put the phone on the desk and looked up at Zack. "It's been a couple days. Why haven't I heard anything?"

Nerves had her a frustrated mess. Between waiting to hear back from Chicago, and waiting to see what would happen with Zack, it was a wonder she'd managed to get anything accomplished at all over the last two days. Renewed potential for a career had inspired her, though. So she'd put all her tangled-up energy into her work.

And if she hadn't been pulled over to the house for the last few hours, she would have gotten even more accomplished.

"It'll come," he assured her. His mouth was inches from hers now. His lips somehow managed to look both soft and hard at the same time. "And then *you'll* get to decide what you want to do. You're in charge here."

She nodded. She didn't feel like she was in charge of anything.

Her eyes remained on his mouth. They had a date. Dates ended with kisses. Dates often turned into more.

"I need to shower," Zack murmured.

She slid her gaze back up to his eyes. She needed to be in that shower with him.

"You'll be ready in an hour?" he asked.

She nodded.

She was ready right now.

Just like the last time he crossed the park on movie night, everyone stared at Zack. Only this time, they weren't staring because he was an outsider. Well, okay, maybe a bit because he was an outsider. But more because of the woman he held close to his side.

Holly walked next to him, one hand in his, and so near that their bodies occasionally brushed as they moved. She looked nothing like the prim innkeeper who'd been manning the desk at the B&B when he'd returned to the house earlier.

Now she had on a short, pale-pink dress that brushed the tops of her tanned thighs and was held up with tiny string-like straps. It had a high waist, and two rows of ruffles with three little pink buttons marching vertically between her breasts.

And those breasts.

Oh, hell. They were cupped and lifted on her chest, lovely creamy mounds peeking out above the material.

And they bounced with every damned step she took.

He'd already had so much blood run south, he wasn't sure how he would make it through the movie.

"Still nothing," she muttered at his side. Of course, as he was trying not to ogle her breasts, she once again had her eyes glued to her phone. She'd checked her e-mail at least five times since they'd left the house.

"You're worrying too much," he told her.

Her gaze lifted to his. "She said I'd hear from her today."

"She said a couple days. And a couple days doesn't always mean two," he informed her. "Not for everyone." He reached over and plucked the device from her hand. He wished she had an answer from the store owner in Chicago, but stressing over an e-mail she couldn't control wouldn't help matters. And it certainly wouldn't go far toward having a good time tonight. "You'll hear from her soon enough. Don't you want to enjoy tonight while we're here?"

"I do, but . . ." Her eyes grew panicked as she watched her phone disappear into the front pocket of his jeans. "Zack," she begged.

He put his mouth to her ear and whispered, "Quit worrying and enjoy the evening."

She eyed his pocket as if considering going after the phone.

He eyed her as if considering letting her go for it.

"Touch me and it's over," he murmured.

She blushed. A lovely shade of pink that almost matched her dress. It colored her cheeks and the tip of her nose.

But if she put her hands anywhere near the front of his jeans, he would toss her over his shoulder and be out of there in a heartbeat. And they absolutely would not come out of her cabin until morning.

"There's your niece," he said. He nudged his chin toward the girl standing half a football field away, one arm waving wildly. "Are we sitting with them?"

"Yeah," Holly murmured. Her mind was clearly not on where they were sitting, or anything else about their date. She turned pleading eyes up to his. "Can't I just check it one more time?"

"Not on your life." He hauled her through the crowd until he got to her family. They were all there. Kyndall; Kyndall's parents; Brian and his flavor of the week; Patrick, Jillian, and their boys; and Mr. and Mrs. Marshall.

Every last one of them watched them expectantly. He had Holly's hand in his in a manner that spoke of possession. Not of friendship.

Nerves pinched his gut.

His own mother also sat nearby. She was watching too.

As was Ms. Grayson, whom his mom had ridden to the park with.

His mom was fitting in perfectly, having already made several friends since she'd been here, and had excursions lined up for every day of her trip. Lucky for him, the one person she seemed to enjoy spending the most time with was the town busybody. The same woman, from what he understood, who was the ringleader of Holly getting so many men chasing after her.

He didn't like men chasing after her.

"Did you want to sit with your brothers instead?" she asked. She looked guilty as she glanced from her family over a couple blankets to where his brothers, Joanie, Lee Ann, and his nieces sat.

"It's okay. We can sit here." But when Candy and Kendra spotted him in the crowd, he found himself wanting to be with them too. Kendra was talking to her boyfriend, and they looked to be trying to decide where to sit, and Candy was standing beside them showcasing a load of boredom and holding a massive tub of popcorn.

Both girls waved at him, and he waved back. They'd been out at the construction site with Nick today, and had trailed around behind him as much as they had Nick.

"Come on. Let's sit with them," Holly urged, while at the same time Kyndall said shyly, "Will you sit beside me?"

Ah, shit.

What was he supposed to do? He looked down at the young face shining up at him. Yep. He couldn't walk away from that.

"I'd love to," he said. He glanced at Holly. "If it's okay with your aunt. Wouldn't want her to get jealous, would we?"

He dropped to the ground and tugged Holly down beside him while Kyndall giggled.

"I like that you two are dating," the girl said.

Holly's smile went a little too wide. "Where'd you hear that?"

Kyndall's mother peered around from the other side of the girl. She shot Holly a pointed look, then lowered her gaze to where Zack's hand still held Holly's.

"Mom said you were," Kyndall informed them. Her smile was angelic.

"As has everyone in town," the woman added.

And yeah, Zack might have told his own mother that he and Holly were going out tonight. He'd assumed she would tell her new best friend, and that friend would then be free with the information. He needed the other men to know to back the hell off.

Kyndall's mother reached a hand out to Zack and he had to turn loose of Holly to shake it. "We met a couple weeks ago. I'm Erika. This here is my husband, Rodney."

Yet another blond Marshall stuck out his hand. He gave Zack the same look that Patrick and Brian had been known to shoot his way on occasion.

Don't touch my sister.

Right. Only, he had every intention of touching their sister. Every square inch of her.

"We've heard it about ten times in the fifteen minutes since we've been here," Erika informed them. "I think you two make a great couple, by the way."

Rodney grunted, and Kyndall edged closer to Zack. Holly twirled a lock of hair around her finger as if embarrassed.

Then Candy and Kendra headed their way. "Can we squeeze in?" Kendra asked.

Zack's heart did its own squeeze. They wanted to be with him. That felt way better than he'd ever imagined it would.

"Absolutely," he replied. "But don't you want to sit with your boyfriend?" he teased Kendra.

"Nah." She plopped down on the quilt, followed by her sister. "I'm going to dump him anyway. I have my eye on another guy. One who'll be in the ninth grade next year. I like older men."

Holly chuckled and scooted over, giving the girls enough room to slide in next to him, and he shot her a grateful wink. So much for snuggling up tight during the movies. Maybe that would help him focus and not drag her off in the dark for a quick make-out session.

"Want some popcorn?" Candy offered the tub around. As she did, he watched Holly eye the front of his jeans.

"Leave it alone," he told her.

Erika snickered from the other side of her daughter.

Zack pulled the phone out of his pocket to show it to Holly's sister-in-law, ignoring the glare of every Marshall man in the vicinity, then tucked it back into his pants.

"You just checked two minutes ago," he told Holly over Candy's head. "You're fine."

Holly grunted in disgust.

"What's she checking?" Kyndall had scooted so close her elbow poked him in the side every time she wiggled. She was way too cute, and he found himself a bit smitten with her.

He bypassed her question, not wanting to either explain the neurosis of her aunt or give away anything about the mirrors, instead spending the next few minutes talking with Kyndall and the other two girls. They discussed everything from best friends, to what they were all doing on their summer vacations, to reruns of *Happy Days*. Apparently Kyndall had just discovered the show on television.

"I like the older shows," she told him very maturely.

"Me too," Candy agreed. "My favorite is *The Cosby Show*. Bill Cosby is *so* funny."

The girls had a way of making him feel way too old.

"Mom says tonight's movie is a classic too," Kyndall explained. "I'm sure I'm going to love it."

The movie was *Doc Hollywood*.

It was not what he would call a classic.

Nor did he expect to love it.

Rumor was that it had been picked because of the squash festival in the movie. It was no Sugar Springs Firefly Festival—to hear it told—but there were enough similarities to warrant the showing.

He caught Holly staring at his jeans again, and leaned around behind the twins to put his mouth to her ear. He used the moment to steal a quick nuzzle, then smiled against her neck when he felt her shiver.

"You have it set to vibrate when you get e-mail, right?" he whispered after he finished toying with her neck.

She nodded.

She also breathed heavier.

He nibbled on her earlobe. "Then don't worry about it. I'll feel it." He pulled back before one of her brothers decided to try to kick his ass. "And if you'll behave and enjoy the evening, I'll even let you know if it goes off."

Her eyes narrowed on him.

"You can't do the scary look, babe." He winked at her. "So don't even try."

She made a face.

He laughed. All three girls laughed with him. And then the movie started.

Halfway through the movie, Candy and Kendra had shifted to the front of the blanket, stretched out on their sides, and Holly had made her way to his side. She snuggled in close and whispered, "Have you heard anything from your friend in Atlanta?"

He almost laughed at her. He was sitting there thinking about sliding his hands up under her skirt, and she was still stressing over not hearing anything about her mirrors.

"Yeah," he told her. "She loved them."

Holly reared back. "Why didn't you tell me?"

"Shhh," he whispered when several people scowled in their direction. "There's a movie playing." He pulled her back to him and wrapped his arms around her so that her back was to his chest. It felt right to sit there with her like that. "Because nothing is official," he added quietly once she'd settled back down. He spoke into her ear so no one could hear. "She wants to take a closer look, and then wants to show them to her boss. She'd love to see them in person."

When Holly grew still, he suggested, "We could invite her up."

He liked saying *we*. It also felt right.

"For a product with your uniqueness," he continued, "I'm sure she'd make the drive."

Holly turned her head to take him in as if she still didn't believe his words. But then she shook her head. "We don't have a room to put her in."

He could give up his room and bunk with Holly. Which was actually a terrific idea.

But not one he was ready to suggest.

"We'll talk about it later," he said. He kissed her temple, and they settled in to watch the rest of the show.

As the credits began to roll, he couldn't say what any of the movie had been about. All he'd been able to do was listen to Holly breathe, smell her flowery scent, and steal more nuzzles against her neck. Each time he did, the silk of her hair brushed across his face and he'd wanted more.

He wanted more now.

He'd been a gentleman all night, but the way her rear had been snuggled up next to him for the last forty-five minutes could have tempted a saint. Not to mention, he'd been semi-hard for her for most of the last two weeks.

He was hella frustrated.

She glanced at him as if aware he was watching her.

"What?" she whispered. Her voice had dropped. It was deeper. Softer.

It was middle-of-sex husky.

She was having the same thoughts he was.

Zack put his mouth to her ear once again. This time he didn't nuzzle. He didn't tease.

He demanded.

"Let's go to your house," he said. Yet, it wasn't merely going to her house that he was suggesting.

"You guys want to come over?" Nick and Joanie stood in front of them now, with Cody and Lee Ann two steps behind. "We could play cards or something."

"Yeah," Candy and Kendra both chimed in. "That would be cool."

Kyndall and her mother rose to begin gathering the trash the group had accumulated from the concession stand, while Zack watched Holly's gaze dart to each member of the Marshall family and then to the Daltons. If they didn't go over to Nick's, everyone would assume—*correctly*—they'd be doing something else instead.

Would she let that happen?

She scanned over Zack's features as if to be sure he was asking what he was asking. Yeah, it wasn't cards he wanted to play tonight.

Then she turned back to Nick and gave an apologetic shrug. "Sorry guys, not tonight." She faked a yawn behind her hand. "I'm beat."

Zack was on his feet, pulling her up in two seconds flat. "I'd better get you home then." He looked at his brothers, and he *ignored* Holly's brothers. "Sorry, guys. Maybe next time."

Brian Marshall looked at him as if he intended to slash Zack's tires so he couldn't go *anywhere*.

"Ah, Uncle Zack, you're no fun. Now Mom will think we need to go to bed early."

Candy's words froze him to the spot. *Uncle Zack?*

He looked at his niece. His mouth went dry. She made a silly face at him before turning to her sister, and both girls began helping Kyndall fold up one of the quilts. Cody seemed to be watching him carefully, as if waiting to see his reaction to the familial name.

Hell, he didn't know how to react. She'd tossed it out as if she'd been saying that her whole life.

He wanted to hear it again.

"We can go over if you want," Holly whispered at his side.

She understood. This was a big moment for him. But so was being with her.

He glanced down, taking in her sweet, understanding face as he weighed the situation. He was an uncle. Not just in name, but a blood relative. And he couldn't decide between that and making love to the woman at his side.

Did that make him a bad person?

As if he'd made his own decision, Cody took a step forward and spoke to Zack alone. "Go on, man. You're in. They're crazy about you. I promise this isn't the only time you'll hear that word."

What wasn't said, but was understood, was that he was in with Cody too. They were good.

This was turning out to be one hell of a night.

"You're sure?" Zack asked. Because he really did want to go home with Holly.

Cody nodded and clapped him on the back. "Just remember the deal. Don't hurt her."

Meaning Holly. Right.

If one of her brothers didn't take him out, one of *his* brothers would. He got it. But he also didn't intend to hurt her. He hadn't lied, and he hadn't made promises. She understood that.

But whatever this thing was between them, they needed time to figure it out.

He nodded, shook Cody's hand, then called out a good-bye to his nieces. Both of them came over and gave him a hug. Yet another act that floored him. Kendra offered up a quick peck to the cheek. "I had a good time tonight," she told him. "Way better than sitting with some lame boy."

And then the lame boy called her name and she laughed with glee and rushed off to him.

Zack turned to Holly. She was smiling at him the same way Kendra had smiled at the lame boy. Like he gave her the warm fuzzies.

He liked that smile.

"Ready to go?" he asked.

She nodded. "I've never been more ready."

Chapter Twenty-One

They pulled into the driveway of Holly's tiny cabin fifteen minutes later, and Zack cut the engine. They hadn't touched or kissed since they'd gotten in the car. They'd barely spoken.

But now what?

Zack turned in the seat. The moon was full and he could make out Holly's features perfectly. She was stunning.

And for right now, she was his.

Only, at that exact moment her phone buzzed in his pocket.

He mentally groaned. But he also knew he had to give it to her. Hopefully it would be good news.

He dug the phone out and handed it over. "It just buzzed."

"Really?" She ripped it from his hands. Whatever else she might have been thinking was gone.

"I figured you didn't get any signal out here," he grumbled. He had not wanted to be interrupted.

She scoffed. "The only real dead spot on the property is where you parked your car that first day. The signal here is fine."

He just shook his head, remembering her on that horse the first day. As well as the geese. He hadn't known what he was getting himself into. He looked around as she checked her e-mail, wondering where the crazy geese were.

As if sensing him looking, he heard a honk off in the distance.

"Oh," she whispered beside him.

"What?" He turned back. And then he saw her face. She was about to cry. "Oh, babe." He reached for her.

Before she could say anything else, he had her seat belt unbuckled and pulled her crossways into his lap. He settled her over his thighs, wrapping both arms tight around her, and she dropped the side of her head to his chest.

"I can't believe I got my hopes up again," she moaned. "When will I learn?" She turned her face to him and buried her nose in his throat. Her arms circled his neck. And then her whole body shook as she began to sob.

"They're wrong," he told her. He stroked his hand up and down her back, desperate to make her understand. "I'm sorry they don't see it, but trust me, they're wrong. You don't need them anyway. You could stand on the sidewalk in the middle of town and make a fortune all day long. Didn't we prove that already?"

Her answer was simply more shaking sobs.

He knew his words weren't likely to do much good so he simply held her until she was spent.

Several minutes later, she lifted her face. The sadness reflecting back at him was his undoing. Before he knew what he intended, he had his mouth open.

"I fell in love with a fellow law student ten years ago," he said. That fact had nothing at all to do with Holly and her mirrors, yet still, it compared. As did the meeting with his birth mother. He found himself wanting to share all of it with her.

"It was fast and furious," he continued. "I pictured us together forever." His mouth twisted into a smirk as he thought back to Barb. That's when he'd still believed in forever. "I brought her home to meet my parents that first semester. They loved her. I was certain she was the woman for me."

Holly's eyes had dried and the moonlight shone on her pale face as she watched him. He gulped around the knot in his throat.

"The end of our first year of law school, I bought a ring. She was ecstatic. I loved her, and I wanted her in every part of my life." He gripped Holly tighter. She was soft in all the right places, and he concentrated, forcing his heart rate to slow. He still couldn't think about that day without getting pissed off. "That was also the same time I'd gotten my adoption records unsealed."

Wide eyes stared back at him.

"I hired a private investigator. Not that finding her was hard. Her name was Pam, and she still lived in the same run-down town she'd come from. Not far from Nashville. Still drinking herself stupid. I wanted to know what I was getting into, though, so I hired a guy to check her out."

He took a breath before continuing, "I also wanted Barb to be there with me when I met her."

"Did you?" Holly asked, speaking for the first time since he'd started. "Meet her?"

"Oh, yeah." He quit talking as he sketched out the woman in his mind. Her eyes had been the color of his. Her hair too.

And she'd smiled like him.

Of course, when he'd met her, her smile had been more of a haggard grimace, but the PI had unearthed pictures from before she'd gotten herself so messed up. She'd been pretty once. Zack and his brothers had gotten their features from her.

He lifted his hand and stroked it down Holly's arm as he talked. "I knew she had issues. The PI warned me. But I couldn't wrap my head around the fact that drugs might be more important to her than meeting me. That she wouldn't be excited to *see* me. I was her son. Her firstborn."

He stared off into the night. How stupid. Of course she wouldn't be excited to see him.

"I take it she wasn't?"

His eyes were so dry it hurt to blink. He forced himself to keep going, to admit what he'd never said to anyone. "I thought she'd tell me she'd hated to give me up. That she thought of me every year on my birthday."

He heard Holly suck in a breath.

"I mattered to her in only one way, though," he stated, his voice flat. "My wallet."

"Oh, Zack."

Her fingers brushed over his cheek, but he didn't look at her. He was too embarrassed. He'd come from that woman. She was a part of him.

"I'd also found out that I had brothers," he admitted softly.

Her fingers stilled. "You knew Cody and Nick existed?"

He nodded.

"Before this year?"

"It was in the report from the PI. I'd planned to look them up after I met Pam." He shook his head, refusing to let the anger have control. "However, she explained that she saw them on a regular basis. *Drank* with them, even. They wanted my money too. She swore they'd eventually come after it."

"But . . ." Holly's whispered word seemed to stick in the space between them.

He glanced at her and finished her thought. "They didn't meet until last year."

Her entire body sagged. "That's why you didn't want anything to do with them?"

"Bingo."

"Yet you changed your mind."

"After they appeared on my doorstep, I hired another private investigator. The first one had only gotten me dates and ages. This time

I dug for more. Got confirmation of the story they told me. Then I knew that not only had I been played by my birth mother for money, but she'd also turned me against my brothers before I'd even had the chance to meet them."

Holly sat quietly in his lap. When he didn't continue, she prodded for more. "And how does Barb fit into all this?" she asked. "Did she go with you to meet Pam?"

Fucking Barb. He dropped his head to the back of the seat.

"We barely made it off the plane in Atlanta before she'd put my ring back in my hand. She had plans, she informed me. Those plans didn't include a redneck family and a bunch of hillbilly drunks."

"She dumped you?" Confusion etched across Holly's brow. "Because of the woman who'd given birth to you? Even though you'd never met her until that day?"

"Piece of work, huh?" He'd met a few in his lifetime.

"She hurt you."

Hell. Why had he started this conversation? And then he remembered Holly's e-mail from Chicago. He'd wanted to show her that she wasn't the only one to be rejected. It happened to all of them. In all sorts of ways.

And they lived through it.

It might change her. But she would survive.

"She hurt me," he admitted. "She dumped me not because of who I was, but who I had the potential to be. As if I were genetically predisposed to wind up like Pam."

"But you would never be like that."

He looked at her then. "How do you know?"

She blinked. "Because that's not how you were raised. That's not who you are."

"But that's what's inside me. What if I am trash? Not good enough?"

"Bull."

He shrugged. It was a long-running theory in his head. Thankfully, he'd managed to keep all signs of where he'd come from away from his life for the last thirty-three years. Hopefully that would continue.

Holly's heart broke for the strong man before her.

He'd had his heart broken.

Twice, if she counted the worthless woman who'd given birth to him.

No wonder he was so hesitant to let anyone in. Brothers, women. Why risk the heartbreak?

She smoothed her palm over his day's growth of whiskers, and thought about the fact that he'd shared his past with her. If she wasn't mistaken, that wasn't normal procedure for him. She would guess he tended to hide behind the scars built up from the years. First as a kid, then a man.

She understood that.

It was easier to hide than to share yourself.

And though he hadn't said it, she could sense that what he'd sought ten years ago was what he still wanted today. Love. A family.

Whether he'd allow himself to risk it again, she had no idea.

But he hadn't been wrong in going for it.

"She missed out," she told him. "You're a catch."

He chuckled dryly.

There were so many things she could have said to back up her words, but she didn't think he wanted to hear them. Just as she didn't want to discuss the fact she'd had yet one more rejection concerning her mirrors. Some things were better left unsaid.

Tonight she just wanted to feel.

She wanted Zack to feel.

She put her lips to his.

He sucked her air into his mouth, but he didn't move beneath her. His lips were warm, and she appreciated the time to explore them at her leisure. So she did.

She tasted him. And nibbled at him.

She tested out his mouth from corner to corner until she felt his hands tense against her back. He wanted her. That wasn't a question. Nor was whether she wanted him.

The question was, could she protect her heart?

But the answer didn't matter. Her decision had been made before they'd gone out tonight.

"Make love to me," she whispered. Her mouth grazed across Zack's as she spoke. His fingers spread over her back.

"In my bedroom, with all the windows letting in the moonlight. I want to see you in my mirrors."

Finally, he could sit still no longer.

With an animal-like groan ripping from the back of his throat, Zack brought both hands to her face, holding her to him. He was almost too rough, but he held back at just the right moment.

"I don't know where this will go," he said. "I have my job. My work."

"Shhh." She closed her eyes and tilted her forehead to his. She knew that.

He'd had enough disappointment in his life, and she couldn't see herself being the person to break through those barriers.

And that was okay.

She needed this as much as he did.

She needed to feel as special as she wanted to believe her talent was.

"I'm not asking for promises," she replied.

He looked at her. It was too dark to read whatever was going through his mind, but she felt the power of it. He may not believe in forever, but this meant something to him. *She* meant something to him.

And that was enough.

She put her mouth to his again.

Zack didn't just let Holly kiss him that time. It was his turn to take control. He dipped inside her with determined strokes, holding her steady against him. She was sweet and hot. She was heady.

And he could gladly drown in it.

His tongue dueled with hers, stroking and teasing, before he moved away and traced along her jawline. He cupped the sides of her head, his brain registering the soft skin and silky hair at the same time, the textures alone enough to drive him to the brink. Then he tilted her face so he could slide his mouth down over her throat.

His teeth scraped along her skin and she began to wiggle. His tongue lapped. She groaned. The faint hint of salt filled him as he suckled his way to the base. She was intoxicating.

She was hot in his hands, and scalding where she ground against his dick.

When his fingers stroked over her cheek, she angled toward his hand to capture his thumb between her teeth. She sucked him inside her mouth.

"Holly," he pleaded. She only sucked harder.

He groaned against her throat. Then he dipped his mouth toward the rise of her breast. He wanted to strip her bare.

His erection grew painful, but that didn't stop him. He pushed up against her.

And he had the momentary thought to take her right there.

Instead, he lifted his mouth from her body, his breaths coming in harsh gasps, and watched her in the moonlight. His thumb was wet from her mouth. He trailed it over her bottom lip and down the center of her throat. He kept going until he reached the spot right between her breasts.

It was warm there.

It was heaven.

As he studied her, his words came back to him. He'd told her he wasn't making promises, but he worried that had been a lie. He wanted to make promises.

He wanted to love her.

He wanted to make certain she never kissed another man in her life.

Then she shifted, lifting up so she could bring her leg over until she straddled him. He lowered his hands to her thighs. The desire to crawl underneath her skirt was strong, but he forced himself to hold back. Too much too soon, and it would be over. He intended for both of them to have a night that would be hard to surpass.

That wouldn't happen if he went off like a teenager in the front seat of his car.

"We need to take this inside," he croaked out.

She nodded, but her movements didn't indicate she planned to get out of the car anytime soon. Instead, she scooted forward, seating the vee of her legs around his very prominent bulge. She was wet and burning. That couldn't be missed, even through the material of his pants.

"Holly," he warned.

Her hands moved to the front of his shirt. "I need to touch you," she told him, her words urgent. And then her fingers went to work.

She fumbled, but she didn't relent. In seconds his shirt hung open.

Her eyes glowed as she paused long enough to take him in. That was a look he could get used to. Then her hands flattened on his chest.

It was as if a thousand needles pricked him at once, and he surged up, lifting her with him. And then the horn of his car blared.

He dropped to the seat and let out a breathless groan. Off in the distance he once again heard her geese honk. He laughed. "I think your geese are protesting my being here."

She pressed her lips to his chest. "Then I'll have to get rid of my geese."

He tilted his chin up so he could draw in air as he tried to slow things down. Holly was still running her lips over him, though. She struck him as a woman on a mission, and he struggled to remember why he would possibly want her to stop.

The horn sounded again and he was reminded.

His car wasn't made for him to do what he wanted to do to her.

As she continued greedily sipping at him, he fumbled for the door handle, and practically tumbled them both to the ground.

Somehow he managed to keep her in his arms, and they made it to her front door. She slipped two fingers between her breasts and proudly produced a key, smiling wickedly as she handed it over to him. He merely groaned out his frustration. He wanted *his* hands inside the front of her dress.

Then they were in her house, with so much light from the moon spilling in through the kitchen windows that he didn't need to turn on a lamp.

"Hurry," she whispered. Her mouth once again found the skin of his throat.

Her legs were tight around his waist. And he hurried.

Seconds later, when he entered her bedroom, her words from the car came back.

With all the windows letting in the moonlight . . . I want to see you in my mirrors.

It was like a carnival fun house in the room. Blue light streaked through the glass, reflecting off the mirrors to angle and hit others. Her bed beckoned from the middle of the space. Everywhere he looked, he could see the two of them reflected back.

He took his time now, knowing he wanted to experience this moment to the fullest, and moved slowly through the room. He didn't stop until he found just the right spot. They were in front of a vertical mirror positioned a couple feet off the ground. It rose up at least four feet.

"Unzip your dress," he commanded.

She lifted her head and looked at him. Her eyes were hazy with lust, her lips full and lush where they'd been grazing on his skin, and he almost forgot what he'd said. He licked his own lips, wanting desperately to taste hers again, but managed to drag his gaze away instead. Once it landed on the mirror behind her, he remembered. He wanted to see her skin reflected back at him. And he didn't want to put her down to do it.

Her head turned to follow his and she caught his eyes in the mirror. She let her gaze trail down over their reflection. The look on her face was hot. Naughty. Then the corners of her mouth curled up.

It was an animalistic smile.

And it was hungry.

He grew even harder.

She brought her head back around, watching him. He couldn't take his eyes off her. Her hands slipped behind her back, her fingers reaching until they grasped the tiny zipper just below her shoulder blades. She paused.

He let out a breath.

Then she tugged.

The fabric parted all the way down and he could make out the briefest glimpse of silver lace at the top curve of her rear. Her back was a thin sliver of skin in the middle of pale pink, and a silver band ran horizontally across the middle. It matched her panties.

"Slip your arms out of the straps."

He didn't pull his gaze from the mirror, but he could feel the heat of hers still on him. His words had come out thin. A reedy whisper in the silent room.

The straps dropped to her elbows.

He fought with himself. Watch the material fall in front? Or in back?

"Push it down," he practically begged. "Off."

The mirror won out.

The part in the material widened as she shifted in his arms. Her left arm slid free and the right side of her dress sagged.

Then her right arm.

The other side drooped. The dress still didn't fall. He quickly brought his gaze around to her front. She had her hands covering her breasts, holding the dress up. He swore his erection began to weep.

The muscles of his arms burned with the need to put her down. Not because she was heavy, but because he wanted to explore her himself.

He flicked his gaze back to the mirror, demanding himself to retain control.

The gap from the zipper was now several inches wide. The silver of her panties and bra glistened in the blue reflection.

And his hands burned to touch.

He kept one hand at her rear, holding her tight, and tugged with the other. Her dress fell.

Holly sucked in a soft gasp of air. She wrapped her arms around his neck.

Except for the strapless bra, she was now bare from the waist up. The slope of her back glistened in the night. Her shoulders curved with femininity. And her breasts . . .

He could make out the slight curves rounding out from her sides. He couldn't take his eyes off those curves.

She rubbed against him; the lace of her bra tickled his skin.

He wanted her bra gone.

How many other men had seen her like this? In this room? Reflected in the moonlight like some sort of goddess.

And then he remembered. She'd never let anyone else in here. Only him.

Heavy need rose until it almost cut off his breath. The woman in his arms was special.

And he wanted to keep her.

As if sensing his thoughts, she leaned back just enough to meet his eyes. She didn't speak. Simply studied him. Her eyes were solemn, and seemed to be saying that she understood. This wasn't just some hookup. This was them. And *they* were special.

Then she tilted forward and settled her lips over his.

She took her time, the same as she'd done in the car. She tasted. Licked. Nibbled and sucked. But every time he tried to take it deeper, she pulled back. So he quit trying. He panted against her as she laved over him, and he let *her* seduce him.

He was just about to beg for mercy when she once again lifted her head. Her eyelids were heavy. She licked her lips as if tasting him on hers, her green eyes locked on his, and he groaned out loud. Then she shifted her gaze to take in the room. She paused every little bit, studying the vision they made, seeming to enjoy the sight as much as he.

He turned his head along with hers, and they both stared into a side mirror. Her body was wrapped around his, her curves everywhere.

"Holly," he pleaded. He had to see more. When her eyes lifted to his reflection, he begged, "The bra."

She nodded, and then her hands once again went behind her back. She didn't look away from the mirror, her gaze clinging to his, and his breath could no longer make it out of his lungs.

She pinched the material between her fingers and the band dropped to her sides. Then she pressed into him to keep it from falling off. He closed his eyes in pain. He throbbed so hard he had no idea how there could be any blood anywhere else in his body. He needed release. And he needed it soon.

Forcing his breaths to return, he pulled in lungfuls of air, and he pried his eyes open. He wanted to bring his gaze around to her body. The real one, not the reflection. But he couldn't. He liked watching her watching him.

Both hands cupped her butt, holding her tight against him, and as she let the scrap of material fall, her back arched away. He didn't blink. And he didn't breathe.

The bra landed at his feet.

She was stupendous. Her breasts were heavy and round. Her nipples puckered into hard beads of desire. He had to put his mouth there.

"Touch me," she urged. She slid her own hands along the sides of her breasts, pushing them together, and his knees went weak. "Please," she begged.

He nodded. "I'm going to touch you," he promised. "If I don't, my own hands will strangle me where I stand."

A smile played on her lips, and then *her* hands touched him. She slid them into his open shirt, her soft fingers burning a path over his body.

"I've wanted to touch you like this for days," she whispered hotly. Her fingers worked over his skin, and he couldn't move across the room fast enough. Instead of heading to the bed, he moved to the dresser.

He swiped one arm out, sweeping everything to the floor. Her laughter filled his head.

Then he plopped her down on top.

"I've wanted to do *this* since the first day I met you," he pointed out.

He gripped her wrists in his hands and held them down at her sides. His gaze devoured her. She still had her dress on, bunched at her waist, and her breaths kept her chest rising and falling.

"I don't believe you," she whispered, a note of teasing in her voice. "Since you *first* saw me?"

He nodded. He kept her arms pinned at her sides, and dipped forward. As if he needed the additional punishment, he skipped the darkened tips and nipped gently on the inside curve.

She gasped. Her chest pushed up. "You barely even looked at me when you first saw me." Her words were breathy. "Other than to snarl at my shoes."

"Baby," he mumbled against her, turning his mouth to nibble on the inner curve of the other breast. She smelled like flowers and sunshine. "I noticed every last damned thing about you."

He moved her arms behind her back and gripped both wrists in one hand, and then he took in her profile in a mirror.

"You had on a white shirt," he started. He traced the tip of his finger from the top curve of her breast, down to circle around the slightly darker skin of her areola. He continued watching her in the mirror. She watched him as well. "Your breasts strained so tight against it." He circled his finger in tighter. "As if desperate to get out."

He cupped her then, and held her up to his mouth. She whimpered when he took a tiny swipe with his tongue.

They both continued watching in the mirror.

"Your shorts barely covered your ass," he went on.

"I had on leggings." She twitched, jerking forward, her body reaching out to him.

"Not in my mind," he admitted. He landed on her nipple and sucked. Hard. A deep, guttural sound came from the back of her throat. "I wasn't sure you were old enough to be legal." He turned his face back to the mirror, letting his cheek brush over her now-damp tip while he continued holding her in his hand. He flicked a thumb over her and she shuddered. "But even then, I pictured my palms cupping your ass." He squeezed her breast. "My face between your tits."

She growled, low and hot. "How old did you think I was?"

"Eighteen," he muttered. He released her arms from behind her back and brought both hands around front. He was killing himself with the torture.

"I did not . . . look . . . eighteen." The words were spoken between tiny bursts of air as he held her breasts together and alternated his mouth between her nipples. He plucked at her, sucking and tugging, gulping as if he were drinking her very essence.

She was exquisite. Both *her* and the sight of her in his hands. And he knew that he was just out of his mind enough to want more. More of her. More of this.

More than the next week and a half.

He lifted his head and locked in on her eyes, now a deep, needy green. He just wanted her.

"Lift your ass," he demanded softly. When she did, he yanked her dress down her legs.

She sat before him in a tiny scrap of silvery lace, her breasts heavy and right in front of his face, and her eyes telling him that he wasn't the only one who might want more.

He could love this woman.

"I'm so glad you didn't turn out to be eighteen," he told her.

Then he gripped her panties and tugged them off too. The second they landed on the floor, he spread his hands wide on her thighs. Her breath hitched.

"I'm going to touch you now," he said. His thumb swooped between her legs, barely alighting on her skin and the narrow brush of hair. His words came out sounding like a threat, yet it was a promise. "With my mouth."

He parted her thighs, eyeing her with greed. She was wet.

"And with my tongue."

She whimpered.

He lifted one hand to grasp her chin and turned her toward the mirror. "And I want you to watch me while I do it," he growled out.

And then he dipped his head.

Holly quit breathing the instant Zack's head settled between her thighs. The contrast of his dark hair against her pale thighs was striking.

As was the swipe of his tongue.

She braced both hands on top of the dresser, her breaths coming in gasps, and strained her hips toward him. Her lip slipped between her teeth as she fought to keep from crying out. It had been way too long since she'd had a man *there*.

His tongue worked diligently, sending pleasure to the secret places in her body, and even if he hadn't told her to watch, that's exactly what she would have been doing. The mirrors added an erotic feel she'd only ever dreamed about. Add to that his soft demands for her to undress herself—*while he'd watched*—and she'd been half gone before he'd ever laid a hand on her.

It had been the look in his eyes, though, that had done her in.

This wasn't just sex to him. That's what the look had said.

She didn't know if she could believe it, but she would swear that's what she'd seen just before she'd taken off her bra. This was more. *They* were more.

Fear of getting her heart broken screamed that she couldn't think like that.

He could still walk away.

But what she felt inside had a stronger hold on her now. Love.

Was she in love?

She closed her eyes, refusing to answer the question.

Zack's hands slipped under her rear and tugged her forward, his mouth grabbing a stronger hold, and his tongue making her forget her worries.

"Zack," she whispered the word. It came out as a plea.

She brought a hand to his head, both wanting to press him closer, while at the same time lift him away. He didn't let up.

She held her breath and arched her back until her head bumped against the mirror on the wall behind her. The pressure inside her built. It screamed to be let free.

"Take me to bed, Zack," she begged. "I want you inside me."

She wanted to be connected to him in the most elemental way the first time she came. She wanted to know that he was there with her. A part of her.

Just in case she was right and he walked away.

He paused and she sucked in a deep gulp of air.

Then his head slowly turned. He was still bent between her legs, but his face appeared in the mirror now. His mouth glistened with her juices, and she wiggled with the urge for more.

She forced herself to sit still.

"Make love to me," she said softly.

That look was back in his eye.

She nodded. "You and me. Now."

Hungry possession flashed across his face as he rose and scooped her off the dresser.

"Yes," she urged. "Hurry."

He wrapped her in his arms, and before it even felt like they'd moved, he was lowering her to her bed. The instant she hit the mattress, her hands went wild to rid him of his clothes.

She shoved the shirt from his shoulders, leaving it halfway down his arms while he started on his belt. Then her hands were on his fly, unzipping his jeans. She couldn't go fast enough.

He shrugged out of his shirt and she pulled him from his pants.

"Ah," he groaned as her fingers closed tight around him. He momentarily paused, rearing back as if her touch burned. His teeth gleamed in a feral clench.

He was so hot. And so hard.

It was everything she could do not to put him in her mouth right then and there. She wanted to taste him. But she wanted more to feel him.

"Inside me," she begged.

She let him know with her look that she would do more. Later. She would take him in her mouth. Until he begged.

But right now . . .

He shoved her to the bed, and then he was on top of her. Somehow, a condom appeared in his hand. His eyes were on hers.

Then everything slowed.

They rolled the protection down over him together, and he stretched out, his body touching hers all the way down. His elbows braced against the mattress and his hands gently cupped her head. His thumbs slid over her temples. His mouth dipped for her kiss.

It was a slow burn. And that kiss said the same thing she'd seen in his eyes.

She meant something to him.

She was special.

When he pulled back, he simply stared at her. Moonlight made him seem to glow in the room as she slid her hands down his sides and eased her legs apart. Heat nudged against her core. His harder, rougher skin tantalized her. Everywhere. She nodded.

And then he slid inside.

They both pressed their mouths closed, their chests heaving against the other, and it was complete silence in her room.

And she knew.

She was absolutely in love with this man.

Then he began to move, and it was the best damned feeling she'd ever experienced in her life. He was slow and hard. Masterful. And he knew exactly where to find her favorite spots.

His body pumped above hers, sliding deep, in and out, leaving her breathless with each move. All while keeping her head steady between his hands. His eyes on her eyes.

And then he kissed her.

And then they both tipped over the edge.

Chapter Twenty-Two

Holly opened her eyes as sunlight peeked over the mountains and hit her windows. She was on her back, and though her head wasn't turned to Zack, she knew he was still there. His weight pressed into her, and his heat seemed to cocoon her.

He'd been wonderful last night.

No. That didn't tell the whole truth. He'd been freaking awesome last night.

And she wasn't just thinking about the sex.

He'd understood what receiving that e-mail had meant to her. She'd gotten her hopes up. Again. Which had made her as upset as receiving the e-mail had.

She was done with all of that once and for all. She'd either sell them herself, or she would never sell them at all. And she was okay with that decision. She couldn't go through that sort of rejection over and over again. Maybe some people could handle it. The big artists had been through hundreds of rejections. She knew that. She'd studied about it as she'd worked on her degree. Tough skin and all.

But she didn't want tough skin. She just wanted to create.

She wanted to be happy. To smile each day, and hopefully make someone else's day brighter just for being in it. She was good at that. And she loved it.

So she was finished seeking an external outlet for her mirrors. They would be sold out of Sugar Springs, or they wouldn't be sold at all.

The decision made her more content than she'd ever thought it could.

She focused out the windows and thought about the other things that had been discovered throughout the night.

Like Zack's muscles. And his stamina.

His compassion.

He really was a wonderful guy. And a great lover.

And she just happened to be in love with him.

Yep. That was the big revelation to come from the night. She had fallen in love with Zack Winston. Just as she'd feared. Someone who would leave her in barely more than a week.

Unless she convinced him to take her with him?

The pressure of tears built in the back of her eyes because even if she could convince him, if by some miracle he fell in love with her too, she didn't want to move to Atlanta. His house was great. His mother was greater. His car was off the charts.

But her life was here.

Her mirrors were . . . here.

She closed her eyes and thought about Zack. He'd been in love before. He'd even had his biological mother stomp all over his emotions. Holly couldn't imagine him taking another chance. Not with his heart.

Work and his life might commingle, but women and his life didn't.

No matter what his eyes had told her last night.

A tear slipped from the corner of her eye and trekked toward the sheet because she knew he wouldn't take the chance. Not on her. And she couldn't blame him. She turned her face toward the ceiling to stanch the tears. She didn't want to lie there and cry.

But when she shifted, she found that Zack was awake. He was on one elbow, a pair of übersexy, little rectangular glasses perched on his nose, and he was watching her. And now he was looking at that one tear track leading from her eye to her hairline.

"What's wrong?" he asked. He'd whispered. It seemed the right volume for the quiet morning. Everything was so still. The moment solemn.

She understood this.

She would have whispered too.

She shook her head. "Nothing."

"But you're crying." He lifted his hand to swipe against her drying cheek. Then he turned her face toward him and pressed a kiss to the track. It put a lump in her throat.

"It was one tear," she mumbled into his chest. "One tear doesn't constitute crying. I think I had something in my eye."

He gave her his scary look. She didn't feel like laughing.

"Oh my," he said. "Something really *is* wrong when you don't even laugh at me."

This cracked a tiny smile, and he gave her one just as small in return.

"Last night was good," he said softly.

She nodded. "Last night was great."

"Then why the tear?"

"It was just a lot." Too much, she thought. Because of the love. And because he would be leaving soon.

Because she figured that she was just this week's woman.

"Why are you wearing glasses?" she asked. She needed to lighten the mood. Change the subject. "Afraid you didn't turn me on enough last night?"

One corner of his mouth inched higher. "You like my glasses?"

She moaned in pure pleasure and the other side of his mouth rose to match the first.

"I like that," he said. "I had no idea glasses would turn you on. Maybe I should have brought them out before."

"Everything about you turns me on," she admitted. "It always has." Which maybe wasn't so smart to say, to give him that power, but they *were* lying naked in bed together.

"My contacts were bugging me when I first woke up, so I ran out to the car to get them." He tugged the sheet so that it slipped below her breasts. "I wanted to be able to see you like this."

His words came out heavy and needy, and she couldn't help but need a little more herself. She stretched, lifting her arms over her head, and grinned at Zack as hunger crossed over his features. He was watching the movement of her breasts and nothing else.

"Well, I like them," she confessed. "A lot. They're almost as sexy as your car."

He was still focused on her breasts. His hand curled around one now, squeezing it in his fingers in an experimental way, as if he hadn't completely explored that particular body part the night before. She wiggled beneath him.

"Which car?" he asked. His voice was gruff.

"The Roadmaster."

He smiled and leaned forward to suck her nipple into his mouth. She let out a slow, long moan.

"If I promise to bring it up for the wedding, will you go as my date?" He'd lifted his mouth from her body, but remained positioned over her, his breath whispering over the wet tip of her breast. Only now his dark eyes were trained on hers.

She gulped. Lee Ann and Cody's wedding. "I wasn't sure if you'd be coming up for it or not."

"I'll be in it." The pride in his voice almost brought the tears back. She could see it in his face. His brothers had accepted him.

She lifted on her elbows and set her mouth to his. She kissed him with every ounce of the passion she was feeling, combined with all the love she had for him.

It was not a minor kiss.

When she pulled back, they were both breathing hard and his eyes had grown darker. She nodded. "I'd love to go as your date."

The wedding was in three weeks. He would go home next weekend, but if he wanted to take her as his date, maybe he was thinking she could be his woman of the month. Instead of just the week.

Unless she would just be his woman when he was up here.

The joy left her and she eased back to the bed.

"Hey," he said gently. "What happened?"

"Nothing." She tried to force cheer. She wasn't about to tell him that she was simply trying to figure out how much time she had left.

Because she wasn't going to kid herself. He might be attracted to her, but he wouldn't let her be more.

A phone rang from the floor and they turned their heads to the discarded clothing.

"That's mine," Zack said.

She wanted to tell him not to get it, but he was already climbing out of the bed. So instead, she watched his naked body as he scooped up his jeans and dug into his pocket.

His ass was spectacular.

He caught her watching and winked at her, and she blew him a kiss.

"Hurry back," she whispered.

She sat up in bed, letting the sheet fall to her waist, and smiled when Zack's gaze latched onto her body.

He jerked his eyes away as he pulled out the phone and tossed his jeans to the floor. "It's my boss." He spoke almost to himself. She pulled the sheet up over her breasts as if the other man could see into the room with them.

As Zack answered, he sat on the side of the bed and snatched the sheet out of her hands. Then he palmed her breast as he talked to his boss.

It felt dirty. And hot. And she was ready to go again. Right then.

Until Zack said into the phone, "But I'm taking one more week."

His hand still on her, her throat grew tight.

"Right now?" he asked.

He nodded as he listened, and it was as if a transformation came over the man before her very eyes. He sat up straighter. His face hardened. And he seemed to forget that she was sitting naked beside him. She covered herself with the sheet.

"No, sir," he spoke clearly. He had his lawyer voice back. "Nothing whatsoever. Just a short vacation. I can be there today."

His words broke her heart.

Nothing whatsoever.

When he got off the phone, he stepped away and began pulling on his clothes. He didn't look at her. An air of tension surrounded him that she hadn't seen in a couple weeks. She'd forgotten how much he'd changed since he'd arrived in Sugar Springs.

"I've got to go back to Atlanta this morning," he said as he shoved an arm in his shirt.

He shot her a glance. Then he looked at the bedside clock as if he'd already been there too long.

"Get some clothes on and I'll give you a ride to the house. There's a case that'll—"

"Go on without me," she interrupted. She could already feel him pulling away.

She didn't care to hear about the case. And she didn't want to get back in the car with him. Not right then. She could walk. She suspected she might need the fresh air.

Especially given the distance that had already slammed down between them.

He had all but two buttons fastened and he paused long enough to give her a belittling look. "Don't be silly. Put your clothes on and I'll drop you at the house. I need to shower and get Mom anyway."

His dismissive attitude was the deciding factor.

She didn't let people treat her like that anymore. Like she was just some silly little country girl, out looking to sell her silly little mirrors.

No one would ever get away with that again.

"No need to worry," she informed him with an impressive amount of calm. She wouldn't waste her breath pointing out what an arrogant jerk he was being. What good would it do? Their time was clearly over. And she wouldn't beg. "I'm a big girl. I know my way through the woods."

Her tone must have caught his attention because he paused as he shoved his wallet into his pocket. "You okay?" he asked.

Sure. She was dandy. The man she loved was heading home, and she thought he might just forget her before he even got out her front door.

She wanted to cry at the thought.

"I'm great," she answered brightly. "Think I'll sleep a bit more before I head back, is all. It was a big night, you know. You performed quite well."

His eyes turned to thin slits. "It wasn't a performance," he said carefully.

She shrugged. "It was good, whatever it was. Thanks for the memories."

Complete silence ticked away for ten full seconds as they stared at each other. Zack didn't move. Neither did she.

Then his jaw hardened even more.

"Memories?" he asked. The coldness in his voice startled her.

"Yeah." She nodded and offered a halfhearted smile. It was fake, but it was all she had. "I had a good time. And like you pointed out, neither of us promised more." She pushed up the smile. "Hope we can keep in touch."

If she wasn't mistaken, it was fury staring back at her now. She couldn't imagine what for. If she hadn't done it to him, he would have to her. She'd bet her mirrors on it.

She supposed he wasn't used to the morning-after brush-off being directed his way. No doubt he was a master at doling it out, though.

"What's going on, Holly?" He asked the question cautiously. "What am I missing?"

She recalled his earlier words to his boss, and managed to hold on to her smile just long enough to repeat, "Nothing whatsoever."

He stared at her blankly for another second, and then he nodded. And he left her house.

The short drive to the bed-and-breakfast consisted of a lot of cursing, a couple slams of his hand against the steering wheel, and more than once calling himself a fool.

How had he managed to again be falling for someone who cared so little about him?

Thanks for the memories, his ass.

As if he was nothing to her.

And when he let himself think about it, he supposed that might be the case. He was nothing to her. Except her friend.

Or he had been.

That bullshit in her bedroom had destroyed that.

Because he couldn't care for someone who could look at him so casually. Not even as a friend.

He turned into the driveway of the B&B and admitted to himself that when he'd realized he had to go home, he'd given his usual thought to brushing her off. Exactly as she'd done him.

For about two seconds.

But then he'd looked at her sitting in her bed, the sheet covering all that soft goodness that he'd held in his arms last night, and he'd known that he couldn't do that. Not to her.

It may have been his style, but he was a changed man. Holly had done that.

And then she'd smacked him in the face and kicked him in the balls.

A healthy dose of irritation, mixed with all-out anger, had him jerking the car to an abrupt halt. He climbed out and took the porch stairs three at a time, and was at his mother's bedroom door before he heard her laughter coming from the dining room.

Perfect. He'd been hoping not to run into anyone before he got them out of there.

He wasn't in the mood for chitchat.

"Mr. Winston," Sylvia Marshall said as he stepped to the arch of the dining room. "So nice of you to join us this morning." She held up a bowl. She wore the look of someone who knew he'd just left her daughter's bed. "Would you like some eggs and grits?"

Which only made him think of Holly and how she'd made pancakes for him two weeks ago on eggs-and-grits day. She'd tried to put chocolate chips in them.

"No, thanks." His words were curt.

His mother narrowed her eyes at him from her seat at the table, no doubt over his rude tone, but he didn't care. The woman he'd thought he was falling for had just swatted him away as if he were nothing more than a gnat. He had to get back to Atlanta, and he had to get his head on straight.

Work was his number one priority.

Number two was also work.

Holly couldn't factor into the picture at all. Nor could lazing about in this Podunk town. It was time to go.

"Mom," he said. He motioned for her. "Come on. We have to go back to Atlanta."

She didn't get up.

Seven other faces turned to him around the large dining room table.

"I'm having my grits," his mother explained as if he couldn't see what she was doing. "They're cheese grits."

He clenched his teeth. "I'll buy you breakfast on the road. I need to get to the office."

A high-profile case had come in. It would redeem him for the Butler debacle. This case *would* make him partner.

His mother shook her head. "I'm not going back to Atlanta today, Zachary. The Firefly Festival is tomorrow. We're going with Cody and Nick."

"We *were* going with Cody and Nick," he corrected. "My boss called. I've got to go."

"Then you go on. I'm staying here."

Once again, his back teeth ground together. If he kept this up, his dentist would be able to buy a new boat the next time Zack went in to see him.

"Mother," he said.

She turned her back to him and began talking to the man on the other side of her.

She had to be kidding him. He didn't want to have to drag her from the room.

"Mother," he tried again. He did not have time for this.

Everyone at the table continued to stare at him, including Mrs. Marshall, who stood in the doorway to the kitchen. Still holding her bowl of grits.

"I told you," his mom started, "I'm not going. I'm enjoying my time here. You should too."

"I have enjoyed it." He smiled at Mrs. Marshall to show his appreciation for her hospitality. "It's simply time to go now."

"Slow down, Zackie. Enjoy life for a change."

"I do enjoy my life, Mom. Success makes me happy. This case I've got to get back to is the one I've been waiting for. It will make me very happy." He put his hand on his mother's shoulder and softened his voice. "Come on. I really have to go. This is the one that'll make me partner."

"Stay through tomorrow." His mother couldn't be swayed. "Go to the festival with Holly. Have a good time."

That was the wrong thing to say at that moment.

He took a step back from the table. "I'm leaving in fifteen minutes," he announced. "You need to choose whether you're staying or going."

Without hesitation, she stated, "I'm staying and going to the festival with your brothers."

Rejection slapped him across the face yet again.

"I'll send a car for you Sunday morning."

For the second time that day, he turned and walked out of a room without looking back.

Chapter Twenty-Three

I heard he left."

Holly looked up from her phone as she stepped to the front of the bus. She was the last person to exit after the ride over from the parking lot, and Jesse Beckman now sat watching her from the driver's seat. He wore a baseball cap, along with the official "Firefly Festival Committee" T-shirt that Trina had made up for everyone. Holly had forgotten to wear her T-shirt.

It was the middle of Saturday afternoon, and Holly was just now arriving at the festival. She wouldn't have shown up at all if she hadn't promised to help man the rubber duck race. But as a Marshall, it was hard to get out of that particular task.

"Who left?" she asked. She shifted out of the way, stepping into the front row to allow those wishing to head back to their cars to board. She wasn't in the mood for chitchat, but she also wouldn't be rude—not even when the last thing she wanted to do was be civil. Her mama had taught her better.

"Winston," Jesse said. His eyes held hers, and she caught herself fixating on how long his eyelashes were. Most women would die for eyelashes like that.

Most women would also appreciate not being reminded that the man they were supposed to be there with was gone.

She found her fake smile. "Yep. Headed back yesterday."

"Heard he didn't take his mama."

"He was in a hurry. My understanding is he's sending a car for her tomorrow. She wanted to stay and see the fireflies."

Sympathy shone in Jesse's eyes. Small towns were wonderful until something happened and everyone knew your business. And chances were the story going around was ten times worse than the reality.

She'd gone home with Zack Thursday night and he'd raced out of town as fast as possible the next morning. Those were the facts.

Clearly, that had to have been her fault.

Probably the whole town believed she must be some kind of crazy funky in bed or something. That certainly boded well for ever getting another date in her life.

But then, maybe crazy funky would bring her more dates than she'd ever want.

Only, not any man she would want.

But then, she didn't want just any man.

"I'm sorry." Jesse's words were solemn. "I'd gotten the impression you two were—"

"I'm fine, Jesse." She didn't want to know what impression he'd gotten. "Zack was nothing." Her voice cracked on the last syllable and she quickly looked down at her phone. Thankfully, she'd just gotten a return text from Brian. She'd asked where she was supposed to be just before the bus had stopped. She held up her phone. "I need to run. Good seeing you again."

Before she could take the steps down to put her out in the sunshine and away from the conversation, Jesse added one thing more.

"I'd still like to take you out," he said.

Her throat closed. How was she supposed to go out with another man?

She turned back, and the look coming her way was patient and kind. It said he was a good guy, just wanting to get to know her better. And she wasn't an idiot. She knew she didn't need to push away the good guys. There were too few of those to choose from. Someday she just might want to go out with one.

Damn Zack anyway.

"Whenever you're ready," Jesse added.

Tears threatened, but she pushed them back down. She would not stand in the middle of the entire population of Sugar Springs—plus several thousand tourists—and cry over a man who'd run away from her at the first opportunity.

Plus, Jesse did seem like a sweetheart. She didn't say anything—*couldn't say anything*—but she gave him a nod. Someday, yes, she just might go out with him.

She turned away from the bus and took in the field before her, mentally pumping herself up to handle the day. She'd already missed the parade, but there were still hours of fun before everyone got bussed to the hillside where the fireflies made their annual showing.

Synchronous fireflies showed up in June, and people came from all over the country to see them. Being a part of that was a tradition. Not only for her family, but for the whole town. Everything would be shut down and deserted come dark.

Yet this year she'd considered missing it because of a man.

How silly.

She breathed in the smells of fried everything and moved toward the crowds. There would be funnel cakes, fried Twinkies and Oreos, even fried ice cream. And if they were lucky, there would be a booth serving a half-pound cheeseburger with a scoop of fried ice cream plopped right on top. It was a specialty.

The whole place was a heart attack waiting to happen.

The sight of a booth she'd never seen before made her slow her steps, and then she began to laugh. It was the booth for Sam's Food-mart. Miley Rogers had apparently *not* lost her fondness for loud colors, as the once white and slightly rusted traveling concession stand now had bold purple, yellow, and pink cartoon-like fireflies painted all over it. Behind the fireflies was a vibrant-blue night sky. And of course, all the tails glowed bright. With real lights.

Sam was behind the small crowd that had formed at the open windows, pacing back and forth. He would take ten steps, turn and look at the booth, then reverse and go back the other way. The man's face seemed to be a shade too red, but then, he also had two lines thirty deep waiting for his food. He couldn't be that upset.

It was the brightest booth in the area, and that seemed to be doing the job. The man would make a killing today. If he didn't die of a heart attack, he might even have to thank Mrs. Rogers and her daughter for their sneakiness.

Trina rushed by, a sheaf of papers in one hand, before pulling up short about fifteen feet away from Holly. She whirled around.

"Where is your T-shirt?"

Holly looked down at the yellow blouse she had on as if surprised to see her official festival T-shirt missing. "I guess I forgot," she finally answered.

She was beginning to regret not coming out earlier. At least she would have had fun watching Trina run around hyperactively all day.

"I brought extras." Trina held one hand up as if stopping traffic. "Come with me."

Oh good. Just what she wanted. But Holly followed along behind the other woman, stepping into a small, stuffy trailer that smelled like mothballs and old newspapers. It was better than standing alone in the middle of the crowd, she supposed.

Until now, she hadn't come out of her cabin since Zack had left. Instead she had spent yesterday and this morning alternately moping over the sad state of her love life and working on her new career. Not just finalizing a couple of unfinished pieces, but outlining a business plan for her own store.

She had an appointment set up to see the empty storefront on the square tomorrow.

Screw everyone who thought she was a joke. Who laughed at her or looked down their noses at her. She didn't need them or their pity.

This was what she wanted, and she intended to do it.

She would bring her family out to the cabin tomorrow morning, and she would let them know that her time as bookkeeper-slash-cook-slash-check-in girl was over. She had her own career to get off the ground.

Nerves were eating her up at the very thought of it, but Brian assured her everything would be okay. He'd kept her secret. However, he also had faith that the rest of the family would be as supportive as he. Until she saw it for herself, she would continue to worry.

"Ta-da!" Trina stood from the plastic tub she'd been rummaging through and held a blue-and-white T-shirt up to Holly's chest. "Perfect," she declared.

"Perfect," Holly agreed. Since she couldn't get out of the day, it was easiest to go along.

When she stepped from the trailer in her new, only mildly stiff and stinky, T-shirt, she once again headed into the throng of people. She needed to be at the river soon. The races would be starting.

As she weaved through the booths and games, she saw Gina off in the distance flirting with a tourist, and Sandy and Bubba Brown, both looking like they were up to no good. And then there was Keith. He lifted his head and met her gaze, and he, too, sent her a sad look. It was identical to the one Jesse had given her.

Yeah, yeah. The whole town knew she'd fallen for the wrong guy. She got it. Move on.

She should have stayed home. At least there she could have gotten back to the other thing that had taken up hours of her time.

Missing Zack.

Wanting Zack.

Wishing she were more than "nothing whatsoever" to Zack.

Her subconscious kept nagging at her, suggesting that she might have read things wrong. He had been talking to his boss, after all. If the case was important enough, he wouldn't want to explain that he couldn't come back yet because he wanted to get laid a couple more times first.

And yes, he had looked down his nose at her. But again, could that have been more about the case than about her? He'd been in a hurry. Possibly his feelings for her hadn't really factored into his actions at all.

She had no idea. Because she hadn't bothered to let him tell her about the call.

Which, in hindsight, she regretted.

That might have answered a few questions.

And now that she thought about it, he *had* looked rather shocked when she'd flippantly thanked him for the evening. In fact, he'd looked outright furious. If he'd been about to brush her off himself, would her doing it first have really made him so angry?

She just didn't know.

Maybe—possibly.

But also, it was possible he *hadn't* been about to depart from her life and never look back. Which would still have left them with issues. What else could come of their time together? A few more rolls in the hay? A handful of laughs?

They would have been good rolls, and good laughs.

But still. Love?

She didn't see that happening. Not for Zack. Not with his past.

Plus, at the first phone call, he'd returned to big-city, lawyer Zack in a heartbeat. That's who he was. He would never be content to fit into her life.

And in her life, love led to marriage. Marriage to forever. Together. As in . . . Atlanta?

Which she couldn't see happening either.

She sighed.

She did miss him, though. Terribly. And it had only been one full day. She couldn't imagine how much worse it was going to get.

Good thing she hadn't told him she was in love with him. How embarrassing would that have been?

A coral-colored rose appeared in front of her nose as she stood staring blindly at the contestants already lining up for the firefly "duck" race. Her breath stuck in the back of her throat.

He'd come back.

He regretted leaving. Not calling.

He needed her as much as she needed him.

Slowly, holding back the desire to let a smile find its way to her lips, she turned and followed the arm holding out the flower. Her heart pounded with both relief and joy.

And then she saw that the arm was attached to Hounddog Thompson.

The breath rushed out of her and tears sprang to her eyes. *Damn.*

She brought her hand to her mouth.

Hounddog stood in front of her with sunglasses on and his hair mussed. He also looked like he was up to no good. *And* he looked amazing.

Only, he wasn't who she wanted to see.

"You okay?" Bobby asked gently. He removed his sunglasses.

She nodded and swiped a tear from her cheek.

He flipped the flower back up so its petals tickled her nose. "You looked like you could use this."

His tone said he got it. She was broken. He wasn't there for anything more than to be a friend. And she was more grateful for that than anything in a long time.

She took the flower and mumbled, "Thank you, Bobby," and his arms went around her and pulled her to his chest. She dropped her head to his shoulder. It was a lovely gesture. All of it. The flower. The friend.

The hug.

The knowing she was standing there miserable.

"I won it for you." He motioned to a carnival game with vases of roses sitting behind the table as prizes. "I picked this one out because it matched your shoes."

Her heart shattered.

Any other day, and she would have loved that someone picked her out a flower because it matched her shoes. And if she went by her own rules, that meant that Bobby was an okay guy. He'd noticed her shoes.

But she already knew he was an okay guy. He always had been. He'd just been a bit of a hound dog.

"Want to talk about it?" he asked.

She shook her head. She was still in his arms, and when she noticed Janet Winston watching the two of them, she turned her head in the other direction. Janet was standing at Joanie's cupcake van with the rest of the Dalton clan. Holly would have been over there with them if Zack were here.

"I'm good," she told Bobby. Because she was. Or she would be. She pushed out of his arms and surreptitiously wiped at her cheeks. "It was just . . . one night . . ." she added. And didn't that make her sound impressive? She gave him a resigned shrug. "A fling. It was nothing."

She wished her heart believed that.

Instead her heart kept making her look around, thinking every tall, dark-haired man looked like Zack.

She peeked at Janet once more, and the expression on the woman's face said it all. Zack wasn't coming. This wasn't where he wanted to be.

"Thought you might want company today," Bobby suggested.

She looked at her companion then. Really looked at him. He was still the same Hounddog. Sexy, droopy eyes that could reel in a girl in two seconds flat. Pouty mouth that would make said girl forget her own mama's name. And a body that did not want to stop.

He was a *very* good-looking man.

But she also saw more. It was behind those soulful blue eyes.

She didn't know why he'd come home now, but something had changed him. Possibly enough that he *could* be a different person.

If she could let herself fall in love with a man who had nothing whatsoever to give her in return, she supposed she could also believe that Bobby Thompson might have grown up while he'd been away. Weirder things had happened.

And for certain, hanging out with him today would only help her reputation at this point. After all, she was the girl who'd run a guy out of town after only one night.

If she would soon be thrust back out on the dating scene, why not build up her courage with Bobby? So yeah, she wanted some company today. And she wanted to go over to the hill and see the fireflies and have a really excellent time. She couldn't believe she'd contemplated not going just because Zack had broken her heart.

"I would love company today, Bobby. Thank you."

He gave her his award-winning smile, and she shook her head at the power of it.

"You need to bottle that stuff," she muttered.

He laughed out loud and held out his elbow, and she slipped her arm through his. For the first time since she'd woken up yesterday morning, she had a real smile on her face. She wasn't happy, but she would be. Eventually.

Until then, she would just fake it.

Zack paced the length of his mother's kitchen yet again. It was two in the afternoon, and he'd already been there for three hours. She should have been home by now.

He'd gotten a message from her late last night, letting him know that he didn't need to send a car. The "boys" would be bringing her home today.

The boys.

His brothers were now her boys?

What the hell had happened in the last forty-eight hours since he'd been gone?

And why couldn't she have just stuck with the original plan? If he'd sent a car, he would know that she was back safe and sound already.

Hell, she would have even gotten back in time to have lunch with him.

Not that he'd expected her to rush home and cook. He'd planned to take her out. He'd worked around the clock since he'd been back, just so he could be here for her when she got home.

It was Sunday. That's what they did.

Yet she was nowhere to be found. Probably off having fun with her two favorite "boys."

He was being an immature, jealous child, and he knew that. But he couldn't help it. It seemed like everything he wanted was being taken from him.

Holly had shoved him out of her life. His mother had chosen his brothers over him.

And likely, his brothers were choosing his mother over him too.

Issues, much?

He knew he had them. He wasn't a moron. But that didn't stop the anger from festering.

A door slammed outside, and then another. They were here. He went to the front door and yanked it open.

"Zackie," his mom called as Nick helped her from the backseat of Cody's SUV. She waved. She was smiling and happy, and she had on green from head to toe. She reminded him of Holly.

Zack bit his tongue to keep from yelling at her to quit calling him such a childish name.

"Hey." Nick lifted his chin as he pulled her luggage from the trunk. "Your mother's a hoot. She had us laughing the whole drive down."

The anger continued to bubble.

He knew his mother was a hoot. She was also *his* mother.

"Why are you so late?"

Cody had Janet by the elbow, escorting her to her own front door as if she were a queen. The action caused Zack to shoot his brother a vicious look. Cody ignored him. His mother preened.

"We had breakfast with Holly and Bobby before we left," she explained.

His heart pumped fire. "Who the hell is Bobby?"

"That nice-looking boy she was talking to at the diner the day we all had lunch," his mom told him. She gave him an innocent look, as if unaware what her words were doing to him. "You remember? Big guy, great smile. And his eyes—"

"Got it." He cut her off. Bobby was the man whose nickname was Hounddog.

"Then the boys were kind enough to stop at yard sales on the way down," she continued. "Such sweethearts. Holly told me how she likes to look for buttons and such at yard sales, so I picked up some things I thought she might like. I'll take them to her when we go up for the wedding."

Nick held several plastic bags up in front of him, as if to show Zack the proof. The bags looked to be bulging with junk. Nick also had her three pieces of luggage in one arm.

While Zack stood there doing nothing to help.

"She was having breakfast with Bobby?" He ignored the bags of junk and stepped to the side to let all three of them pass. What in the hell was Holly doing having breakfast with Bobby?

Cody and Nick eyed him as they entered the house. There was sympathy in the looks.

"She was working at first, but then Bobby showed up and she came out and ate with him. They joined us."

"What did they eat?"

His mother shot him a questioning look as she directed Nick to her bedroom down the hall. She patted Cody on the cheek and thanked him for helping her into the house. "What does it matter what they ate?"

"Just tell me."

They'd better not have been having—

"Happy pancakes," his mother said. Her smile was back. "She made me some too. I just love those sprinkles on top."

Nick returned from the bedroom sans luggage, and patted Zack on the shoulder as he passed. "Sorry, man," he uttered.

"They were also at the festival together," his mom informed him. "Cute couple."

They day after he'd left?

Sure as hell didn't take her long to move on.

Of course, he'd apparently just been her fuck buddy. Memories, and all.

"You should have stayed for it, Zackie." She shook her head. Her eyes glowed with delight. "I've never seen anything like it. The whole hillside was covered with fireflies, and doggone if they didn't light up in sync. It sure beat the grits festival we used to have back home."

His mother seemed like she could go on for days.

Cody and Nick just stood in the living room, looking as if unsure what to do next.

Zack wanted to throw things.

What he really wanted was to go yank Holly away from Hounddog.

"Oh." His mom turned to his brothers now. "I invited the boys to stay for a late lunch. Said I'd pull out a chicken casserole I have in the freezer."

His brothers shifted their gazes away when he turned to them. "Is that so?" Zack asked.

She opened the freezer and rummaged around inside. "I hope you can stay too. I know you have work to do."

"Actually—" He stopped talking when she turned her face to his. His brothers couldn't see her, but she had her scary look going, and he had to admit, he was a little scared.

"Surely you can stay?" Her question didn't come across so much as a question, though her voice did drip with sweetness. "You're here now, after all."

"I was just making sure you got home safely. I need to get back to the office."

"You need to get that stick out of your ass and sit down and eat like the rest of us."

He gaped at his mother. She'd never said anything like that to him.

His brothers stood a little straighter, as well. They stared at Zack over his mother's head.

It would be comical, the three of them looking terrified of the seventy-five-year-old woman all dressed in green, if he wasn't afraid he was about to get a frozen chicken casserole thrown at his head.

"It was your decision to leave early," she told him. "Get off your high horse because I had a good time without you. And if you can't stand the fact that Holly was with another man all weekend, then you shouldn't be here now."

"I have no issues with Holly being with another man." *All weekend?* "She can date who she wants."

He tried to hold on to his anger at his mother, but he knew she was right. She hadn't done anything wrong. Nor had Cody and Nick. And—he supposed—neither had Holly. As she'd pointed out, they hadn't promised each other anything. The funny thing was, he'd thought all along that he was the one not promising. It had never occurred to him that she had been doing it too.

Still, the woman could have at least waited more than twenty-four hours before hooking up with someone else.

His mom turned to him, bringing a finger up in the air to point straight at his face. "You should be in Sugar Springs, convincing her to give you a chance. I can't believe you just up and left like that." Her voice was heated with anger. "I raised you better than to hide behind your feelings. What were you thinking, Zachary? You pushed the woman you love right into another man's arms."

He stood there with his mouth hanging open. Finally he managed to pull his jaw up off the floor. "I don't love her, Mother."

He couldn't love her. How stupid would that be?

"You're too scared to live," she accused.

"I live just fine. I *love* my life."

He loved his job. He loved his penthouse.

He loved that he didn't have to worry about a woman walking out on him when he least expected it.

But he didn't love having this conversation in front of his brothers.

To look at them, they didn't care for it either. They shuffled their feet where they stood, staring at anything but the two of them.

"I need grandbabies," his mother declared. "I need you to quit hiding behind your job, and give me grandbabies to love before I'm too old." She stopped the lecture long enough to smile winningly over at Cody. "At least I have Candy and Kendra now. They're my surrogate grandkids." Her finger came back up and shook at Zack. "But that does not let you off the hook."

"She didn't want me," he roared suddenly. He was sick to death of this conversation.

His mother went quiet.

"She wanted you," she said, her voice less sure.

He shook his head. "She didn't, Mom. We're just friends. That's all we've ever been."

Then pity fell in his mother's soft eyes, and he couldn't take it anymore. She knew him well enough to know his words for the lie that they were. They were not just friends. Not on his side, anyway.

He glanced at his brothers. "Thanks for seeing that she got home." Then at his mother. "I'll see you next Sunday."

And then he headed back to work.

At least there he could hide his sorrows by billing his client an exorbitant fee.

Chapter Twenty-Four

Holly glanced into one of her many mirrors and smoothed her hand over her hair as she waited for her family to arrive. It was time for the big reveal. And she was terrified.

They'd all gathered at the house first, and Brian had just texted her to let her know they were heading her way. No one knew what she planned to show them, but to hear him say it, they were all excited to find out.

Kyndall had been out to the studio before, so she had an idea. She'd seen the mirrors in the living room. She would suspect today would involve those. Also, everyone knew Holly sold pieces at the consignment store. It had been referred to as her "little hobby" for years.

But her hobby was so much more than that, and today she intended to make them see it.

She glanced in the mirror once more. Her hair was twisted into a sophisticated knot, and she had on a lovely summer dress of turquoise eyelet with a white shrug and matching jewelry. She even had on strappy sandals that were color coordinated. She looked quite presentable.

Not that it really mattered to her family, but after finishing here, she would head off to meet with Jane, the real estate agent, to sign a lease for the empty storefront. So yeah, this was important. She wanted to come across as professional. Serious. This was the start of her career.

No more being the breezy little sister who had no purpose in life.

She dabbed on a fresh application of lipstick and rubbed her lips together, then nodded in the mirror. Win or lose, she was ready to go. Ready to show who she was.

Gravel crunched and doors slammed, and Holly stepped to the front door of the cabin.

Her mother was first up the stairs. She stopped at the sight of Holly standing in the doorway. Her eyes took in her daughter from head to toe. Without a word, Holly could tell that her mother got it. This wasn't some stunt or "another wild hair" like they thought running off to Chicago had been. Holly had something important to share with them today.

"Everything okay?" her mother asked carefully. She'd been tiptoeing around Holly since Zack had left. They hadn't talked about it yet, mostly because Holly had made up excuses and found something else to do if she thought Zack so much as ran through her mother's mind. But Holly was aware that her heartbreak was showing. How could it not?

She nodded. Everything was great.

And really it was. She was a new woman today. Missing Zack had been put on the back burner.

Erika, Jillian, and Kyndall all reached the porch behind Holly's mother. Excitement burned in their eyes to find out what Holly had to show them. The men hadn't made it out of the yard. Patrick and the boys had come from church, and were still in their slacks and dress shirts. They reminded her of Zack when he'd first shown up.

"You look so pretty, Aunt Holly," Kyndall gushed. She and her parents were also dressed for church.

Jillian had gotten stuck manning the tour office that morning so Patrick had taken the boys without her, and Holly's parents had been busy overseeing departing guests. Brian had probably just come from some woman's bed.

Yet they'd all made time for her when she'd asked them for it. That meant a lot.

"Thank you, Kyndall." She smiled at the girl. "I'm trying to look professional."

The women all nodded. "You do," her mother assured her.

Brian was at the bottom of the steps looking up, but he didn't say anything. He simply eyed her carefully. Holly got the impression he didn't approve of her new, improved look. All grown up and everything.

"So what's this about, kid?" Patrick was the one to finally ask.

Holly wet her lips, and Brian gave her an encouraging nod.

It was about her new life.

"I've been doing something for a few years now," she began, "and I thought it was time to show you. I also intend to take it to the next level. I wanted to talk to you all about that today."

Brian was not yet aware of her store plans. She caught a raised brow at her words.

With little fanfare, she stepped back and invited her family in.

She'd moved several of her best pieces from the bedroom to display in the front of the house.

"Oh my," she heard her mother whisper as she made her way in. The words were spoken in awe.

Everyone else crowded in behind her mother, and Holly stepped in last. She twisted her hands together with nerves. It wasn't a large room, and with eleven additional people inside, it was hard to really take everything in. But Holly saw that they were doing just that. She had the lights on and shining bright. The whole room glowed.

"When did you . . ." Patrick began, but then shook his head in confusion. He turned to take in another piece. And then another. "This is . . ."

"Art," Jillian supplied. She looked at Holly. "This is incredible work. I had no idea."

"Me either," Holly's mother whispered.

"Oh my gawd, Aunt Holly," Kyndall whispered in tween marvel. "This is what I want to do instead of the flowerpots."

Holly laughed softly, moved at the girl's words. "You stick with your flowerpots, hon. You'll make them just as terrific."

Kyndall continued looking around, her face mesmerized by the work.

"There's more in the bedroom," Holly stated. "And the even bigger announcement I have is that I'll be opening my own store soon."

Her mother's eyes rounded.

"I'm signing a lease today. That empty property on the square. I tried to sell these in Chicago, but no one wanted them."

"They're idiots," Patrick supplied without pause.

"Yeah." Holly nodded. "That's what I've decided. Plus, these belong here. I'm a Sugar Springs girl. My mirrors should be too."

Holly's dad wasn't a man of many words, and that moment was no different. He stepped to her side and put his arm around her shoulders. "I'm proud of you."

Tears welled up in her eyes.

She was a daddy's girl. Always had been. To have him proud meant a lot.

"Thanks, Dad." Her voice barely registered as she snuggled into his side. "That also means I won't be working at any of the family businesses anymore," she whispered. Those words elicited as much anxiety as showing them her art had to begin with.

"Of course you won't," her dad stated firmly.

No one else spoke. They were all too busy staring at the pieces surrounding them.

After several more minutes, everyone moving throughout the room and in and out of her bedroom, Erika stood before Holly. "I need the price of that one, please." She pointed to one of Holly's favorites. It was currently showcased on an easel sitting in front of the TV.

"I wanted that one!" Jillian hustled back into the room. "I planned to ask for it myself, but I was being polite. Not begging immediately. No fair. You jumped the gun."

"I saw something I wanted." Erika pasted on a superior look. "If I wait, I may not get it."

"I want it," Jillian demanded.

Holly watched her sisters-in-law argue over her work, and her heart grew a couple sizes larger. They were not doing this simply to make her feel better. They wanted that mirror.

"I can make a second," Holly snuck in through a tiny opening in their words.

Two heads swiveled in her direction.

"Not exactly the same," she added. "I don't do the same design more than once. But I can work with whichever of you doesn't take this one, and we can come up with something similar."

"Then I want the new piece," both women said at once.

Holly gaped, mouth open in shock, and saw Brian's wide, proud smile pointed her way. Then she laughed. There had been nothing at all to worry about with this bunch. Probably not with the public either. Her store would be a success.

Erika and Jillian fought for a few minutes longer, good-naturedly of course, and Holly's mother came over to take her hand.

"I had no idea," she said.

Holly nodded. The lump in her throat made it hard to speak.

"Why didn't you ever tell us?"

She lifted a shoulder. "I didn't know what you'd think. If I was good enough."

"Baby." Her mom shook her head. "I should have known you were out here creating something special. You've always been my unique one. The one I always knew would find her way."

The words poked at a vulnerable spot inside Holly's heart. The last few days had been hard. The additional rejection from Chicago, realizing she was in love with Zack. Zack leaving.

Her deciding to open herself up to the world.

She was barely hanging on.

Her mom cupped Holly's cheek. "Are you okay, sweetheart? With everything? I know you cared a lot about Zack."

Tears threatened to return. The back of her nose burned.

Then she shook her head and her eyes began to leak. "I'm fine," she lied, her voice cracking on the words.

"Oh, baby." Her mother pulled her into her arms and stroked Holly's back.

"Mom," Holly whispered. She wished she wasn't in the middle of her whole family, crying over Zack. But then, where was there a better place to do it? "It hurts."

"I'm know, sweetie," her mother cooed.

"I'm going to kick his ass," Brian pronounced.

Holly peeked up through the blur of tears and saw Patrick and Rodney step up beside Brian. The sight of her three gorgeous, angry brothers made her laugh. They *would* kick his ass. If she'd let them. They would do anything for her.

"He did nothing wrong," she told them. "Never promised a thing. I just wanted more."

"He shouldn't have—"

"It was both of us," she interrupted Brian. "You will *not* kick his ass."

All three of her brothers' jaws tensed, identically, and Holly almost laughed again. It was nice that they had her back.

"I'd rather you save your strength for helping me move all these mirrors to my store. It'll be a better use of your time and efforts."

Because Zack was gone. And she had to move on.

"I could do both," Brian suggested.

"You're the best, Brian. But no." There would be no kicking of Zack's anything.

Brian gave her a wink. "Of course I am, kiddo. But you're pretty tough to top yourself."

A smile spread wide. She was. And she knew it. She may not be perfect, but she had a lot going for her. A lot that Zack should have been able to see. He was missing out.

Or so she kept telling herself.

In actuality, she felt like she was the one missing out. She'd considered calling him more than once over the last few days. Just to see how he was doing. If he was thinking of her. At all.

But then she'd reminded herself that he could have called too.

It wasn't like they'd left things in a heated argument. They'd hooked up, and she'd let him go without stifling him with clinginess. The moment had been a little tense, yeah, but no reason two reasonable adults couldn't still talk to each other if they wanted to.

Only, she doubted he wanted to. He also probably already had this week's date lined up, and if Holly knew about it, she would want to drive to Atlanta and kick his butt herself.

She shoved thoughts of Zack from her mind and motioned to the door. "My appointment with Jane is in fifteen minutes. You all stay as long as you want, but I need to run."

Excitement washed through her. This was it.

But before she could get to the door, her phone rang. And with unfailing hope that it was Zack, she pulled it from her pocket. It was a number with the same area code as his. Her heart thudded.

"Is it him?" Her mom asked. Nerves tensed her mother's face at the same time they gouged a path through Holly's insides.

"I'll still go kick his ass," Brian mumbled.

Holly put her hand on his arm as if to stop him from leaving, as she continued to stare at the phone. "It's an Atlanta number."

They all gave her a tight smile. Her brothers' were more of a grimace, but it was their way of being supportive. "We'll give you some privacy."

"Thanks."

Everyone stepped onto her tiny porch, and she headed to the windows overlooking the river. She brought the phone to her ear.

"Hello?"

"Ms. Marshall?" a smart, Southern voice said in her ear. "I'm so glad I caught you today. I'm Ashley Summers." The woman paused a moment before adding, "Mr. Winston's friend."

Mr. Winston's friend?

Jealousy took hold, but just as quickly let go. Zack's friend? From Atlanta? The friend he'd e-mailed her portfolio to.

"Yes," Holly stumbled over the word. "This is Ms. Marshall. What can I do for you?"

"Oh my, Ms. Marshall . . . is it okay if I call you Holly?"

"Sure." Holly nodded as if the woman could see her. "Yeah."

"Great. And please, call me Ashley. I just wanted to call and let you know how much my manager and I love your work. Really, we *love* it. It's unique and original, and the talent is clear. You're a brilliant artist, Holly. Brilliant."

Holly dropped to a seat.

She had someone on the phone who loved her work.

"We'd love to sell your pieces if you'd allow us. We want to give you your own room. Seriously, the work is stupendous."

Holly's mouth opened but no words came out.

Someone wanted to showcase her work.

Because of Zack. He'd done this.

Then a tear slipped onto her cheek. She wanted to call and tell him, but she knew she wouldn't. They may have pretended to part as friends, but they weren't. She loved him. He didn't love her.

She couldn't share the best day of her life with him.

And then she remembered her appointment. She glanced at the time. She had to go.

"Holly?" Ashley spoke in her ear. "Did you hear me? Oh, please tell me we aren't too late."

"I . . ." They were too late. "Actually, Ms. . . . Ashley. I'm on my way right now to sign a lease for my own store."

"Then let us be your Atlanta outlet."

The woman didn't miss a beat. Holly appreciated that.

"May I think about it?" she asked. She could see that happening. She could have her store here, but also sell pieces in Atlanta. Why not? It would be the best of both worlds.

And just because it was in Atlanta, that didn't mean she'd ever run into Zack.

"Absolutely," Ashley replied. "Let me give you our contact info and website. Please take a look. Come down and see us in person, if you'd like. We'd love to have you. But please, keep us in mind. I think we could work well together."

They finished up, Holly jotting down the pertinent information and Ashley promising to call back in a couple days, then she got off the phone. She sat there for a moment, her heart in her throat, wanting desperately to call Zack.

She even punched in a text.

But then she deleted it.

He couldn't be that kind of friend right now. Maybe someday. After she'd figured out how to get over him. Right now she had to keep her distance.

Brian poked his head into the house. He looked at her cautiously. "Everything okay?"

She nodded. Then tears pooled in her eyes and she explained about the call.

When she finished, her brother picked her up in a bear hug. Everyone else had come back in and gathered around, hearing all the details. There wasn't a dry eye in the bunch.

"I'm so proud of you, sis," Brian muttered. "We all are."

She buried her face in his chest and let the tears flow. She was proud of herself too. She may show up for her appointment with puffy eyes and streaked makeup, but she was currently filled to the brim with pride.

Her dreams were coming true.

The vibration of the Roadmaster felt good under Zack's sturdy hands as he took the exit off the interstate and turned toward his mother's house. She didn't know he was coming to see her.

He *shouldn't* be coming to see her. It was the middle of a workday.

But he'd been unable to concentrate.

It was Thursday. Movie night. And the only thing that had run through his head the entire day was that the last three Thursday nights had been spent with Holly. The first was when he'd started getting to know her. They'd become friends that night. She'd called him lonely.

The second they'd skipped the movie together and she'd kissed him senseless.

Last week she'd made love to him.

This week she could very well be with another man.

There was no way he could stay at the office when all he could think about was Holly in another man's arms.

So he'd decided to take the car out for a ride, and his mother along with it. She loved this car almost as much as he did. Only, for different reasons.

Cars had been his dad's passion. He'd taken Zack's mom out on their first date in one identical to this. That's the reason his dad picked this car to restore. He'd wanted to rebuild a bond with his son, but he'd also wanted to romance his wife.

And Zack had been too busy to help see that dream come true. He held heavy regrets about that. But he'd done what he could to correct it in the years since. He'd finished the car, and he was taking care of his mother. Exactly like his dad would have wanted.

Zack pulled into the driveway, and he'd no sooner turned the car off than his mother stepped from the house. It was as if she'd been expecting him.

The expression on her face was one he remembered from childhood. He'd come home—too many days—upset because some kid had picked on him. She'd hug him tight and give him ice cream. But that expression was always the first thing he'd seen.

His mother loved him to the bottom of her soul.

She would do anything for him.

And today, when he was hurting so bad over the loss of Holly, he'd just wanted his mom.

"You okay, Zackie?" She'd come out to the car without making him come to her.

He nodded and gave her a sad smile. He loved it when she called him Zackie. "I miss her, Mom."

"I know, baby." She opened the passenger door and climbed in. "Because you love her."

He wanted to deny it again. But he couldn't. "She doesn't love me."

"I think you might be wrong about that. This one is different."

He'd like to believe her. He'd also like to think it wasn't too late. "Why do you say that?"

She reached over and patted his hand. "Because this girl is special. She's not afraid to be herself. And she's not afraid to do things her own way."

He wasn't sure he knew what she meant.

"Zack, honey." She shook her head as if talking to a child who just didn't get it. "Barb wasn't the woman for you. She needed a perfect life. She couldn't trust in anything else." His mom squeezed his hand. "If it hadn't been your birth mother, it would have eventually been something else." She peered up at him through her glasses. "Holly just needs to be loved."

He wanted to love her.

But she didn't want him.

"She showed me her mirrors," his mom said. That shocked him. "When?"

"Saturday night. She gave me a ride back to the house after the festival, and she asked if I wanted to see them." She shook her head in awe. "What a gift that young lady has."

He nodded. "I know. She showed them to me too."

"She showed them to you *first*," his mom stressed.

"How do you know that?"

"Because you told me about them."

He shook his head. "I told you about the other ones. The ones in her living room."

"I knew there was more to the story, I just didn't know what. But when she took me out there . . ." She shrugged. "I knew that was what you'd seen. And then I understood."

"You understood what?"

"That it wasn't just the mirrors you had fallen for." She let that soak in for a second before adding, "Same for her."

"Mom." The word came out sad. It sounded lonely. Which reminded him of Holly calling him lonely that first night. And he was. He wanted more than work. More than an empty house and what felt like an even emptier penthouse. He wanted what his parents had had. "She pushed me away. She doesn't want me."

"Are you willing to bet the rest of your life on that?" she asked.

When he didn't immediately respond, she added, "I asked her about Bobby before I left. Asked if it was something that could get serious."

Zack's throat closed. He did not want to hear that she was moving on.

"She looked shocked, baby. Floored. As if the thought of getting serious with another man was outside the realm of her possibility."

Zack turned to look at his mother.

"Because we both saw that she's already serious about you," she said.

He started to argue, but he found he couldn't. He had meant something to Holly. He knew that. He couldn't have called that one so completely wrong.

"You're special to her," his mom said. "And I'm pretty sure as much more than a friend."

"Was I good enough for you, Mom?" he asked suddenly. "For Dad? I always worried that I wasn't."

Shocked eyes greeted his. "Why would you ever question that?"

"Because you chose me," he said. "I always worried that I wouldn't live up to your expectations. And then I met Pam, and my worries doubled. What if I had too much of her in me? What if I turned into her?"

"Oh, Zackie." She scooted across the seat and wrapped her arm around his waist. "Of course you would never turn into her. You have more of your father and me running through you than that woman. And yes, you were good enough. Of course. You were the best son a mother could ever want. Or a father. He loved you more than you know."

"I let him down."

"No," she said. "Never."

"I should have been around more. Should have made sure he got this car finished."

"But you did. Otherwise we wouldn't be sitting in it right now."

He chuckled a little. Because that's all they were doing. Sitting in it. They were still in her driveway, and no doubt her neighbors were wondering what was going on.

"I never wanted you to regret choosing me," he confessed. That fear had been in him for as long as he could remember. Maybe it was ridiculous, but he'd never been able to shake it.

"The only thing I've ever regretted was that I couldn't fight your demons for you. The kids at school when you were little. Heartbreak in law school. And then what that witch Pam put in your head. I tried, but there are some things a mother just has to be on the sidelines for. I was there waiting to hold you up when you needed me, but I couldn't protect you from the bad." She hugged him tight. "I've never regretted a single thing about *you*, though. And you shouldn't either. Don't live with regrets, son. Be willing to take a risk. Go for what you want."

He eyed her carefully, trying to decide if he should tell her what he wanted.

"What is it?" she prodded. "I know you want Holly. What else?"

He loved his mother so much. She always knew when he needed something. Especially when he needed her.

"I want to move to Sugar Springs, Mom. I want to be close to my brothers. I want to be there for Holly." If she would have him. And he was starting to hope that she might. "I want to work with people who deserve to be helped."

Like Mr. Martin. He'd done nothing wrong, and hadn't deserved to be bullied by his neighbor. Zack had gotten more satisfaction out of that single act than he'd had at his job in years. Most of his clients were guilty. He was just good enough to get them off.

Joy crossed his mother's face. "As long as you take me with you," she stated. "I want to be there for those boys too. And their kids. And wives. I always did want a bigger family. Now I can have a houseful." She paused and patted his cheek. "But *you'll* always be my favorite."

He smiled. He knew he would.

"I love you, Mom."

"I love you too, Zackie."

"It would mean I don't make partner."

That had been bothering him a lot. He was ready to walk away from the career he'd worked so hard for. Just to be with the woman he loved.

And to be with his family.

"Would you be disappointed in me?" he asked.

"Would you be happy?"

He nodded. "I would."

He could always open his own practice in Sugar Springs. There wasn't a lot of need so it may not pay the bills, but he could also join a firm in Knoxville. Maybe with his buddy. A couple days a week in Sugar Springs and the rest working with a larger firm, less than an hour's drive away. He could see that working.

"Then I'm not sure what we're waiting for," his mother said. "Isn't there a movie playing tonight?"

There was. And he happened to know that big things happened on movie nights. He wanted to make sure Holly was with the right man when those things happened.

"Want to take a ride with me, Mom?"

He'd left the top off the car again. Partly because he knew his mother liked riding with the top down, and partly because it made him think of Holly.

Total contentment settled over his mother's face. "You couldn't get me out if you tried."

He laughed with a relief he hadn't felt in a week. "We're going to need some clothes."

"We can buy clothes; we'd better hurry. Beatrice called earlier. Rumor is that Holly has a date tonight. You can't let her spend the evening with the wrong man."

His thoughts exactly.

Chapter Twenty-Five

The opening credits to *Casablanca* scrolled across the screen, and Holly looked at the man seated to her left. He was focused on the movie, but she caught Kyndall on the other side of him, checking him out too.

He was a good-looking guy. Kyndall seemed to think so too, if the way she took him in from head to toe, her little face focused in concentration, was any indication. Yet Holly got the impression that Kyndall didn't want Jesse sitting in between them any more than she did.

Holly shouldn't have said yes when he'd called her up yesterday. She should not be on a date.

And since she was, especially with someone as fine looking as Jesse Beckman, then she most definitely should feel something other than the need for the night to hurry along.

Kyndall shifted her gaze to Holly's and her nose wrinkled in opposition. Holly agreed.

He might be cute, but he was no Zack.

And she really, really wanted it to be Zack.

She missed him something awful.

Cody and Nick had filled her in that they'd seen him when they'd taken Janet home Sunday morning, but that's all they'd told her. They hadn't provided any details. It had felt as if they were on Zack's side. Whatever his side might be. As if they were respecting his thoughts because he was their brother.

She hadn't cared about that. She'd wanted to know if he was miserable like she was.

She'd gotten nothing out of them.

That was a good thing, she supposed. It was the relationship the three of them needed, so yeah, she was glad it had fallen into place. It hadn't kept her from wanting to kick the two brothers in the shins when they wouldn't share details, though.

Jesse turned to her and gave her a little smile, but still . . . nothing. Damn. She really wanted to like him. She'd even been given the go-ahead from his sister that it was okay if Holly went out with him. She could now officially date her friend's little brother.

Only, she didn't want to.

He reached for her hand, and Kyndall eyed them both as if trying to figure out if she should intercede.

Holly winked at her, but Kyndall just scrunched up her nose again.

"This is fun," Jesse whispered.

"Yeah," Holly replied noncommittally.

She sighed internally. She had to put an end to this.

Zack may not be the one for her. Heck, maybe there was no "one" for her. But she couldn't force it with someone else either. Clearly she wasn't ready to go out with another man.

She'd focus her time on her store instead. Plans were already being put into place. Shelving had been ordered, and she had Nick lined up for some customization work. Soon she'd be a business-woman on her own. That was pretty awesome.

That was all she needed to make her happy for the moment.

Jesse inched closer and slid an arm around her waist, and Holly froze.

What was he doing? Surely he wasn't about to make a move. Not here. In front of her niece?

Before she could put a stop to it, or even figure out if that was his intent, she caught Kyndall taking another peek in her direction, but then her gaze shifted above Holly's head and her eyes brightened. The girl smiled.

And then the most god-awful pair of shoes reached Holly's peripheral vision. They were men's black oxfords, but they looked to have been violated with a glue gun. Poorly.

Sequins of every imaginable color were haphazardly slapped along the surface, with chunks of dried glue balled up in random spots throughout. As if someone had never handled a glue gun in their life.

There was also fringe stuck to the tongue. Well, fringe on the tongue of one shoe. The other just held a blob of glue. The fringe was a red tassel, like what might be found hanging from a curtain.

The shoes were right behind Jesse now, but were pointed toward *her*. Holly wanted to see who wore those shoes. She began to lift her gaze.

They were under a pair of black trousers. Over long legs.

Her pulse began to hammer.

She also noticed that no one was complaining about whomever it was standing in the way of the screen.

Then she saw Kyndall's face once again. The girl's smile was infectious, and Holly knew without a doubt who was standing by her side.

He'd come back.

"I hope like hell you don't think you're about to kiss her," Zack proclaimed.

Jesse froze. Then he mumbled under his breath, "You've got to be kidding me."

He separated from Holly and climbed to his feet.

Kyndall clapped.

"I was kind of hoping you wouldn't show back up." Jesse's words were directed at Zack.

Zack merely stared. The line of his jaw seemed set in stone, and there was zero emotion coming from his eyes. The look was actually a bit chilling. Holly switched her gaze back to Jesse.

He turned his head toward her.

He studied her for a moment, seeming to ask her a question. Did she want him to go?

Actually, yes. But she was sorry. She let her eyes go soft just long enough to show him the love she felt for Zack. She didn't know why he was there, but she had to find out.

Jesse gave an almost unnoticeable nod.

"She's all yours, Winston." Then he winked at Holly. "Thanks for the date, gorgeous."

Zack took a step closer, but Jesse only laughed. Though Zack had a good six inches on him, Jesse was built like a tank. And he could probably bench at least a hundred pounds more. It would be an interesting fight.

If Holly were into men fighting over her.

"Stand down, soldier." Jesse patted Zack on the shoulder. "We're good here." Then he once again looked at Holly. The easiness and warmth in his gaze let her know that he was okay with this turn of events. "I had to try." He gave a little shrug. "In case he didn't come back." He took another long look at Zack before shooting a parting glance at Holly. "Good luck," he said sincerely.

Then he was gone.

Zack watched until Jesse was out of sight, while Holly remained where she was on the quilt. She needed to know what was going on.

And she needed to know now.

Before she got her hopes up.

"You're back." The words were all she could get out. Her chest burned as if from lack of oxygen.

Zack nodded. "I'm back."

It was interesting that no one around them complained for him to sit. Holly took a quick glance around to find all eyes on them. She returned to Zack. "So now what?"

He might have come back, but she had no idea what that meant. And she hadn't forgotten the brusque way they'd parted.

"I don't want you kissing other men," he stated.

She nodded. "I picked up on that."

Kyndall giggled behind her hand and Holly shot her a quick look. When she did, she saw that her entire family now stood behind her niece, all watching the two of them. Janet Winston was also there. He'd brought his mother?

Holly's heart beat faster.

"Stand up." He spoke the words softly. They reminded her of other commands he'd given. *Unzip your dress. Lift your ass.*

She stood up.

Nerves made her hands shake.

"I screwed up," he told her. "I shouldn't have left."

"But you said you had a case."

He nodded. "I did have a case. A career-making one."

"Then what are you doing here now?"

He cracked a wry smile. "I couldn't let you watch a movie with the wrong man."

She licked her lips. Jesse had most definitely been the wrong man. "And you're the right one?" she asked.

The crowd around them was silent.

Zack's eyes roved over her as if checking to make sure she hadn't changed in the six days since he'd seen her. "I want to be," he finally admitted. "If you'll let me."

She gulped. Then nodded. "I—"

"I'm not done," he interrupted as if needing to get something out. "I forgot to tell you something before I left."

"Okay," she whispered. He was killing her. "What was it?"

He looked away from her then. He took in the crowd that had

closed in until the two of them were merely a dot in the middle of a thick circle. Someone had even turned off the sound to the movie. The moment was theirs.

Then he returned those sexy browns to her and said solemnly, "That I love you."

Sighs came from every spot around the circle.

"That makes you cry?" he asked. He reached out and swiped a thumb under her eye.

"Apparently." Though she hadn't realized she was crying.

"Why?" He left his hand at her face, and his fingers cupped her cheek.

"Because I love you too," she whispered. More tears fell.

His mouth turned up in a gorgeous smile. "That's nothing to cry about, babe. That's good stuff. Because it means that I get to ask you a very important question."

Oh. Shit.

He was going to ask her a question. Now? Here? In front of everyone?

All she could do was nod for him to go on. Off to her right, she heard her niece whisper, "Oh my gawd."

Zack let her go and took a step back. But instead of going to one knee, he merely pointed to her feet.

"Why in the world," he asked, "are you wearing plain white shoes?"

A breath burst from her chest. As it did from several others around her. "That's your question?" she asked. "About my shoes?"

She had on a pair of white leather Keds. For some reason, she hadn't felt like anything more tonight. In fact, she hadn't all week. Not since Zack had left. Brian had pointed this fact out with disgust more than once. He'd declared the world not right if she actually matched.

"Kind of makes me look silly standing here in these when you're wearing something so boring," Zack remarked.

He had a point.

"What if I said I would never wear boring shoes again?" Because she wouldn't. That wasn't who she was. She planned to burn these just as soon as she got home.

He pulled something from his pocket then and held it up. "Then I'd say, 'Marry me?'"

This time there were gasps all around. Including hers.

Hell's bells, the man had brought her a ring.

Before she answered, she took in the scene before her. He stood in the middle of all of her friends, a few strangers, and both her family and his. And though she knew he had to have at least some trepidation about the night, he didn't look nervous in the least.

He looked confident.

And he kind of looked like he wouldn't take no for an answer.

She peeked at his mother. Janet was wiping a tear from her own cheek.

"Do we get to live at the big house?" Holly asked instead of answering. Because yeah, she'd follow him anywhere. She'd keep her store here, though. Her mirrors belonged here. She'd just hire someone else to run it. But she could already imagine turning one of his big garages into a studio.

Only, Zack shook his head no.

Oh.

"The penthouse, then?" She could deal with that. She'd just take over the kitchen.

Again, it was a no.

"Then . . ." Her shoulders sagged. She was confused. "What?

"Will you just answer?" he asked. "My arm is getting tired."

He also gave her his scary look.

Which still wasn't scary at all.

She laughed instead.

"Holly," he growled out.

And then she slowly nodded. A wide smile broke out over her face and she had to fight to keep from shouting.

"Yes!" she said. It didn't matter where they lived. As long as they were together. "Yes, Zack Winston, I'll marry you. But only if *you* promise to never wear *those* shoes again."

Zack closed the distance with a predatory gleam and swept her into his arms. As his lips closed over hers, he muttered, "It's a deal."

When they came up for air, he added, "And we're building onto your cabin. *That's* going to be our home."

"Oh," she murmured and snuggled in tighter. "I like that."

He gave her one more kiss. It was a long one, but this time when they parted, he looked at her with the kind of love in his eyes that she once hadn't even realized she'd been missing. She had her mirrors, her family, her town, and her man.

She had it all.

"Can we keep the geese?" she asked.

Zack merely shook his head and laughed. "I couldn't imagine my world without your geese in it."

Epilogue

D o you take this man . . ."
Nerves revved inside Holly when the preacher asked Lee Ann
if she would take Cody to be by her side forever. A contented smile
formed across Lee Ann's mouth. Her eyes shone bright.

Her look said that she most definitely *would* take her man.

They were all standing on the stage where the movie screen typ-
ically hung. The majority of the town's residents were there, all sitting on white chairs lining the grassy area before them. It was
nighttime, and there were tiny white lights strung through the
branches of the trees and dipping in and out around the stage. The
wedding party was huge, fanning out on both sides. Girls in red
sleeveless dresses, guys in black tuxes with royal-blue ties. Bridal
white completed the Independence Day theme.

"I do," Lee Ann stated without hesitation.

Every pair of eyes turned to Cody. His dark gaze burned hot as
he took in his bride, prompting Holly to shift her eyes to Zack. *He*
was watching *her*.

And yes, his gaze burned just as hot.

Holly's nerves settled into a low hum as she felt his love reach
across the stage and wrap solidly around her.

Fifteen days ago he'd shown back up in her life. And fifteen days ago she'd known without a doubt that she would take him forever. He was it for her.

He'd quit his job in Atlanta, already had a new one lined up in Knoxville, and was readying his own location in Sugar Springs. He'd also been by her side at the Atlanta gallery as she'd signed a contract for them to carry some of her work.

Then he'd jumped into the fray of getting her own store ready. Her front windows displayed her original pieces while Zack and Nick created a showroom meant to wow. She had taken calls daily asking how soon she would be open, and had even fielded a few from boutiques across the country. Tourists had passed the word along, and it seemed she might soon spread out farther than Atlanta.

"I do," Cody stated with clarity.

The preacher turned his sights from Lee Ann and Cody. "And do you . . ."

Joanie and Nick stepped forward from their respective spots next to Cody and Lee Ann, to come together and stand before the preacher.

Joanie's wedding dress was different from Lee Ann's, but in sticking with the patriotic theme, she, too, had on white. Whereas Lee Ann's was a sleek beaded lace, perhaps a bit more "mature" in taste, Joanie's rocked the fun. It was the perfect mermaid dress for someone who changed the color of her hair each week to match her cupcakes. Strapless, full-torso ruching, with an explosion of ruffles making up the bottom.

Nick's white tux sported the same royal-blue tie and cummerbund as Cody's.

And Zack's.

Holly's wedding dress was a replica of her grandmother's.

It had been a rush job when the brothers had suggested they all get married at the same time, but Holly had managed to locate a seamstress who would take it on. Wanting to bring her grandparents into her wedding day, she'd opted to wear the traditional look her granny had chosen when she'd once stood before *her* betrothed.

Only, Holly had to make a few alterations.

She'd kept the sweetheart neckline and cap lace sleeves of the silk sheath. Even included the peekaboo lace that striped down the sides and into the train. However, she'd raised the front hem to mid-calf. To show off her shoes, of course.

Because as usual, her shoes spoke a different language than everything else.

The heels were high, ending with crisscross ties climbing past her ankles, while the shoes themselves were a mix of colors atop hot-pink soles. Orange, red, pink, yellow, purple, blue, and green. All bright splashes on a background of white. They looked like sprinkles. And she loved them.

She especially loved that Zack had been the one to pick them out for her.

The preacher looked at her, and Holly's nerves were suddenly nowhere to be found. Zack stepped forward, meeting her in the middle of the stage, and wrapped her hands in his. She shared a look with her future husband that let her know all was right in the world. Whatever was handed to them, they could handle together.

Six weeks ago she'd come home broken and rejected, certain she'd never have a life that would truly make her happy. The thought of a husband certainly had been nowhere in the mix.

Today, she had a man, a career, and a renewed love for the town she'd grown up in. Life couldn't get much better than that.

"Holly?"

She jerked her head around to the preacher. "What?"

Giggles skated through the crowd.

"*Do* you?" the preacher asked.

Her eyes went wide. She'd missed everything he'd said. But that was okay; she knew the words by heart.

Just as she knew that the man those words went with was a deeply ingrained part of her heart.

As she looked at Zack, she overflowed with love. In one way, she couldn't believe they were getting married so fast. Yet at the same time, this was where they belonged. Zack wasn't just standing with his brothers as they got married, but was committing to a lifetime alongside them. He was promising to love *her* forever, but he was making a promise to them, as well.

As they were to him.

Someone cleared her throat in an obvious manner, and Holly peeked to the front row where Ms. Grayson sat primly beside Zack's mother.

She wore a haughty look, and Holly knew she was thinking, "I did this." And heck, maybe she had. Maybe Zack wouldn't have been inspired to ask her out if he hadn't gotten jealous watching her date other men.

But she didn't believe that. Something told her the two of them would have found their way to each other no matter what.

However, if it made a busybody happy, who was she to burst her bubble?

"I do," she said simply, turning back to Zack. Tears appeared in her eyes and she whispered, "Forever."

He nodded and, waiting his turn, agreed. "Forever."

"By the power vested in me—"

The boom of fireworks blocked out the remainder of the preacher's words as everyone in the park tilted their faces skyward. Hounddog had set off the fireworks fifteen seconds too early.

As red, white, and blue rained down on them, the preacher finished with, "You may kiss your brides."

And that was exactly what all three men did.

ACKNOWLEDGMENTS

Acknowledgments for this book go screaming out to one amazing person: my agent, Nalini Akolekar. Oh my goodness, thank you so much. This book almost killed me in so many ways, and without you helping me through it (and reading it numerous times!), I'm not sure where my sanity level would be today. (And we know it wasn't high to begin with!) Thank you so much, and fingers crossed no other books are this painful to get to production.

ABOUT THE AUTHOR

© 2012 AMELIA MOORE

As a child, award-winning author Kim Law cultivated a love for chocolate, anything purple, and creative writing. She penned her debut work, "The Gigantic Talking Raisin," in the sixth grade and got hooked on the delights of creating stories. Before settling into the writing life, however, she earned a college degree in mathematics and then worked as a computer programmer—for far too many years. Now she's pursuing her lifelong dream of writing romance novels. She has won the Romance Writers of America's Golden Heart Award, has been a finalist for the prestigious RWA RITA Award, and has served in varied positions for her local RWA chapter. A native of Kentucky, Kim lives with her husband and an assortment of animals in Middle Tennessee.